ART HOUR AT THE DUCHESS HOTEL

ALSO BY SOPHIE GREEN

The Inaugural Meeting of the Fairvale Ladies Book Club
The Shelly Bay Ladies Swimming Circle
Thursdays at Orange Blossom House
The Bellbird River Country Choir
Weekends with the Sunshine Gardening Society

ART HOUR AT THE DUCHESS HOTEL

SOPHIE GREEN

hachette
AUSTRALIA

For my brother, Nicholas, with all the love in the universe and beyond.

Published in Australia and New Zealand in 2024
by Hachette Australia
(an imprint of Hachette Australia Pty Limited)
Gadigal Country, Level 17, 207 Kent Street, Sydney, NSW 2000
www.hachette.com.au

Hachette Australia acknowledges and pays our respects to the past, present and future Traditional Owners and Custodians of Country throughout Australia and recognises the continuation of cultural, spiritual and educational practices of Aboriginal and Torres Strait Islander peoples. Our head office is located on the lands of the Gadigal people of the Eora Nation.

Copyright © Sophie Green 2024

This book is copyright. Apart from any fair dealing for the purposes of private study, research, criticism or review permitted under the *Copyright Act 1968*, no part may be stored or reproduced by any process without prior written permission. Enquiries should be made to the publisher.

 A catalogue record for this book is available from the National Library of Australia

ISBN: 978 0 7336 5056 7 (paperback)

Cover design by Christabella Designs
Cover images courtesy of Shutterstock
Author photo courtesy of Jen Bradley
Typeset in 11.3/16.2 pt Sabon Lt Pro by Bookhouse, Sydney
Printed and bound in Australia by McPherson's Printing Group

 The paper this book is printed on is certified against the Forest Stewardship Council® Standards. McPherson's Printing Group holds FSC® chain of custody certification SA-COC-005379. FSC® promotes environmentally responsible, socially beneficial and economically viable management of the world's forests.

AUGUST 1999

CHAPTER ONE

It's so lovely, this house. Three storeys, newly renovated, off-white paint on the walls and the best furniture she could find. Clean lines, clean surfaces, stainless steel in the kitchen and expensive tiles in the bathrooms. The most expensive architect in Sydney, because that's what her husband wanted for the house that he has worked so hard to afford and which he wants to show off to his friends and acquaintances and associates. Which makes it a showroom more than a house. And that makes her . . . his showroom model, perhaps.

Joan walks to the glass doors that open onto a wide balcony. The balcony furniture is also new. Isaac was so determined that everything would be new that she once asked him why he didn't just pull the whole house down and start again.

'Because it has history,' he said. Which made her laugh, because if he liked the history so much he should have kept it the way it was: a little musty, a lot old-fashioned.

The history of this house is that Isaac coveted it for years. They once came to a party here when he was a junior partner at a large law firm and ever since then he's wanted to own it. Owning it means something to him. Joan was happy to support him, of course, and she knows what he's like when he covets something because he coveted her once too. And worked just as hard to get her.

So now she's here in this house he bought for them both, a house they've barely lived in because the renovations took years and they rented somewhere while they were done, but which is now complete and resplendent and no doubt they'll be the envy of everyone they know, and all she's interested in is what's outside.

Because as lovely as the house is, it has nothing on the view.

From this balcony, she looks over Sirius Cove and across to Curraghbeena Point between the cove and Mosman Bay. It's a glorious day with a clear blue sky, the way Sydney can be in winter: the light softens and the air is crisp and everything looks sharper. The movement on the water below her tells her there's a light breeze, and the few boats moored there bob a little.

To her left, there are the high walls of Taronga Zoo and if she moves her head, she is looking at the city. The Opera House, the Harbour Bridge, the office towers, the Botanic Gardens, Camp Cove, Campbells Cove, The Rocks. She can see it all.

Between the house and Sirius Cove there is a small strip of bushland; a stone staircase nearby leads down to a track that takes her through the bush and, in one direction, to Curlew Camp.

The camp was inhabited by Arthur Streeton and Tom Roberts and other artists in the late nineteenth century. They strung up shelters next to the water and painted what they saw in this place that is now her home. Streeton depicted the water she is looking at now, trees, and rocks she can't see from this spot. They lived rough and painted elegantly.

It's a romantic story, even as it contains the elements of what art means to her: commitment, the sacrifice of earthy comforts, the pursuit of beauty and excellence and the feeling of something being just right, in you, in the world. It isn't electric so much as magic, and there is no room for magic in a culture like Australia's, hewn out of military history and colonial obedience and, in the name of both, conquering wilderness. Conquering wildness. And wildness is an essential component of magic.

Actually, that is what art used to mean to her. She hasn't painted for a long time now. She used to be good at it, too. Sold works, won prizes, as modest as they were. Her talent was evident from primary school, or so her mother always said; Joan was only aware of it in high school, when she was lucky to have an encouraging art teacher, Miss Sharam, who taught her about acrylics and oils and watercolours, about Impressionism and Classicism and the Renaissance. Miss Sharam rhapsodised about Vincent van Gogh and Artemisia Gentileschi, thought Picasso entirely too brutal and Renoir overrated.

Joan chose oils as her main medium because Miss Sharam offered her space to leave her canvases to dry, in a part of her classroom behind a screen. It wasn't long before Joan was arriving early to school and staying late. She wasn't interested in chasing boys or being chased; she just wanted to paint. Miss Sharam encouraged her to enter competitions and, emboldened by successes in them, Joan kept painting.

Then Miss Sharam became Mrs French and stopped teaching. By then, however, Joan was in full flight, and she stayed that way for quite a while.

After she married Isaac, she thought she'd find magic in their marriage too, then in motherhood. Both of those roles, as it turned out, had more to do with militarism, colonialism and conquering wildness – so they felt familiar, but they weren't what she wanted. She knows that now.

The phone rings, deep in the sitting room behind her, and she walks swiftly towards it before it rings out.

'Hello?'

'Darling.' It's what Isaac always calls her. Sometimes she thinks he's forgotten her name, even as she feels mean thinking it. She knows women who wish their husbands would use such endearments.

'Hi.'

'Having a good day?' He sounds distracted, as he always does when he's at work. Secretaries coming and going, appointments to keep, briefs to study. The law. His great love, she joked once, but really it's the lifestyle the law affords him that he loves.

'Sure,' she says, because he's not interested. Her job is to make his home run smoothly and keep his social connections humming, keep up with their children – both grown, both in their own homes, and their daughter with her own baby – and inform him of their comings and goings. She is chatelaine and confidante and companion, and what she wants almost more than anything in the world is for someone to be that for her.

The thing she wants most in the world is to pick up a paintbrush again. But there's no space for that in this life she's allowed to be built around her.

That's unfair: she has let it happen in that she hasn't resisted it. She lives in a house with art on the walls and none of it's hers. She has a life in which everyone tells her what they want and she makes it happen for them but she does not, ever, open her mouth and say what *she* wants. Because she's not meant to want anything, is she, other than the happiness of her nearest and dearest.

Except she does. Oh, she wants things. She wants that hum in her veins that used to happen when a painting flowed out of her. She wants the stillness she would feel in the air around her when she was sitting in nature, looking at nature, trying to capture nature on a canvas in front of her. That feeling was like a drug, and she was gleefully hooked on it. It is almost impossible to understand now why she ever gave it up, no matter how much she rationalises it to herself and how she knows that it came only in the wake of the greatest shock of her life, when she was so shaken she didn't trust herself to make anything other than tears. So many years ago now, too many to let it stop her from painting again.

And now she feels guilty that she has this glittering existence in this perfect house, and she doesn't care for it. For any of it. Because it seems empty.

'Listen, darling,' Isaac says, and she snaps back to the present.

'Mm?' she says, watching as a car drives along the road on the opposite point.

'Late notice, sorry, really, but I invited some people to dinner.'

That's got her attention. 'Tonight?'

'Yes. Just eight of us. Nothing big.'

'Eight invited or eight in total?' The question sounds robotic because she has become an automaton where these requests are concerned, given how often Isaac makes them of her. She has long since given up asking him to give her fair warning of dinner parties and stopped being cross about them too. There's just no point.

'Eight total. Including you, of course. Although,' he starts laughing, 'there will be a lot of work talk so you may be bored.'

I'm sure I will be, she thinks. And she's not sure he doesn't count on it: that she'll be so bored she takes herself off and they can all sit there and talk about work.

'Right,' she says. 'What time?'

'Seven.'

She looks at her watch. It's almost midday. She does not have enough food in the house to feed eight people, which means she has to do a lot of work in a short space of time.

'All right,' she says. There's no other acceptable response. She knows the drill: cook and serve and be the hostess he expects her to be. At least the house doesn't need to be cleaned; Isaac is barely here enough to sully it and she cleans up after herself every day. They could afford help, of course, but part of her feels like she needs to take responsibility for their domestic life, that she's not worth anything unless she is being useful. Or perhaps she just needs to feel useful and she's telling herself that she's really self-less instead.

'You're a treasure, darling. See you later.'

The call is over. He doesn't tell her what time he'll be home because she knows it will be just before whatever time dinner is. So she's on her own preparing everything. Again.

There's so much to do.

Standing by the open balcony doors, she feels the breeze. It's cool but tolerable. She closes her eyes and listens to boats clinking, a dog barking, children calling out, a cockatoo squawking. When she opens her eyes she can't see the sources of the noise but she knows they inform the scene she is looking at below. The beauty of nature and the traces of humanity that form a portrait she wishes she could paint.

That's when she feels it for the first time in decades: the hum.

The hairs on her arms stand up and a shiver runs up her spine. She remembers this, not just in her brain but in her body. The feeling that she just has to *do something, make something*.

And what she absolutely does not want to make is dinner. Not again. Not ever.

She shuts the balcony doors forcefully and turns away from the view, her breath quickening.

This house is lovely, and it is a trap. Her husband is decent, but she suspects he does not care for her, not really. Her children – well, when she's feeling less than generous she thinks they only care about the ways in which she can help them, even though she has been so keen to offer that help, over and over. So this is a trap she has probably laid for herself, even as she doesn't want to take responsibility for it. She's not sure she wants to take responsibility for anything ever again. Not for this house or her husband's dinners or her friends' disappointments. With one exception: she loves her granddaughter, Natalie, and would gladly take care of her forever. That angel face, that baby smell, the wispy hair on her head, the little scratches on her cheeks from her sharp baby fingernails. She loves it all; she wishes she could preserve it all.

Joan smiles as she thinks of her granddaughter's dimples, but stops when she remembers her daughter, Corinne, presuming that she is always available to help. As if Joan has nothing else going on in her life. And that rankles because, well, it's largely true. Joan let her interests – indeed, the passions of her younger self – slide out of her life once she married and had children. She can't really blame her husband or her children, either, because with a bit of effort she could have kept them up. But it was just all too hard. Or it seemed that way at one time. One time that changed her forever.

There was another baby, twenty-five years ago, she couldn't keep with her. That was the greatest shock of her life. Every day, she hopes she'll get over it. That hope is sometimes, she thinks, the only proof that she's still here when she can tend to feel like she exists in some kind of limbo.

Joan shivers and closes her eyes again, willing the hum to abate. When she was young and painting all the time she would let the hum take her over and lose track of time, and sometimes of place. It was a rapture, of sorts. She can't allow a rapture to take place now. There is too much at stake. For one thing, there is the Joan she has become, the only Joan she knows now: wife, mother, good citizen.

That's not the Joan she wants to be, though. She wants the other one back – the one who succumbed to the rapture. Who felt that hum in her veins and let it flow like the drug it was. Who had not known great loss and still believed in magic. That Joan does not know how to poach salmon for eight and make a pavlova and set the table just so and arrange flowers like a florist.

No, she's not going to make dinner tonight.

Hurrying upstairs to her bedroom, she pulls out a decent-sized suitcase and chooses some clothes to go into it. Given almost everything in her wardrobe coordinates, this task is fairly simple.

She goes to the secret stash of money she keeps in her underwear drawer – the one she has 'just in case' because her father, who had felt the sting of the Great Depression and World Wars, told her to always have cash on hand in case something happened to the banks. She puts it all in her handbag and picks up the chequebook for the bank account she opened when her grandfather died and left her a tidy inheritance. As Isaac never asked if she had received anything in her grandfather's will, she didn't tell him, and now she's glad of that.

Toiletries, a winter coat, a couple of pairs of shoes, the book she's reading and her reading glasses go into the suitcase.

Joan hauls the case downstairs then picks up her keys. She pulls off the car key and leaves the house keys behind. They're not needed any more.

Out to the driveway of that lovely home with its harbour views and guest bedrooms and swimming pool and a tennis court they never use. Her new-model Mercedes is in its usual spot. Suitcase in the back, handbag in the front.

Within seconds, she has reversed onto the street and soon she is driving towards the Harbour Bridge, heading south, for the Hume Highway, letting instinct guide her away from the dinners that will remain uncooked and the perfect house she won't be able to appreciate and the phone calls that will be made from that house in search of her.

She drives past Goulburn and Yass and places she knew as a child when her parents would put her and her sisters in the back seat and take them away for school holidays. Into Victoria, which as an adult she hasn't known well apart from the occasional trip to Melbourne and its boutiques.

Melbourne isn't where she wants to go, though. Too much of a city, not enough of an escape.

The Mornington Peninsula is her destination. This part of Victoria has lived in her memories for decades, because it was where her parents would bring her and her sisters. They'd take two days to drive here, stopping in Gundagai on the way, and when they arrived at the Duchess Hotel they would all sigh with relief. It was their haven away from home.

So it is to the Duchess Hotel that Joan has escaped from her adult life. Because she has decided that the Joan who lived that life is not the Joan she wants to be for the rest of her years, and there is no better time to start than now, so she will let this road take her as far as it needs to so that she can start again.

CHAPTER TWO

This noise and bustle is the reason Frances likes to sit in the lobby of the Duchess Hotel. Not that she sits here for long. A few minutes. Long enough to appreciate, as she does every day, that there are so many different types of people in the world and a lot of them come and go from this hotel. At least, that's her theory: that the Duchess Hotel is a microcosm of the world. It's more of the world than she saw through most of her youth and now, at seventy-five, this place makes her feel more engaged in life than anything else.

Perched not far from the tip of the Mornington Peninsula, the Duchess is not a pub but a grand hotel of the old style, perched on a large amount of land not far from Sorrento Back Beach. With its views out to the Southern Ocean and winds sweeping up from Antarctica, it's an impressive place. Built like a castle. She's heard that the original owner – it was a private house – fancied himself a lord of the manor and a castle was, therefore, in order. She can't imagine why anyone would want to live in a place this large. How lonely. Hotel accommodation is a better use for it; that way people can fill it with life.

'Frances,' says a tall man with thick, dark hair and a slight stoop, as he passes, giving her a nod. That's William, the hotel's manager. Polite fellow. Always greets her even though she is in no way a regular paying customer. She's a denizen, yes, but not a guest. Not a resident. She is a local, however, and as the Duchess is only fifteen or so minutes' walk from her home it's a convenient place to visit when she feels like an outing. Plus the outing doubles as exercise, which makes her feel virtuous.

Frances sighs with contentment as she looks up to the very high ceiling of the lobby. It is decorated with a mural in a classical style, probably by someone who thought mimicking Michelangelo was a good idea, and it sort of was. Frances is more keen on Impressionists than Michelangelo. Her and everyone else, she guesses. There was some exhibition at the National Gallery in Canberra and half of Australia went. She didn't. Too hard. Melbourne seems too far for her these days and it's only a car ride away. Canberra is . . . an idea only. Maybe that means she is unadventurous. Oh well. In her youth, she would ride bareback through the High Country and help her father and her brothers put in fence posts and chase stray cattle and do all sorts of things. Plenty of adventure. She's earnt a more sedate life.

Not that she's having as quiet a time as she might. Frances is sure that when her mother was the same age she was enjoying cups of tea and crosswords and crocheting, and Frances was busy running her own family by then, as were her brothers. She might have caused her mother worry while she was still living at home, but once she was established in her own home she barely troubled her with more than a request for a recipe or a tip on removing a stain.

If only her own children could be the same.

Her son, Keith, was a talented boy and everything came easily to him at school, right up until his classmates decided to study in their final years and Keith – who had always topped the class by barely studying – found himself slipping down the rungs. It didn't motivate him to work harder; instead, he sowed the seeds of later discontent, lamenting that it wasn't fair that everyone was suddenly doing well. As if it was a mystery as to why it was happening.

Frances told him that it wasn't enough to be talented and smart, that you had to apply yourself in order to make the most of that talent. Even as she said it she feared it was too late: his path was fixed and would only change if he truly decided to change it. Which he has not.

Still, he's had opportunities. When Frances's husband, Gerald, died he left his business and the family house to Keith, reckoning that Keith would take care of Frances. But Keith ran the pharmacy into the ground and sold the house to pay the debts. Now she's in the cheapest house she could find with the money that was left, and while it's not like she hasn't lived on air before – her family were not rich – she has her pride and this has dented it. She drew the line at living in a flat – a woman who grew up in the High Country the way she did could not be confined to a box, which makes her wonder how she'll like being dead and tossed into a coffin. So she has a house, and it's small and needs repairs, but at least she's not on the street.

She knows that people aren't talking about her – because most are wrapped up in their own lives – but she feels embarrassed that her son has done this to her, and even more embarrassed that she can't bring herself to cut off contact with him. Because he's Albert's.

In 1941, when she was nineteen, she became engaged to Albert, a young man from a neighbouring property. He was from a good family, and she had no plans to leave the High Country so it seemed like a sensible idea. Plus she loved him, such as love can be at that age. He was handsome and wild – compared with the other young men she knew – and they would ride together across the mountains. She'd never felt so free as when she was with him.

Then he was called up to fight in the Pacific and that was the last time she saw him. Two years later there was a letter saying he'd died; sometime after that she found out he was on the Burma Railway, and she never liked to think about what he had gone through. And she never forgot him, not even when she married the older, respectable Gerald, to whom she was introduced on a rare trip to Melbourne. He was a friend of her aunt's, a man previously thought to be a confirmed bachelor who came alive in her presence and wasted no time proposing.

Gerald was also prepared to accept the son who had been born to Frances eight months after Albert left. It was a shock to find herself pregnant because she and Albert had only decided to be together in that way after he was called up. They didn't know if they'd see each other again, and every encounter took on an urgency that they allowed to carry them away. She didn't regret it, even once she found out how much the pregnancy would complicate her life. Keith was the only evidence she had that she was loved sincerely and truly by a good man. Perhaps that's another reason why she can't ever tell her son when he's let her down.

Gerald had his roots and his pharmacy on the Mornington Peninsula so Frances left the High Country and her family. And the headstone they installed for Albert in the local cemetery. There was no body to bury; no one knew where he was. She thinks about Albert every day; she misses the land where she grew up. She especially misses her brother Cec, who was her strength throughout the turbulent years of pregnancy and early motherhood, and his wife, Margie, who was her confidante. But wives had to go with their husbands and that's how Frances became embedded here on the lowlands.

Gerald died a decade ago, and Frances is getting towards the age he was when he died. She hates growing older. Her body doesn't behave the way she wants it to. She has trouble climbing stairs, and she fears her sight is going.

The other thing that's not behaving so well is her bank account, thanks to Keith's fondness for 'investments' that never seem to work out and the money that she doesn't have as a result of him not taking care of her the way Gerald wanted him to.

Thank goodness his sister doesn't have the same fondness for failure. No, Alison's problem is that she gets on Frances's goat. Constantly ringing to check on her. Telling her she's 'just worried,

Mum' but not being specific about the worries, which leads Frances to believe that she thinks Frances's whole existence is a worry. It's not pleasant when your own child thinks that way about you.

Frances told her friend Shane about Alison's behaviour and he told her to see it as evidence of how much Alison loves her. Shane is the bartender at the Duchess Hotel. She knows him because she goes to the Duchess almost every day, just to be there. That's her social life. Mainly because she talks to Shane. He's around Keith's age – a little older, perhaps – and he doesn't mind old ducks. That's what he said once.

Now here he is, standing in front of her with his big grin showing a little evidence of his fondness for cigarettes on his teeth. Two of her brothers had teeth stains from smoking, so she doesn't mind them.

'There you are,' Shane says, holding out his hand like the gentleman Frances knows him to be. 'I thought you'd either be here or in the garden. Fancy a drink?'

'That would be lovely.' She takes his hand, and he gently pulls her to her feet then offers her his elbow, and she takes it. She likes it when men do that – they make it easy for a lady to accept support.

Frances squeezes his arm, then they walk through scattered people and busy staff, past gilt-framed paintings and semi-worn couches, to the bar, to the place where Shane makes everyone feel welcome.

He sees her to her favourite spot then promises to return with her usual drink. And he will, she knows that. He's one of the reliable things she likes about this hotel. That, and the fact that it is unchanging even though it's constantly changing: the structure of each day is the same, the rhythms, the feeling of it, they don't change. It's the place that feels most like home to her, and the people who work here are a huge part of that.

'Here you go,' Shane says, putting a shandy in front of her and waving off her money, as he always does. But she has to offer; that's only right. The only time she ever gets to pay is when someone else is behind the bar, which isn't often. She likes to do it, though, to feel like she's not entirely taking advantage.

'On me,' he says.

Then he's on his way, and she sits back and surveys the room, as she likes to do. Time to watch, time to think, time to be. That's what the Duchess gives her. In here she has no age and no concerns and no children trying to put her in an old-age home. In here she is just Frances, part of the furniture. It's heaven.

CHAPTER THREE

'Bridge, sweetie, where are you?' Kirrily calls to her daughter as she hauls towels out of the dryer and puts them in her 'clean' basket.

'*Bridge!*' Her daughter is somewhere in the house, probably with her head in a book, and Kirrily wants to find her so she can feed her and her brother before their father comes home, so then all Connor needs to do is put them to bed. The benefit of the kids being six and eight is that she can feed them early. And Connor is never late, so that helps her organise things.

Kirrily puts more towels into the clean basket. She likes to keep the laundry separate – one basket for dirty and one for clean even when there's nothing in either of them. It's a distinction she thinks logical and her husband, Connor, believes to be extravagant.

'We end up wearing it all anyway,' he said once. 'Can't it all go in together?'

Not for her it can't, because she likes things just so. Some might say she likes them a little too *just so* to the point where she's obsessive. Or fanatical.

Right around the time Connor puts the kids to bed, Kirrily will be in the laundry at the Duchess Hotel, making things clean for the guests. At the Duchess, they appreciate her love of cleanliness – all right, her preoccupation with it. William tells her all the time that she's the neatest, tidiest, cleanest employee he's ever had.

That's why he likes her being in the laundry on weekends when they're busier. At other times she's a maid. Or a factotum. William just calls her 'a staff member' but a maid is what you are when you run things up to people's rooms and clean up spills and check to see where their husbands or children are.

The clientele of the Duchess Hotel can be quite demanding, you see. The hotel is expensive so the guests like to think of themselves as being a bit ooh-lah-lah. Or la-di-da, maybe. They remind Kirrily of the song 'Puttin' on the Ritz'. She loves that song. And she thinks of it each time a guest demonstrates a few airs and graces that they definitely weren't born with and probably didn't grow up with but which they've put on especially to annoy her and the other workers.

Kirrily's developed theories about people and classes thereof since she started working at the Duchess. These are not theories she had while she was growing up because her experience of the world was what one of her teachers called 'limited'.

She spent her younger years in Tasmania, the eldest of five children. Her mother died when Kirrily was thirteen, which meant she had to look after her siblings so her father could go to work and support them. He worked in a timber mill in Burnie, in the island's north, where it was freezing in winter and less freezing in summer but, still, warmer than other parts of Tasmania.

Kirrily would stand on the beach looking north into Bass Strait and dream about what might lie across the water: a life where she could do whatever she wanted, when she wanted, no siblings to look after. She had dreams of being a dancer in the Australian Ballet or maybe a singer in a rock band. Something glamorous. Grand. Different to how her life was. It felt small and she felt constrained.

So one day she took the ferry across Bass Strait to Melbourne and tried to make it as a singer because she knew she didn't have what it took to make it as a dancer. She didn't have it as a singer either and ended up working in a pub. That's where she met Connor when he was out one night drinking with his mates. He stayed until closing then after closing; he walked her home, because she lived close enough to walk but far enough for it to be a little scary at night. With him she felt safe. He was tall, and fit from his work as a plumber, and after she'd known him for a little while she realised that he was prepared to take on all the responsibility she'd been carrying ever since her mother died. For her siblings she had been mother, father, caregiver and caretaker. Connor took that off her hands and said he'd look after her.

He told her stories about growing up on the Mornington Peninsula, how he loved the wild coastline and the ocean and the southerlies, but Melbourne was where the work was so that's why he was here. When she got pregnant – not intentionally – he proposed straightaway then suggested that maybe they could make a go of it on the peninsula, them and their baby with his parents nearby to help. She liked the idea of help. And she loved him, with his ruddy cheeks and ginger hair and sandy eyelashes, his warm hands and subtle kindnesses. He didn't like to make a show of helping people but on weekends he'd be fixing taps for the elderly gentleman two doors down or mowing someone's lawn.

Now they live in Rosebud, and Connor works all over the place. There's always work for a plumber, as he likes to say.

'Mama.' Bridget is standing in the doorway of the laundry holding her favourite teddy bear.

'Hello, sweetie.' Kirrily blinks, wondering how long her daughter has been there hoping her mother would notice. Lack of sleep is something Kirrily has become used to but it does mean she can space out from time to time.

'Where's Daddy?' Bridget inspects the teddy's nose.

'On his way home.' Kirrily smiles weakly. 'Then I'm going to work, remember?'

Bridget nods and hugs her teddy. She's probably getting too old to cart that thing around, yet Kirrily can't blame her for wanting something to hug every now and again.

'Is Aidan still playing with his toys?' Kirrily asks.

Bridget nods again and Kirrily places the basket full of neatly folded laundry on top of the silent dryer. Connor will put it away later.

'Let's go and get you some dinner, shall we?' Kirrily kisses the top of Bridget's head and waits for her to move out of the way so she can lead her to the living room, where Aidan looks content, playing with his Matchbox cars.

As the children are finishing dinner, she hears Connor's car in the driveway. Not that long ago she wouldn't see him until later on Fridays because he'd be having his usual Friday catch-up at the pub with his mates. Who knows when he'll make it back to that. It's more important that she takes the work when it's available.

'Hi, love.' He kisses her, smelling of deodorant and a trace of aftershave and a little bit of sweat. The cocktail is different every time.

'They're fed,' she says, and she can hear the weariness in her voice.

'You go; I've got it.' He kisses the top of her head.

'Bye, darlings,' she says, placing her own kisses on little heads before she scoops up her keys.

Kirrily never used to work Fridays. Her original shifts were Saturdays and Sundays from 4 p.m. until midnight or thereabouts, with Connor looking after the kids after he worked all week himself. Fridays are an extra shift and when William asked her to do them she accepted immediately.

Neither she nor Connor likes the fact that there isn't a day when they aren't both working but it's what they have to do, with rent to pay and two children and all the usual costs of life. Connor makes fairly good money, plus he's usually home just after the kids finish school because he starts so early. He can help with homework while she makes dinner, and they both have long days but they're in it together.

Even though his income is sufficient to cover most things, it can't provide a buffer against future things. That's why she looked for work. Their son, Aidan, is going to need more surgery down the track. He's already had more than any little boy should.

When he was four, they were at a neighbour's place. A different neighbourhood; a different part of the peninsula altogether. It was winter but they were all outside, around a bonfire. Kirrily and Connor weren't standing together. They were busy chatting to other people. Drinking beer or wine or something. She can't remember. There were plenty of kids there too and they were running around in a pack.

She remembers the scream. For the rest of her life, she will remember it.

Aidan tripped over and fell towards the fire, his arms out in front of him. The man standing closest snatched him back but her son's torso and his arms were badly burnt. Somehow his hands were not, for the most part. Some knuckles. But not his thumbs. She imagined he had them tucked into his palms, like he did when he slept as a baby.

The screaming only stopped once the ambulance took him away and by then Kirrily wasn't sure if it was Aidan screaming or her. Connor could barely look at her while she clutched Bridget and tried to understand how it had happened. How she and her husband had both looked away long enough for permanent damage to take place.

Aidan was in hospital for weeks. There were grafts then follow-up surgeries. Because he was so little and he'll keep growing – maybe even become as tall as Connor – they have to take him back every now and again for more surgery, to do what they can to keep him comfortable.

It's not something she and Connor want to rely on the public health system for, because they like to take care of things as they're needed. They both feel too much guilt about what happened to make Aidan wait. That's where her Duchess money comes in:

private health cover and a little savings account. For the rainiest of days.

She parks her car in the staff area out the back of the hotel. Just as well there are enough spaces here because if she had to park outside the grounds, she'd have a long, dark walk back at night, down the driveway fringed with pines. It's kind of spooky amongst those pines. Or maybe she just has an overactive imagination. Her mother used to tell her that, usually when Kirrily would say she dreamt of living somewhere other than Burnie.

'Well, if it isn't Glinda the Good Witch.'

She hears the greeting as she arrives in the staff common room and she doesn't have to turn around to know it's Shane. He's been calling her that since she started because her hair is long and wavy like Glinda's in *The Wizard of Oz* – although she ties it up once she arrives at work. He says she's a goody-two-shoes because she doesn't gossip about staff nor will she say anything bad about guests. As far as she's concerned that doesn't make her good, just sensible. Gabbing about people always comes back at you.

'Shane,' she says drily as she pushes her handbag into a locker. 'Reusing your old material, I see.'

'You know me,' he says with a wink. 'Not very original.'

She doesn't think that's true. Shane can be funny, and he seems smart.

'What are you doing back here?' she says, checking her watch. It's bang on four, and usually that's a busy time in the bar.

'Looking for you, as a matter of fact.'

'Oh?'

'A few extra in the bar – some footy function or something. We need a hand.'

'We?'

'Hopeless Harry.' He raises his eyebrows and she knows why: Harry gets assigned to Shane when William wants to get him out of someone else's way, mainly because he's hopeless, hence his nickname. William won't fire him because his aunt used to work here and she's still alive and calling William to check on her nephew's progress.

'So basically you want me to do the jobs Harry is meant to do?' she asks.

'No, that's what I'll be doing. I need you to clear the empties and generally keep an eye on things.'

'I don't know anything about bar work.'

'Mate, if an idiot like me can do it, anyone can.' He winks again. 'See you in there.'

He's gone before she can ask if William knows about this but she presumes he does. Shane has worked here long enough to know the procedure.

It could be quite fun being in the bar. Buzzy. That's what she's telling herself as she pushes through the staff door that connects with the foyer and is greeted with a wall of sound. There's the noise of what could be fifty people calling out to each other accompanied by high-pitched laughing from all directions. The place is busier than she's ever seen it, and it gives her a slight thrill, because she knows that the busier it is the more wrapped up in it she becomes. She doesn't think about money or chores at home or the fact that she hasn't called her father in weeks, or that Connor's parents are thinking of going to Europe for a few weeks, which would mean they couldn't provide occasional babysitting for a while. The only breaks she and Connor have are when they can take the kids.

So she and Connor hardly spend time together and she misses him, and he says he misses her, although sometimes she wonders if that's true because he doesn't look at her the way he used to. Not as a woman. She hopes that look will return one day, but for now they just have to keep working to get ahead. It's the sacrifice they agreed to make to have a more comfortable life than the one they each grew up with.

CHAPTER FOUR

Alison has been married to Tadeusz for . . . fifteen years? Maybe it's sixteen . . . Is it bad that she can't remember? Probably, but it's not as if she's been counting the days. If she had been, then that would make her marriage sound like a prison sentence and usually being married to Tad is the opposite of that, because he never tries to restrict her.

Anyway, she's been married to him long enough to have given birth to Sean fourteen years ago and Rosie twelve years ago, and Tad's been a great father to them, and the whole time he's been a reasonable father to Erik, who lives with his mother. Alison has to say 'reasonable' because Tad's fathering of Erik has been intermittent. Also because Erik is a very different character to Sean and Rosie, and Alison doesn't know where to put the responsibility for that. Which makes it sound bad. And it is. Erik hasn't been a model teenager. Now he's legally an adult but he's still behaving like a wayward kid.

Then this morning Tad told her that Erik wants to come and live with them. Actually, that's not true: Erik's mother, Sunny, has had enough of him and she told him to get out. Given that Erik doesn't have a job, or a purpose in life, and that Tad feels guilty about the fact that Erik hasn't lived with him since he was two, Tad told Erik that he could come and live with them. He just didn't ask Alison first.

Obviously she was upset. She has tried to be fond of Erik – as fond as you can be of a boy-now-man who glares at you every time he sees you. It wasn't her fault his parents' marriage broke up. Sure, she met Tad not long after it happened and Erik probably thinks there was some overlap – which there was not, she would never do that – and no doubt he has wished that he could have the same attention from Tad that Alison's children have had, but life never follows a script. And if it did, whose script would that be? Alison believes in God sometimes but she doesn't think it would be His script.

No, there's no script; there's no plan; we're just stumbling along – all of us, together, separately, alone, apart – trying to make the best of it.

So – deep breath – she has to try to make the best of this situation and also try to help her children do the same, because it will be a huge disruption for them.

'Alison, did you put that meeting in my diary?'

She looks up to see her boss, Glen, standing over her, frowning.

'Yes, why?'

He's always double-checking her work even though there is absolutely no need. Sometimes she thinks he just likes having an opportunity to speak to her. She gets the impression he's lonely. That's what she prefers to think, at least.

'No reason.' He flashes her a smile. 'Just checking.'

Just-checking could be his middle name.

'Okay.'

He stays standing by her desk and she raises her eyebrows in question.

'Would you like a coffee?' she guesses.

'Lovely. Thanks.'

Then he's gone and she sighs as she pushes herself up to standing. He's an adult male who, she is sure, can make his own coffee – two spoonfuls of Moccona, one of sugar, it's not hard – but she's never seen it. And she can't tell him to make his own because she wants to keep her job.

After she's made and delivered Glen's coffee, Alison picks up the phone and dial's her mother's number. It's a habit she's fallen into. Actually, that's not correct: it's one she's developed. Ever since her father died and Frances has lived alone, Alison has felt she needs to check on her. Not unlike, she guesses, the way Glen checks. But not the same, because he's doing it to be irritating whereas she's doing it because she worries.

Sometimes her mother snaps at her about it.

'I'm not a child, Alison!' she'll say. Or, 'What do you think has happened in the last hour since you phoned me?'

Ten years of snapping at her about it, though, and Alison hasn't been moved to break the habit. Even though she knows she shouldn't bother Frances so much – knows that it's her own anxiety that's propelling her behaviour – she is not inclined to stop. Because one day something *will* happen in between her phone calls. That's the day she dreads. And she really doesn't want to have to find out on a phone call. She wants to be there for her mother. Her father died alone in a hospital bed and Alison has never forgiven herself for not being there. So she's trying to put things in place to ensure her mother is not alone when the time comes. If only Frances would stop resisting.

'Hi, Mum,' she says when Frances answers.

'Hello, love.' Frances sounds distracted. Alison checks her watch. Right. That's why she's distracted – it's nearly Duchess Hotel time. Frances will put on her sensible shoes and traipse up the street to go and be surrounded by strangers – and Shane. Frances loves Shane. She's always talking about Shane. Sometimes Alison thinks her mother is more interested in Shane than in Sean and Rosie. Or her, for that matter.

Not Keith. Frances is always interested in Keith. Even thinking about Keith makes Alison feel tense. He wasn't the nicest brother while they were growing up and he's even less nice as an adult.

Except he's her brother and you have to make exceptions for family. Like she's about to do for Erik.

'I know you have to go,' Alison starts.

'It's all right. I have a few minutes.'

'Heard from Margie?' Alison's aunt, married to Frances's brother Cec, is the other person who keeps tabs on Frances. Alison knows that if Frances is keeping something from her, Margie probably knows about it. Which rankles a little, but her mother is allowed to talk to other people. Maybe.

'This morning.'

'Is she well?'

'Sounds like it. Cec has a toothache or something.' Silence for a few seconds. 'How are you?'

'Tad's son is moving in,' Alison says in a rush.

She likes to keep Frances updated with news. Or maybe she just likes having someone to tell it to, someone who has to put up with her nattering away because they're related.

'Oh?'

Alison believes she can hear her mother pursing her lips.

'Yes, um . . . He doesn't want to live with his mother any more.'

'How is that your concern? Or Sean's? Or Rosie's?'

Immediately Alison feels tense, and she knows why: Frances is implying that Tad should take care of this without involving anyone else, which means she's taking Alison's side, except Alison isn't sure she should take her own side in this. If she even has a side. Her side should be supporting her husband, shouldn't it? That's why she's tense: she doesn't know what she should do. Which is the subconscious reason why she called her mother. Frances will tell her straight.

'Tad's my husband,' Alison says meekly.

'And this falls under the "for worse" category of "for better, for worse", I imagine.'

'Mum!' she cries, although she can't help but agree.

'That Erik has always been troublesome,' Frances says. 'I'm just concerned . . .'

Alison hears a sigh.

'He's a good kid at heart,' Alison says, because she wants to believe it. Also because her mother used to say that about Keith.

'Alison!' Glen calls from his office.

'I have to go, Mum,' Alison says.

'Ta-ta, love.'

Frances hangs up first; she knows that when Glen calls Alison has to jump. Still, Alison holds onto the phone a bit longer, listening to the hung-up sound. It's weird how you can be a mother yourself and still want your own mummy sometimes. She wishes Frances could fix the Erik situation like she fixed Alison's grazed knees and elbows. The way Alison fixed them for her own children.

She'll have to be her own mother this time and – to borrow a favourite phrase of her mother's – be a grown-up and get on with it.

'*Alison!*'

'Coming,' she calls, putting the phone down, already thinking ahead to when she's going to call Frances tonight. Just to check she's back from the Duchess. Not to talk about Erik because she'll be at home and Tad would hear her.

Oh, the ways we navigate around the people we love sometimes, like they're snags in a river instead of the river itself. On days like this Alison doesn't like being an adult much.

Pen and paper in hand, she goes into Glen's office, ready to take her orders.

CHAPTER FIVE

As Joan had driven south she knew where she was heading in the literal sense but no more than that; certainly she didn't have the feeling that her future was as open as the road she was driving on. If anything, it felt like a narrow tunnel leading to a place she knew but a state of mind she didn't.

The only conscious decision she had made was to stop at Bowral in the Southern Highlands to buy some pencils and drawing paper. There would come a time, she knew, when she would want to express something, and she would need the means to do it. The only means she has ever known is through her hands: to put something on paper or a canvas, to interpret what she sees within the context of what she feels. Art for her has never been about rendering what's in front of her as faithfully as she can; it's been about expressing what's within her using what's in front of her as the vehicle.

Choosing to paint a tree one day meant she was feeling one sort of way; a water scene meant another. She would never actually remember, once the painting was complete, what she had hoped to achieve or express. The act of creation had taken care of whatever itch she was trying to scratch. It's why she laughed at a friend who swore by her psychiatrist, and Joan said she would never need such help because she had her art.

Then, of course, she stopped painting.

It didn't feel like a choice; it just happened. After that she had Nathan and Corinne and she needed to dedicate herself to her family. Except she didn't replace art with anything else, and there were times – terrible times – when she needed it. Her hands would ache to do something yet she never went back to it. Because she wasn't that person any more, or so she thought. She wasn't that supposedly flighty – as her mother used to call her – paint-covered young woman trying to make sense of the world through shades of yellow and blue and red. She was a wife. She was a mother. She was a daughter and a sister and a friend. All these roles lived in relation to others and nothing for herself, all these years.

She should never have stopped painting.

Yet, as everyone who is older than about twenty-five knows, hindsight is the source of all wisdom.

What hindsight is telling her now is that everything she did not express for those years can still find its way through her hands and to the paper or canvas, because it's still inside her, not festering so much as fermented. Maybe the bubbling over had happened as she put her keys in the ignition in her driveway in Sydney. Or maybe it is yet to come, here at the Duchess Hotel. There's only one way to find out, and that involves sitting still, pencil in hand, paper in front of her, and seeing – feeling – what emerges.

She has worked out that the windows in her hotel room are facing south-east, although the morning light is harsher than she'd like at this time of year. Winter light can be whiter, sharper, than summer light. Or spring or autumn light. There are nuances in light that she used to know better than she does now but that knowledge is still part of her, even if she has lost the habit, over the years, of noticing the world around her the way she used to. When she was painting all the time each day was an opportunity for a new scene, a new palette, a new way of viewing. It kept her engaged in life and she was foolish, she knows, to believe that she would be more occupied by life at home. That was a line she was fed by her friends, by her mother, by her teachers. She kept trying to swallow it, and it always felt stuck in her chest. Right where her heart used to be. Or the heart she knew. That heart didn't die so much as shatter several years ago and she has been wondering how to reassemble it ever since.

It is a strange thing, Joan thinks, when a woman leaves her husband. Strange because it's not the normal thing, is it? Nor is it the acceptable thing. Women are meant to stay in their marriages and put up with the things that irk them and the children who take them for granted and the husband who tends to prefer his workplace over his home, and they're meant to just take it.

Not her.

That's what she feels as she looks out the window of this second-storey room in a hotel that means more to her than she's expressed to anyone.

She never stayed in this room when she used to visit, of that she is sure. The second-floor rooms were always the expensive ones when she was a child. The Duchess was an annual treat even in the cheaper rooms, for a hardworking man and his harder-working wife and their children. Joan's father had a small-goods shop in their south-west Sydney suburb, and he was always gone before dawn and back after dinner. Her mother had to manage everything in between. They toiled most of the day and still there wasn't much in the way of fripperies. Because, as Joan knows now, they were saving everything they could for this one week a year at the Duchess.

This hotel, therefore, is bound up in her feelings towards her parents. The resentment she felt as a teenager when they had no time for her because she didn't understand that they worked so hard in order to give her that freedom; the gratitude she feels now for how they provided for her and her sisters.

Not that it stopped her leaving them behind too. Isaac won't tell them she's gone, not for a while. Joan should probably call them at some stage to inform them that she is a civilian with a military acronym: AWOL. And that she is alive, because they may presume something has befallen her. As it has: the life she never led has arrived to haul her out of the one she found herself in.

The trees she can see from her window were there years ago. Pines. She can't tell if they're the same height as they were back then because she always saw them from the ground, and she was shorter at the time.

Beyond the pines there is ocean. Not immediately – that is, not right next to the hotel. But there are the pines, then the end of land, and a cliff face, of sorts, down to a wild beach not far from the beach where a prime minister died while swimming one day.

If Joan opens the window, she will feel a southerly; there are always southerlies. And she's facing south, so that makes sense. Or south-ish.

So: the light. That is her first consideration for what she's to attempt here. Sitting in front of the desk in her hotel room, she has moved a mirror from the bathroom and perched it in front of her, trying to angle it so she can see herself properly in order to draw a self-portrait.

It was rarely her inclination to draw herself, back when she had plenty of time to choose other subjects. It seems fitting now, however, since she's cloistered herself in this room, to start with the subject that needs the most exploration.

She begins the way she always used to: by looking. In front of her is a woman who would be said by most to be past her prime, yet she feels she hasn't even reached it. And they would say that because the skin on her face isn't as firm as it once was; her eyelids are sagging, although her blue irises are still bright. It doesn't pay to look too deeply into them, though, because she knows there is no end to the depth of loss there. Loss she tossed all the way to the bottom of the well, too far down to retrieve. Yet here she is, staring at it, thinking of ways she can get to it because it's time to pull it up and have a good look at it. Time to remember the child who was hers for four months then gone. The child whose portrait was the last she drew.

After Rachel was born, Joan always found time to draw her, as if she couldn't believe she existed and needed to document her. In between feeding and naps and nappy changes, she would snatch a few minutes to pick up her pencils and put something, anything, on paper. Once Rachel died, Joan wondered if she knew it was going to happen, subconsciously, because her pressing need to gather evidence that Rachel was here became evidence itself that she knew Rachel wouldn't stay. It scared her to think that; to consider the idea that her child's death was in train even as life began. How could she live in a world that worked like that? There was no way to make sense of it.

Joan's fringe covers the fine lines on her forehead so she pushes it back and puts a headband on. Those lines deserve to be seen – they are hard won. As are those around her mouth and at the corners of her eyes.

Her hair is the same shoulder-length grown-out bob cut worn by half the women in her suburb. Boring, conventional, practical. All the things she wished never to be and plans never to go back to being.

Having made a good survey, she starts drawing and doesn't look up for a while. The image she wants to commit to the paper is in her mind's eye and that's what she's drawing. Once the basis of it is down, she looks up again and checks details.

Her hand moves fluidly, like it has never stopped. That old warmth in her veins – or is it her nerves – flows. This feels right; natural. This is her way of being, so long dormant.

She sighs. A release of tension or concern, maybe. She's not that interested in examining her own state of being in order to find out. The sigh was involuntary; she'll leave it at that.

Once she's satisfied that she has something – not a perfect something, but evidence that she was here – she stands and stretches.

The change in light outside tells her that more time has passed than she knows, and when she checks her watch, she sees it's four o'clock.

It's time for a pre-dinner drink. She wonders if the bar downstairs is as ornate as it used to be, then picks up her room key and decides to find out.

CHAPTER SIX

As Frances walks slowly through the foyer of the Duchess Hotel, she sees Wendy coming towards her at what could only be considered a collision-course pace.

Wendy likes to attend the hotel bar most days to have a few drinks and see if there are any attractive guests she can pick up. When a maid once mentioned a lady of the night going to a resident's room, Frances wondered if she meant Wendy, then decided that was mean. Not that she said it out loud, but it's not good to have mean thoughts. Is it? She's still on the fence about that. At her age, she should probably have a position but it just goes to show that growing older doesn't mean you've sorted everything out.

'Hi,' says Wendy, pulling up just in front of Frances.

'Hello, Wendy.' Frances smiles as warmly as she can. She doesn't want to be Wendy's friend nor does she wish to be rude. 'How are you?'

'Worn out!' Wendy sighs dramatically. 'Done three loads of washing, run the kids around to their friends' places, done the ironing. Do you wonder I drink!' She laughs, a little nervously.

'Not at all.' Far be it for Frances to judge anyone for having vices.

'You heading in to the bar?' Wendy gestures to the open door towards the back part of the foyer where the entrance to the bar is partly obscured by a large statue, again in the Michelangelo style.

'No,' Frances says. 'To the tea room.'

'Shane won't be happy about that.' Wendy nudges her.

'He'll live.'

'Is he single?' Wendy says.

Frances is taken aback by the sudden change of tack. 'No,' she replies, which is partly the truth: Shane is married, but his wife has left him. 'And he's not for you anyway,' she adds, and Wendy's face falls, so perhaps her tongue is still sharp. 'Not when he works here, Wendy. If it went bad, you wouldn't be able to come back.'

'True.' Wendy purses her lips. 'I'd kill for a durry.'

'How extreme,' Frances mutters.

'I'll just go out for a smoke before I go to the bar. Have fun with . . . tea.' Wendy looks dubious about the suggestion just before she turns away.

Frances ambles into the tea room, with its civilised-looking ladies and their set hair and dainty pearl earrings, blouses with bows and neat suits. She's not a tea-taking person usually, but her daughter, Alison, wanted to meet her at the Duchess – 'Since you spend so much time there, Mum,' she said, and there was a little archness to it that Frances ignored. It's not Alison's place to tell her where to spend her time. Alison can do what she wants with her own time and Frances will do the same.

Now, here she is getting worked up. It's because her daughter is treating her like a child and Frances does not enjoy it. When Alison's eldest was born she gave Frances a list of instructions for when she babysat and Frances laughed, not sure whether to take it as a commentary on her own parenting or as evidence that Alison was a little dense, thinking her mother didn't know how to mother. Alison has been giving her instructions ever since, like she can't manage or something, and it rankles. It really does. You raise a child – and her brother – and you keep them healthy and safe and in return they act as if you don't know enough to be left alone in a room.

So Frances comes here, to the Duchess, partly to play truant from her child. Because Alison also has a habit of popping round to check on her. And now she can't escape her at the Duchess either.

It's nice, this room, with its high ceiling and lattice work, large oil paintings on the walls and damask curtains, somewhat faded now. Those curtains have been there for years; so has she.

She first visited the Duchess Hotel not long after she moved to the area, somewhat reluctantly, when she married Gerald. Reluctantly because the ocean has never really been her thing, yet she finds herself surrounded by it.

Frances is a child of the mountains. Inland is what she knows. Altitude and alpine scrub. She grew up on a cattle farm in the High Country. They were bred tough out there – both people and cattle. Her mother had rough hands but a warm heart, not that she was prone to showing it. Once when Frances was a teenager, her mother admitted that she had to be hard on Frances and her brothers because they could die in that environment otherwise. In that one statement Frances detected her mother's love and fear of what might happen to her beloveds, but it was not a sentiment she expressed again, and not one Frances expected her to. Talking wasn't the done thing in her family; action was always their preferred method of communication.

Frances did the same jobs as her brothers and, for that matter, as her father. She rode horses; she mended fences; she drove trucks once she was old enough, all of which made her feel strong and capable.

'Would you like something a little stronger in that tea?'

Frances smiles before she even looks up, because she knows who has asked the question: Shane, on duty during afternoon tea service to accommodate the requests for other beverages. Wendy wouldn't know that about him because she only ever goes to the bar.

'What are you offering?' she says.

He grins and bends down to kiss her on the cheek. Presumably he's not allowed to be so familiar with guests but she is not a guest so much as a part of the furniture. Seeing him always makes her happier. Perhaps a part of her would like to swap him for Keith. He's more of a son to her than her own. Shane looks out for her; he chats to her, makes sure she is taken care of while she's on the premises. In short, he treats her like a person, and now that she's older she can feel like she's invisible to others. Never invisible to him, though.

'Whatever you like.' He straightens and puts a hand on the back of her chair. He shaved his head a couple of years ago – because he was balding, she imagines, and the hairline that was developing didn't flatter him – and it suits him. His face is strong, almost patrician. It can carry a bald head.

'Maybe a nip of bourbon,' she half-whispers.

'As long as it won't get you in trouble with Alison.' He's smiling as he says it but Frances knows he's serious.

It is Frances's firm conviction that Alison is waiting to pounce on evidence of her frailty as a reason to put her in a nursing home. Frances would rather die – literally – than go into a home because it would be an admission of weakness and she wasn't brought up to be weak.

That's also why she persists in living by herself.

Now, Alison may have a point right at this moment because Frances had a fall the other day and strained her right hand, which is very inconvenient because she's right-handed. Her corgi, Colin, surprised her. He has developed a habit of popping out the doggie door and not returning for hours, which not only makes her nervous but means he may reappear without warning.

It's not his wellbeing she worries about when he disappears; it's her own. Colin is her constant companion – unless he's out and about or she's at the Duchess – and when he's not there she is prone to think too much. Thinking is the issue. Thinking drags her into the past and rushes her into the future and neither are safe locations, really. Ghosts in one place, spectres in another.

Perhaps that's what happens when you seem to know more dead people than alive ones.

Colin came from the local pound; Alison objected to his presence, saying that Frances would trip over him. Which is why Frances is not going to tell her the truth about her sore arm, because as it is the injury has given Alison an opportunity to start up again with the 'maybe you shouldn't live alone, Mum' line but Frances still doesn't want to hear it. Her father would roll over in his grave if she depended on others to do things she can still do herself. Coming to the Duchess is something she can still do by herself – particularly with Shane as her accomplice.

'She won't know,' Frances says, and it's about the bourbon but also about how she runs her relationship with her daughter.

'How's the arm?' Shane nods at the sling that is supporting it.

'Sore.' She makes a face. 'And not healing as quickly as I would like.'

'You'll get there.' He squeezes her shoulder, and she wishes he would keep doing it. One thing about living alone she really doesn't like: there's no one to hug, no one to even tap on the arm. Some days she thinks she may atrophy from lack of human touch.

She sees Shane glance towards the doorway to the tea room, and his face changes.

'Um,' is all he says, then he raises his eyebrows at her.

'Mum!'

Frances feels her heart sink swiftly followed by a pang of remorse: she really shouldn't dread seeing her own flesh and blood. To cover for it she forces a big smile and swivels slowly in her chair.

'Hello, love!' she says with fake brightness that Alison will surely detect, then they'll have a squabble about how she makes Alison feel this, that and the other. *You make me feel bad, Mum*, that's Alison's usual refrain. To which Frances usually says: 'I don't make you feel anything – that's all your own doing.' Which is never well received.

Unexpectedly, Alison seems to buy the put-on happiness and beams, kissing her on the cheek.

'I like knowing I can find you here,' she says, sitting down, putting a big plastic bag on one of the empty chairs. 'I've brought you some wool.'

Frances represses a sigh. Alison has decided that she needs to crochet as some sort of therapy for her arm. Frances has never liked crochet and has no plans to change that. She wants to reply with something along the lines of, *And what do you want me to do with that?* But that wouldn't be well received either.

'Thank you,' she says. 'How's work?'

'Fine.' Alison waves a hand. 'Busy.' She leans across and squeezes France's non-injured arm. 'But how are *you*?'

This question is, Frances thinks, always loaded. If she admits to being lonely on occasion or feeling a little less than vigorous – as is to be expected at her age – Alison will start the old refrain and they'll fight.

'I'm fine,' she says.

Alison points to the sling. 'What about your arm?'

'It's nothing serious, Alison,' Frances says tersely.

'But it could have been serious. You're –'

She stops and because Frances knows what she was about to say she doesn't need to prompt her. *You're elderly.* That was going to be it.

Every now and again there's a moment in human interaction – especially with close relations – when two parties who love and care for each other find themselves on a precipice formed by competing interests and conflicting aims. Alison wants Frances to admit she's old and, therefore, in need of extra care, presumably in a facility that can provide such a thing; Frances is aware she's old but in no mood to admit it, lest she lose her freedom. They love each other and each doesn't want to upset the other yet they are convinced of the rightness of their position. Love and self-love – or conviction or ego – will duel on this precipice until one party falls over the edge. Frances is determined that she will not be that party.

'I'm many things,' she says firmly. 'Some of them unknown to you.'

Alison's mouth drops open. *Yes*, Frances wants to say, *mothers have secrets too.*

And so do daughters. Frances knows this. Remembers the night Alison came home dishevelled and sobbing, back when they still lived in the same house; Frances recalls the questions she asked her only daughter, trying to find out what happened. Alison wouldn't answer, and the next week she quit her job and moved to Brisbane. The reason why is still her secret, and Frances respects that even if she will always want to know it.

'I just worry,' Alison says quietly. 'That's all.'

'And I worry about you. But I accept that you have your own life and you're responsible for it.'

Alison starts to talk, and Frances holds up a hand.

'I can't live according to what makes you less worried,' she says. 'I never asked you to do that for me. It wouldn't have been fair.'

'But that was different.'

'How?'

'I was never . . .' Alison bites her lip.

'Never infirm?' Frances prompts. 'I'm not that yet either.'

'Could you just not . . . look after yourself?'

They're not as close to the edge of the precipice now but Frances can see how they can get back there in an instant: by her not making some accommodations. What Alison is asking of her isn't much, really; what she is asking of Alison – to not worry and meddle so much – probably seems like an equivalent demand. Instead of duelling they could compromise, and Alison will take her cues from her mother in that regard, because Frances is older and therefore presumed wiser, and besides, Alison has always been a respectful child.

'All right,' Frances concedes.

'And will you come over for lunch next weekend? The kids would love to see you. I'll pick you up.'

The kids are of an age where they'd have a million other things they'd rather do than see their grandmother. Alison would know that too, but that's another pact that exists between people who love each other and always will: you don't mention the temporary things that might cause permanent upset.

'Of course. That would be lovely.' Frances smiles to show she means it, and she does: she loves her grandchildren and their father, Tadeusz, whom Alison met during her time in Brisbane.

'Now.' Alison glances around the room. 'What else is new?'

It's an anodyne question and, not for the first time, Frances wonders if they will ever be honest with each other. If they even know how. Decades of pretending that everything is fine – not just to each other but to themselves and to the world, because that's what's expected, God forbid that they're ever not fine – and it's only led them here: to polite smiles and lies on a wintry afternoon, in this grand hotel with its traditions and afternoon tea. She loves the ritual of coming to this hotel and observing how it works; she loves how its rituals are fundamentally unchanging. There is comfort in rituals. Perhaps the two-step she and Alison do around each other is a ritual in itself. If so, they're going to play it out once more this afternoon, and Frances will go home alone and wait for it to happen again.

CHAPTER SEVEN

The public phone in the Duchess Hotel is discreetly tucked underneath the stairs, in a booth with a door that closes. Joan wonders what sorts of calls have been made here. Setting up rendezvous of illicit lovers? Brokering deals? Breaking up marriages? Probably nothing so dramatic. Likely the calls have been pedestrian in nature and no more scintillating than a trip to the dry cleaner's.

That's her way of geeing herself up to call her best friend, Genevieve, to tell her that she's all right.

Genevieve is someone else who'll be wondering what on earth has happened to her. They usually talk on the phone at least twice a week. Nothing major: prattle more than conversation. But they probably both know it's the connection more than the conversation that's important. The other day they talked about the Sydney Olympics – still over a year away – as if they were intimately involved in them, discussing the progress of the site at Homebush and whether or not they should flee the city during what is likely to be an intolerable time due to the influx of visitors. There was no reason to talk about the Olympics other than to make conversation, as a way of verbally keeping each other company. It was reassuring, and it's a reassurance Joan has left behind. While she's been caught up in her great escape, Genevieve has been without their connection and it's time for Joan to restore it.

It's strange, though, that she's so worried about how her closest friend of many years' standing will react. You'd think that knowing someone for so long would mean you could rely on them always being there . . . except if she applies that to her own behaviour, she knows that Genevieve would be able to say she can no longer rely on Joan.

While Joan quite likes the idea of being unreliable – of not *being there* for all and sundry any more – she doesn't want to hurt Genevieve. They've been such good friends to each other.

Probably Joan should call her husband or her children before she calls Genevieve, except her friend can, she hopes, offer her something her family can't: non-judgement. She and Genevieve have confessed all sorts of treacherous thoughts to each other over the years: in bad moments, how they'd like to leave their husbands and children; in milder times they've giggled about men they find attractive but who of course they could never go near.

Given that Joan has now acted on one of the things they've talked about, she believes Genevieve will understand. She would understand if Genevieve did it; or perhaps she's only saying that with the benefit of her own experience.

The phone in Genevieve's cavernous Cremorne house rings. That house is bigger than Joan's and Genevieve often moans about how much work it takes and how she and her husband should probably move now the children have left. But she's shown no inclination to put it on the market.

'Hello?'

Joan exhales. 'Hi, Gen.'

'Joan!'

It's almost a shriek but Joan can't tell if it's a happy or angry one.

'Where are you?' Genevieve says.

Joan swallows. 'I'd rather not say.' It's tantamount to telling Genevieve that she doesn't trust her with the information but in truth she just doesn't want to burden her with it. Isaac will be asking her if he hasn't already.

'Oh.'

The silence lasts a few seconds.

'*How* are you?' It's a gentler enquiry.

'Gen, I'm free.' She says it without thinking but knows how it sounds: like she's never coming back. And she hasn't yet decided if that's the case.

'Free?'

'I'm just . . .' Joan wants to be able to describe the lightness in her body that she's felt over the past few days: the sense of her chest opening, her chin lifting. But she knows it probably has to be experienced to be understood so she needs to think of another way to describe it. 'I wasn't happy. You know that.'

'I didn't think you were *this* not-happy.' There's a harder edge to her voice now.

'I need some time. To myself. Away from . . . everything.'

'You'd barely moved into the house!' It's an admonishment.

'I know.' Joan sighs. 'I know.' While they'd been there for a little while, she'd never unpacked her books and albums, hadn't finished ordering furniture. Sometimes she'd catch herself not wanting to do things and wonder why; now she thinks it was because unconsciously she knew she was leaving.

'Isaac's upset.'

Joan feels her jaw tighten. She hates the idea of them talking about her.

'Right,' she says.

'Don't be annoyed, Joanie.'

Don't tell me how to be, she wants to snap, and feels her neck tensing in a way it hasn't done since she arrived at the Duchess Hotel. But she won't say that out loud. She'll bite it back the way she has always bitten things back, not to preserve Genevieve's feelings but because it won't do any good. Genevieve is trying to be the peacemaker when there's no war going on. Joan is not fighting Isaac; she's simply realised she has been fighting herself all these years.

'How are you?' she says instead.

'I'm fine. Don't change the subject.'

Joan takes a breath. Clearly she's not going to be let off any kind of hook.

'Gen, I'm not coming back.'

Silence for a few seconds. 'Ever?'

'I don't know.'

'Why didn't you tell me you wanted to leave?'

'It was a snap decision. Really.'

'Nothing this big happens that quickly.' Genevieve's tone is incredulous.

'What do you want me to say?' Joan says, irritated. 'That it was building up for years? It was. That I didn't realise how much it had built up? That's the truth of it.'

'But you never said anything!'

'What could I say? I didn't know. Remember how you told me after your cancer was diagnosed that you had no idea it was in you? That you felt fine?'

Genevieve had breast cancer three years ago and Joan had helped her through her treatment, taking her to doctors' appointments because her husband was at work and her children were busy. Truthfully, though, Joan felt she was the right person for the job. If anyone in Genevieve's family had done the appointment run, Genevieve would have felt like she still had to think about their feelings and their needs; with Joan, she never had to. Joan didn't need her for anything apart from just being herself.

'Yes, but I don't –'

'This was my cancer, Gen. This . . . *bitterness*. That's what it's been.'

They're both quiet.

'What have you been bitter about?' Genevieve says softly.

'That I got so far away from myself. That I let go of things that were important to me so that I could make sure everyone else got what was important to them.'

'But isn't that love?'

Joan's laugh is short. 'Love for others, yes. What about love for myself?'

They've never had a conversation like this. Not even when Genevieve was sick. They don't do deep-and-meaningfuls, as Joan's daughter would call them. Their friendship has been long but, Joan knows now, they have barely scratched the surface. And maybe they shouldn't. Maybe this is the point at which they diverge.

'Joanie, just tell me where you are and I'll come and get you,' Genevieve says, sounding small.

'I don't want to be gotten,' Joan says.

'Joan –'

'Gen, please don't push me.' She pauses. Swallows. 'I've been pushed around enough.'

'But your family –'

'Are all grown-ups and they can manage.' She's not going to be guilt-tripped by Genevieve when Isaac, Corinne and Nathan each have two arms, two legs, working eyes and ears and brains, can make themselves toast and turn on taps. They'll survive without her. But she won't survive without herself any more.

'Joan, just come back,' Genevieve pleads softly.

'No,' Joan says.

'Then . . . tell me where you are,' Genevieve tries again. 'Just so I don't lie awake wondering any more.'

In that moment Joan remembers that life still has the capacity to surprise, because for all their familiarity with each other she would never have picked Genevieve as the type to worry about her to this extent. She is touched. And she trusts her friend.

'I'm in Victoria,' she admits. 'On the Mornington Peninsula. In a hotel.'

'Which hotel? How do you even know about a hotel there?'

'It doesn't matter. But it's a nice hotel. Grand. I'm safe here. If that's what you're worried about.'

'I was. But if it's a nice hotel . . .'

Joan smiles into the phone. Genevieve has always put faith in expensive institutions.

'It is,' Joan assures her, then she remembers that she's not in her sitting room at home and she and Genevieve aren't chatting about mundane things. 'Look, I'll call you again.'

'Really?'

'Yes. Bye.'

She hangs up quickly, not wanting to invite further questions, then opens the door of the booth and emerges into a din. In the short time she's been on the phone the number of guests in the foyer has grown. Having no wish to be amongst them, she walks quickly into the bar, where it's quieter if not as empty as she'd like.

The bar itself – as opposed to the room – is made of a heavy, dark wood and it seems like it's half the length of an Olympic swimming pool, but Joan also knows she is prone to exaggeration, mainly in her own mind. There is the usual array of liquors and liqueurs behind the bar, some taps for beer, and one man who wasn't there when she was in here the other day. His face is tanned and lined, his head bald. Late forties, she thinks. Or her age. Or older. Hard to tell when a man has spent time in the sun.

The bartender smiles at her in the way people in his job tend to do: warmly yet vaguely. They don't want to imply familiarity because the potential patron could read too much into that, nor do they want to put you off entering their establishment. Joan wonders if it's the hardest part of the job to keep up that smile. Pouring drinks must be easier.

'Hello,' she says as she sits on a barstool.

'Hi. I'm Shane.' He flattens the *a*. *Shuyne*.

'Joan,' she says and smiles. No reason not to – if she's to take up residence at the Duchess, which is what she's already sort of doing, she'll get to know him.

'I don't mean this to sound . . . creepy,' he says, 'but I've seen you here the past couple of days. Not *here*.' He nods around the bar. 'Here in the hotel.'

'It's the blonde hair,' Joan says, self-consciously touching what remains of the last blowdry she had in Sydney. It's almost gone and she's hardly going to look for a hairdresser near the hotel. Unless there's one *in* the hotel? She should ask. 'It stands out.'

'Could be, yeah.' He shrugs. 'Would you like a drink?'

'Um . . .' She hadn't thought that far ahead. 'Yes. Please. An Old Fashioned.'

He nods as if he approves. 'Don't get many requests for that but I'm sure I remember how to make it.'

After a couple of minutes, he's back with her cocktail in a short glass.

'I'm in room 204,' she says. 'Should I sign something?'

'I'll start a tab.'

'What makes you think I'll return?'

'Won't you?'

They stare at each other, and she doesn't know whether to think him perceptive or impertinent.

'In all probability, yes,' she concedes.

He grins triumphantly. 'Tab it is.'

As he scribbles on a piece of paper, he says, 'Would it be rude to ask why you're staying at the hotel?'

'No.' She takes a sip and considers how much to tell him. The truth is always easier to maintain than even the mildest fiction. 'I've left my life.'

'Ah,' he says, looking not at all surprised at her declaration. 'A bold move.'

'Yes.'

'I admire courage,' he says seriously. 'Not enough of it going around.'

His eyes hold hers and she sees something there – pain, wisdom, understanding, all together – but she doesn't want to know his story. Not yet. She's not ready for a fellow traveller.

'Perhaps not,' she says, then Shane's attention is caught by a trio of men in suits at the other end of the bar and he's gone, while she's left to her Old Fashioned and the refashioning of whomever it is she's meant to be.

CHAPTER EIGHT

Only a terrible mother would look forward to coming to work, Kirrily thinks as she folds towels in the hotel laundry, Cher's 'Believe' playing on the radio at a sound loud enough to be heard over the washing machines and dryers. She loves that song, and because it's been in the charts she gets to hear it a lot. Her mother liked Sonny and Cher; 'I Got You Babe' was probably her favourite song.

As she stacks towels and piles them on a shelf, she thinks that a mother who looks forward to coming to work is the sort of mother who doesn't want to be around her children all the time – and aren't mothers meant to want to be with their kids? Aren't they meant to think the sun shines out of them twenty-four hours a day?

Not that her mother felt that way. 'You kids aren't my life,' she said once – probably after they'd all gathered around her like hungry birds, mouths open, demanding food and attention – and at the time Kirrily was upset because she thought it meant her mother was indifferent. Now she understands, and she thinks her mother probably meant to say 'my whole life'.

You kids aren't my whole life.

She wants to say that herself sometimes. Not because she doesn't love them but because it's true. The Duchess Hotel is part of her life, and she does look forward to being here, not because she's away from her children but because it's lively and interesting and there are different people here. Time passes quickly at the hotel; at home it can seem slow.

The other day she was watching the kitchen clock when Connor arrived home.

'That's not going to make it tick faster,' he'd said, playfully pinching her waist.

She'd smiled. 'You'd think I'd know that by now.'

Gesturing to the stovetop, she'd said, 'I'm waiting for those eggs to boil.' The kids' dinner. Aidan loves hard-boiled eggs, and Bridget tolerates them.

'Oh yeah?' He'd kissed her behind the ear, where he knows she likes it. 'Gonna take a few minutes, right?'

A hand on her waist, a kiss on her neck. A few years ago, she'd have turned the stove off and wrapped her arms around him, but a few years ago she likely wouldn't have been boiling eggs because they didn't have children then. She knew he was taking whatever opportunity he could to be affectionate, given the children might appear at any time, and she appreciated him trying. If only she hadn't had a million things on her mind and a watched pot to boil.

'Yeah,' she said, but it hadn't sounded encouraging.

So he'd straightened up and looked at her seriously. Then he'd taken her face in his hands and kissed her on the lips. Slowly. Like it was just them in the house, and for a few seconds she wished it was.

'We should do that more often,' he'd said softly when he let her go and she'd smiled up at him. He still loved her even though she was tired and distracted. She should appreciate him more.

'Your break, hm?' William has appeared from nowhere to stand in front of her, looking at his watch, eyebrow raised. He likes to enforce breaks if he thinks staff aren't taking them, stating that they need to stay sharp around the guests and they can't do that unless they occasionally give themselves a rest. So if he knows it's someone's break time – and he seems to know *everyone's* break times – and sees them working, he'll say something.

'Going now!' Kirrily pats the pocket where she keeps a handkerchief, her cigarettes and matches, checking they're all still there, then heads out a side door to the garden that's on the ocean side. She likes the view. Some of the staff prefer the garden on the land side because it's more secluded, and not as cold in winter, but that bracing wind off the ocean is good for the senses. For her senses.

Plus she can stand, looking out, and pretend she's looking at Tasmania even in the dark. Even though she was so keen to leave the place, she misses it. She doesn't think about it too much, though. Or she tries not to. Thinking too much is a habit she wants to break.

So instead she considers the fact that here she can smoke without the kids telling her she smells funny. At home she always smokes outside and hopes that means the smell doesn't cling to her, but every time she comes back inside Bridget – usually Bridget – wrinkles her nose and makes a comment. That should be enough to make her give up the cigarettes; instead it is yet more proof that she's a terrible mother.

Here at the Duchess, though, she's not a terrible anything. She's competent, and she's appreciated.

Turning her back to the breeze, she lights a cigarette and it's not until she lifts her head that she sees Frances sitting on the nearby bench seat, underneath a light.

Frances was one of the first people she met at the Duchess. Everyone knows her. She's here so often and the place would seem odd without her. Frances treats the Duchess with respect, and she is given respect in return. Once Kirrily asked William if he minded Frances being around so often.

'Never!' he replied. 'She makes us all stand up a little straighter, don't you think?'

Kirrily knew what he meant: Frances knows the Duchess Hotel so well that she's almost like the guardian of its culture and secrets. The other interpretation is that she's like its mascot, but that makes her sound like a doll and she's not that. She's someone they want to please, because she always has a cheery word for every staff member and a polite enquiry of guests. In her way she makes everyone feel like they belong at the Duchess even if they're only there for a night.

'Hi, Frances.' Kirrily smiles then blows smoke out of her nose.

'Hello, dear.'

'You're out here on your own?' It's an obvious statement yet not, because she never sees Frances on her own.

'I –'

The side door opens, and Shane emerges with a blanket.

'G'day, Kizza.' Shane winks then places the blanket gently on Frances's knees. 'The lady wants some time outside and to be warm at the same time,' he explains, then pulls a packet of Winfield Reds from his back pocket.

'And not your smoke, thank you,' Frances says, glaring, but Shane just laughs. 'How are you, pet?' Frances is looking in her direction.

'Fine!' Kirrily says quickly.

Frances's eyes narrow. 'Of course.'

Kirrily frowns. 'What do you mean?'

'Looking as tired as you do, of course you're fine.'

'Um . . . thanks?' Kirrily wants to feel offended, but she can't because what Frances has said is true. Instead she drags on her cigarette and blows the smoke downwind.

'She's got a bit on her plate,' says Shane. 'Haven't you, Kizza?'

Kirrily half-smiles. She doesn't really like that nickname but at the same time she's pleased she earnt a nickname other than Glinda the Good Witch. Shane must be softening towards her. Which means he might be on the way to being her friend. She doesn't have friends; she didn't have any in Burnie, not after her mother died, because her spare time was spoken for. Made the one connection in Melbourne, Justine, and she's gone now. Hasn't been able to on the peninsula because her time is completely spoken for. So she'd like to have a friend in Shane.

'I do,' Kirrily murmurs.

'What do you have on your plate?' Frances asks.

'Hm?' Kirrily inhales the nicotine and tries to feel the effect it once had on her, back before she was really hooked. She doesn't like that part about cigarettes, or coffee, for that matter: the more you have, the less they work.

Frances purses her lips.

'All right,' Kirrily says, giving in. 'Nothing more than anyone else. Job. Housework. Kids.' She turns her palms up. 'The usual big load.'

'Yeah, but your little fella needs some care.' Shane squints as he takes a puff and Kirrily glares at him. That wasn't information she intended to share.

'He's all right,' she says dismissively. 'Just needs to go to hospital every now and again.'

'Even once is enough,' Frances says. 'Enough to make you worried.' She nods slowly. 'I feel for you, pet.'

'Thanks, but I'm fine,' Kirrily snaps. She hates pity. Had so much of it growing up. Poor little Kirrily looking after all those kids. Poor little Kirrily without her mum. Poor little Kirrily having to cook and clean and never getting her homework done. She never wants to be poor little Kirrily again.

Now Shane is the one glaring at her and she knows she's gone too far.

'Sorry,' she says, dropping her cigarette and stubbing it out with her shoe. 'That was rude.'

'Understandable.' Frances smiles and Kirrily can tell that she means it. 'I felt like that myself once.'

There's obviously a story there but Kirrily isn't sure she's been invited to know it. Plus she's out of time.

'I have to get back,' she says, her voice softer now. 'Thanks for your concern, Frances, really. I'm just a little ... well, tired. As you said.'

'I'll see you again,' Frances says, and Kirrily likes the way that sounds: it's a promise, of sorts.

'See ya, Shane.' She nods in his direction and out of the corner of her eye sees him sit down near Frances, holding his cigarette away. Those two are friends, she supposes, and she feels a pang of jealousy, then she's back in the hotel and into her list of jobs for the night.

CHAPTER NINE

Alison is singing along to the Backstreet Boys on the radio when she hears it: a knock on the front door that is loud and distinctive. One. Two. Pause. Pause. One-two-three. Pause. One.

Her heart feels like it's going to drop to her knees because she knows it's Keith and she wishes Sean didn't have the TV on so loudly because she can't pretend no one is home.

Still, she waits. It's so ungenerous, she knows this, to not rush to the door to greet your brother. She should be happy to see him. Except, as Tadeusz has said, no one is entitled to get away with being a let-down over and over again.

'Only so many excuses, *kochanie*,' he says when the subject of her brother comes up.

Kochanie means darling, and she loves it when he calls her that. Which he knows, so he does it all the time. Especially when he's trying to make a tough point.

She hears Tad open the front door – he would have recognised the knock as well – and turns off the radio in the middle of the bridge of 'I Want It That Way' so she can listen to what's happening.

'Keith,' she hears him say, his voice flat.

'G'day, Taddy,' Keith replies and Alison winces: Tad does not like being called that. Which Keith knows.

There's a low murmuring of voices down the hallway towards the kitchen, where she's sitting, cup of coffee in hand. Coffee that will probably now go cold, and she'd looked forward to it so much. But it's hard to have an argument and drink a hot beverage at the same time, and there will be an argument because they follow Keith around. Or, rather, he instigates them.

Her father once said that he thought Keith liked drama but he wasn't blaming his stepson for that; indeed, he thought Keith had a built-in excuse because of the circumstances of his birth and young life. Gerald often made excuses for Keith; that could be why they're all in this situation now, where Keith thinks he's owed the world and complains when he's only given an ocean.

The pharmacy, the house – these were his ocean. He drained it. Leaving their mother not on dry land but in limbo. Alison has been trying ever since to pull her mother to dry land – she and Tad saved up to build a granny flat in their garden so Frances could be close but not feel intruded upon. So Alison could take care of her from a respectful distance. Then Keith persuaded them to loan him money 'just one time' after they'd refused him an earlier request and felt guilty about it.

When he asked Alison knew – from experience – that Keith didn't return things loaned to him: not her favourite albums from when they were young, not her hand-knitted Essendon scarf, not the car he borrowed one night and crashed. So, not being wealthy, with only a small amount of savings, she and Tad had said no and he didn't speak to them for months.

The next time Keith asked for a loan Alison, who always wants to believe the best in people even when there is proof to the contrary, and who has often talked herself into granting people second chances, gave him what they could afford to lend. They've never seen that money again. Alison never told Frances about it, nor about her plans to build a granny flat.

Instead she worries about her mother and what to do with her, and she was on the verge of saying she should move into the house when Tad told her about Erik moving in.

She knows she irritates Frances with her fussing but how else is a daughter meant to show her love to a mother who is stubbornly refusing to make concessions to old age? Frances shouldn't be gallivanting around the neighbourhood with Colin, no matter how much the dog likes walks. She shouldn't be at the Duchess most days, chatting to strangers. That bartender Shane sees her more than Alison does.

A little ember of jealousy sparks in her belly but she tamps it down, as she always does. She can't begrudge her mother friends. Also: her mother doesn't belong to her. Even if Alison wants, just for a little while, to feel that her mother loves her just a little bit more than she loves anyone else.

'G'day, Ally,' Keith says as he walks into the kitchen.

It's been a few months since Alison has seen him – usually he phones when he wants something – and he's grown a straggly beard in that time. His eyebrows look bushier. His eyes wilder.

'Hi, Keith.' Her tone is as flat as Tad's was.

'Coffee, is it?' Keith nods at her cup.

'Would you like some?'

'Yeah.' He sniffs and rubs a knuckle under his nose. 'Thanks.'

She raises her eyebrows – normally he doesn't bother to thank anyone.

Alison stands up and turns on the kettle, then takes a mug from the cupboard, opens the coffee jar, makes the preparations.

'How's work, Taddy?'

'Fine.'

Alison glances at her husband, who looms over Keith, his arms crossed, his mouth downturned, looking like he's a bodyguard although she knows he's guarding her, not her brother.

'Building roads and stuff, yeah?' Keith sniffs again.

He knows that Tad is a civil engineer and has been for a very long time. So he knows that, yes, he's building roads and stuff. Yet each time they see Keith he acts like he can't quite remember what Tad does for work, even as he turns up expecting Tad to fund whatever his new scheme is.

'A road here or there,' Tad says. His eyes meet Alison's and she knows what they're saying: *How long before I can throw him out?*

She smiles weakly because she doesn't have an answer. The kettle has boiled so she makes the coffee and hands it over.

'Do you have a cold, Keith?' Alison asks, wanting to move things along, at least.

'Huh?'

'A cold. You're sniffing.'

'Oh.' *Sniff sniff.* 'Nuh.'

'Right.' She smiles as pleasantly as she can without it looking like she's actually pleased, then waits. There's no way he's here for a social visit.

The volume of the TV in the sitting room goes up. Tad and Alison's eyes meet; with the tacit language of a long-married couple, each understands what needs to be done, so Tad leaves the room.

'Sean!' she hears him call.

'So how have you been?' she says to Keith, still hoping to move things along. She really wishes – as she always does – that when he shows up wanting something, whether in person or on the phone, he would just get on with it. It's such an odd ritual, to want a transactional relationship with your only sister then stall at the stage of transaction. It's almost as if he's telling himself that he's really here to see her, not because he needs her.

'Yeah, fine.'

He sips his coffee and makes a face.

'Hot,' he complains.

'Mm.'

He takes another sip and makes another face. But that's Keith: doing the same thing over and over again and expecting a different result each time.

'Why are you here, Keith?' she says, out of patience now.

'To see you!' He grins and for a second she sees the teenager she adored. With seven years between them, she had been young enough to think the sun, moon and stars shone out of him when he was in high school. Certainly their mother always treated him as if that was the case. Keith could do no wrong. Alison didn't know why until later, of course; didn't know that it was because Keith was the precious relic of Frances's great love. Hadn't felt the heartache, then, of knowing that *she* would never be her mother's great love, which is all a child ever really wants to be.

'Sure,' she says. 'And?'

His brow knits. 'What does that mean?'

'Keith, you want something. You always do.'

Tad wanders back in and Alison is grateful for it. It helps to have reinforcements whenever her brother is around.

'Oh. Yeah.' Keith takes some more sips-with-winces. 'There's this investment scheme, right,' he starts, his eyes brighter. 'Mate of mine. In Geelong. He's got this land, right. Gonna be a big office block. *Heaps* of potential.'

He looks from Tad to Alison, back and forth, back and forth, grinning like he's won the lottery. It's quite the display; Alison has to give him credit for that.

'We don't have any money to invest,' Tad says, his tone indicating that he would brook no argument.

Keith doesn't look deterred. 'You don't need much, Taddy, mate! Ten thousand. Twenty.'

Alison laughs involuntarily. In whose world is ten thousand dollars not much? That wasn't the world she and Keith grew up in, so she wonders where he gets it from.

'We don't have it,' Alison says sharply. 'You still haven't paid us back from the last lot.'

'What?' Keith blinks.

Of course he's going to pretend he doesn't remember. There's no point in ever raising the past with Keith because he acts like it's a country he's never visited.

'The money we lent you,' Alison goes on. 'The money we were going to use for the granny flat so Mum could live here.'

'She wouldn't want to live here,' Keith says lightly, as if that's the issue.

'How would you know? You never talk to her.'

Alison knows this is true because Frances tells her. It's not even a complaint when she does it, just a statement.

'I'm busy.' His eyes cloud, and he puts down the coffee cup. 'Oh well,' he says. 'Gotta be off.'

He doesn't say goodbye. Doesn't look at her. Doesn't look at Tad. Just hurries from the room and out the front door and when her eyes meet Tad's she sees in them the remnants of the same Cyclone Keith that will be in hers. It's a storm that blows in and blows out and they're always picking up the pieces afterwards.

'Don't feel guilty,' Tad says, because he knows her.

'I won't.' She has to use the future tense because, right now, that child who adored teenage Keith feels bad. Feels like she's let him down. Even if all she was doing was protecting herself.

'Come here.' Tad opens his arms and Alison walks into them, appreciating the expanse of his chest and the warmth of his embrace.

'I love you,' he says above her.

'Thank you,' she says, hugging him tighter.

They stand like that until the volume goes up again in the sitting room and Tad goes to deal with it.

CHAPTER TEN

During her first week at the Duchess Hotel, Joan has made several perambulations around the grounds, mainly to find things to draw – although she hasn't been overly pleased with her efforts. Trees, flowers, bushes and plants used to be some of her favourite subjects but her technical skills need some work. She has not been deterred, however, despite the fact she didn't bring adequate clothing for the temperatures here, which are more wintry than she is used to in Sydney.

Not that she will let the temperatures stop her from going outside. She cannot – never has been able to – live a day without going outside, even when she feels poorly.

When she was a child her father said, 'Girls, no matter what's going wrong in life, a shot of outdoors will fix it,' and she has lived by this credo. During her younger years, it was because she loved to run outside and play; once she was an adult, she loved sunbathing and swimming and sitting in nature, first just to think, then to paint. That early appreciation of the natural world turned into a way of seeing trees and grass and rocks and dirt and birds and other creatures that led her to pick up paint and brushes and try to capture what she loved about it all so much.

It was also, no doubt, what drew her back to the Duchess Hotel. Its position – on a bluff, in grounds dense with pines and gums as well as ordered gardens, with the ocean beyond – puts her right in nature. When she wakes up and looks out the window, that's what she sees. On the other side of the hotel, as she has discovered, there is some open land that looks like it's waiting for sheep or kangaroos – whichever creature may wish to populate it – and beyond that the houses of Sorrento begin, little cottages and sturdier, weather-proof propositions. But they don't impede the view from the hotel, which is unobstructed on most sides, apart from the front, where there's the drive leading to dense trees, then the road.

At home, in Sydney, she is also in nature although its colours and shapes are different. Living by the harbour means there's a certain kind of light and different trees. It's gentler. What is here, next to her on the peninsula, is wild. And that's what she feels she needs: to tap into the wilder parts of her, the parts that marriage and motherhood, and years on this earth being buffeted by other people and their wants and needs and opinions, have squashed into tiny parcels that she has tucked up inside her, waiting to spring open.

She walks the grounds of the Duchess, which are less extensive than in memories of her childhood but larger than she expects in a day and age when land like this is at a premium. Then she usually heads to the bar to warm up and chat to Shane. She likes him, with his direct gaze and indirect sense of humour. It's not impossible to believe that he likes her too, mainly because when he sees her, he smiles in a way he doesn't to other patrons: unguardedly.

Usually when Joan is at the bar she finds Wendy, whom Joan guesses to be in her mid-forties. Wendy lives within walking distance – admittedly quite a walking distance, given the amount of land surrounding the hotel, but she likes to declaim, loudly, that she 'lives local and I'll die local too'. Not that anyone asks. By the time Joan comes across her, Shane is usually trying to cut her off because she's a few drinks in and trying to pick up men who are on their own.

The other day Joan heard Wendy – as everyone in the bar did – telling one such gentleman that she was definitely not a 'pro'. Joan wanted to offer some gentle advice along the lines of Wendy softening her sales pitch if she didn't want the same response in future, but Wendy likes to talk more than listen.

So talk she does, to Joan and anyone else who stands still long enough. 'Long enough' being about five seconds. It was during one such experience that Shane appeared, with a look on his face that suggested he was rescuing Joan.

'Joan, I've been meaning to suggest something to you,' he said, taking her elbow and pulling her away from Wendy, who didn't seem to notice.

What he suggested was that she try the Saturday afternoon tea that was popular with locals and guests. Which is why Joan is walking into the tea room now, finding Shane, who is smiling expectantly.

'Thought you might show up,' he says, and she wonders if he plans to take tea with her. This would be an odd, but not unwelcome, thing, although she can't really imagine him drinking tea.

'I can't say the same of you.' She smiles vaguely and he laughs.

'I bet. Anyway, I saw you coming so I ducked in here to introduce you to someone.'

Joan's heart sinks a little as she realises he had an ulterior motive for this tea suggestion: pity. Clearly he thinks she needs friends, or at the very least company. She wants to tell him to mind his own business but before she can he moves to one side and reveals an elderly woman sitting at a small table set for two. She has short, neatly combed hair and strong eyebrows and watery green eyes with a look of mischief in them. Which is a relief because that mischief is how Joan knows they will get along, even if it's only for the afternoon. Having introduced mischief into her own life, Joan is pleased to find a comrade.

'Joan, I'd like you to meet Frances,' Shane says with a gesture towards the table. 'Frances is one of our regulars and has been for years. She's definitely my *favourite* regular.' He grins at Frances and Joan can see the affection between them.

'Well, of course I am,' Frances says, then she turns her smile to Joan. 'Please excuse me not getting up, dear. It would take so long that my tea would be cold by the time I sit back down again.'

'That's quite all right.' Joan runs a hand down her dress, hoping she's neatly presented enough because she feels herself wanting to impress this new acquaintance. Not for the first time, she is cognisant of the fact that one has immediate responses to people one meets and doesn't know why they're one way or the other, except to guess that they're instinctual – that the subconscious mind knows something we don't. Perhaps Frances has a measure of her, too; perhaps one day she'll find out.

'You look lovely. I wish I had the figure for a dress like that.' Frances's nose wrinkles as she smiles and Joan almost laughs at being found out so easily.

'Thank you,' she says. She learnt long ago that accepting compliments without putting up a fight always makes the giver of the compliment feel better about their day. The only exceptions she makes are for men who give fake compliments in order to get something out of her – those she acknowledges only with a cheerless smile and a half-turned-away cheek.

'Thank you for the introduction, Shane,' Joan says as she sits.

'My great pleasure,' he says, then he's gone.

Frances sighs. 'I love that boy,' she says. 'His heart is pure gold.'

'Really? That's nice to hear.'

'Keeping an eye out for an old duck like me – not many like him.'

Joan half-closes her eyes so she can make a proper assessment of Frances, who may technically be an old duck but clearly has the spirit of a duckling.

'He strikes me as someone who only does things he wants to do, not things he thinks he should,' she says after a few seconds.

'True.' Frances peers back at her and Joan has the distinct impression that they're auditioning each other for something she can't yet name.

'Do you know about him?' Frances goes on.

'Shane?'

'Mm.'

'What do you mean?'

'He was in the war. Vietnam.'

Joan blinks. Returned servicemen are not in her usual orbit. Her husband's friends are lawyers and bankers with the occasional orthopaedic surgeon thrown in because they all seemed to play rugby in their youth and that's how Isaac knows a lot of these men: from playing rugby at school.

'Really?' she says, which is a weak response and she feels weak saying it.

'Terrible time they had,' Frances says in a serious tone. 'Over there and back here.'

The Vietnam War barely passed Joan's consciousness in her youth, simply because she didn't know anyone who served and it was a war that never threatened to reach Australia's shores, so why would she worry? She remembers her father getting into an argument about it with someone once; the other man said the war was actually a police action and her father aggressively denied it. That was one of the few times she saw him *en couleur*, as her mother called it. Then again, he always liked to stick up for principles he believed in, and clearly that was one of them.

She should call her parents and tell them what's going on. She's sitting here with a woman old enough to be her mother instead of speaking to her actual mother. If only she knew how to tell them she's upended her life.

'I don't know much about it,' she murmurs to Frances.

'You don't want to. But he's . . . suffering from it, I think.' Frances nods slowly. 'Now – tell me about you.'

'Me?' It's a stupid, obvious response but it feels involuntary.

'You.' Frances smiles. 'Ah, here's the lady with a teacup for you.'

One of the waitresses fills her cup and refills Frances's and another brings over a tiered arrangement of sandwiches and sweet things. And thus it is that several minutes pass in which Joan doesn't answer the question, then she steers it to something else and hopes Frances won't notice.

'So,' Frances says, draining her cup. 'You.' She smiles.

'Ah.' Joan smiles back – acknowledging that she's been foiled – and considers how much to reveal. 'Well . . . I'm not that interesting.'

'I don't believe that.'

Joan laughs. 'Okay. I'm interesting. Maybe?'

'Where are you from?'

'Sydney.'

'What are you doing here at the Duchess? You've obviously been here a little while because Shane knows you.'

'I'm . . .' How to phrase this? 'I ran away from home.'

Frances's eyes light up. 'Really? I think about doing that sometimes.'

Joan relaxes: if Frances doesn't automatically think her answer odd, she may be able to tell her more.

'I left my husband behind.'

Frances nibbles a little bit of cake. 'Has he noticed?'

With that Joan laughs more heartily than she has in . . . years, probably.

'I don't know,' she confesses. 'I haven't contacted him. Or my children.'

Frances scrutinises her face and Joan doesn't mind.

'I'm sure they miss you,' Frances says. 'But you don't look like you miss them.'

'I do and I don't.' Joan shrugs. 'I'm focusing on other things.'

'Such as?'

'You're very good at interrogation. Have you worked for ASIO?' Joan says with a smile.

Frances arches an eyebrow. 'I couldn't tell you if I had.'

'Fair point. Um ... I want to ...' Joan hesitates because she hasn't said the next part out loud to anyone and in her head it sounds trite. But Frances is direct so she'll be direct with her. 'I want to paint again,' she says.

'Paint? Canvases?'

'Yes. And draw. Which I've been doing since I arrived. I used to do a lot of both once upon a time. Then ...'

'Husband. Babies.' Frances nods and nibbles more cake. 'I understand. So one of those creative types?'

'I suppose.'

More nodding. 'I've heard about you lot. Flighty. Head in the clouds.' She winks.

'I wish.' Joan finishes her own cup of tea and looks around for the waitress bearing the teapot. 'Anyway,' she continues. 'It may sound drastic but I had to run away from home to get back to something I love.'

'Not at all drastic. If you need a model ...' Frances gestures to herself, looking quite serious.

'I'll keep you in mind.'

'I'm joking, love! Now, where's the girl with the tea?'

Frances looks around too and smiles in a certain direction, so Joan presumes tea is incoming. Or maybe it's Shane.

'I meant it,' Joan says quietly. 'I will keep you in mind.'

Frances's eyes meet hers and she dips her head. 'Shane knows how to find me.'

They grin at each other then wait for the tea, and once they say goodbye later on, Joan ascends to her room, feeling lighter than she has since she arrived.

CHAPTER ELEVEN

In his corgi way, Colin registered his displeasure when Frances left this morning. He never acts displeased when she goes to the Duchess Hotel – perhaps because she leaves with a light heart and sense of anticipation. But this morning it was as if she was transmitting her worry to him.

Dogs are sensitive, she knows this. Even though she only had working dogs when she was a child and young woman, they were still sensitive creatures. They knew when she or her brothers or father weren't happy. After Albert left for the Pacific, one of the dogs kept trying to round her up. At first she was annoyed, then she realised he was trying to take care of her by keeping her in one spot.

Don't you go too, she felt like the dog was telling her. *I'm keeping you right here.*

Of course, this could all be fanciful thinking and Colin might just have had wind this morning, causing him to make a disgruntled face as she left. It could have been nothing to do with the fact that her son was taking her out for the day and she didn't want to go.

Not that she objects to spending time with Keith per se. Or maybe she does, but she's certainly not admitting it to herself if that's the case, even though Alison has told her time and again that 'you don't have to see him, Mum'. She said a variation of it when Frances told her Keith would be taking her out.

'Really?' Alison said, sounding a little funny. A mother knows when her daughter sounds funny. Alison need only utter a syllable and Frances would know how to interpret it.

Alison cleared her throat. 'Where to?'

'I don't know,' Frances said, and she could hear Tadeusz in the background.

'You don't have to go, Mum.'

'Why wouldn't I? He's my son,' she replied, even though Frances knows why Alison said it and that Alison knows that Keith can unsettle her – because a daughter can read her mother too.

Alison and Keith stopped getting along around the time Keith let the pharmacy founder. Alison did not have a financial interest in it but she was appalled that Keith could no longer support Frances the way her late husband had wanted. The provision in the will was for Keith to inherit and make sure Frances was looked after. There was, however, no provision for what would happen if Keith became derelict in his duty. Gerald never shirked a duty so he likely couldn't have conceived of the idea that Keith would.

It's hard for a parent to accept that their child has let them down or, worse, that the child doesn't care about them. Or doesn't care about them enough.

Keith is not a bad person, as far as Frances can tell, and she certainly didn't raise him to be one. But he doesn't seem to care about others the way a person should. That's how humans co-exist, isn't it? Caring for each other. If we don't care for each other, societies fall apart, cities crumble and the world ends. An extreme view, perhaps, but when you're getting on in years sleep becomes harder to find and there are more opportunities to lie awake and contemplate the meaning of life. If there is one.

'So how've you been, Mumsy?' Keith says as they leave her place and head in the direction of Melbourne. He tends to call her Mumsy when he wants something.

Apparently they're going to lunch somewhere in the city – how Keith has the money for this she doesn't want to ask, and why he would want to drive down to get her then drive back to the city then repeat the whole thing to take her home is beyond her. Unless he's planning to put her on the train home. Always a possibility.

'All right,' she says. They drive past Gerald's old pharmacy and Frances stiffens; Keith does not react.

There's an awful din coming from the car radio.

'Can you turn that down, please?' she says.

'But it's Smash Mouth,' Keith says, sounding hurt. '"All Star". It's my new favourite song.'

'It's very loud.'

He makes a face but complies. 'Keeping well?' he says.

'Aches and pains, but nothing apart from that.' Her arm is out of a sling now and Keith doesn't know about the sprain. There's no point telling him because he's unlikely to care anyway. 'How have you been?'

'Good, yeah, good.'

Keith has never been much of a conversationalist but he invited her out today so Frances believes the onus is on him to keep the chat going. Moreover, after a lifetime of making polite conversation she's tired of it. That's one of the reasons she and Shane get along: there's no polite conversation, just straight to the meat of things.

A few minutes pass as Frances gazes out the window then gives in to her more polite instincts.

'So we're going to lunch?' she says.

'Yeah. Place in Toorak.'

'Toorak?' Frances blinks. That's probably the priciest part of town.

'Yeah. Nice little bistro.'

'We have bistros on the peninsula,' Frances says tersely.

'Not like this one.'

'What's the occasion?'

'No occasion.' His voice wavers a little so she knows he's lying. A mother always knows when her children fib. Whenever Keith would tell her business at the pharmacy was 'fine, Mum, don't worry', his voice would waver. It was an early-warning system for what was to come; what Frances didn't know at the time was that she should have read that wavering for the air-raid siren it really was.

'I don't believe you,' she says, feeling bolshie.

'Just got an investment to show you, Mum,' he says so quickly she barely catches it.

'An investment!'

'Yeah.'

'How can you have any money for an investment?' She feels unwell suddenly. All the money he lost, all the changes she had to make in her life because of it, and now he's talking about an investment.

'Borrowed it.'

'How?'

'Don't worry about it, Mum.' He pats her hand. Like that's going to placate her.

'I do worry, Keith. I . . .' She swallows. It's almost impossible to tell your son that he's a hopeless case, although she's hinted at it before.

'I just want to take care of you, Mum.' This time he sounds confident, but she knows that too is a front because it's the voice he'd use when he was caught smoking at school and told her it was 'just a little thing'. It was 'just a little thing' until he was expelled in his final year and she had to find him somewhere else to go for his last months.

'I'm doing all right,' she says through gritted teeth.

'Are you still going to that hotel?'

'Yes. Why?'

'You could probably save the money. You know, unnecessary expenditure.'

The switch is so rapid, between saying he wants to take care of her and telling her to be careful with money, that she almost doesn't catch the hypocrisy. Yet there it is, trapped in a net in her heart, sinking, taking her spirits down with it.

Her son does not care about her, let alone want to take care of her. This whole trip is probably a ploy to ask *her* for money. And she has none. Well, she's not going to give him the chance.

'I can spend what I like,' she says, even though she spends hardly anything at the Duchess Hotel because Shane likes to give her drinks and probably pays for them out of his own pocket. How strange that a man she hasn't known for very long can show her more kindness than the son she scrabbled to raise on her own, the son she married another man for – because Gerald would take him on. The son she is quite sure she favoured over her daughter for far too many years just because he looks like a man she still loves.

'Sure, Mum, sure!' His laugh is hollow. Like his moral centre, she supposes.

Bitterness floods her mouth, and she swallows again.

They spend the next half an hour in silence, before arriving at their destination.

It's a warehouse nestled amongst other warehouses, and the whole place is deserted. Frances feels uneasy, not wanting to admit to herself that she's a little scared. What mother, after all, wants to be afraid of her child?

'Is this it?' She gestures to the building.

'Nah, it's what's inside.'

Keith hops out of the car and doesn't wait for her. A man of the sort her mother would have called a ruffian emerges from the building, and now Frances is prepared to admit she is properly afraid.

'Won't be long, Mumsy!' Keith calls just before he enters the building.

He has no intention of showing her anything here, she knows. Indeed, this whole thing could be a charade designed to make her think he has a prospect of doing some business in this place.

Then he'll come back and spin her a story about what he was doing inside, with a view to her giving him money for it, and she'll say no to him – because she has no money, thanks to him – and he'll go sullen, then not talk to her for weeks or months. And when he contacts her again, she'll talk to him, and probably listen to his next request for money, because that is the cycle she knows, and she is powerless to break it, because it needs someone with a stronger will than hers.

To her Keith is, and always will be, Albert's son, and no matter what he does she will never let him out of her life.

CHAPTER TWELVE

It took Kirrily longer than it should have to get out of the house to work. Aidan was clingy, hanging on to her leg, to the hem of her skirt, whatever he could get hold of. She knew he was out of sorts – he had a mild temperature, but when didn't he? – and when he's low he always wants his mummy. Much like she has wanted hers from time to time, although it's been years since the thought of her mother gave her any comfort and she has only the vaguest memory of what it was like to be in her mother's presence.

As Kirrily tried to get out the door by levering Aidan off her leg, Connor was on the phone to someone who was trying to book an emergency job while Bridget played quietly in the corner, probably plotting the downfall of everyone she knew, because Kirrily is convinced that that's what little girls do when no one is watching.

'Bridge!' she called. 'Can you please help me with your brother?'

A scowl from her eldest, then a sigh as Bridget got up from the floor and made a show of stomping over to her mother and brother.

'C'mon, Aidy,' she said, holding out her hand. 'There's a fairy in the garden I want to show you.'

Aidan likes the idea of supernatural creatures – he's still adamant that he has an invisible friend – so this worked and Bridget, still scowling, led him towards the back garden while Kirrily made her escape.

Is it wrong to be relieved when you leave your kids and husband behind and sit in your car and turn on the engine and wish you could just drive somewhere and not come back? That's what she felt like, tonight, with pop songs on the radio and the petrol tank mostly full.

Instead she pointed the car towards the Duchess Hotel then parked it in one of the staff spots, fixed her skirt as she got out and slung her handbag over her shoulder.

Now she's in the laundry room, which is always hot, with dryers going most of the time and the door closed so that the sound doesn't bother anyone outside. Kirrily pauses to blow air up to her fringe, which is stuck to her forehead the way it always gets stuck in the laundry room, but she's not willing to grow it out. For one thing, it would take too long and she'd have a weird half-fringe; for another, she has lines on her forehead from frowning and she's self-conscious about them. At least she can have a fringe to hide them; one of her colleagues has tight curly hair and says a fringe would make her look like a circus clown.

Because Kirrily works on weekends she mixes up her duties. It's a paradox she sometimes wonders about: weekends are their busiest times but the penalty rates that make staff more expensive mean the hotel limits the numbers. Which in turn means the staff who are rostered on have to hustle and do as many different things as possible. However, there's a variety to her work at the Duchess Hotel that Kirrily likes, even if switching between the laundry and other duties means she's constantly combing out her damp fringe. When she's outside this room, in the hallways and the foyer, she has to look presentable.

The phone on the laundry room wall rings.

'Hi,' she says, curt. The heat in this room can make her that way sometimes.

'Kirrily, are you busy?'

It's William, the regular weekend manager. And weekday manager. William, from what she has heard, is here all the time.

There's a rumour that he lives in one of the rooms but Kirrily can't see how that would be possible, given the popularity of the Duchess: surely they'd need all the rooms for guests? If Kirrily didn't live nearby and work here, she'd want to stay at the Duchess. There's something reassuring about how old-fashioned and opulent it is, like it's a generous grandmother in the form of a hotel. Connor sometimes tells her they'll have a weekend away, just the two of them, while his parents mind the kids, and she has dreamt of staying at the Hotel Windsor in Melbourne, mostly because it reminds her of the Duchess. Yet that weekend away is unlikely to happen. They can't afford it.

'Um . . . yes,' she says to William. 'There are a few loads on the go here.'

'We need bar towels.' His voice is distant for the last word, which is how she knows he probably has someone in his ear, in the bar. A lack of bar towels is a common problem on a Saturday night, mainly because the night bartender is not Shane, who is much better organised.

'Okay,' she says, her eyes flitting across the laundry room to the shelf where they keep clean and folded surplus items. There's a small wad of bar towels on the second shelf. 'I'll bring some up,' she says.

The line goes dead, and she emits a short laugh. William isn't rude – when you get him in person he's politeness personified – but he can certainly seem like it when he's being pulled in a hundred different directions.

She runs her fingers through her damp fringe and picks up some towels, then pushes open the laundry door to enter the milder climes of the corridor that leads to the rest of the hotel.

Although William didn't express urgency, she guesses he'd expect it, so she hurries down the corridor into the area adjacent to the grand staircase, passing the telephone booth – and almost collides with the man who is emerging from it.

'Ah!' she cries as she attempts to move out of his way, looking up at what is undoubtedly the most handsome face she's ever seen. It's tanned skin and thick, layered brown hair and blue eyes and long eyelashes and lips that are full enough to be suggestive – to her, at least – and a strong jaw. She likes a strong jaw.

It's a shock, that kind of beauty. So rarely seen in the wild, let alone in captivity, and almost always on the face of someone famous for their looks.

Once, a little while ago in the hotel, she saw an actress whose face was well known to most Australians because she appeared on a popular television show. She was so beautiful in the flesh that Kirrily gasped, because that's the only reasonable response to perfection. But that's the only other encounter she's had, so Kirrily feels she's underprepared to deal with what's in front of her and, most particularly, to control what she's sure is a mixture of surprise and desire on her face.

It's quite different to the time she saw that actress because there wasn't desire then, just admiration. Now, though . . .

The man takes her hand, the one that doesn't hold bar towels, and she recoils because she likes him touching her but doesn't want to show that.

'I'm so sorry,' he says. And his voice is deep and mellifluous and Kirrily has the sense of being inside a romantic comedy, except she can't be because she's married and in those movies the heroine is never married.

'No, it's, um . . .' She feels her breath catch in her chest and wishes he'd keep holding her hand forever and also that he would let it go, and it's all so embarrassing and juvenile that what she really wants is for William to bowl up and ask her why she isn't in the bar already.

'I have to go,' she says, pulling her hand away against his resistance, and as she glances back he's staring at her and frowning slightly, and she has the sense that she will see him again and also that she doesn't want to, because whatever happened just then, in those few seconds, will be replayed in her memory for the rest of her life.

When she arrives in the bar William isn't there, not that she expected him to be. Handing over the towels, she wishes she could order a nip of something strong enough to calm her, but instead she turns and walks out the front door of the Duchess Hotel and round the back way to the laundry so she doesn't have to again encounter the man who has hit her like a lightning strike.

For the rest of the night, she tries not to think about him and for stretches of time she succeeds, but that night, once she's home and in bed next to a spreadeagled Connor, she curls up and imagines the man's hand holding hers, and that's how she lulls herself to sleep.

SEPTEMBER 1999

CHAPTER THIRTEEN

Joan woke with resolve and fortified it with two poached eggs for breakfast, but it's weakened as the day has gone on.

She has to call her parents today to let them know what's going on. Isaac would have got to them first, and she ceded that ground because she needed time to consider what she's doing and how long she's going to do it, and the answer to the latter question is 'As long as it takes', which is obviously open-ended. So that's what she needs to tell them. That plus the fact that she's doing well. More than well.

It's now two o'clock and putting off the call isn't helping. She doesn't feel nervous about talking to them, it's more that it feels like a chore, and she's never been fond of those.

Actually, she's got it now: it feels like roll call at school – 'Joan?' 'Present, miss.' That's what she's dragging her feet about. School was not her favourite place. Now here she is planning to tell her parents that she is 'present, miss'.

In lieu of calling at two she picks up her pencils and sketchpad and draws her feelings in the shape of a cactus that she saw – improbably, given the location – in the garden of this south-facing hotel. She's drawing from memory, as she often does, and adding spikes just because she can.

Then the clock in the room chimes three and she puts down her pencil and picks up the phone. One more hour of procrastination has proved enough.

'Hello, Dad,' she says when her father answers.

'Joanie! Thank God.'

She breathes, still not really wanting to have this conversation.

'Are you there?' he prompts.

'Yes.' *Present, miss.* 'I'm here, Dad. I'm fine.'

'Where are you, exactly?'

'South.' If she tells him Victoria, he'll guess she's at the Duchess Hotel, then he'll tell Isaac because he'd think that it's a man's right to know where his wife is, and perhaps he's not incorrect about that but Joan doesn't want to have that discussion either. *South* could be Canberra or Wagga Wagga or Deniliquin. It will do.

'You can't tell your father?'

'I can but I don't want to. I'm just calling to let you know I'm in one piece.'

There's a noise she can't make out.

'Your mother's here.'

Another noise.

'Joan?'

'Hi, Mum. I'm all right. I'm just taking a break.' Might as well pre-empt the questions.

'Corinne's in bits.'

Because she's lost her babysitter. Oh, that's an unkind thing to think about your daughter. But, well, that's what popped into her head.

'Is she?'

'You need to call her, darling.'

Joan deflates a little: ringing Corinne was not on today's agenda but if she doesn't, she'll start to feel bad about it. After all, she's being a bad mother by being a selfish Joan.

'I will. How are you?'

'Fine, yes, all good here.' Her mother sounds matter-of-fact, which makes Joan think that she may not be surprised at what Joan's done. 'Don't take too long, wherever you are,' she says a little more quietly. 'You may get used to it.'

'What if I'm planning to do just that?' Joan doesn't know if she is, but she can't really help it.

'Mm. Well. Up to you. I'll let you go and call Corinne. Bye, darling.'

Brisk and efficient. That's her mother.

With that call disconnected, Joan doesn't let herself pause to think before she rings Corinne's home number.

Four rings. Five. Six.

'Hello?' comes breathlessly down the line and Joan feels her heart contract. Maybe she's misjudged this part of her flight from Sydney and she misses her daughter after all. In theory it's fine to think you miss no one and need no one and you can manage on your own; in practice, you can't help your heart responding to the voice of someone you love so much.

'Darling, it's Mummy.'

'Mummy!' It's almost a shriek, then there's a noise like a hiccup. 'Where are you?'

Sniffles. Another hiccupping noise.

'I've been so worried,' Corinne says.

'Don't be,' Joan says. 'I'm fine. I just needed to get away from home.'

'For how long?'

'For as long as it takes.'

'For what?' Hiccup, sniffle. Maybe the hiccups are little sobs. That makes Joan's heart contract more.

'For . . . time, Corinne. I need time.'

'For what?' her daughter repeats.

'For me.'

'For you?' said in the tone of a child whose mother has always been on tap. For this Joan is responsible, she knows.

'I'm tired, darling. I haven't had a day off in decades.'

'You went to Fiji in June!'

Joan smiles wryly into the phone. How to explain that it's never a holiday when you're constantly thinking about how to make sure your husband and the friends you're travelling with are all having a lovely time? The *thinking* – that gets to her as much as the doing. She's so tired of trying to remember everything that needs to be done for everyone. Being here, with only herself to think about, has been a revelation.

'That I did,' Joan says, because she doesn't want an argument. 'Clearly the holiday wasn't long enough.'

'So it's a holiday you're having?'

'Of sorts.' More like a life-change, but there's no way to say that and not insult her daughter by implying that Joan didn't like anything about her life as it was.

'So you'll come home at some point.'

Joan hears Natalie cry in the background and knows their conversation is about to end.

'At some point,' Joan says. To visit, no doubt. To live – she can't say.

'I have to go, Mummy. Please call me again.'

'I will. Give Natalie a kiss for me.'

'Come home, Mummy.' Another hiccup.

'I love you, Corinne,' she says, then hangs up before she hears another of Natalie's cries. That baby's cries hook into her as if they were Corinne's. If anything takes her home, it will be the desire to watch her grandchild grow up. But there's time to consider that. Time that Natalie will spend being a baby, still not forming memories, so she won't miss the grandmother who isn't there.

Joan has missed that woman, though. And that's why she needs to stay where she is for now.

CHAPTER FOURTEEN

Glen wasn't understanding when Alison told him she had to leave and go to Sean's school because her son is sitting in the headmaster's office after, apparently, kicking another student in the shins. Her mild-mannered son, who has never been the type to burn ants with a magnifying glass or torment a neighbourhood cat, the usual precursors to kicking someone in the shins. Sean has barely even teased his sister; in fact, Rosie is more likely to tease him.

So that's the case against Sean being violent – except in the pit of her stomach, in the place where instinct makes itself known, she knows it's true. Because ever since she and Tad told Sean and Rosie that Erik would be moving in, Sean has been different.

First he moved all his books into his wardrobe.

Then he told Alison he wanted to give away his goldfish.

He's been asking to take up swimming even though it's far too cold yet and he's never been interested in going to the local pool all the times Rosie has gone for squad training. She's the athletic one.

The meeting with the headmaster is perfunctory and stern: if Sean behaves this way again, there will be a more formal consequence, but for now she can take him home.

'So?' she says when they get in the car, Sean slumped in the seat beside her. He got a number-two haircut the other day and it makes him look like a thug. Maybe that was a sign she missed. Maybe her son is turning into a thug.

'So?' he parrots, his head turning away from her.

'What happened?'

'Luke's an idiot,' he mutters.

'Did that warrant a kick in the shins?'

His head is turned half-away but she can see the tug at the corner of his mouth. 'Yep,' he replies.

'*Sean.*'

Now his head whips around and although she can't look at him while she's driving, she can feel his stare.

'Sean what?' he almost hisses. She reminds herself to stay calm. That's what it said in a parenting book she read a year or so ago. *Adolescence is hard, stay calm.*

'This isn't like you.'

'Yeah, well.' He turns away from her again.

'It's Erik, isn't it?' She doesn't want to pretend she doesn't know what's going on, doesn't want to try to draw it out of him in some game, even though the book said to let the child *reveal things to you at their own pace*. There's no indication of what Sean's pace might be and Erik is moving in tomorrow, so the subject needs to be addressed now.

Sean kicks his heel down onto the floor, once, twice, thrice. Then he jiggles his leg. Or it jiggles on its own. Alison doesn't know how nervous tics work.

'I don't get it,' he says softly.

'Don't get what, sweetheart?'

'Why he has to move in.'

'Because he's your brother.'

'Half.'

'He's your father's son.'

'Not the only one. And he's old.'

'I know. But when you're older you'll realise that we don't stop being parents just because our children aren't at school any more.'

'Great.' He sighs heavily and she smiles, because she knows he's trying to bait her and she also knows it won't work.

'I realise Erik has been tricky.'

Sean shrugs. 'He's a dickhead.'

'*Sean.*'

'*What.*'

Her sigh is involuntary.

'I don't want him in the house!' Sean says vehemently.

'We need to help him,' she pleads, even though she's not convinced of it. 'If it were you, would you want Dad to say you couldn't come home?'

'It's not *his* home!'

The point is well made, but she can't let him know that.

'His home is wherever your father is. For now.'

Sean frowns.

'I thought you didn't mind him so much,' Alison tries. 'You used to think he was the bee's knees.'

'The what?'

'The best.'

'Oh.'

Another shrug.

'We need to try to make this work, Sean. I know it's not ideal. I know it will change . . .' She swallows. 'Everything.' This is the part that makes her pause: there is no way that Erik's presence will have minimal impact. That's not the sort of boy – man, now – he is. Even as a child he could not sit still, would not listen to his parents, would definitely not listen to her.

'He's mean to Rosie,' Sean mutters and Alison feels a clutch at her chest, her instinct to protect her child innate and immediate.

'What? When?'

Sean presses his lips together. 'He says she's fat and ugly,' he says almost inaudibly.

'When has he said that?' she demands. Erik hasn't seen the children for so long that she can't think of an opportunity he'd have had. Not that she doesn't believe Sean. She just needs to have her facts straight in case the matter has to be raised with Tad.

'Every time we see him,' Sean says.

'Well, you know she's neither of those things.'

'Yeah, but she doesn't. She believes him. That's why it's mean.'

Alison remembers when an older boy said those things to her once. More than once. Every time she walked past him in the playground. She tried not to pay attention but the words became lodged in her brain until all she had to do was see him and she thought them. Like she was brainwashed.

'It is mean,' she concedes. Except she can't do anything about it unless Rosie wants her to. And given that it's never been mentioned, Alison feels stuck with it.

The rest of the drive is mostly silent, apart from Sean laughing at something on the radio that isn't funny at all, although Alison barely notices, clutching the steering wheel, worrying over what is about to change in her home and knowing she can't stop it.

After dinner, she goes to Rosie's room while her daughter is doing homework.

'What do you have to do tonight?' Alison asks and Rosie turns, looking confused. That would be because Alison never asks her about her homework – Rosie is conscientious and doesn't need monitoring. Nor does Sean. Usually. Alison can't really explain how both her children turned out to be so well-behaved but she is grateful for it.

'Maths,' Rosie says.

'Oh.' Alison has no idea what they do in high school maths these days.

'What do you want, Mum?' It's said perfectly politely, because that's Rosie's way.

'Sorry. Yeah.' Alison smiles nervously. 'So. Erik.'

Rosie answers her with a frown.

'Um . . . I know having here him will be a big change.'

Now lips are pressed together.

'I just . . . wanted to check that it's okay.' Alison has already asked this, of course, but she has to ask again given what Sean told her.

Rosie's eyes widen then she looks down at her textbook. 'Yes,' she says meekly.

'Rosie, if there's something –'

'It's fine!' Her voice is shrill. 'I told you it's fine!'

'Sean said –'

'He's lying.'

Alison knows immediately that this is confirmation of what Sean said, and she wishes that when she'd told the children about Erik originally she'd done it separately – maybe she would have received a less polite response.

'I don't think he was,' Alison says softly.

'It's none of his business!'

'He cares about you.'

'Rack off!'

That is the rudest thing Rosie has ever said to her, but Alison is not going to react, because Rosie is probably justified in saying it.

'Please, Rosie. I know that Erik has said some things to you.'

'I don't want to talk about it.'

'I think we should.'

'Leave me alone!' Rosie slams the textbook shut and stands up, her shoulders dropped forward, her chin jutting out. Defiance mixed with self-protection.

'Sweetie . . .'

Rosie's arms are crossed now and she has half-turned away. The signal is clear and that's something else Alison read in that parenting book: *Be sensitive to what your child is telling you through non-verbal communication.* And what Rosie is saying is KEEP OUT.

Instead of pushing further, Alison puts a hand on Rosie's arm and squeezes, then gently kisses her cheek before leaving her alone, wondering how on earth she is going to manage the change to come. How they all will. One day at a time, is what her mother would say if asked. If only Alison knew what the next day would bring.

CHAPTER FIFTEEN

Part of the appeal of the Duchess Hotel for Frances is that it feels like a far better version of home. Especially given that she's not overly fond of the home she has, because it's poky and drably furnished due to the fact that the old-age pension doesn't leave room for extravagant purchases. Or even moderate purchases. She's careful with her money but even still she finds herself butting right up against the line of having some and having none.

Frances could say that Keith also vacillates between having some and having none except she tends to suspect he *does* have money and pretends he doesn't. Certainly he doesn't appear to have conventional employment. She has worried about this for a while – not only about what he lives on but how he lives, whether he pays taxes, whether he's involved in something illegal. As a teenager, he would push the limits of legal behaviour – always the passenger in a stolen car, never the one doing the stealing, or so he said each time his friends got caught. Gerald would attempt to punish him but it's hard to punish someone who is taller than you. Keith has, Frances knows, been getting away with too much for too long and it's impossible to change course now. Not that he wants to.

That's what she's thinking about as she walks the fifteen minutes or so to the Duchess Hotel. It's always the right amount of time to get herself worked up about something and not solve it.

On her walk, she thinks of Alison telling her that she's too old to be 'walking around town' but there is not much town to speak of, so Frances isn't sure what she means. There are quiet streets with a mixture of holiday homes that the wealthier residents of Melbourne visit every now and again, and residences of those who can't afford to go elsewhere on weekends.

Frances likes the quiet; it reminds her of being in the High Country, on horseback, with only the wind and trees to keep her company. She took her life there for granted, not thinking – not knowing – that other places could be louder, crowded, full of people rather than trees and animals and clouds. It had been a shock, to descend. The home she grew up in, that she misses so much, exists in another dimension – the past – and she knows she can't go back there, but she can be here and feel more like herself than in any environment that contains bricks and concrete.

The Duchess has a large front gate that has huge stone sentries, although the gate is never closed so the sentries are never needed. Whenever she enters the grounds Frances hoves right, in the direction of the sea. There is no fence around the perimeter – instead massive pine trees form a barrier between the sanctuary of the Duchess and the outside world.

Once the trees reach the edge of the land, with rocks and the ocean below, they give way to weather-beaten shrubs in shades of acid green and a deeper green, verging on brown. It's a mystery to Frances that any vegetation can survive the southerlies but she also knows from her upbringing that tough weather breeds tough trees – and people and animals. *Soft* is something she has never been and never wants to be, and perhaps that's why she likes these grounds with their hardy shrubs.

Usually she takes a slow stroll around the perimeter, chatting with anyone she recognises. William has spotted her here often enough to tell her to go away if she isn't welcome, and he never has. Instead he almost treats her like a talisman – that is, he looks relieved to see her, like she's assured him of good luck. Or perhaps that's a figment of her vivid imagination.

Today, as she reaches the spot where the shrubs stop and there's just grass, she sees that there is someone in her way and that it is Joan.

'Hello,' Frances calls. She has to call because the waves are loud. This is the sort of noise she doesn't mind: nature at its wildest and strongest.

Joan rotates to her right, her face pinched, as though she's expecting to not like whomever it is who called to her. Frances takes it as a compliment when the pinch disappears.

'Oh, hello, Frances.' Joan steps towards her and smiles a little, although the arms folded across her chest suggest she won't want much of a conversation.

'Quite a view,' Frances says, nodding towards the ocean. 'I never get tired of it.'

Joan's smile is brief.

'Nor do I. Even though I'm out here every day.'

'Are you?' Frances always thinks that if someone gives you a tidbit of information like that, they want you to do something with it.

'Mm.' Joan keeps looking towards the water. 'Thinking about how I'd paint it.'

There's a tone in her voice that suggests wistfulness, maybe even sadness. Frances has no time for either.

'So where are your paints?' she asks.

When Joan turns she looks surprised. 'I don't have any,' she says.

'Then why are you thinking about how you'd paint it?'

Joan's mouth hangs open. 'I . . .' She shrugs, then laughs. 'That's an excellent point. Perhaps I've been a little afraid to start.'

'There's an art shop in Mornington,' Frances says. 'I imagine you have a car?'

'Yes.' Joan purses her lips.

'It's safe to leave here, you know,' Frances says gently.

'Mm.'

But Joan looks unsure and Frances wonders what sort of citadel she has made the Duchess into.

'I'll go with you,' she says, surprising herself this time. She doesn't know Joan from Adam, not really, not enough to offer an outing. Companionship. *Support*. Although maybe all of those things are for her as much as Joan.

Joan looks relieved. 'Shall we go now?' she says.

While Frances hadn't expected such a rapid response to her suggestion, she also can't think of anywhere else she has to be today.

'Why not? I can direct you.'

Joan grins and it's the first time Frances has seen her look remotely happy.

'Thank you,' Joan says. 'I'll just go and get my handbag and keys.'

'Rightio. I'll wait downstairs for you.'

Joan keeps grinning as she and Frances walk towards the front of the hotel, and Frances looks forward to her first visit to the Mornington shops in a long, long time.

CHAPTER SIXTEEN

It's nice, sitting in the passenger seat of the car, being driven for a change. When Connor's mum, Julie, offered to babysit the children so Kirrily could have a night out with her husband for their wedding anniversary, the passenger seat didn't figure into her plans. But it should have. Not having to do the driving – being taken care of, because that's what it feels like – is a real treat.

They're not even going far. Julie had suggested they drive to Frankston and see a movie – *Runaway Bride* is popular, she said. Connor wanted to see something called *The Matrix* but it's no longer showing; hasn't been for months. It's months since they've been to a movie. Or years. Kirrily can't remember the last one they saw. At any rate, they decided against it.

Instead of the movies they're going to the local pub just across from the beach. It's Connor's occasional watering hole on a Thursday night but as it's a Wednesday night his mates shouldn't be there. Kirrily wouldn't mind if they were.

Actually, that's not true: she would mind, because she'd like to have her husband to herself for a little while. A good wife isn't meant to mind, though, is she? She's meant to want her husband to hang with his mates and drink a few beers and probably check out a few chicks and swear a lot. That's what she's seen some men do. Never Connor, but who knows what he gets up to when she's not around?

Yet it's hard to imagine, her gentle husband being rowdy. His father isn't. When Kirrily met Roy – and Julie, for that matter – she knew she was on the right track with Connor. His parents were warm and mild of temperament. After spending her teenage years with a grieving father who couldn't quite handle his emotions, their calmness was greatly appealing. Julie's always been generous with her time, too. When Aidan was burnt, during those horrible months of treatment and recovery, Bridget pretty much lived at Roy and Julie's house. Kirrily doesn't know what they would have done without that help. So these days, when Bridget seems to be more excited to see her grandmother than her mother, Kirrily puts aside her little jealousies.

Connor parks the car across the road from the pub, comes around to open her door then offers her the crook of his elbow. She smiles as she takes it, then immediately gets a memory of the stranger at the hotel the other day. The handsome one. The one who made her insides get in a tangle. He's been popping into her head at odd times and while she should be unhappy about it, in truth it's been pleasant. Except she's been alone those times and this time she has taken her husband's arm. The memory has no place here.

'Pretty empty, by the looks,' Connor says as they approach the lounge, which is entered from the side. They used to come here more when the kids were little enough to be asleep in baskets.

'Good,' she says, squeezing his arm. 'I won't have to shout when we talk.'

They pick a table then their food and Connor goes up and orders it, returning with a schooner of beer for himself and a glass of white wine for her.

'It's been ages,' he says as they clink glasses.

'Too many ages.' She smiles, then pauses. At home they always seem to natter. Now, with all the time in the world to have a proper conversation, she's stuck for subjects.

'Weird, isn't it?' he says. 'We haven't done this for so long we don't know how to do it any more.'

She smiles gratefully. 'Yeah,' she says.

'So tell me about the Duchess.' He takes another sip. 'We don't chat about that much.'

Kirrily wonders where to start, but knows where not to: the handsome stranger will definitely not come up in conversation.

'It's . . . always interesting. William is . . .' She pauses.

'Who's William again?'

'The manager. It's like he's always there. Shane thinks he lives there.'

'Shane?'

Kirrily is sure she's mentioned Shane to Connor, but then again he's probably mentioned people to her whom she's forgotten.

'The bartender. He's there sometimes when I'm there. We take smoke breaks together.'

Connor's face shifts and Kirrily knows why: he doesn't like her smoking. It's not a regular topic of conversation but it comes up usually when she smells like smoke and he says he wishes she wouldn't. Maybe that's why he hasn't touched her in a while. Sure, he kisses her some days and puts his hand on her back sometimes, but he's been saying he's too tired for much else. She is too, most of the time, but there's the occasional night when the children are long asleep and she just wishes he would *want* her the way he used to. The way she used to want him. Because the truth of it is that she doesn't often think of him that way since they have become parents, and she knows that's probably why she fancies the handsome stranger.

No, stop. She doesn't fancy him. She just has thoughts about him. Not thoughts – no, that would imply she's imagined scenarios. And she hasn't. Not really. Her imagination is *not* that colourful. So it's the memory she has, of running into him. It's the shock of it – yes, that's it. She was startled by the encounter. Banging into someone is startling no matter what they look like.

'You were saying?' Connor says.

'Hm? Oh. Yes. William.' She smiles, relieved to have something else to think about. 'He's at the hotel all the time. Never seems to get sick of it. Shane thinks he must have some dark past he's running away from and that's why he never leaves. It's like if he goes outside the hotel, he'll get caught. Or something.'

She doesn't believe that's true but this is called making conversation, isn't it?

'Interesting.' Connor nods slowly. 'What about the guests?'

'What?' She says it too quickly, too loudly, and Connor frowns.

'Guests,' he repeats. 'In the hotel.'

'Oh. Yes.' She bites her lip nervously. There's no way he could know about the handsome stranger. Is there? No. That's not what he's asking about. So she grasps at someone else.

'There's this woman. Joan.'

On Sunday she saw Joan drawing in the grounds. Joan looked serene, and like she didn't want to be disturbed. But Kirrily wanted to disturb her. Wanted to see what she was doing. As a child, Kirrily loved drawing and painting. Her mother always put her artworks – if that's what they could be called – on the pinboard in the kitchen. Told her they were wonderful. After her mother died, there was no time for art. No time for anything but running the household and trying – failing – to keep up at school. Mostly she has trained herself out of missing her mum, but sometimes – like when she saw Joan draw – she misses her like it was only yesterday she lost her, and the missing is a full-body ache that seems to travel from her skin through her muscles and bones, gathering strength as it aims for her heart. And it never misses, that ache. It makes her gasp. Almost knocks her over. How it can be so strong after all this time she doesn't know, and will never know because who could ever have an explanation for it?

'She draws,' Kirrily goes on, fearful now that if she lets her brain whir around the subject of her mother the ache will come back.

'Draws pictures? In her room?'

'Maybe. But I've only seen her outside. Once. She's been at the hotel for . . .' Kirrily tries to remember the first time she saw the elegant blonde with her tapered eyebrows and distant smile. 'At least a fortnight. No. Yes.' She squints, still trying to remember. 'Three weeks? No, that can't be right.'

'Why would anyone be there for three weeks?'

Kirrily shrugs. 'Shane says he thinks she's left her husband.'

Connor raises his eyebrows. 'Must be loaded if she can stay that long.'

'Yeah.' She takes her first sip of the wine. It's all right – a little sweet. There's not much choice in this pub.

'So she draws, you said?' Connor prods and Kirrily smiles. 'Is that her job or something?'

'I don't know. I haven't spoken to her. Just seen her around. Shane knows her.'

More raising of the eyebrows. 'This Shane gets around.'

Kirrily laughs. 'Yeah – from his house to the hotel and back again. I don't think he does much else.'

'He's not married?'

'He is. Was. I'm not sure where he's at with that.' Shane has only mentioned his marriage a couple of times and not in a way that invited questions.

Connor's face clouds. 'Is he sweet on you?'

'What?' Kirrily gasps. 'No!' Then she laughs, because the idea is ludicrous.

'He talks to you a lot.'

'Because we *work together*, babe.'

'Right.' He takes a long sip this time.

'Honestly, he seems to be more sweet on Frances than anyone.'

She's told Connor about Frances, who is such a constant at the hotel that it's hard to avoid mentioning her.

'The old lady?'

'Old-*er*.' She doesn't think of Frances as old even though Frances thinks that. 'Shane looks after her. It's nice.'

A young man appears holding two large plates and Kirrily knows that one of them will contain a steak for Connor and the other a chicken parmigiana for her.

'Thanks, mate,' Connor says as the plates are deposited.

'Thanks for taking me out,' Kirrily says as she picks up her cutlery. 'We should try to do it more often.'

Connor reaches across and gently pinches her cheek. He used to do that all the time, and she giggles the way she always used to.

'We should,' he says. 'We will.'

They eat in silence for a while, then Connor starts telling her about his apprentice, and the night passes quickly.

CHAPTER SEVENTEEN

This. This is what Joan remembers. In her blood, in her bones, in her skin. Her pores, her cells, her plasma. This feeling of something flowing through her, unknowable yet deeply *of her* at the same time. Ancient, intangible, mysterious and necessary. So necessary that she can't believe she ignored it for so many years. The feeling of creating. Of *creation*, if that's not too grandiose a word for what happens when she puts her brush to a canvas, which she's been doing these past couple of days since she and Frances drove to Mornington and returned with supplies.

When they'd entered the art shop Joan had looked around in wonder, remembering how she used to feel when surrounded by paints and brushes and crayons.

'You look happy,' Frances had remarked.

'I *am* happy,' she replied before she knew what she was saying.

For the first time in so long she couldn't remember the last time, she felt this lightness in her body. Even when her granddaughter, Natalie, was born she had felt happy *for* Corinne, of course, and delighted to be a grandmother, but it hadn't felt like this. *This* is a feeling of freedom, of limitlessness. Of joy. Yes, that's what it is.

'When's the last time you bought paints?' Frances asked and Joan tried to pinpoint it but couldn't, so she shrugged.

'Forever ago,' Joan said.

'What's been stopping you?'

She didn't yet know Frances well enough to tell her the truth although she suspected she would one day. So she decided to give her a version of it.

'Me,' she said. 'I've been stopping myself.'

She turned to run her fingertips over the tubes of paint that showed jewel colours and earth tones on their packaging, started to imagine what she could do with them, what colours she could make from combining this one and that one.

Frances had stood by looking quite pleased with herself as Joan selected ten oil paints, linseed oil and a palette, as well as some watercolour and acrylic paints, and appropriate brushes.

Now, as she stands amidst some of the trees on the fringe of the Duchess Hotel's land and observes a leaf closely as she attempts to bring it to life on the paper in front of her, she remembers this magic of creation. She needed it. Chased it, all the way south to this place where, she recognises – remembers – it was a common part of her childhood. These grounds, these trees, these flowers and blades of grass, all came in for close observation on her part and found their way into her childhood drawings and paintings which, in turn, were her apprenticeship for what came later.

The mistake she made was in thinking that her creative work wasn't actually work – as in, it wasn't something she could pursue as a livelihood, despite the fact she won prizes and received praise for it. Partly she didn't want to rely on it for money, fearing it would cause her to lose the love of it. Also she had been trained since childhood to think that marriage and motherhood would be her occupations. And so it proved, because being married to Isaac was the real job, as she found out as soon as he started asking her to cook for and play hostess to his colleagues and his parents and his friends.

It was such a change from how things had been between them initially. They met when he'd approached her one day while she was painting *en plein air* at Balmoral Beach in Sydney, a spot she loved for its various vistas and the way the water changed colour with the light. On a winter's day the sunlight would turn the water a brighter blue than in summer; the changing tides added their own elements. She could sit there for the duration of an incoming tide and find so many different ways to paint the beach.

'That colour is just right,' he had said, nodding at her canvas. 'The water...'

He smiled and she noticed the way his eyes crinkled. There was kindness in his smile and interest in his eyes.

'The water is that exact blue,' he went on. 'How do you do it?'

She smiled in return, although usually she didn't like to be interrupted while she was painting. It felt like bashing on a piano sounded: jarring, incoherent, upsetting. Yet today she didn't mind.

'I don't really know,' she answered. 'That sounds weak...' She shrugged. 'It's the truth. I just sit here, and it flows out of me.'

He shook his head like he didn't believe her. 'It's terrific. Beautiful too. Do you sell your paintings?'

'Yes,' she said, although she'd barely sold any herself. There was a little gallery nearby that took her work and while she couldn't make a living out of what she sold, it was enough to make her think she was reasonably proficient.

'I'd love to buy one.' He put his hands on his hips, in a relaxed way, like he was settling in. Yet after she gave him the details of the gallery he left.

Two days later, she had a call from the gallery to say a man named Isaac had bought everything they had of hers, and would she be interested in meeting this new collector?

She was. There was a dinner together, then another, then many. There was a meeting of the parents and an engagement and a wedding. Isaac didn't so much sweep her off her feet as make an irresistible case that their life together would be wonderful for them both. He wanted her to keep painting; he told her this often. It was just that once they were married there were so many other things to think of, and while she kept painting for a little while – and he would ask her about it from time to time – it was not her main purpose any more.

Running a household was so much work she couldn't believe she didn't have to go to university to learn how to do it. Her mother once muttered something about the role of chatelaine being such a demanding occupation that staff were required to support it, and Joan understood that within one year of being married, but never broached the subject with anyone. Because it was what a married woman did. Wasn't it?

Once her children arrived, she was aghast to realise there was no degree in childrearing either and she was expected to know how to do it anyway, with a failing mark on offer for any little thing she did wrong. It wasn't that she'd been given to believe that being a mother was easy – her own mother's repeated complaints over the course of years took care of that – but she had expected . . . what? Now it's so hard to remember. Some joy, perhaps. And there had been a little of that, but only in moments. Such fleeting moments. Her son lifting his head to her the first time he tried to push himself off the floor. Her daughter skipping around a garden and giggling. Moments that are memorable for their scarcity. Moments in which she realised that while she gained much she had also lost, and what she had lost most was herself. And there was Rachel. After she died, Joan felt like she was plunged into the deepest pool with no idea how to swim to the surface. In order to do so – to arrive here, at the Duchess – she had to kick off all the vestiges of who she had become in order to survive in that pool.

It has taken years for her to reclaim herself and now she is here, paintbrush in hand like it is an extension of her very being, and she feels, at last, at home in her body and in her mind.

'There you are,' says a newly familiar voice behind her, and even though Joan has been deeply concentrating she does not startle. Something about Frances makes her feel safe.

'And here *you* are,' she replies, half-turning and smiling, although she is concerned to see Frances looking a little upset. 'What's wrong?' Joan asks.

'How do you know something's wrong?'

'Because you don't seem that cheerful.'

'A person can't be cheerful all the time,' Frances says, then blinks, like she's surprised herself.

Joan laughs. 'No, they can't. I certainly am not.'

'I apologise,' Frances says. 'That was curt of me.'

'You're forgiven. Now what's the matter?'

'I've interrupted you.'

'You knew you were doing that when you approached me.' Joan raises an eyebrow. There's something about Frances that lets Joan believe she can be direct, and although she may be pushing it a little, she's no longer of a mindset – the mindset she's had most of her life – to beat around bushes. Her time here at the Duchess may end soon, or it may not, but she is not going to waste any of it.

Frances purses her lips and walks slowly to the seat that is next to Joan.

'I'm just worrying about things,' Frances says.

'Do you want to talk about them?'

'Not yet.'

'All right.' Joan decides to go back to painting, reasoning that Frances may just be here for the company.

'Who are your favourite artists?' Frances asks.

'That is like asking if I have favourite children.'

'Do you?'

Joan laughs. 'I chop and change. You?'

Frances is silent for a minute or so. 'I may have favoured one who didn't deserve it. And now he's –' She stops. 'I guess I've given it away.'

'You have, but I won't hold you to it.' Joan keeps painting. 'Whistler and van Gogh. Two of my favourites.'

'I've never been to an art gallery,' Frances murmurs and that makes Joan pause.

'Never?' she says.

'No. Not a lot of them where I'm from. Or down here.'

Joan considers this – and the fact that she grew up in a city where there were galleries, and artists, and opportunities to have experiences with both. She thought her world was broad accordingly but she can see now that it was narrow, because it never occurred to her that other people might have different experiences.

'You're welcome to watch me paint any day,' she says, 'as an easing-in, shall we say.'

'Thank you, pet,' Frances says. 'Then you won't mind if I sit with you for a while today.'

'I don't,' Joan affirms.

Minutes pass; maybe dozens of them, Joan doesn't keep track. When she next glances in Frances's direction, she sees that her acquaintance's eyes are closed, but her posture suggests she's not asleep, and Joan wonders if she's sorting through her worries or picturing a different reality. Then Joan returns to painting the real world in front of her. For this is life, and her coming back to it, one drawing, one ocean view, one cold day at a time.

CHAPTER EIGHTEEN

'It's really nice, Char.' Alison looks around the sitting room of her cousin Charlotte's new house in Elsternwick and grins. 'Don't you think, Mum?' Alison turns towards Frances, who is peering at the bookshelves.

'How long have you been an Agatha Christie fan?' Frances says.

'Oh, not me!' Charlotte laughs. 'They're Freddie's. He *loves* a murder mystery.'

Frances nods slowly, still looking at the shelves.

'Not here, is he?' she says.

'No, he's seeing his mum.'

Alison sits on the couch that Charlotte had ushered them to when they arrived, only for Frances to start poking around. Probably in order to report back to Margie about what her newly married daughter's house is like. Margie and Cec haven't been able to get down to see it yet because Cec has the flu or something – Margie was a little vague when Alison called her to say hello. It's been a long flu, if that's the case, because Charlotte and Fred moved in a month ago, and normally Margie wouldn't miss an opportunity to inspect a house. She has inspected Alison's on multiple occasions. That's what it felt like, at least – as if Margie was considering whether or not to give her a passing grade on her housekeeping.

Frances does it too. Alison thinks it's their generation – children during the Depression, brought up in households where nothing could be controlled, really, apart from how tidy the place was. Coppers for the washing on Sunday, make the plum puddings eight months ahead of Christmas – if not earlier – iron and iron and iron again so that a person could keep her dignity even when there was absolutely no money and almost no food.

Margie has told her stories; Frances has long insisted that her family was protected from the worst of that time because they had land and animals, but Alison still thinks rigid, almost obsessive control of one's environment is a feature of that generation. Maybe it was the wars. Or wars and Depression. What a time: they came out of what they thought was the Great War, into the Great Depression, then along comes another great war. Decades of uncertainty, of circumstances being dictated by men in far-off lands, losing the men from close to home either to years overseas or to death by an enemy's hand, or to the slow erosion of their souls through no work and, therefore, no ability to provide for their families. Both Margie and Frances have tried to control their daughters, in particular, because they grew up amongst adults who had no control over anything. While Alison has tried her best to understand this, she has also railed against it. As has Charlotte. It's part of the reason they've always been friends. That friendship began when they complained to each other about their mothers always telling them to tidy their rooms, as if that was the only important thing in the world.

'How are your parents, love?' Frances asks as she finally stops poking around the shelves and sits down.

'You'd probably know better than I would,' Charlotte says lightly but Alison catches the edge to it: her cousin knows that Margie calls Frances often, possibly more often than she does Charlotte. They act more like sisters than sisters-in-law – or maybe it ends up being the same thing if two women get along with each other.

'I doubt it. We only talk about the chooks.'

Alison rolls her eyes. They never talk about the chooks. Instead, they gossip about people they know and politicians they don't like.

'I saw that, Alison,' Frances remarks.

'You did not,' Alison says.

'She's always rolling her eyes at me,' Frances says, sounding hurt.

'And you at me!' Alison has to stop herself doing it again.

'I may be old but I still have my wits about me.'

'I never said you didn't, Mum. Honestly.' Alison heaves out a sigh. 'Char, can you get home soon?'

'Hopefully! Mum keeps saying Dad isn't well enough for visitors but I'd like to see them.'

Cups of tea are poured and biscuits offered, and Alison half-wishes she had come alone to Charlotte's house so they could talk properly – there are some things she doesn't want to say in front of Frances because she knows her mother will be judgemental. Yet she also knows that if she withholds certain information and Frances finds out later, she'll be in trouble for not telling her sooner. Some days of daughterhood are an infernal tap-dance between doing the dutiful thing and protecting oneself.

'So how's Erik fitting in?' Charlotte says at a certain point. This is the very subject Alison had wanted to bring up but not in front of Frances, to whom she's given scant information about her stepson other than telling her that he was moving in.

'Um . . . yeah.' Alison waggles her eyebrows, hoping that conveys enough.

Charlotte's eyes widen. 'That bad?'

Alison risks a glance at Frances only to find a stare in return.

'You haven't said anything,' Frances says sternly.

'Not much to say, Mum.' Alison laughs nervously. 'He hasn't been there long.'

'Long enough to cause some kind of upset.'

Oh great, now Frances is doing that lip-disappearing thing that signifies major disapproval. One day Alison would really like to tell her mother to stop it – to tell her that if a friend did that, she'd stop talking to them because she'd take it as evidence that the friend didn't like her very much – but instead she presses her fingernails into her palms to distract herself and fakes a smile to Charlotte.

'We're doing our best,' she offers. 'Nineteen-year-old men don't make for the best house guests.' She stops. 'Except he's not really a guest, is he? He's Tad's son.'

For most of her marriage her children have had their father to themselves, and she knows she got used to that way of being – because it was all they knew. In some ways they still have him to themselves because he barely interacts with Erik, who comes and goes and takes food from the fridge and speaks in fragments.

'Tough situation,' Charlotte murmurs.

'Send him to me,' Frances retorts. 'I'll sort him out.'

Alison blinks with surprise. Her mother, who let Keith get away with everything, is now wanting to sort out Erik? Not that she can say that. Frances will think she's helping, and Alison's role is to support the fiction.

'I might take you up on that,' she says, which is not a commitment but also not a dismissal.

Her eyes meet Charlotte's, and she sees understanding of the tap-dance there.

Frances nods once, like something has been decided.

'Maybe we should all go and see your parents,' Frances says to Charlotte. 'It's been ages for me.'

'I'll talk to Mum.'

Charlotte pours more tea and offers more biscuits. The visit seems to be over too quickly, and all the way back to Frances's place in the car Alison chats to her about Rosie and Sean, and Frances talks about Colin.

When Alison pulls up outside her mother's small house with its beige brick and heavy roof, she turns off the engine and starts to open her door. She likes to check for hazards in her mother's path and has taken to escorting Frances inside.

'I'm serious about Erik,' Frances says, sounding like she means it.

'Okay.'

'Don't let him ruin your family.'

Their eyes meet then Frances's drop, and Alison tries to read something into that but knows she's only reading into it what she wants to see: some admission of guilt about Keith and his behaviour.

'I don't plan to,' Alison says. 'But I really appreciate your support.'

Frances looks up and Alison smiles kindly.

'I do, Mum.'

'Thank you, Alison.'

Alison hops out of the car and goes round to open Frances's door, then takes her into the house.

CHAPTER NINETEEN

No time for a quick ciggie because she was running late, and tonight she's not in the laundry but helping with general duties so her lateness would be noticed. And William's pursed lips as she arrives in the staff kitchen tell her that it has been.

'Hm,' he says, making a show of looking at his watch, although Kirrily suspects he's only doing it because there are a couple of others present and he doesn't want them to think lateness is allowed. He's never once pulled her up for taking longer on her break than she should. Because sometimes she does, needing a few extra moments to herself so she can face guests again. She likes her job most of the time, but guests are a variable she could do without.

'Mrs Reynaud in 205 would like new towels and there are some room service trolleys to clear,' William says as Kirrily puts her handbag in a locker.

'Right,' she says, smoothing her hair. It's in a tight bun but wisps always escape no matter how much hairspray she uses, and she doesn't want to look messy. She's started wearing it up not because of Shane calling her Glinda but because she thinks it looks more professional. And she wants to be thought of as professional.

William raises his eyebrows at her.

'I'm going now,' she says and almost trots out of the room, heading for the linen stores. She'll do the towels first. Trolleys will take longer.

Once she has the towels in hand, she walks towards the goods lift. Staff don't take the guest lifts, nor do they use the central staircase to reach the first floor.

'Miss,' she hears from behind her, and she figures it's her being referred to, so she turns.

And there he is. Young Paul Newman. Or whatever his name is.

His smile is broad. Her heart constricts.

'I thought it was you,' he says.

'Hello,' she says, because it's polite and gives nothing away.

He steps closer and Kirrily feels her breath catching.

'Do you remember me?' he says.

Kirrily isn't sure whether she should pretend not to know who he is – which she'd find hard, because she's not good at keeping up lies – or give in to the fact she's been thinking about him for days. Except he's still a guest and she can't be too familiar.

'Um . . . yes.' She smiles and hopes it looks formal, not like an invitation to continue talking.

Another step closer.

His skin looks tanned, his eyebrows are neat and he smells of something expensive.

'My name is Derek.' He holds out his hand and she looks at it, then shakes it quickly, mildly disappointed that his name isn't Paul.

'Kirrily.' She wants to look away, she really does, but there is something transfixing about beauty at close quarters. It's hard not to stare when perfection is standing right in front of you. And staring is what she's doing now, so she blinks to break it.

'I gather you work here.' He smiles again and his teeth are white and even, the way she wishes hers were but her parents couldn't afford an orthodontist when she was growing up and it's the last thing she'd think of now.

'I do. And, uh . . .' She holds up the towels. 'I have to get going.'

He takes her free hand with both of his and she flinches, not because it's an unwelcome gesture but because she's frightened of what it may mean. Of how much she likes it. His hands are warm, and he squeezes hers gently.

'I couldn't help noticing you last time. And now,' he says, and he looks more serious. 'You're so lovely.'

She laughs sharply, out of shock at the compliment. Then she glances around, hoping none of the other staff are seeing this; she could get in so much trouble.

'That's a nice thing to say.' She's staring again, and once she realises, she tugs on her hand, taking it back. 'Thanks, Derek. I really need to get these upstairs.'

'Of course,' he says. 'I'll be in the bar for a while. In case you're passing by.'

The look he gives her is long and hard and it makes her heart constrict again. She swallows.

'Right,' she says. 'See you.'

Before waiting for him to answer, she almost runs to the lift and doesn't look back as she presses the up button.

Even after she's delivered towels to Mrs Reynaud, her heart is still beating faster than usual, and she reckons it stays that way until she takes her break, grabbing her cigarettes and lighter and tucking them into her pocket as she heads to her usual spot.

With her first long drag on a cigarette, Kirrily feels herself relax.

'Those things'll kill ya,' she hears Shane say, approaching from the side.

'Probably,' Kirrily murmurs. Connor says that to her all the time, and she always agrees. How can she explain to him – a non-smoker – that the handful of minutes she has to smoke each cigarette are the only lumps of time she can give herself? No one questions a smoke break here at the Duchess and at home no one bothers her when she's outside smoking.

So, yes, cigarettes are bad for her but so is not having a second to herself. Maybe when she's older and there are fewer demands on her time she'll give up. Maybe she'll take up gardening or something instead and that will be her way of relaxing, of having time for herself. That's a long way off, though.

For all his teasing – and he does it every time they find themselves on a smoke break together – Shane understands why she needs this. Because he does too.

'If I didn't have these,' he'd said once, holding up his durry, 'I'd probably kill the patrons.'

She'd laughed in the way that only someone with a profound understanding of a statement can. Somehow smokers seem to know in their bones that short breaks from their jobs – or maybe it's more that it's short breaks from other people – are necessary to keep sane.

'So,' Kirrily says, taking another drag and contemplating what she has to say next. She needs to tell *someone*.

'So.' Shane looks amused, like he can guess she's in a predicament.

'I wanted to ask you about a guest.'

'Oh yeah?'

'A man.' Kirrily closes her eyes briefly and sees Derek's face. She's been thinking about him so much the image of him is almost burnt on her retinas.

'I'm guessing not the one you're married to,' Shane says drily, 'going by the look on your face.'

'Shane!' Kirrily's cheeks feel hot, and she can't believe she's been so obvious. Or maybe he's just good at reading people because of his job.

'Okay, yes.' She coughs, more to stall for time than because she needs to. 'This man . . . he was handsome. Really handsome. I saw him a week or so ago. And then again. An hour or so ago.'

'You need to be more specific. I don't know how you define handsome. Like, Tom Cruise in *Top Gun* handsome?'

'No. Paul Newman.'

'Ah. Blue eyes, then?'

'Yes.'

He nods slowly. 'Can't say I noticed a Paul Newman type. And why do you want to know?'

The temperature of her cheeks goes up.

'I bumped into him the first time,' she says quickly. 'I felt bad.'

'Did you injure him?'

'No.'

'So why are you so interested in who he is?'

'Because . . .' She sighs loudly and ponders what to say. 'All right, it's because I have a crush.' She won't meet Shane's eyes despite what feels like extreme bravery on her part.

He nods again. 'Figured.'

'Is that all?'

'Sure. Crushes are fine, Kirrily. We all have them.'

'Really?' She hasn't had one since she met Connor.

'I reckon they're normal. They remind you that you're still in the world. That you're still interested in who's around you.' He flicks the last of his ash to the ground. 'Acting on them is different.' He's staring at her again. 'No one can get into your brain and find out what you're thinking about some handsome stranger, but they sure as hell know about it if you do something.'

Kirrily runs through the scenarios she has dreamt up about her and the perfect stranger – schoolgirl things, mainly. They've been a good distraction while she works. Maybe that's what Shane means about them being fine. Normal.

'I think you probably asked me about this bloke so I could remind you of that,' he says quietly, seriously.

'Maybe.' She considers that he might be right; also that her crush is at a stage when she just wants to talk about it. Like a high-school girl. It's not good to talk about it, though, like it's not good to think about it.

'Thanks,' she says as she turns to go.

'For?'

'Listening.'

Shane winks. 'Anytime.'

Then he lopes in the opposite direction, towards the front of the hotel, while Kirrily treads her familiar path to the back.

CHAPTER TWENTY

Painting outside on a cold afternoon that has more of winter than spring in it has not been Joan's brightest idea – although she wouldn't say she's had many of those over the course of her lifetime. Once upon a time, she would have said her children were the best thing to ever happen to her and she would have meant it. But as children become adults and form their own lives, they move to the periphery of consciousness. At least, in her case they have. Not all the time – occasionally she finds herself worrying about them then she realises they don't need her to do that because they are fine. For now.

Life never really stays fine, though, does it? Not every day. Not all the way. She has found herself in slipstreams, where it feels like everything flows and it's easy; she has found herself flung to the ground when the current stops. She has tried to work out how she can predict or control when the slipstreams happen but she now knows she can't; she just has to hop on them when they appear and make the most of them because they'll end.

For a while marriage and motherhood were slipstreams, up until the point Isaac became more focused on his work and building his reputation and neglected to realise the role Joan had to play in it all. That's when she crashed to earth.

The moment she decided to get in her car and drive to the Duchess Hotel, she felt the slipstream picking her up, and it's continued to carry her all the way to this day, this easel, this moment of her brush on canvas. She has picked a spot that to her left has a broad view of the rugged cliff – almost a small peninsula – over the beach and the scrubby vegetation that lines it. The green of that vegetation is what she's trying to capture now: acid green in parts, darker in others, it contrasts with the blue of the ocean in the afternoon light, the white caps of the waves and the pale yellow of the sand. Although she may make it more yellow on her canvas. Not too much. Just enough for the contrast. Painting is not mimicry of life; it is, rather, an enhancement of life. An adornment, almost. She is adorning her impression of this scene so that someone else may appreciate it. Or it may just be for her.

So she doesn't mind the cold when she has a view like this and something to do about it. And shortly she won't even notice it because her work will absorb her, and she will let it.

A noise nearby makes her turn, and she sees one of the maids – Kaye, or Caitlin, or something like that – walking through the trees, holding a cigarette, frowning.

Joan really doesn't like to be interrupted when she's at this stage of a painting, which is one of the reasons why she chose a spot where she thought no one would notice her. Now she wonders if she'll look strange to this other woman, standing here with an easel in front of her, then decides she doesn't care. Moreover, in this hotel Kaye-Caitlin will no doubt have seen sights more dramatic than a middle-aged woman with a paintbrush.

'Hello,' she says as Kaye-Caitlin draws near.

'Oh.' Kaye-Caitlin looks around, as if she might be about to drop her cigarette, which Joan wants to tell her not to do because she's half-tempted to bum one off her. She misses smoking. That was something else she gave up when she married. Isaac didn't like it. Too bad that she did.

'I'm Joan. We haven't properly met.' She smiles and holds up the paintbrush. 'I have a new hobby. New-old.'

'Kirrily.' A quick puff then another glance around.

Kirrily. That's right. She knew it started with a *k* sound.

'I don't mind you smoking,' Joan says, 'if that's what you're worried about.'

'I'm not –' Kirrily stops. 'Yeah, I was. Not the best look, staff smoking on a break.'

'Why not? Isn't that what breaks are for?'

Kirrily looks relieved then steps closer.

'Watercolours,' she murmurs.

Joan registers surprise on her face. 'You paint?'

'Used to.' A weak smile. 'Before . . .' She nods towards the hotel. 'Work takes up a lot of time. And kids. You know.'

'I do.'

Joan whips away the painting she has started to reveal a fresh sheet of paper, then holds out the brush.

'Why don't you have a go?' she offers.

Kirrily shakes her head vigorously.

'I couldn't. You're a guest.'

'And we're not allowed to fraternise?'

Kirrily's eyes widen. 'Probably not.'

Joan laughs lightly. 'I'm a person, first and foremost. And so are you. And we have an interest in common.'

She again holds out the brush. 'How much time do you have left?' she asks. 'I'll keep an eye on the clock. You just paint. And I'll look after that cigarette for you.'

With her other hand, she takes the cigarette as Kirrily, looking a little relieved, takes the paintbrush.

'About fifteen minutes,' Kirrily says. 'I'm not normally here during the day. Got called in to cover for someone.' She smiles tentatively. 'I'm glad I did.'

Joan knows she's paying her a compliment, so she smiles then checks her watch. 'Go,' she says. 'I'll wander over here.'

It's hard for Joan to know exactly why she has encouraged Kirrily to take over her own activity; she can only say it was instinctual. The young woman looked like she needed something – hard to say what, but the only thing Joan had to offer was paint. Maybe Joan needed something too – again, hard to say what. But as she walks away from Kirrily and takes a furtive puff on her cigarette, feeling once again, after decades, the nicotine go to her head, she decides not to try to find out. Her whole stay at the Duchess Hotel has been a quest to find out what she needs in order to move forward in her life; sometimes, she is discovering, it's best just to let the day take its course.

After almost fifteen minutes have elapsed, she returns and sees that Kirrily has painted the beginnings of a pine cone and surrounding bracken.

'That's good.' Joan looks more closely. 'Actually, very good. You'll have to come back and finish it.' Joan startles herself by saying this, because the offer seems to have come from an unconscious part of her, given that she has no interest in painting in company.

'Are you sure?' Kirrily looks unsure herself.

'Mm.' Which is code for, no, she's not.

'Could I . . .' Kirrily looks to her left then right before locking her eyes onto Joan's. 'Could I set up a time, maybe? You know, once a week? To come and paint with you?'

Joan thinks about it, then sighs. Loudly enough for Kirrily to flinch.

'That sounds like you're after lessons,' Joan says, attempting a smile to offset any offence caused by the sigh, because she didn't mean to upset the other woman. 'I'm not really the teaching type.'

'Oh.' Kirrily presses her eyes closed and Joan thinks she might be about to cry, which is an unintended and regrettable circumstance but Joan is not going to give in.

When Kirrily opens her eyes, they do indeed look watery but also brighter, and determined.

'It doesn't have to be a lesson. I could just . . . be nearby.'

Joan stares at her.

'I want to paint. Really,' Kirrily adds quickly. 'I just need a regular commitment, you know?' She laughs nervously. 'Never been good at making myself do things unless I know someone is waiting for me.'

This is not a mentality Joan understands – if she decides to do something she does it and she doesn't need a timekeeper or chaperone – but she appreciates that Kirrily is trying to share something of herself. Joan might even take it as another compliment.

'And I, ah . . .' Kirrily goes on. 'I used to be good. Pretty good. My mum always said so.'

In Joan's experience mothers are not reliable judges of their children's talent, and she's been guilty of that herself. When Corinne was little Joan was convinced she was the next Margot Fonteyn, only for Corinne to give up ballet for netball at the slightest provocation.

'So you'd like to make her proud again?' That's Joan's kind interpretation of the matter.

'I can't. She's dead,' Kirrily says quickly.

'Oh.' Now it's Joan's turn to falter. 'That's awful.'

Kirrily shrugs like it's nothing. 'I was young. It was a while ago. But I . . . I stopped painting when she died. And I miss it.'

'I see.' If this is a ploy to pull on Joan's meagre heartstrings, it's working.

'I could come on Friday afternoons.' It's said so quickly that Joan barely catches it. 'I could ask my parents-in-law to watch the kids until my husband gets home. They're always saying they want more time with them.'

She looks so hopeful.

'I'd only need an hour,' she almost whispers and in that moment Joan feels quite sorry for her. That she almost has to beg to do an activity that is not work and not mother work or housework. And that is something Joan understands.

'And the days are getting longer,' Joan says, then she smiles. 'So we have more light than we did.'

Kirrily's eyes widen.

'What time does your shift usually start?' Joan asks.

'Five. Or six. Depends. William changes it.'

Joan sighs again but it's softer this time; Kirrily doesn't seem to notice it. Something like resignation settles in her marrow but she doesn't feel resentful about it. This young woman is asking her for something and if she puts herself in that position – if she imagines herself begging for time to paint, time to herself, time to *express* herself – she would not want to be denied.

'So if we start at four o'clock?' she says and Kirrily's response is to grin.

'Yes!' she says.

'I'll be here earlier on Friday in case you wish to come earlier,' Joan says. 'And I mean *here*. This view is your first assignment.'

Kirrily moves towards her as if she's going to hug her but as much as Joan is not the teaching type, she is not the hugging type either, so she keeps her hands by her sides and Kirrily stops.

'Thank you!' Kirrily almost squeals. *'Thank you!'*

Joan holds her paintbrush in the air to signify the end of the conversation.

'See you Friday?' she says.

'Yes. Yes!'

As Kirrily keeps standing there, looking expectant, Joan half-turns away, hoping she'll understand her meaning.

'Bye!' Kirrily says to Joan's back, and Joan smiles to herself as she puts her brush onto her palette.

CHAPTER TWENTY-ONE

This won't do. Not at all.

Frances has looked all over the Duchess Hotel, and she can't find Shane anywhere. She knows it's his day to work – he is always here on Tuesdays. And he knows that she is always here on Tuesdays because she's here every day, even if it's just to walk around the grounds.

Last week William said he'd have to give her a job, such is her dedication to the hotel. Frances laughed but he looked serious. She wondered what sort of job she'd be able to do here in this grand place full of grand people – including William. There's a rumour that William is the son of a member of the aristocracy who decided to slum it in the southern hemisphere, although his accent isn't plummy enough for that. He sounds to Frances like the ABC news presenters of old: Australian with overtones of Received Pronunciation. In other words: not English. Although if the rumour is true, maybe he's worked on his accent so he sounds less posh?

William isn't here today, that she can see. So she can't ask him about Shane. And she doesn't feel she knows the other staff well enough to query them – they might think her odd, asking about the barman. Not that Shane is just the barman. He is more than that to her, at any rate. He's her friend and, if she allows herself the indulgence, her protector. Always looking out for her; always asking how she is. Shane cares more about her than her own son does.

Keith called her the other day, saying he needed to see her.

'What for?' she asked.

'Things . . . Y'know.'

'No, I do not. Otherwise I wouldn't ask.'

He grunted and at that point Frances knew the conversation would go no further. Not then. Apart from Keith telling her he'd 'make a time'. She wondered why he couldn't say what he wanted to say or at least make that time while on the phone, but there would have been no point asking him. Ever since he took her on that strange mission to Melbourne to see his 'investment' she's been wary of him in a way that feels entirely unsuitable for a mother yet which she should have felt earlier, given his behaviour. He's given her no reason to trust him, even if she can't help loving him. Alison is incredibly trustworthy yet Frances knows, in her marrow, that it is Keith's approval she wants – she knows she has Alison's – and it makes her feel pathetic.

So she told Shane about the conversation and he was sympathetic, the way he always is. Which makes it sound like he's just automatically sympathetic, like it's an act. Except it's not. Frances has had conversations with him. *Real* conversations. The life-and-death kind – not about either of them dying but about what life and death mean. She has seen enough of both and so has he, in different circumstances. Carrying a gun, trying to survive in Vietnamese jungles, trying to forget what he saw and heard and felt. Then returning to Australia and having no one to tell. Not until her, he said. Not even his mates from the army could listen the way she could, let alone give him advice the way she did.

He only hoped, he told her, that he could be as good a friend to her.

But he was. He is. By smiling at her each day, by noticing that she exists, by talking to her like she's a person and not a 'little old lady' – that's how he is her friend. What he does is keep her anchored in the world, and she fancies she does that for him as well.

It is Shane who has listened while she talked about the man she never married because a different war carried him away. Shane to whom she has talked of regrets and hopes dashed. Her children were never as curious about her, and in turn she was curious about him.

Probably she should be surprised that she's grown close to someone half her age and so different in life experience, but just as you can't help who you fall in love with, you often can't help who you fall in friendship with. Friendship is about luck and circumstance and timing just as much as love is.

Now she can't find him anywhere and her disquiet about that is not at all selfish – she does not feel the need to unburden herself to him or anything like that – but, rather, concern for his welfare. Because she knows the black dog visits him. That's even the way he refers to it. 'Just like Winston Churchill,' he said once and he didn't need to explain further. She understood. The black dog does not visit her although grief can take its shape sometimes and lead a person to confuse one set of dark emotions for another.

'Frances?'

The voice pulls her out of her ponderings, and she remembers that she's sitting in the hotel foyer, with the world passing her by.

She turns to see that the voice belongs to Joan, who looks uncharacteristically windswept. Even when Joan is outside, she seems to be immune to weather.

'Hello,' Frances replies.

'Are you all right?'

Frances presses her lips together. How should she answer this?

'You look upset,' Joan goes on, and Frances appreciates her forthrightness. So much better to just say things than meander around them.

'No. I'm not all right.'

Joan nods as if this is the most normal thing in the world.

'What is it?' she asks.

'I can't find Shane.'

'Right.' Joan gives her a quizzical look.

'He's meant to be working today. He isn't anywhere on the premises.'

'Perhaps he's unwell.'

Frances looks at her meaningfully. 'That's what I'm afraid of.'

By the expression on Joan's face, she understands what Frances is saying and it's a relief not to have to explain it. 'Has he been . . . unwell before?'

'Not for a while.'

There was a week, about two years ago, when he wasn't meant to be on holidays but he wasn't at the hotel. Frances wasn't as friendly with him then so she didn't ask questions. When he returned he looked both a stone lighter and like he was weighed down.

'I see.' Joan frowns. 'Have you tried calling him?'

'I don't have his number.' Said out loud, it sounds ridiculous: they know so much else about each other but she doesn't know where he lives or how to contact him outside of the Duchess Hotel.

'I'll ask William,' Joan says confidently.

'He won't give it to you!'

'Maybe not, but I'll try. Leave it with me. Could you give me your phone number, Frances? Then I'll let you know what happens.'

Frances feels a modicum of relief, the way a person does when someone else takes charge. It's so nice when that happens. A lifetime of taking responsibility for others is wearing and Frances appreciates that Joan is giving her one less thing to do.

'Thank you,' she says, and Joan looks amused.

'I haven't done anything yet.'

Frances feels moved, then, to pat Joan's cheek, even though they're not familiar enough with each other for that.

'You're helping,' she says, and she's as surprised as anything when Joan hugs her.

'I'm happy to,' says the voice close to her ear.

Then Joan is gone and Frances is left sitting alone, but not lonely, with the bustle of the hotel around her. She hopes that, wherever he is, Shane isn't lonely either.

CHAPTER TWENTY-TWO

Alison potters around Frances's kitchen, opening and closing cupboard doors, not sure what she's looking for – if she's looking for anything. Her mind is not here; it's at home, thinking about the argument Tad had with Erik this morning in front of the children. That had also involved the slamming of doors – larger ones that shook the house.

Erik took Tad's car last night without asking, and while Tad probably could have let it go, he was meant to take Sean to cricket practice while Alison picked up Rosie from her friend's house. So that meant there was no other car for Tad and Sean had to wait until Alison came home, which meant he was half an hour late for practice and the coach didn't care about his excuse. When Tad picked Sean up later he was upset – the coach had yelled at him in front of the team and said clearly Sean didn't care about his teammates or cricket and he was a disgrace and all the things irate coaches tend to say to boys when they think they're pulling them into line but actually they just embarrass them so much they take a year to recover.

'Your actions have consequences!' Tad thundered at Erik as the household prepared itself for the day. Erik hadn't come home by the time they went to bed so it was Tad's first opportunity to say anything.

'So do yours,' Erik said, sneering, while Alison hoped Tad wouldn't take the bait. Except he did.

'What do you mean by that?' He drew himself up to his full height – a substantial six-feet-two, taller than Erik – and looked down his nose.

'You think you can be a father *now*?' Erik replied. 'Fuck off.'

It was the swearing that did it, because the children were listening and that swear word is the one word that is not used around them. Tad looked like he was going to punch Erik and that's when Rosie started crying. Erik took off and Tad went after him, the slamming of doors ensued, and now Alison finds herself still shaking a little. Adrenaline, she supposes. And dismay at what is going on in her previously semi-serene household. The most upset they've had to date has been the mourning of a dead dog and a lost parrot. Maybe that means her children are sheltered. Certainly Alison doesn't think *she's* sheltered: growing up with a tough mountain woman for a mother and a pharmacist father who brought all sorts of stories home from work made for a wide-open world view.

Alison distracted Rosie with promises of TV after school then took the children to school. After that, taking advantage of it being one of her days off work, she headed for Frances's, knowing she needed her mother even if she wouldn't tell her that. Their relationship seems to run on a tacit understanding that Alison wants more love and support than Frances is prepared to give, and she'll take what she can get.

'What is going on in there?' Frances calls from the sitting room, and Alison stops before she yanks open yet another cupboard.

'Ummm . . .' she replies.

'Are you looking for something?'

This is a loaded question, because Alison is intimately familiar with the contents of the kitchen cupboards, and Frances knows it.

'Maybe,' she answers.

Frances appears in the doorway, frowning. 'What's going on?' she repeats.

'What do you mean?'

'Alison – I know you well enough to know that something's bothering you.'

It's pathetic, really, that Alison feels chuffed that her mother would say something like that – it reminds her that all any of us really want is to be acknowledged, for someone to say that they *see* us, that we exist. It's too easy, in the run of everyday life, of keeping up with responsibilities, to feel like you're invisible. Like no one appreciates you for anything. One word of familiarity from her mother can keep her going for a while – and she should remember that Frances may, from time to time, need it in return. Because while she may feel hard done by because her mother thought Keith was the sun and Alison merely the moon, if Alison's being honest with herself, she knows that she treated her father like the sun and her mother like the moon.

She turns and smiles gratefully.

'Erik is causing problems,' she says.

'What a surprise,' Frances says drily. 'That boy has been nothing but trouble since day dot.'

Alison frowns. 'How do you know?'

'The scant amount you've told me was enough. He's selfish and spoilt.' Frances inhales noisily. 'I don't wish to blame your husband, but I also don't wish to solely blame the boy's mother.'

While her first instinct is to bite back, Alison takes a few seconds to consider this, because Frances is only saying what Alison wishes she could to Tad: that a firmer hand with Erik when he was younger could have averted the behaviour they're experiencing now. Erik seems to believe he can get away with everything because he can. Even when Tad went after him this morning it was only to chastise him – there were no practical consequences. If Sean had been the one to misbehave, they would have deprived him of something he liked. What Erik likes is the freedom to do whatever he wants, and that he has in spades.

'I don't know what to do,' Alison admits.

She and Frances stare at each other.

'And I am not the best person to help you, because . . .' Frances's eyes widen momentarily then she says no more.

Alison knows she must be referring to Keith, but she doesn't want to be the one to say it. She has never, in her life, been allowed to criticise Keith.

'All I'll say is, try not to let your children see it,' Frances says at last.

'Too late.'

'That's a shame.'

They sigh at the same time.

'But I'll try from now on,' Alison says. 'To keep them out of it.'

'That's all you can do.' Frances moves slowly towards the kettle and flicks it on. 'That's all any of us mothers try to do with messes.'

They spend the next few minutes in a silent ballet of organising mugs and biscuits, and by the time they sit down together the subject has changed to the TV shows they like to watch.

When Alison leaves, Frances walks her to the door.

'You have to hold your nerve,' she advises as Alison steps outside.

'Hm?' Alison doesn't understand what she means.

'It's your family. You've made it the way you want it. Don't let this outsider ruin it. Hold onto what is precious to you. Don't let him scare you away from it.'

Alison goes to respond – to say that she'd never allow that – but she remembers the shaking, and Rosie crying, and realises she's already let something slip.

'He'll ruin it if you let him,' Frances goes on. 'And Tad isn't strong enough to stop it. You have to be.'

This is the warning she needed to hear, but she wants nothing more than for her mother to take care of it the way she took care of a schoolyard bully who used to kick Alison in the shins and steal her lunch on a regular basis. Frances marched up to the school, then to the child's parents, and said that if the girl's behaviour didn't change, she was going to the local newspaper to report a lapse of discipline in local children and she would be quite happy to name names. Of course, the paper was unlikely to have printed names but the threat worked. Alison remembers feeling proud of her mother. And safe. At least for a while.

Frances can't take care of Erik, though, and she's made it clear that it's Alison's job to do so. If only it didn't feel like yet another task on an infinite list, and she didn't resent Tad for not being stronger. This resentment, it's been simmering away inside her ever since Erik arrived and it's not good for her. She has to find a way to reduce it, or remove it, except that doesn't seem likely. She's never thought of Tad as being weak, yet . . . in the back of her mind, the thought is starting to creep in. Even as she knows it's unfair.

What she really wants is a magic wand. Wave it, and *poof*! The problem disappears. If only she knew where to find one.

CHAPTER TWENTY-THREE

In her former life Joan was known for being helpful. When her children were at school, she often took in other children whose parents couldn't pick them up or were late home. School fete: she was up early baking. One of her sisters needed a babysitter: she'd offer without being asked. That was when both of her sisters lived in Sydney; now one is in Hong Kong, the other in Cairns, and she has missed them. Long-distance phone calls are not the same as physical presence.

The helpful activities she undertook were not done in order to be liked in return. She didn't want for friends, and she maintained her friendships carefully so she had no need to try to be more liked than she was. Of course, those same friends will now be thinking her the worst person in the world for disappearing from their lives. But she still believes she's not doing anything wrong. Taking some time to herself is, she has decided, a fundamental good and every woman should try it. Especially the ones who are helpful.

Because it wore her out, the helpfulness. She did it because she wanted to be of assistance; in some ways it felt like it was an act of service. Religion has not factored hugely in her life but she has always liked the idea of service. Of making other people's lives easier. It became a reflex action, though – help here, help there, help everyone but herself. Then she stopped one day and realised the reflex wasn't doing her any good.

When she offered to help find Shane, it was not a reflex. It was an action that came from a genuine desire to ameliorate Frances's distress, which was plain. She has spent little time with Frances but enough to know that she likes her and doesn't want her to be distressed.

It felt good to make a sincere offer, not one she thought she ought to, even if it made her reflect more on her previous behaviour. Perhaps she's never been sincere. Perhaps everything has been reflexive. Does that mean she's not really a person, just an entity who looks like a person moving through the world and doing person things without question? What a horrible thought. But it might be true.

Not that she's using this gesture towards Frances to prove anything. She likes Shane, too, and she wants to check that he's all right. That's all that's in her mind when she rings the number given to her by William after she promised she just wanted to ask Shane about a drink he made the other night.

William had narrowed his eyes then lifted his chin as if he was assessing her character – and probably he was.

'That is all?' he queried.

'Of course.'

His nostrils flared and he raised his eyebrows. 'I wouldn't usually,' he murmured, then wrote a number on a piece of hotel stationery, and Joan felt the flutter of a minor victory: she's been here long enough to be trusted. Or, rather, she's spent enough money here to be trusted. She pays her bill every three days, as William asked, writing a cheque from the account she has kept separate all these years.

Now she dials that number and listens as it rings three times, four times, five times.

'Hello?'

'Shane?'

There's silence on the line.

'Shane?' she repeats.

'Who is this?'

'Joan. From the Duchess.' Maybe that's not enough information. 'From the bar. I know Frances.'

More silence.

'She's worried about you.'

'So why isn't *she* calling?' He sounds spiteful. Not at all like the man she knows.

'Because she doesn't have your number.'

There's a noise that could be a guffaw or a grunt.

'I'm worried too,' Joan adds quickly. Because it's true. 'We haven't seen you for a little while.'

'I'm fine.' It's said with such vehemence that she knows it can't be true.

'Are you unwell?'

'What did I just say?'

She feels a little frightened of him, even though he's elsewhere, on the end of the phone. This man isn't one she knows, and she can't help thinking the version in the bar has been a facsimile. She knows from experience, with some of the people Isaac associates with, that people can keep up a pretence for a very long time. Years, if necessary. The calculatedness of it has always unnerved her – except, she has to acknowledge, she's probably been doing it herself. Just not so coldly. At least, she doesn't think she's been cold. Maybe Shane hasn't meant to be cold either. Maybe they're not so different to each other.

'I have obviously disturbed you,' she says, trying the path of concession. 'I'm sorry.'

That grunt/guffaw again.

'Right,' he says, then he hangs up.

She's never been hung up on before. That must be why tears have sprung to her eyes and she feels like she's been slapped.

'Oh,' she says to the air, then she puts the handset back on its cradle.

She walks to the window to look at her tree, and blinks back the tears. When she's felt this unsettled while being at the Duchess, she has gone downstairs to the bar for a drink and a chat with Shane.

Instead she sits on the bed and stares out the window and wonders what she can tell Frances. That Shane is out of sorts? That's not strong enough. That he doesn't seem himself? That's closer to the truth. Of course, she doesn't know the actual truth, and it's not really any of her business. She just wishes she could help him, if only because he helps Frances.

It's not something she can solve today, however. So she does what comes naturally: picks up her pencils and paper and begins to draw.

CHAPTER TWENTY-FOUR

'I like what you're wearing.'

Connor's hand lightly brushes between her shoulder blades and Kirrily moves away from it. Not willingly. Unconsciously. Because she was thinking about Derek at the exact moment Connor came up behind her and said that, while she had her hands in the kitchen sink, trying to clean its sides.

'This apron?' she snaps, to cover her embarrassment at recoiling from her own husband.

There's silence but she doesn't turn around.

'Your dress.' Connor sounds . . . not hurt but bewildered. Still, she's not going to turn around, because guilt is probably written across her face. Guilt for something that is illogical. Silly. No – stupid. Teenage. Hormonal. Irrational.

A crush. A ridiculous, baseless crush.

Well, maybe not baseless. The handsome stranger is handsome, after all. And how is she meant to be immune to that?

Except Connor is handsome. Sort of. He used to be.

It's terrible to think that about your husband, isn't it? And each time she does she also has to accept that he may think she 'used to be' something too.

Sometimes – there's a niggle at the back of her brain about this – she thinks it's more comforting to believe that he doesn't think that. The story she has been telling herself, about how she doesn't deserve good things because she's not special, is more familiar. She doesn't usually stop to consider that perhaps not being special is just fine. That you don't have to be special to deserve good things because, surely, everyone deserves them. Everyone deserves to be loved. Everyone deserves to be told they're beautiful or handsome or whatever makes them feel good.

Of course, that means Connor deserves it too. She should be telling Connor that he's great, not just waiting for him to tell her. Which he doesn't any more. Probably because she's never said it to him and he's sick of it being one-sided. She wouldn't know. She doesn't ask him. And that's the exhausting merry-go-round of her life: *Should I have done this? Should I not?* Beating herself up for it all.

Which is why a crush feels like a holiday. It's bliss, to be swept up in pure . . . what? Feeling? Chemicals?

Connor has noticed there's something different about her. Every day he's asked if she's all right. If work is okay. Every day she has brushed him off.

Now she turns to face him at last, and he's standing in front of her, home from work mid-afternoon – not unusual, since he starts so early – looking at her like he doesn't know who she is.

His hair is messy, its waves going in all directions on his head. She used to find that charming and now she just thinks he looks like he doesn't care, even though she knows he's been crawling through holes and whatever else plumbers do. There's a streak of dirt on his forehead and one of his eyebrows is going in five directions at once. Again, that sort of thing was endearing once upon a time.

How would she look to him? Tired, most likely. Shoulders slumped. She straightens them. No make-up apart from some mascara she put on before she went to the shops. There was lipstick then too but it's gone now. She ate it off with her lunch.

The kids are making noise somewhere in the house and her tea is getting cold in its cup.

Domestic life. Nowhere near as exciting as Duchess Hotel life.

'What's up?' he says, putting his hands on his hips.

She frowns like she doesn't know what he means. 'Huh?'

'Something's up.' He tilts his head to one side, and she shakes hers.

'Nup.'

'*Kick*.'

His nickname for her.

Standing up, she angles a shoulder towards him. 'You're imagining things,' she says but she doesn't look at him.

'Just talk to me.'

'No!' she almost hisses then her cheeks burn with shame. What's going on in her head – this crush – is not his fault.

His face tightens then relaxes. Not once has he ever spoken to her the way she has just spoken to him, and she doesn't expect him to start now. But who knows? People change. She has.

'We don't fight,' he says flatly.

'We don't *anything*.' That was mean but she felt like she couldn't help it.

He half-closes his eyes then sighs.

'Something is going on, Kick. Obviously you don't want to say what it is but I'm letting you know that I've noticed.'

The fact that her first thought in response to this is, Good on you – do you want a medal? tells her that she has reached a point of disdain for her husband that he does not deserve. She feels ashamed about it and helpless to change it, and she wishes – oh, how she wishes – that there could be someone to talk to about all of this because she feels so lonely inside her head with her thoughts and her confusion and just generally wondering what is happening to her. It's far too early in her life for a midlife crisis, and she loves her kids so it's not as if she is sick of being their mother. She loves Connor too but somehow she is sick of being a wife. Not his wife. Just a wife. It is entirely bound up with how she's feeling about Derek at the Duchess and nothing to do with the reality of anything. But still, here she is. Wretched and confused and taking it out on a man who has never let her down.

She needs to say something to him, right now, so she can hide what's really going on. So she opts for a version of the truth.

'I'm sorry,' she says. 'It's my hormones. I guess.'

Connor knows all about the troubles she has had with her periods because he's been there when she's felt so desperate she could jump off a bridge, then felt completely fine a day later. He's reassured her when each month, on cue, the world would feel too hard. It's disingenuous of her to play on that now but it's also not entirely an untruth, because she does feel like she's in a chemical washing machine just like she does with her menstrual cycle; it's just that this time there's a different cause.

'Oh, babe,' he says, then he puts his arms around her and kisses the side of her head and she feels even worse.

But she can't cry – she doesn't want to let loose that way – so instead she hugs him back.

'Thanks,' she whispers.

'What for?'

It's a good question. One that she's going to answer again with a version of the truth. 'For being you,' she says.

They stand like that for a minute or so, then their son starts calling for them and Kirrily lets her husband go, her cheeks still aflame, and she doesn't look him in the eye as she leaves the room.

CHAPTER TWENTY-FIVE

There's a tucked-away corner in the gardens of the Duchess Hotel that is known only to those who have explored the premises thoroughly, as Frances has done. Even some of the staff don't know it's there and are surprised when she mentions it. Although she supposes it's not that obvious – there's a tall buxus hedge that has a small gap that could look like it's not meant to be an entrance to anything, except it leads to a spot that contains a seat that looks out to sea, the view fringed but not impeded by pine trees.

Frances has sat in this spot contemplating the past and the future – almost never the present, because it doesn't hold much interest for her. It's preferable to think about what was, to occasionally indulge in revisionist versions of it, and to speculate about what will be. Today, however, she has pressing matters of now on her mind and she feels the need to talk about them with someone who has no stakes in the game.

Alison called her this morning, as she does every morning. Often she'll say she's so busy, getting the kids off to school, going to the office, doesn't have time to scratch herself and so on. She did it again today.

This morning Frances had said, 'If you're that busy you don't have to call me, you know.'

As she said it Colin was snuffling around her feet, so she was half-wondering what he was doing and it was only once she'd finished speaking that she realised how harsh she'd sounded.

'Right,' Alison said tersely. 'Right. Fine. You know, I only do it because I *care*, Mum.'

'I do know that, Alison,' Frances said in a tone that did not help matters.

'I know it's not as good as *Keith caring*.' Alison's tone rose on the last two words.

'Alison, don't be ridiculous.' Again, Frances's tone was not good but sometimes when talking to an irrational daughter it's hard not to snap back into the mode you had when she was a teenager.

'Oh, so now I'm ridiculous as well as busy, am I? Right. Fine.'

By now Frances had recognised that 'right' and 'fine' were code for 'not right' and 'not at all fine' but she had no idea how to rescue this situation. She and Alison were both adults but not behaving like it.

'We'll talk another time,' Frances said as meekly as she could.

'When I've calmed down, you mean?'

It was what Frances meant, but she could hardly say it.

The call fizzled out around then with murmured semi-normal goodbyes, the trademark of the stalemate of those bonded for life who are also mad at each other.

Then Colin had regurgitated something on her feet and Frances felt the day was on a trajectory she did not like, so she set off for the Duchess.

She had a feeling that Joan would have found the alcove, as Frances calls it, because she seems to have found so many other good spots around the grounds, and when she wasn't in her room nor in her usual painting positions, Frances went to the alcove.

'Here you are,' she says as she steps through the buxus and sees Joan set up with an easel and paints.

'Here I am.' Joan turns and smiles and seems entirely unsurprised at Frances's presence.

'Were you expecting me?'

Now Joan's smile turns mysterious. 'Perhaps. You tend to find me wherever I am.'

'I'm a homing pigeon,' Frances says lightly.

'Would you like to join me?' Joan gestures to the easel in front of her.

'Oh, I don't know about that.'

Joan looks amused. 'I presume you've done *some* sort of art before?'

'Just drawing at school. That was a long time ago.' Frances remembers the little classroom in the little town that took half an hour on horseback to reach, and the teacher who gave them stubby pencils and told them not to press hard so they didn't wear them out too quickly. In warm weather they'd sit outside and draw leaves and sticks. In winter they'd freeze inside and trace the outlines of their hands. Rudimentary stuff. Nothing that would prepare her for Joan's tutelage.

'That's better, actually,' Joan says. 'You have nothing to unlearn.'

Joan hands her some paper and a couple of pencils.

'What do I draw?' Frances asks.

'Whatever you like. That's the beauty of it.'

Frances stares at the paper and unfortunately has not the faintest idea of what to put on it. Instead she decides to say what's on her mind.

'About Shane,' she states.

When Joan looks pained, Frances feels worried about the man she hasn't seen for over a week.

'I spoke to him,' Joan says. 'Briefly.'

Frances waits for her to go on.

'He hung up on me. But he insisted that he's fine. So . . .' Joan shrugs. 'His actions say otherwise. I presume you haven't heard from him?'

'No.'

Frances sighs then eyes the seat on the other side of Joan.

'Sit down,' Joan says. 'Please.' She pats the seat.

As Frances sits, she feels heaviness in her bones, in her flesh. In her heart. She had felt she could rely on Shane for ... what? Steadiness? To be there for her? Yes, she's being selfish but she had come to rely on him and partly she thinks he let her. Hence her disappointment.

'I wouldn't take it personally,' Joan says, sitting back and looking ahead, to the sea being whipped by a wind that has not quite reached them on the cliffside. 'He seems to be angry at the world in general. That's my take on it.'

'He has a lot to be angry about,' Frances murmurs.

'Oh?'

Frances wonders if she should reveal anything, except she and Joan appear to have become what would have been called fast friends when she was a girl. Then again, she thought Shane was her fast friend.

'His war experiences,' she starts, because she wants Joan to know. 'He is tormented. And he and his wife ...'

'He's married?'

'Sort of. They're separated. She couldn't get pregnant. It was ...'

Frances remembers the conversations she and Shane had about it. How she tried to reassure him that children aren't the be-all and end-all and that she sometimes wished hers had never been born. She'd surprised herself, saying that, although it was true. Keith has betrayed her, and Alison seems to be working up to a betrayal, with her constant reminders that Frances shouldn't be living alone.

Which is something else she wanted to talk to Shane about. He knows all about her children so she feels free to chat to him about them. Or she felt free. Now she doesn't know where she stands and she really needs to talk to someone other than Colin, because dogs are not ideally suited to giving advice.

Joan is looking at her expectantly. Probably because she didn't finish her sentence. That happens sometimes. Often. Not because she's losing her marbles but because she has so much on her mind most days that she is trying to fit it all in. Perhaps she's secretly worried she'll die before she gets to say and do everything she wants to. Or maybe she just needs to clear her mind. There was some lass on the television the other day going on about that. *Meditating*, she called it. Clears the mind. Frances might try it.

'Frances?'

'Hm?'

'Are you away with the pixies?' Joan's eyebrows are raised, and she looks more amused than concerned.

'As often as I can be,' Frances replies.

'Oh good. I do endorse that kind of thing.'

Frances peers at her companion. Joan is what some people might call a dark horse and while Frances is curious to find out more about her, today she has other priorities.

'I had a fight with my daughter,' she announces. Only one way to find out if Joan can be the sounding board Shane has been, and that's to launch straight into the matter at hand.

'You too?'

They stare at each other.

'What was yours about?' Frances asks.

'I ran away from home partly because I didn't want to become a nursemaid to my grandchild. Yours?'

'I was a little short with her. It escalated from there but I'm not sure how. You know how these things get out of hand?'

'Oh, yes,' Joan says, smiling sadly. 'I do.'

Frances peers closely again.

'Did you say anything before you ran away?'

Joan makes a face. 'No.'

'Why not?'

'They wouldn't have paid attention.'

She looks stricken but it's only brief. Frances remains intrigued but she won't pry.

'Oh,' is all she says.

'You don't want to know the story?' Joan says in a way that indicates she wouldn't mind telling it.

'It isn't caring to pry,' Frances says. 'That's why I haven't with Shane.'

'It's not prying to ask someone how they are.' Joan's hand comes down and the corners of her mouth droop a little before she sniffs and raises her brush again.

'There have been times when I wished someone would ask me how I am,' Joan goes on.

Frances considers that Joan has run away from home and thinks that, yes, this is a reasonable statement and that this might be one of those times.

'Do you mean now?' she asks and Joan smiles.

'Not right now, no. I'm fine right now. But once . . .'

The brush is down again and her head is half-turned away, her eyes open, like she's staring at something Frances can't see.

'I had a daughter,' she says softly.

Frances is confused: she knows about Corinne but last she heard Corinne did not belong in past tense. Still, she gets the feeling that Joan does not want her pointing that out. Or saying anything at all right now.

'Rachel,' Joan says. Then she leans forward and brushes purple on the board. 'She was four months old when she died.' This is said as she keeps working, dipping her brush onto the palette on her lap and Frances can only watch. This is not a conversation Joan wants to have; it is a testament and Frances is her chosen witness.

'There was no reason, the doctor said. Just . . . death.'

Joan clears her throat and Frances feels hers tighten with sympathy. With tears she wants to cry for this friend she hardly knows.

'It is so odd to miss a baby who never started talking, never developed a personality, never said "Mummy".' Joan smiles sadly. 'But I do.'

'Of course you do,' Frances says, because this is what she can offer her, one mother to another. 'And of course she had a personality – we know it as soon as we see them, don't we? And didn't we keep them tucked up inside all those months, getting to know them?'

Joan's eyes meet hers, so brilliantly blue, more blue than Frances has seen them.

'Yes,' Joan says. 'But maybe that's worse. Maybe I'd have been better off if she had never existed at all.'

'You don't get that choice,' Frances says. 'Because it's done. It's happened. Like my Albert.' She stops. This is not her time to tell that story.

'Your . . .' Joan looks upset.

'Not my child,' Frances says, because she has to say something to clear this up. 'One day I'll tell you about him.' Frances points to the easel. 'Do you ever paint her?'

Joan sits back. 'No. And yes. I feel like I'm always painting her, like every painting is for her. Does that make me a ghoul?'

'No.' Frances shakes her head. 'It makes you her mother.'

She hears the breath catch in Joan's chest. 'I suppose. Anyway, I stopped painting when she died. I've only started again now. That's why I think she's in all of it. I never let myself . . . *feel* all of this before. You know? There was too much else to do.'

Frances does know. By the time she found out about Albert she had Keith to look after and he was a good excuse for her not to dwell on what she'd lost. It's only now that she has time and fewer distractions in her life that the loss feels stronger and she considers, as she sometimes does, that grief is so cruel in this way, lurking for decades, waiting for its opportunity to swim up from the depths and break the surface.

They sit in silence for a while, Frances still trying to make something of the blank space in front of her and wondering if she might draw Albert – if she has the skill. Something to work towards, at least, although she obviously has to draw him from memory and time has blurred the lines.

'Is that why you left Sydney?' Frances says as the thought pops into her head, although it sounds odd now it's out of her mouth.

'Hm?'

'Because no one asked you how you were after Rachel died?'

More silence and Joan's face shows no expression.

'Yes, I suppose it is,' she says after a minute or two. 'Because they didn't. She was just gone and that was that and people started asking me when I'd try again. Like she was replaceable. And my husband never asked. Not once. Not that I asked him but . . .' She waves her brush in the air – for emphasis or surrender, Frances can't tell.

'It's different,' Frances says. 'The babies come from our bodies. It's different.'

Joan nods and as she smiles in Frances's direction there are tears in the corners of her eyes.

'I just got sick of it,' she says simply. 'The not-asking.'

'His loss is our gain,' Frances says cheerily, although she didn't really mean it to come out like that. Joan laughs, though, so it can't have sounded too bad.

'Quite,' Joan says.

They keep going for a while, in silence apart from Frances's occasional art questions, until the light drops and suddenly it seems like night. That means it's past time for Frances to find her way home.

CHAPTER TWENTY-SIX

'Oh, you're here,' Joan says. She is carrying two easels and a large bag and looking confused.

'Yes. Friday at four?' Kirrily rushes to help her but Joan swats her away and puts everything down on the garden bench next to their allocated meeting place. Or perhaps Joan forgot that she told Kirrily to meet her here, but Kirrily didn't forget – from Sunday till now she has been looking forward to it, and triple checking that her in-laws can pick up the kids from school. In fact, they even said they'd take them for the night and that if Kirrily wanted to do this 'art thing' every Friday, they'd happily take them every Friday night. Connor hadn't liked that idea, though, because he said he'd have no one at home. Kirrily told him he could use it as a chance to see his friends and he looked uncertain about that.

'Are you trying to get rid of me?' he said.

'How am I getting rid of you? I'll be at work all night. You'll be home before I will!'

He'd relaxed then and agreed that he'd make plans to see his friends, and it might even work out better because he wouldn't be trying to cram them into the weekend, which would mean he'd have more time for her. For them. Kirrily hadn't been sure about that part because ever since she met Derek, she hasn't wanted Connor to touch her, but she guesses she should appreciate the fact he's trying. A couple of the women at work talk about how their husbands are more interested in beer than them and they're so sad about it. Kirrily doesn't want to tell them that she might actually prefer that.

'It's three-thirty,' Joan says, somewhat crossly.

'You said you might be early. Besides . . .' She squints up into the afternoon sun. 'It's such a nice day. I wanted to make the most of it.'

Joan looks at her askance. 'If you're going to *paint*, darling, you'll need to come up with better words than "nice".'

For all of Kirrily's existence 'nice' has been a perfectly good word so she's not sure where she's gone wrong, and frowns accordingly.

'What colour is the light?' Joan says as she unpacks her bag, withdrawing paints and brushes and arranging them on the bench.

'Um . . .'

'Not good enough. *What colour is it?*'

Kirrily was a little bit afraid of Joan after their last conversation and now she's even more so.

Kirrily looks up again. 'Yellow,' she says confidently.

'What kind?'

'Hm?'

'What kind? Lemon yellow, banana yellow, mustard, canary?' Joan presses.

Kirrily's mouth hangs open and she lets it, because her brain is fizzing and she can't concentrate on anything else. *Mustard? Canary?* Why is she being quizzed like this?

Joan's face softens. 'There are shades of colours,' she explains. 'It's not enough to say "yellow" – you must be able to define it more narrowly. If you look at this palette –' she gestures to the bench '– you'll see that there are several shades of green. It wouldn't be enough to say those leaves are green.' She gestures to the nearby pine. 'You need to form an opinion as to *which* green.'

'An opinion?'

'None of us sees the same colour for the same thing. I may see that green as a shade darker than you do, or two shades lighter. The difference may not be that noticeable to others but those of us who work in colour – who see the world in shapes and colours – have to be attuned to those differences. They are our language.'

Kirrily can truthfully say that even when she was a child, painting and drawing, she never looked at the world as being made up of shapes and colours. Which suggests she's not cut out for this painting thing.

'I don't expect you to be at that stage yet,' Joan says, as if reading her thoughts. 'But you need to be aware that if you are to paint – or draw, although that is a different way of seeing again – you have to start looking at the world differently. That tree is not just a tree, you see? It is composed of shapes and colours. If you wish to put it on paper or canvas, you can't just decide you're painting a tree. You have to decide *what the tree is made of.* That is what I mean about forming an opinion about colours. We cannot state as an absolute that the sunlight is a certain yellow because it is not one yellow. It is many yellows as seen by many different people.'

She smiles and for the first time Kirrily relaxes.

'So I'll ask you again,' Joan goes on. 'In your opinion, what yellow is the light?'

Kirrily looks up once more and instead of squinting she tries to open her eyes as much as possible. The fizzing in her brain dies down and her face relaxes. She says the first word that pops into her head.

'Lemon.'

'Good. Now, what colour is the sky?'

She laughs in surprise. Another test, so soon?

'I'll give you some options,' Joan offers. 'Azure, cerulean, sky blue, of course.' Another smile. 'Cornflower, baby blue . . .'

'Isn't "azure" the same thing as sky blue?'

'It depends on which sky you're looking at.'

'They're not the same everywhere?'

'They're not the same depending on the season.' Joan glances around. 'Have you noticed that the sky in winter looks different to the sky in summer?'

'No.'

'You will.'

Kirrily pauses to consider this. 'How?'

'By observation. And observing is what you're going to do today.'

This is not what Kirrily left her children with her in-laws for, so she is taken aback. She wanted to *do something*. It feels almost like a primal need, to use her hands to make something, move something. She can't explain it to herself, or anyone else, although she imagines Joan may understand it. If only she knew her well enough to mention it.

'But . . .' She stops when she sees Joan's frown.

'I could give you a paintbrush, obviously,' Joan says. 'But it wouldn't mean anything. It wouldn't do anything for you. I sense, Kirrily, that you want to paint not just to *paint*, if you see what I mean.'

She stares at her and Kirrily feels her cheeks go warm.

'And neither do I,' Joan continues. 'You want to make something beautiful, I imagine. Even if it's just beautiful to you. Or maybe you just need some time to yourself.' She waves a hand. 'Who doesn't.'

Joan tilts her head to one side as if she's assessing Kirrily like a car on a lot. 'I'll make you a deal: spend twenty minutes observing then I'll let you paint what you see.'

Kirrily works out that she'd still have at least half an hour of painting time.

'Sounds good,' she says.

'On one condition.'

'Mm?'

'No smoking.'

Kirrily actually hasn't even thought about it but now that Joan's said it her fingers start dancing like they're on their way to her pocket, where her cigarettes are.

'Why not?'

Joan glances down. 'Your hands need to be put to other uses.'

Feeling like a child caught with stolen lollies, Kirrily makes a fist and puts her dancing fingers behind her back.

'You can last for an hour, surely?' Joan asks.

'Yes,' Kirrily says quickly. She lasts longer than that when she's working.

'Wonderful. All right. Why don't you go over there –' Joan points to a rocky spot '– and look at what's in front of you. Just look. Don't start planning anything. Observe what appears in front of your gaze. And think about the colours you're seeing. I'll let you know when your twenty minutes are up.'

Kirrily nods then makes her way to the rock, pulling her cardigan around her because the breeze is stronger even than it was in Joan's spot by the pine.

The rock is cold underneath her bottom but she'll just have to get used to it. The surface is flat enough for her to sit in relative comfort, her feet on the ground, her hands in her cardigan pockets.

First she closes her eyes and feels the breeze and the late-afternoon warmth on her skin. Then she opens them and strangely it feels like she's seeing this scene for the first time. She fixes her gaze straight ahead of her, at the tip of the promontory, with waves breaking on it, seagulls flying around it. After a while she notices that she isn't blinking that much and she isn't noticing many noises either – it's as if the waves are crashing silently and there is no rustling of breeze in the trees or birds anywhere.

She feels peaceful here, for the first time in a very long while. She can't remember the last time she sat like this, with nothing else to do but be here.

'Twenty minutes!' comes the call from behind her and she blinks at last, then wishes – for all her initial dismay – that Joan had made her sit for longer after all.

'Okay,' Kirrily calls back, but she takes a few more seconds and decides that the sky is azure and the sand is beige and also knows she'll need to study the names of colours before she attempts to label anything else.

CHAPTER TWENTY-SEVEN

Alison knew that her last conversation with Frances shouldn't have gone so badly wrong. She shouldn't have become so worked up. No, that's wrong – she was already worked up when she rang, and that wasn't a good idea. Frances wasn't to know that Sean had stormed out of dinner the night before because he didn't want to eat with Erik, and that Tad hadn't done anything about it because they're all trying their best to integrate Erik into the family. That was Alison's idea – given his behaviour and some of the things he's said to Tad, he clearly resents not having been part of their family life, so Alison asked the children to try a little harder.

'He doesn't like me,' Rosie said.

'He doesn't like anyone,' Alison said, which probably didn't help Rosie even if it was the truth.

It's also no help in the times when Erik loses his temper, which is often, and it's unsettling for them all because no one in this house has been prone to tempers. It's hard for her to reconcile her mild husband with his panther of an eldest son, always prowling around ready to strike.

Looking for prey. That's what she thought the other day as she watched him pacing the back garden. It was so odd – who paces a garden like that? Yet she is trying to think the best of him, which is why she insisted that they all have dinner together. And all it took was one remark from Erik about how Sean was a runt and that was the end of it.

Sean is on the small side for his age, yet Tad himself was too. So was Erik, according to Tad, and they both ended up tall and broad, although Tad is taller. Again, Alison tried to interpret Erik's behaviour through his own lens: a boy teased for being small who in turn teases another boy. It's not acceptable but it's explicable. She just has to persevere with him, that's all, which means persevering with the children so they give him a chance. He's their brother. Or, as Rosie likes to remind her, 'half a brother'. That girl can be too smart for her own good sometimes.

Alison has not told Frances the latest of what's going on in her home not because she thinks it will worry her but because Frances will give her advice unbidden and Alison doesn't want it, as it will just remind her that she needs it, which means she's a failure.

Today, however, she needs to apologise to her mother – to whom she hasn't spoken since their spat – and that may involve a confession about what's been happening.

As it's Saturday morning the kids are out doing activities and Tad has gone to St Kilda to see a friend. Erik is who-knows-where – not in Alison's or Tad's car, at least, so Alison was able to drive to the green grocer and pick up a bunch of flowers. Frances never buys herself flowers but Alison's father used to buy them for her from time to time, and Alison remembers how much her mother appreciated that.

Alison can hear Colin barking as she approaches Frances's front door.

'Oh,' her mother says when she opens it and her eyes drop to the flowers.

'I thought you may like them,' Alison says. 'And, um, hi. Hi, Mum.' She smiles awkwardly and steps a foot inside, trying to kiss Frances on the cheek and getting her ear instead.

'Hello, love.' Frances slowly steps aside as Alison relaxes. Being called *love* is a good sign.

Colin gets in between them, looking from one to the other, tongue out, tail wagging.

'Hi, Colin,' Alison says. Frances told her once that Colin likes it when people say hello to him.

'Out of the way, Col,' Frances says with a hint of irritation as they try to move down the hallway. 'I don't want to trip over you.'

She shuffles ahead of Alison.

'He won't leave me alone,' she says over her shoulder. 'Like he thinks I'm about to get into strife or something.'

Alison watches Frances move carefully. Is she imagining it or is her mother walking more slowly? More stiffly?

As her mother eases herself into her favourite chair Alison locates a vase, fills it with water and arranges the flowers before placing them on the kitchen table.

When she re-enters the sitting room, Frances is looking at her expectantly.

'So – what's going on?' Frances says.

'Um – nothing much.'

Raised eyebrows tell Alison that this response is not believable.

'You know – work,' she goes on. 'Kids.'

'Mm.' The eyebrows are still up.

Is it that obvious that she's worried about something? Or, rather, someone? While she wouldn't say she has a close relationship with her mother, it's probably true to say that Frances knows her better than anyone. Even Tad. Frances knows the full catalogue of her expressions and gestures – and moods – the way only a mother can. The way Alison knows Sean's and Rosie's. The way she doesn't know Erik's, which is why she can't read him the way she can her own children. Sean and Rosie need never say a word and she knows exactly what is going on: if they're unwell, or upset, or happy or worried or nervous. She knows what each arrangement of their facial expressions means. That's what happens when you love someone so much you spend hours observing them, taking in all the details, wanting to know everything. Even once she became a mother, though, Alison never believed that Frances had done that for her. Yet here is evidence of it: Frances is clearly reading her better than she is reading herself.

'Erik's not fitting in that well,' Alison confesses.

'Well, blow me down with a feather,' Frances says.

'What?'

'That delinquent isn't fitting in yet? Why am I not surprised?'

'But I thought . . .' Alison blushes, realising that Frances probably thinks her naïve.

'You thought that if you gave him a home and cooked him dinner and were nice to him that he'd be nice back.'

It's said so matter-of-factly, as if Frances has heard this story a thousand times and knows how it ends. And maybe she does.

'I guess.'

'No guess.' Frances nods once, decisively. 'You're so kind-hearted, Alison, that you can't imagine other people not being the same. I hate to be the bearer of bad news, love, but they're not.'

In her entire life Alison has never heard her mother call her kind-hearted. So it almost registers as a criticism, but she can't treat it that way because if she does, and she's wrong, that could go badly.

'I guess I want to give him the benefit of the doubt,' she says instead.

'Why?'

The question takes her aback because she doesn't know the answer. Or she does – because she's always thought you're meant to give people that benefit – but doesn't want to say it.

'Because he's Tad's son.' That's also a valid answer.

'Not one you raised.' Frances sniffs. 'So no guarantees.'

That sounded like another compliment but Alison still isn't sure if she should take it as such, so she decides to change the subject.

'What's new at the Duchess?' she asks.

'Art class.' Frances smiles quickly.

'Art class? For you?'

Searching her memory, Alison cannot locate a single instance of Frances being interested in art.

'Yep. Me and a lass who works there. Kirrily.'

'So she's teaching you?'

'No, Joan's teaching us.'

Ah, Joan. Alison has heard this name so often that she's starting to think her mother and Joan are joined at the hip. Now Joan's getting even more of her time. And, yes, that's jealousy she feels because if she'd suggested an art class, there's no way Frances would have agreed to it, but here's this Joan – on the peninsula for all of a couple of weeks or whatever – already signing her on.

Alison tries to swallow her irritation but it gets stuck in her throat and she coughs. 'Is she an artist?'

'Yes. A good one. Or she used to be – won prizes and whatnot. Then she stopped for a while.'

'Why?'

Frances's face clouds momentarily.

'Oh, you know – husband, children.'

Their eyes meet and Alison knows what's in that gaze: the mutual understanding of what both women have missed out on due to their family circumstances, and the knowledge that only one of them has caused it for the other.

Frances half-smiles and to Alison it feels like forgiveness.

'You get busy,' Frances goes on. 'No time. Now she has time. And I was hanging around like a bad smell anyway, so she started showing me how to do it. And Kirrily wanted to join in.'

'How often?'

'Once a week. Friday afternoons.' Frances shrugs. 'I'm there anyway.'

'That you are,' Alison murmurs and it earns her a narrowing of Frances's eyes.

Colin, who has been lolling by the coffee table, gets to his feet.

'Need a walkie, Col?' Frances croons. A walkie means a trip to the garden for Colin to do a wee.

'I'll take him,' Alison says.

'Thanks, love.' Frances sighs and sits back against a cushion. 'I'll wait here for you.'

'That's good, because I'd be worried if you ran off.' Alison smiles.

'Would you?'

Alison can't tell if she means it sincerely.

'Of course,' she says. 'I'd miss you.'

'I'd miss you too,' Frances says quietly, and that's enough to make Alison smile as she nudges Colin towards the back door.

CHAPTER TWENTY-EIGHT

'I heard a rumour I'd find you in this place.'

Joan recognises the voice – it's Shane's. She doesn't know if she feels happy about that or not. Given his rudeness the other day, she's inclined to not give him any quarter.

'Some rumours are true, I suppose,' she says, not looking up from her sketchpad. There's a statue in front of her that she's determined to capture – someone told her it was a Norman Lindsay but she's not sure about that, especially since it's tucked away in a part of the garden hardly anyone visits – and she isn't interested in having her concentration ruined.

Not that this means it won't be ruined, because now he's standing next to her and she can hardly ignore him.

'That's good,' he says, pointing to her sketchpad.

It would be reasonable to point out that she didn't ask for his opinion but that would be churlish. And obvious. No doubt he knows it anyway and he's trying to make small talk regardless.

So she looks up at him and sees the uncertainty on his face.

Oh, he's *nervous*. About talking to her. So he should be.

'How are you, Shane?' she says and she hears the tone in her voice typically used for managing social engagements and batting away personal enquiries. It's her rounded-vowel authoritative tone. Her 'phone voice', as her daughter once called it, and Joan supposes everyone has one, it's just that hers is also used off-phone.

'I'm, uh . . .' His face goes through a range of expressions and doesn't really arrive at one. Then he sighs.

'I'm better,' he says. 'Although not great.'

It's an honest answer, clearly, and Joan feels like being honest with him in return. A sort of exchange, she supposes.

'When a person calls to check whether or not you are great,' she says, 'it's not customary to be rude to them.'

'I'm really sorry,' he says, sounding almost relieved. 'I shouldn't have spoken to you like that.'

'No, you shouldn't have. Would you care to explain yourself?'

She's not letting him off the hook so easily but she also wants to give him the opportunity to talk about whatever is bothering him. After all, he's listened to her while she's sat at his bar and blathered on about who-knows-what.

Another sigh, and he shoves his hands into his pockets. 'I have these . . . spells,' he says. 'I can't . . .' He extracts a hand and rubs it over his head. 'I can't really explain them. But it's dark. You know?' His eyes hold hers and she can see the pain in them.

'No,' Joan says, 'I don't know because this darkness comes from your experiences. And I don't know what they are. Were.'

He stares at her but it's the stare of a man trying to connect with another person. It makes Joan feel momentarily uncomfortable because she feels as if she wants to be the person he connects with and while she may have left her husband – and she's still not sure if it's permanent – she is not interested in forming any kinds of connections outside of friendship. So she breaks her gaze and clears her throat.

'You and Frances are the only ones who have ever said something like that,' Shane says softly. 'Everyone else . . .' He raises his eyebrows. 'They try to tell me how I'm feeling. What I went through.'

'Maybe that's their way of helping,' says Joan, giving a generous interpretation for once, mainly because she doesn't want to be special. Not to him. Not because she wouldn't enjoy it but because she would.

'Maybe.' He gazes at the trees in front of her then at the statue, then at her sketchbook.

'How long have you been doing . . .' He gestures to her drawing.

'Sketching? As long as I've been able to hold a pencil. Painting is more my thing but sketching is the foundation.'

'I could never do it.' He laughs. 'Not artistic. Not musical. Not anything.'

It is obvious that he wants her to reassure him. A person doesn't tend to make statements like that unless they want another to say no, you're wrong, you're all of those things. Otherwise why say them and not just think them? Yet she's not going to indulge him; that is not her job.

'If you say so,' she retorts.

His eyes widen then he laughs again. 'Gee, why don't you tell me what you really think?'

'Shane, I'll be blunt: you came here to apologise to me for being rude when I was simply trying to be friendly. Now you want me to make you feel better about yourself. Presumably make you feel better about being rude. I'm not going to do it. We are all more in control of our behaviour than we like to tell ourselves. And we all like to make excuses for ourselves.'

She holds up a hand.

'I am not suggesting that you do not have spells of depression, as that's what it sounds like. But the thing to do is apologise for your rudeness then not expect more from me. From anyone.'

He nods slowly. Perhaps he's just been waiting for someone to be frank with him. To not act as if these spells do not exist and carry on as normal.

'If we are to be friends . . .' Here she pauses, because she knows she's making a commitment of sorts. 'I'd rather we speak plainly.'

Shane smiles then, almost like the Cheshire cat. 'You and Frances,' he says. 'You're so alike.'

'Really? I think she's nicer than me.'

He laughs loudly and Joan feels oddly pleased to be the cause of it.

'She may be,' he says. 'I guess I'll find out. But you both don't beat around the bush. I like it.'

'It's my preferred modus operandi.' Joan picks up her pencil. 'Now, I have work to do.'

'Sure.' He half-turns away from her. 'Pop into the bar later?'

'If you're lucky.'

Another laugh.

'Right,' he says, then raises a hand in farewell.

It's only once he's out of sight and Joan is once more sitting in the quiet of this little glade that the fast beat of her heart becomes noticeable. But she chooses not to analyse what that means and goes back to drawing the statue.

CHAPTER TWENTY-NINE

'What's the matter with you?' Connor says under his breath as Kirrily flaps around their kitchen, picking up plates and putting them down, opening cupboards, opening the fridge and closing it without taking anything out.

His parents are coming for lunch and she is in a tizz about it; she isn't the sort of wife who knows how to put on fancy meals for people and even though Connor would say his parents don't expect that, she feels like she should do it. It's what a wife is meant to do, isn't it? Especially a wife who hasn't been paying much attention to her husband for various reasons, one of which is that she's thinking about another man.

She saw Derek again last night. As she was leaving the laundry room carrying towels for room 317, she felt a tap on her shoulder and when she turned around there he was, smiling at her. She thought she stopped breathing for a few seconds. Handsome men don't look at her like that. She's always been realistic about the sorts of men she attracts, and decent looking is the shape of it.

'Hello, Kirrily,' Derek said, leaving his hand on her shoulder, and all she was conscious of was the warmth of that hand and the lack of distance between them. If she hadn't been holding the towels, there would have been even less space and she was glad for those towels because otherwise she might have wanted to press herself against him. That's how strongly she felt the pull towards him. It was weird and unsettling and she loved it and feared it at the same time.

'Hi – hi, Derek.' She smiled and tried to avoid his eyes because they drew her in too and she was sure he could see what she was thinking by looking into them. Yet she wanted to look because his eyes were so blue and held so much warmth and promise.

'How have you been?' His hand dropped slowly but only, she imagined, because there were people milling around and it wouldn't look appropriate for a guest to be so familiar with staff.

'W-well, thank you.' She smiled quickly and glanced to her left and right to see if any of the other staff might notice them.

He shifted a little closer. 'I've been thinking about you,' he said softly. She had a friend who talked about how a man made her 'melt' and Kirrily thought it was a stupid thing to say, except now she understood it because her whole body felt hot and unstable.

'Oh?' She swallowed.

'Hoping I'd see you again.' He was even closer now; his nose was near her ear and she kept looking around. This time she saw William emerge from the dining room and while he wasn't heading in her direction, he was close enough to turn his head and see her. So she stepped away from Derek but still kept her body angled towards him.

'That's nice of you,' she said. 'But I, ah . . .'

He looked in the direction of the dining room. 'I understand,' he said. 'You're working.'

They stared at each other, and she felt like she was on the edge of something terrifying and exhilarating, something she should never attempt to jump into but also something she wanted to experience because she never had and may never again.

'I'm in room 451,' he said, so quietly she almost didn't catch it. 'In case you happen to be free later.'

He didn't wait for an answer, which was good because she didn't want to give one.

She did not visit his room, although she thought about it. And tried not to think about it. And thought about telling Shane about it when she saw him outside during her break. He knew something was off because he said so but she just couldn't tell him. Saying it aloud would have made it more real and she's not yet at the point where she can admit to herself that a man other than her husband has propositioned her.

As she drove home, she told herself to forget about Derek but of course that was impossible, and when she slid into bed next to Connor she tried to be happy it was him lying there: familiar, solid, caring. All the qualities she has loved.

After a fitful night's sleep, she awoke and Derek's face was the first image in her mind, his voice the first sound, and as Connor rolled over and kissed her cheek she pulled away and he noticed.

Now she's checking the roast leg of lamb and the vegetables, wishing she could never cook again because it would make her life so much easier, and he's standing there looking forlorn and she wishes she could be at the Duchess Hotel, for work if not to see Derek. She will be there in a few hours' time, but first she has to put on a good show in front of her parents-in-law.

Roy and Julie arrive with smiles and hugs and gifts for the children, a peck on the cheek for her and a hug for Connor.

It takes Julie all of five seconds to work out that Connor is unhappy, which Kirrily knows because Julie is looking her way then back to Connor and what Kirrily really wants to ask is why Julie would presume that Connor's mood is *her* fault. Of course, it is. But Julie doesn't know that.

'Everything all right?' Julie says with a tight smile.

'Fine!' Kirrily squeaks and turns back to the stove, inspecting the roast unnecessarily.

'I've been making a bench, Dad,' Connor says, then gestures for his father to go out the back door, in the direction of his shed, leaving Julie standing too close to Kirrily and Kirrily's antennae up.

'How's work?' Julie asks as she folds and refolds a cloth serviette that Kirrily put on the countertop because she was one short at the table.

'Good. Busy.' She looks around for something else to occupy her.

'You've been going earlier on Fridays?'

'Yes. For the art class. I really appreciate you taking the kids.'

Julie beams. 'We love having them. Honestly, if you and Connor need more time . . .'

Their eyes meet then Kirrily looks away.

'Connor says you've been more stressed than usual.'

'I have a lot on!' She tries to make it sound like a good thing.

'I know. That's why I think it might be good for the two of you to spend some more time alone together. We can take the children for weekends for a while. Give you a chance to . . .' She shrugs.

'Do you think they're better off without me?' Kirrily snaps, and she knows it's an illogical question but she's heard that attack is often the best form of defence and maybe it will help her hide what's really going on.

'Never,' Julie says more calmly than Kirrily would have said it. She steps closer.

'Kirrily, you and I have always got along. We love the same people.' She smiles in a reassuring way. 'So I think we understand each other. Please keep that in mind when I say that you are really not yourself. I've noticed it lately. Connor's certainly noticed it. Even my darling husband – who can be a little dense about such things – has noticed it.'

'Maybe this is just who I really am,' Kirrily retorts. 'Maybe the person you thought you knew wasn't real.'

Julie shakes her head slowly. 'I don't think so.'

They stare at each other, Kirrily feeling her heart beat faster, the blood pumping through her. She's angry, she knows, but not at Julie. At herself. Except she doesn't want to tell Julie that.

'Whatever's going on,' Julie says, 'we're going to be here. We are your family. So . . .' She tilts her head to one side. 'If you need me, for anything, tell me. I don't judge. You know that.'

But you would judge this, Kirrily thinks.

'Sure,' she says, because she has to say something.

A loud thud from the sitting room makes both their heads turn.

'I'll go,' Julie says, and it isn't until she's out of the room that Kirrily puts her head in her hands and wonders how she'll get through the next few hours.

CHAPTER THIRTY

It takes Joan a few seconds to work out that it's the phone in her room that's making the ringing sound. It hasn't rung once since she arrived here. There's been no need: she calls down if she wants something, but no one wants anything from her so they don't call up.

No one wants anything from her. Oh, the bliss of that phrase. That idea. That way of life. Someone has always wanted something from her: to be a good daughter, to be a pretty teenager, to be a comely young woman, to be a doting and dutiful wife, to be a devoted and adoring mother.

None of these are ever roles she has designed for herself. Prettiness – well, that was out of her hands. Comeliness was more within her control but still relied on the preceding prettiness. It was a lottery win that she could satisfy both requirements yet instead of feeling lucky she felt cursed.

If she hadn't been attractive – she is hardly going to practise false modesty in her own head, so she may as well say it – her life would have turned out differently. She knows this because she also knows that she has not developed supplementary skill sets that have well served the girls she knew at school who could never rely on their looks. They had interests and hobbies. Talents. Accomplishments. Joan never needed them.

If she is continuing to be honest – and why not, since she's on a roll? – this is probably a factor in how easily she gave up art after she married. She didn't need it. She was married. She 'won'. Or something. The fact that it never felt like a victory was beside the point. There was nothing to be gained by developing another talent, so she let it go.

It is not the case that she's only finding it again now because her looks are fading, because they aren't. If anything, age could be said to have improved them.

The phone has stopped ringing. Good. The call was probably not meant for her anyway.

Now it's started again. Right. Must be for her.

She heaves herself off the chair and ambles over to the handset next to the bed.

'Yes?'

'Joan, it's William.'

She had long ago asked him to use her first name, since he'd only offered his.

'Hello, William.' This is unusual: surely the hotel's manager doesn't call guests?

'I'm, ah . . .'

Joan can hear someone talking in the background.

'A moment, please, sir,' William says faintly.

'Joan,' he says into the phone. 'Your husband is here.'

For a second – rather, a millisecond – Joan doesn't understand what he's said. William knows enough of her story to know that her husband is the last person she wants to see.

'I . . .' she starts.

'*I tried,*' he whispers.

She can guess at what he means: that he tried to pretend she wasn't here, or that she was uncontactable. It doesn't matter now because the life she left and the life she has are about to meet each other and in all the time she has been in this place she has not planned for what was, she sees now, always an eventuality. Isaac is resourceful; he would have deduced how to find her.

'Thank you,' she says. 'I'll be down.'

Hanging up, she panics a little. What to say to him? How to explain herself? This is a reckoning of some sort and she's just not ready for it.

It is odd that in this moment the person she wants to talk to is Frances, probably because she imagines Frances will have something wise to say.

So she puts her shoulders back and checks her reflection in the mirror. The ends of her hair are in need of a trim, and she isn't wearing the amount of make-up Isaac is used to seeing. But so what? She's not the version of Joan he knows any more.

With a steep inhalation, she picks up her room key and tucks it into the pocket of her sensible slacks. These are the ones she wears for painting because they're comfortable for sitting and she doesn't care that there's paint on them. Except now she does, because he'll ask about it. He's not used to seeing her look anything but perfectly groomed.

And here she is, spiralling into patterns of frivolous worry that used to mark her days and nights and which disappeared after she arrived here.

Nothing to be done about them right now, however.

As she descends the central staircase, she takes a few seconds to appreciate the sweep of the grand foyer in front of her. It's almost like she's walking to the gallows, and this is the last thing she'll ever see.

Oh God. *Oh God*. When did she become so apprehensive about her husband? Or is it that she feels like she's about to be scolded and she wants to avoid the punishment? This is not a matter she can sort out, not now Isaac has moved to the bottom of the staircase. The first thing she notices is that his hair is still neatly cut; his nose, with its rugby-caused dent, is the same; his grey eyes still intense as his face shifts through happiness to dismay to concern back to happiness, then to an arrangement he probably thinks is impassive. He likes to control his emotions in front of other people; he once told her that a man could never succeed in the world if he did not. She had wanted to reply that a woman couldn't either because the judgements for showing emotion were harsher, but she knew he wouldn't understand. Moreover, she thought it was sad for both of them that the charade extended to their marriage, as it did for their friends. Everyone pretending that they had no emotions about anything but their children's achievements, federal elections and sport. No wonder she left.

'Darling,' Isaac says but there's an edge to it. 'There you are.'

Joan pauses on the second-bottom step and folds her hands in front of her.

'Here I am,' she says. 'How did you find me?'

'Genevieve.'

Joan's heart lurches as she registers the betrayal; she didn't tell Genevieve the name of the hotel but either she worked it out from the details Joan supplied or Isaac did. Obviously she knew Isaac would go to her friend for information and Genevieve might feel compromised. He is, after all, Genevieve's husband's best friend. Still, she thought that Genevieve's loyalty would be to her over Isaac. How sad she is to realise she was wrong.

'Don't blame her,' he adds. 'I wore her down.'

'With what?' Joan snaps.

Isaac's grey eyes go flinty. It's an expression she knows – he has it when negotiating. With her, with the children, with the council over a footpath that needs tidying, with a tradesman over a bill he thinks is too high.

'She felt it best that I know,' he says calmly, and Joan is sure he's lying. It's not something she'll take up with Genevieve, however; their friendship, if it still exists, will be forever altered by this.

People want to get up the stairs so Joan moves to one side and catches the eye of René behind the concierge desk. He frowns and makes a hand gesture which suggests he'll remove

Isaac if Joan wants him to. She smiles slightly and shakes her head and finds it odd that the staff here seem to be more solicitous of her welfare than her own husband.

Isaac turns to look at René then back at Joan.

'What are you doing?' he demands.

'René was about to eject you,' Joan replies, just as strongly. 'Me shaking my head was me saying he doesn't have to.'

'Eject me!'

'They don't know you, Isaac. They know *me*. They care about *me*. Not you.'

He looks exasperated.

'They only care because you're paying them,' he says.

That's possibly true, but Joan knows that the hotel never wants for guests. They don't have to be friendly to her. She'll be gone eventually and there will be other guests. Besides, they are extremely friendly to Frances and she doesn't seem to spend any money here.

'I'm sure that's right,' she says to Isaac, because what he wants to hear is that he's right.

'Joan, this has to end.' He steps up and so does she.

'What are you doing?' he says.

'Keeping my distance.'

'Why?' He looks a little pathetic as he says it.

'If I wanted you to know, Isaac, I would have told you when I left. I just . . .' She sighs heavily and folds her arms across her chest. 'I need *time*. Here. By myself.'

'You've had time!'

'Not enough.'

'How much is enough?'

'I don't know. And you're hardly making the case for me to come back.'

He's making no case at all, in fact, making only demands.

Now it's his turn to sigh.

'I don't want to keep having this conversation here.' He gestures to the staircase. 'I'm going to get a room and we can have some more time that way.'

She doesn't want him staying here. The Duchess is her sanctuary. But she can't stop him. Just like he can't stop her.

'Fine,' she says, half turning away from him. 'I'll leave you to it.'

'Joan –'

'I'll see you tomorrow, Isaac.'

She walks away before he starts to negotiate with her about dinner tonight or something like that. The staff won't give him her room number – she knows they enforce their guests' privacy, so they wouldn't give her his either, if she asked. Which she won't. Not because she's upset about him being here but because she feels . . . not much at all. Irritation. A tinge of despair. A sense of resignation. These are emotions she can manage. On her own.

This is her intention as she mounts the stairs and leaves him behind.

When she returns to her room, she pulls out her sketchpad almost without being conscious of it, picks up a pencil and, rather than attacking the page, finds her hand moving in strokes and swirls. Almost as if she's trying to soothe herself.

A knock on the door comes half an hour, an hour – who knows? – later. She looks at what she's been doing and sees a bird; perhaps it's an emblem of her wanting to fly free yet feeling, once again, caged.

She knows who is on the other side before she opens it, not because she has a sixth sense but because it's so predictable. Of course he found a way to work out which room she's in.

'I'm not waiting until tomorrow,' Isaac says without preamble. 'You're my wife. I want to talk to you now.'

There's no point resisting him, so she stands back to let him inside.

'What do you think you're doing?' he says as he walks past her, although he doesn't sound angry, just dismayed.

'You've already asked me that. I'm not a witness in a trial, Isaac – you can't badger me until you get an answer you like.'

'Why would you ever . . .?' He shakes his head. 'Did I do something?'

Not something, she wants to reply. *Somethings. And nothings. For years.*

'I'm tired,' she says instead. 'Tired of being at your beck and call. Tired of not being myself.'

'Not being yourself?' He sounds incredulous. 'Who else have you *been*?'

'Whoever you've wanted me to be.' She offers him a smile, to show that she knows she's been complicit in this. 'And it worked beautifully, didn't it?'

'I don't understand,' he says, and she laughs.

'I'm not sure I do either – but I got lost somehow. I'm trying to find out who I am. Again.'

'Again?'

'I was someone before. Not just your wife. Not just a mother.' She presses her eyes closed as she remembers what that was like.

'It isn't enough, being my wife?' Now he really looks confused. Poor man – why wouldn't he be? She has played the part so well for so long and it benefited him so much – he has absolutely nothing to gain by a change in circumstance, whereas she has everything to gain by trying to change a situation that they'd both created. She ran the home and their life and their children; he worked and paid for everything. That was the deal, and for a while Joan had thought it was a good one, then once the children were past the baby years it became clear that Isaac's work stopped once he was home from the office and hers never ended, and then the deal seemed like it should be voided. Although she never said it then; nor did she say it when she left him. She just left. So he has no idea of the history behind her decision and thus she can't blame him for being confused. Yet just as she wished he could guess what she wants she wished he would just know why she was unhappy enough to walk away.

'Would you describe yourself as just my husband? When someone asks you what you do, what do you say?'

His mouth opens but he says nothing.

'You say "lawyer". Or a variant. You don't say "I'm Joan's husband". But I've been your wife, Corinne's mum, Nathan's mum. That's all. Now I just want to be *me*.'

'You can be you at home. I promise,' he pleads, moving towards her.

'Really? What's going to change? Are you going to stop asking me to cook for ten at short notice? No more running out to get a birthday present for your secretary or your friend's wife?' Her nostrils flare. 'These are all jobs that require me to be available at short notice, which means I can't have anything else in my life. Have you ever stopped to think, Isaac, about what that has required of me, to be able to drop everything for you?'

They stare at each other.

'I didn't either, for a long while,' she goes on. 'But I have now. And I don't want it again.'

He takes another step and puts his hand on her elbow.

It is a wonder to her that it took her so long to understand that she had been his factotum rather than his wife for so many years and that this was the reason why she didn't want him touching her: he felt like her employer, not her husband. Certainly not her lover.

For a while – two years, three – he asked her why she kept rejecting him in that way. She didn't have an answer for him then – all she could say was that she didn't feel like it, which was true. It has taken her complete removal from his life – their joint life – to understand that being treated as his dogsbody induced no romantic feelings in her because she didn't enjoy it. Perhaps some women do; perhaps they prefer it because it removes the need to think too much. Take orders, execute the orders, await new orders. It's simple. It requires no extra thought. And it is not for her.

'I'm sorry,' he says softly. 'Please come home.'

He tries to kiss her and her instinct is to put her hands on his chest and push him away, but he puts his hands on her shoulders and holds her still.

'Please, Joan, I've missed you.' His nose touches hers and her body remembers this: they used to like this, noses touching, in the days before they married, in the days when everything seemed like a promise.

'I've missed me too,' she says.

He tries to kiss her again and she moves her head. She is no longer going to give someone what they want just because it suits *them*. This is her era of suiting Joan.

'All right,' he says into her ear. 'All right.'

He lets her go and, without another word, leaves. But he won't be leaving the hotel – she knows him too well for that. While ever he has a chance to prosecute his case again, he will. She needs to be ready for that.

When she picks up her sketchpad again the bird looks different. Less free. One wing looks almost broken.

She rubs it out and starts again.

CHAPTER THIRTY-ONE

Each time Kirrily has walked into the Duchess Hotel lately she has felt nervous. Or excited. Possibly both. Each time there is the prospect of seeing Derek again and she feels exactly the way she did when she had a crush on a boy in high school. There were a few. Which is normal when you're a teenager. It's not normal when you're a married lady. Not that she has a crush on lots of men. Just Derek.

It's irrational that she should even think she'd see him when she arrives at work because she comes in through the staff entrance at the back and while she does seem to bump into him in the back part of the hotel, she is sure it's been a coincidence. Or fate.

No, not fate. She can't think of it like that.

As it turns out, Derek isn't anywhere to be seen near the staff entrance this evening. But Shane's there, smoking.

'Heya,' Kirrily calls as she approaches.

'Kizza.' He grins and takes a last puff before dropping the butt and stubbing it out with the toe of his boot.

'Don't call me that,' she says, but she means it kindly. *Kizza* doesn't sound like her; it's just his way of showing affection.

'What's up?' he says.

Kirrily has no idea how he can detect that other than via some kind of bartender life-experience sixth sense, but she's not giving him the satisfaction of being proved right. So she turns her face away in order to avoid him reading it.

'Hiding won't help,' Shane says. 'I'm always here if you want to chat.'

'Sure.' She smiles at him briefly then bustles into the staff room and puts her bag away.

William has listed her jobs for the night on their blackboard – something he's installed recently in order to improve efficiency, he says, although Kirrily doesn't understand how they're related – and is surprised to see that the bar is on her list. Finish the loads of towels then help out in the bar. *Big function* is written next to *Bar* so presumably that explains it.

Kirrily heads to the laundry room and does not pass a stray Derek, which is both a disappointment and a relief. After she's done there, she goes to the bar, which is fuller than she's ever seen it. There are dirty glasses everywhere and Hopeless Harry – the occasional fill-in – is back, behind the bar with Shane, who makes a face.

'Thank God,' he says as she walks round to see him. 'I haven't been able to get out to pick up the empties.'

'I'm onto it,' she says over the din, then puts on the spare apron that Shane keeps hanging by the less popular liqueurs.

Shane seems to be asking for her to work in the bar regularly these days, which suits her. Being in the bar means she's more likely to see Derek if he comes back to the hotel – he may never, of course. Daydreaming about it won't make it happen, yet she can't help it. If nothing else, it is a distraction – for a few minutes she is carried away with the feeling of what it would be like to be near him again, and that makes her happy.

As she brings glasses back to Shane, she can see that he looks annoyed.

'What's up?' she says.

He frowns and shakes his head, says nothing and keeps mixing the cocktail in his hands.

So she looks around the bar to try to identify a cause for his annoyance and thinks she's found it: Joan sitting with a strange man. Quite a handsome one. Around Joan's age, with thick, wavy grey hair and matching eyebrows. Thin-rimmed glasses and a suit. Sitting forward, looking agitated as Joan sits back, arms folded.

Going about her tasks, she keeps looking at Shane surreptitiously and sees him glancing Joan's way several times. It seems to confirm what she has suspected: Shane is sweet on Joan. Which is not a good idea, because staff and guests are not meant to fraternise. As Kirrily keeps reminding herself whenever her thoughts drift to Derek. Maybe it also means she shouldn't be painting with Joan, but that's not fraternising so much as learning.

Besides which, Joan is married – there are rings on her wedding finger – and the body language going on at her table and Shane's behaviour suggest that the man talking to her is her husband.

She's not going to say anything to Shane because that would be intrusive. His crush isn't her business unless he makes it so.

Instead she watches him work faster than usual and avoid Joan's table. Which means Kirrily's the one who'll have to go and collect the empties from it.

'Hi, Joan,' she says as she puts her hand on a wine glass.

Joan looks relieved. 'Hi, Kirrily. How are you?'

'Fine, thanks. You?'

'Yes, fine.' A tight smile, a glance down.

Is she meant to wait for an introduction to the man? Or pretend she hasn't seen him?

'This is my husband, Isaac,' Joan says after a couple of seconds have passed and Kirrily has picked up his glass.

'Hello,' Kirrily says with a polite smile.

Isaac nods at her and says nothing, which Kirrily reads as a signal for her to get lost. So she does.

'That's her husband,' she tells Shane a few minutes later. 'In case you're wondering.'

'I'm not,' he says, too quickly for it to be true.

'Right.' She smiles.

'What?' He frowns.

'Nothing.'

A few minutes later she watches Joan and Isaac get up from their table and walk towards the foyer, he leaning closer to her, her leaning away from him. At one point he puts his hand on her arm and she does nothing. But she wouldn't react, would she? Kirrily would be the same in front of people if she were Joan.

Turning away from them, she sees Shane staring after the retreating pair.

Their eyes meet then Shane drops his. Kirrily wants to tell him that it's all right – she understands. More than he knows. But he's a private man – she still doesn't know why he was away from work all those days, nor does anyone else seem to – and she needs to respect that, as she'd want someone to respect her privacy.

Which is why she won't ask Joan about Isaac the next time she sees her.

CHAPTER THIRTY-TWO

'We've finally got you off the mountain, Marg,' Frances says as Alison stands back to let her aunt into her mother's house. Alison has the day off work because Glen's away, so when Margie called to see if she'd be available to say hello, she said yes.

It's been months since Alison has seen Margie – she likes to think it's been months, not years, but time passes so swiftly now that perhaps it's been years and she just doesn't want to admit it. She should be better at keeping up family relationships. That's what daughters do: maintain the family fabric. Even if they often wish someone else would do it once in a while.

'You know I don't like the plains, Fran,' Margie says with a wink as she waddles into the sitting room in that stiff-hipped way of longtime horsewomen.

'Rubbish – you love the plains when they involve Toorak boutiques.' Frances says it like she's joking but Alison knows she's not, because the entire family is aware that Margie is partial to a nice leather handbag and pair of finely crafted heels. Where she wears them is anyone's guess because it's not as if she and Cec go many places. Or maybe they do. Alison wouldn't know because she hasn't asked. Another failure.

'True, true.' Margie stops and puts her hands on her hips as she surveys the sitting room.

'Nice,' she says. 'Could use a painting or two.'

'You've had a haircut,' Frances replies.

Margie touches the underneath of her thick, silvery bob. 'Long hair's a pain,' she says.

Alison has the distinct sense that the two of them could go on with this chatter for a while and she need never contribute, but she wants to – she's here because she hasn't seen Margie in ages, and because Frances invited her.

'How's Cec?' she asks, and both Margie and Frances look at her as if they've just remembered she's there.

Margie shrugs. 'Getting along. And getting on.' She chortles. 'As we all are. I left him in bed.'

Frances frowns.

'In bed? He's usually up before sparrow's.'

'Not these days, Fran. We have *staff* now. They do the early work.'

Cec and Margie have never expressed disappointment about the fact none of their children want to run the property – nor have they worried out loud about what will happen to it when they die – but no doubt they would have liked one of them to take an interest. Except, as Charlotte told Alison, 'It's seven days a week, 365 days a year – who'd want it?'

Frances and Margie arrange themselves on the couch, angled towards each other.

'Coffee?' Alison offers. It's her mother's home but she knows it's her job to make the hot beverages.

'White with two, thanks, Ally.'

'Thanks, love,' Frances says. No need for instruction: Alison knows how she takes her coffee.

As Alison moves around the kitchen preparing the drinks, she can hear the other two seemingly talking about nothing, except Alison knows they're talking about everything. In every detail shared, they're describing their world. As a child she thought it was so boring listening to the adults talk; now she knows how much can be revealed not only in what's told but what's left unsaid. In the spaces between their sentences there's the tacit understanding between two women who know each other so well they don't need to explain things. It's almost tangible, that bond: thick and rich and layered. Alison likes to think she has it with Charlotte, but maybe it won't be quite the same until they're older. And while she and her mother talk regularly, see each other often, she doesn't think she'll ever know Frances as well as Margie does.

It makes her stop, that thought. Because she believes Frances is the obstacle to that closeness; has always been. As a child Alison felt like her mother didn't approve of her, kept her at a distance, didn't smile at her as much as she did at Keith. It could have been imagined, but it's not the result of a later-in-life interpretation: she felt that way when she was young. Alone, that was it. She was alone. Keith had their mother, her father had their mother, but she didn't.

The sound of the kettle hides the strangled noise in her throat. This is why she doesn't think about these things too often: she gets upset. Nothing can change the past, she knows that, but that doesn't mean it's no longer upsetting.

Coffees made, she puts them, appropriately, on the coffee table as Frances and Margie continue to natter.

'Thanks, love,' Frances says absently as Margie beams at Alison.

'Beaut, Ally, thanks.'

Alison hovers, not sure if she should join them.

'Sitting down?' It's Margie who asks.

'Um . . .'

'Of course she is,' Frances states and Alison dutifully alights on the high-backed chair that apparently belonged to her great-grandmother and was scratched and chipped enough to make that plausible.

'How's tricks, Ally?' Margie picks up her mug and sips.

'Oh, well . . .' Alison wonders what Charlotte might have told her.

'Stepson's moved in, I hear.' Another sip, and not for the first time Alison notes Margie's ability to ask a question then answer it herself.

'He has.'

Margie raises her eyebrows. 'That must be interesting.'

'It is.' Alison doesn't really want to say any more, and she knows how good Margie is at getting information out of her. Better even than Charlotte. 'So you've been keeping well?'

Margie laughs. 'Your change of subject is noted. Yes, I have been, thanks. And you, Franny?'

'Yes, fine.' Frances's eyes meet Alison's. 'I'd like to come up and see Cec if Alison can find the time to drive me.'

'I'd take you up myself,' says Margie, 'but I'm going to bunk with Char for a couple of days then tootle back. Not sure how I'd get you back here.'

'No, that's fair.' Frances smiles understandingly, although Alison feels guilty. She needs to make time to get her mother to the High Country. It's not *that* far. Tad will just have to look after the kids' sport one weekend, then she and Frances can go overnight.

'We'll work something out,' Alison says and catches her mother's eye again.

'Great. Cec'll be happy to see you. What's it been – six months?'

'Something like that,' Frances replies.

While her aunt and her mother catch up on district gossip, Alison sits and calculates when, exactly, she can get away for a couple of days, and realises that her children have parties to go to, sport, a school play . . . When did being a child get so busy?

She'll find a date, though – she has to. If only to be able to spend more time with Frances. They'll make it work.

By the time she's stopped worrying about it, the coffee cups are empty and Margie is holding hers up for another round.

CHAPTER THIRTY-THREE

It's been two days since Joan managed to get rid of Isaac and she had almost asked Shane and William and any other capable man she could find to bodily remove him. Then it shocked her that she felt that way about her husband.

Or, rather, she was shocked that Isaac did not respect her wishes for him to leave. Then she was surprised that she was shocked, given he'd never paid much attention to her wishes in the past. This in turn led to a self-searching which revealed that she did not really discuss her wishes with him; instead, she had expected him to intuit them, which in hindsight was ludicrous. For one thing, the man had a lot on his mind, and for another he had never once shown himself to be psychic. Yet she had clung to an idea – formed from nothing and going nowhere – that because he was her husband, because he must know her so well, he should know what she wanted.

Should know that she dreamt of a holiday that did not involve her doing all the organising or, as when their children were young, all the cooking, cleaning and tidying. Should know that while she appreciates that he does not begrudge her spending money she doesn't like his requests for her to itemise her expenditure. For the accountant, he says, and maybe that's true but it feels like he's her gaoler.

He should also know that she wishes he would talk to her as a person, not as an aggregate of services he is now currently without.

'I'll wait to hear from you,' he said just before he left, in a tone so casual it was if he was trying to make an appointment with her.

'About what?' she said, irritated.

'About coming home.'

That had only irritated her more, because she had given him no expectation that she was thinking of doing that.

Her attitude must have shown on her face, because he quickly added, 'I mean, I hope you'll come home. Obviously.'

She wanted to tell him that she hoped the same thing, although they might have different ideas of what home is. Her idea of it is as place where she feels settled, comfortable, free. That is not the home she left.

The phone in her room rings. It hasn't rung since William called to tell her Isaac was downstairs, and she suspects this time there will be similar news. Although not about Isaac.

'Hello?'

'Mrs Irving.' It's not William. She doesn't recognise this voice. Which means the man who owns it won't know her and know which callers she doesn't want put through. So far the list includes Isaac, Genevieve, several of Isaac's friends and some more of hers.

'Yes?'

'We, ah – we have a Nathan Irving on the line for you.'

Joan closes her eyes and presses the phone against her ear, sighing. She should have guessed that Isaac would deploy his son. After her conversation with Corinne, she half-expected Nathan to call, but when he didn't she surmised he simply wasn't interested, which means that if he's calling it's because his father has put him up to it. She did not put her children on the no-call list because that seemed like a mother-sin but now she wishes she had. Although she can't not accept a call from her son, and if she asks for reception to tell him that she's out, he'll only call again.

'All right,' she says. 'I'll take the call.'

She waits for several seconds as there's silence on the line.

'Mummy?'

He still calls her that even though he's a man, and she normally finds it endearing, although now it sounds like a manipulation.

'Hello, darling,' she says – aware that 'darling' itself is a manipulation.

There are two loud breaths then a strangled sound.

'What are you doing?' he says.

'Having a little holiday.'

'*What?*'

'A holiday, darling. A break.'

'From your *life*?'

'That tends to be what holidays are for.' She's keeping her voice light, not wanting to upset him – her maternal instinct is responsible for that.

'Dad thinks you may not come back.' His voice sounds hard, like he's the one she left. Although she supposes that is correct.

'Not yet, no.'

'When?'

'I don't know. Nathan, I need some time to sort a few things out.' Now she's using her firm voice, the one that used to tell him not to climb on the cupboards or throw pebbles at his sister.

'What things?'

He sounds petulant and that annoys her. Given that he is getting on with his own life, she should be able to get on with hers.

Just then her eye catches the canvas she has propped against one wall. It was not her intention to turn her room into a studio but she doesn't have anywhere else to put her paintings.

This painting makes her smile. It depicts Frances in profile – the other day, when Joan asked Frances to sit and observe what was in front of her, Joan decided to paint her instead of the tree she'd been planning on. She used acrylics and with a few strokes came up with something she's quite pleased with. So was Frances once she showed it to her.

'My word!' the older woman said. 'No one's ever painted me before.' She squinted at the canvas. 'It really looks like me. How'd you do that?'

Joan shrugged. 'I observed,' she said and Frances beamed.

'Things,' she says to Nathan, because he doesn't need to know the details. 'Darling, I love you and I miss you but I have to go.'

It's a fib: she isn't due anywhere. But sometimes fibs are necessary to protect us from saying the truth.

'Mummy, if you miss me –'

'You have your life and I have mine, all right? I'll call you soon.'

She hangs up and feels . . . exhilarated. As if she has run away from an angry teacher who is determined to keep her after school. That happened to her from time to time so she knows the feeling. Remembers it, rather. It's been a while.

Obviously hanging up on her son is a bigger mother-sin than not taking his call but she knew that the longer they talked the more likely it would be that she'd weaken. As much as she hardly sees him any more – perhaps *because* of that – Nathan can wrap her around his little finger when he wants to.

The phone rings again. It won't be Nathan directly on the line – he has to go through reception – so she won't ignore it.

'Hello?'

'Mrs Irving, I –'

'If it's my son, I don't wish to speak to him.'

'It's not. It's Frances. She's asking if you'd like to meet her in the bar.'

'Oh!' Now she has a detention-fleeing companion. She likes the sound of that. 'Tell her I'll be right down.'

'Yes, Mrs Irving.'

She hangs up and goes to the bathroom mirror, fluffing her hair and pinching her cheeks before descending to the hubbub of the Duchess foyer.

CHAPTER THIRTY-FOUR

It's never a good day that starts with a barney, and Frances has had two: one with her neighbour, Phyllis, who is convinced that Colin is getting into her garden beds, which is ridiculous because Colin does not like dirt; and the other with Alison, who tut-tutted her way through a phone call about how Frances missed a dentist appointment and if she would only allow Alison to take over her life, this wouldn't happen.

Actually, that's a slight exaggeration of what she said but that was her implication. What she'd really said was, '*Mum*,' in that scolding tone of disapproving daughters, then there was a loud sigh, then there was a 'You need help'. That's her favourite new refrain: Frances needs help. She often doesn't specify which sort of help, which leaves it open to Frances's interpretation. Help around the house? Yes, Frances would love that. Help from a psychiatrist, if that's what's being implied? No, thank you. It is her firm opinion that psychiatrists are for people who cannot cope with life and that will never be Frances.

The fight with the neighbour used more words and was a little more invigorating. It was heralded by a loud knock on the door, which Frances opened to reveal Phyllis bearing an uprooted daffodil and a cross expression.

'He did this!' Phyllis declared, shaking the plant in Frances's face.

'Who?'

'That dog!' She looked over Frances's shoulder, although Frances knew Colin was curled up in the back room, out of sight.

'When?'

'This morning!'

'He's been inside all morning.' That was the truth. Apart from the five minutes Frances let him out to do a wee. Which was not enough time for him to somehow get through Phyllis's fence, liberate a daffodil and come back dirt free.

'Stop lying!' Phyllis had shrieked, then stomped her way back to the gate and onto the footpath, past the corgi – similarly coloured and shaped to Colin – who lived a few doors down and was most likely the culprit. She didn't even look at that corgi, so clearly she was wedded to the idea of Colin being the bad dog.

That set the tone of the day, really, because Alison's call followed not long afterwards.

The only thing for it was to take off for the Duchess Hotel and see if Joan was free for a drink. She likes spending time with Joan. Not the art thing so much, because she doesn't enjoy it the way Kirrily does. Kirrily always looks like a pig in mud when she has a brush in her hand. And, in fact, if Joan *is* free for a drink Frances could take the opportunity to talk to her about Kirrily, who will not be around as it's not one of her regular days.

It's not that Frances is a gossip. The Duchess Hotel provides plenty of material for gossip but apart from the time she told Shane she saw Wendy canoodling with someone who looked like the gardener near the spotted gum tree by the staff entrance, she has declined to tell tales. That one was too good to keep to herself, though, because Wendy had never shown an interest in gardening. Except Shane was a disappointment, because after she told him all he did was nod slowly and polish a glass.

That was her first attempt at Duchess gossip. She is now about to try her second.

'Hello,' she calls as she sees Joan descending the grand staircase, looking slightly flustered.

'Hello.' Joan looks distracted.

'Everything all right?' No point beating around the bush.

'What? Oh. Sorry.' Joan's face relaxes. 'My son just called me. I hung up on him.'

Frances raises her eyebrows. 'I understand,' she says.

Joan laughs. 'Really?' she says.

'Yes. Shall we have a drink and talk about it?'

'Sure.'

Frances leads the way to the bar and waves hello to Shane, who grins at her then his face drops when he sees Joan. It's odd – he's never seemed to have a problem with her before, but maybe he didn't like her checking on him. If so, it's Frances's fault that he's being cold. However, Joan doesn't seem to notice, so Frances doesn't spend any more time worrying about it. Instead she puts in her order at the bar then she and Joan find a table, and Joan recaps her conversation with her son, who sounds about as useful as Keith.

They're halfway through their drinks when she decides to change the subject.

'Kirrily,' she announces.

Joan frowns at her. 'She's not here. It's not Friday.'

'Oh, I know,' Frances says breezily. 'That was my way of introducing her as a topic of conversation.'

No reply.

'I think she's getting herself in trouble,' Frances says.

Joan looks amused. 'Doing what?'

'There's a man,' Frances says.

'What do you mean?'

'She's interested in a man. A man who isn't her husband. I'm worried about her.'

'Why? She's an adult. If that's what she wants to do, that's her business.'

'I just think . . . he's toying with her.'

'How do you know? Maybe she's toying with him.'

'She can't be! She's a good girl.' Frances developed this conviction about Kirrily not long after meeting her for the first time. Kirrily is dependable, responsible. Or so she seems.

'Good girls do silly things. And sometimes we have to let them.'

'But her husband . . .'

'Is none of my concern.' Joan looks pointedly at Frances. 'We don't know what's going on in their marriage. *They* might not even know.'

Frances considers all of this then realises she's a duffer – she is talking about Kirrily's marriage and husband and there's Joan with her own marriage clearly in strife since she's left it, even if she talks about that like it's temporary.

'Right,' is all Frances says, because if she pushes the point about Kirrily, it may seem like she's pushing about Joan.

'Right,' Joan affirms.

Frances feels a sense of unease and it takes her a few seconds to work out what it is: in the attempt to share gossip, she may have annoyed Joan. And she doesn't want to annoy Joan. She likes Joan. Joan says what she thinks and does what she likes, and while Frances has always believed she's the same, it's come to her attention that in the matter of her circumstances and her children she's not really saying or doing what she wants so much as trying not to antagonise them and failing. *Reacting* to life is not the same thing as taking action to do what makes you happiest. Awareness has come to her, slowly, that she doesn't know what makes her happiest, apart from coming to the Duchess. Maybe that's enough. Yet she feels that there's more – somewhere, somehow. Sitting here, with Joan, feels like she's getting closer to the more.

'So what are we going to paint this Friday?' Frances asks, just to get the conversation back on track.

'The shed.'

'Which shed?'

'The one in the far corner.' Joan jerks her head in the direction of the hotel's rear. 'The gardener's shed. That's what Shane told me it is.'

'Shane told you?' She wonders if that was before or after he decided to start glowering at her.

'Yes.' Joan's eyes drift towards the bar and Frances follows them in time to see Shane looking in Joan's direction then looking away.

'Everything all right with you two?'

'Who knows.' Joan smiles briefly. 'Men are a mystery.'

'That they are. Of course, they'd say that about us.'

'Good.' Joan takes a sip of her wine. 'I don't want them knowing everything. We can't take over the world if they know our plans.' She smiles and Frances laughs – a good, satisfying belly laugh.

'I'm with you there,' she says, raising her shandy in a toast.

They sit for another hour or so, trading stories about childhoods and motherhoods, until Frances decides it's time to return to Colin and inspect his paws for any new incriminating dirt.

CHAPTER THIRTY-FIVE

Anyone looking at Aidan would think him a normal six-year-old boy, the way he is climbing all over the playground equipment, his cheeks pink. Most of the time he is just like other little boys, and the rest of the time he wants to be. Kirrily wants him to be too.

Yet he's been listless, not eating, his sleep disturbed by nightmares. Not that nightmares are uncommon in children but his are constant, and they scare her, because she knows where they come from and she knows her complicity in their origin, even though not a single one of her own nightmares has come true. Not the nighttime ones, that is. She's had daytime nightmares – fears about things that will happen to her or the people she loves – and they have come to pass.

Her mother dying was her biggest nightmare – isn't it any child's? From the time Kirrily was old enough to have worries she worried about that. And then it happened. That taught her that her thoughts were not safe, that anything she feared might come to pass. Which hasn't stopped her worrying – if anything it's made it worse.

Her next biggest nightmare was that something would happen to one of her children, and it did, and here is Aidan living with the consequences. Whenever he's unwell, she worries that he's picked up an infection somehow – that his skin has broken somewhere she can't see and that it will need repairing, and that will require surgery, which means money and time and Bridget's life rearranged, not to mention her own.

Yet she is hardly going to ignore the symptoms. That's why she took him to the GP today. Their local doctor has known Aidan since he was a baby and since the fire has been entrusted with keeping an eye on him.

'He's growing quickly,' Dr Hamer said not even an hour ago, peering over the top of his half-moon glasses. Kirrily could almost count the hairs in his nostrils and his hair is completely white now, so perhaps he won't be their GP for much longer. Then what? Who can she trust with her children's health?

'I think he's in pain because his skin is stretching. That's why he's out of sorts. He just doesn't want to worry you with it. But it may be time for more surgery.' Dr Hamer made a face that was halfway between a grimace and a sympathy smile. 'I know that's not what you want to hear.'

No, it wasn't, but surgery has always been an eventuality rather than a possibility. Is it wrong, though, to want it to be always somewhere off in the middle-distant future rather than something that needs to happen so soon? She doesn't want her son to be in pain, and it will cause him pain. More pain than he's in now.

The referral letter is in the handbag that's now next to her on the bench adjacent to the playground. She brought Aidan here so she could sit and think for a while. Think about everything she'll need to arrange so they can get him to Melbourne for the specialist, about whether she'll need time off work, about what they'll do with Bridget. And she also thinks about how she can never understand why she has to keep getting referrals to a specialist they've seen before but that's the system, she knows.

Here's what else is the system: parents having children who then cause them a large amount of stress. She knows that this is what happens when you love someone as much as she loves Aidan and Bridget; knows too that she does not want to swap it for a life without them in it. Yet it hurts, this worry. No one told her parenthood would hurt.

Sometimes, when she's lying awake at night, unable to sleep, she wonders if her mother hurt so much from having all those children to worry about that she died because of it. Two children cause Kirrily so much concern; her mother had five. That's an exponential increase in worry.

She can't think about that for too long, though. It will lead her to places she doesn't want to go.

The other night Connor woke up and found her staring at the ceiling.

'Again?' he said, but it wasn't unkind: it was the question of a man who has seen his wife awake in the middle of the night too many times.

'Again,' she said.

He took her hand and she let him, although at the point he awoke she'd been thinking about Derek, because she needs something pleasant to keep her company in those awake hours.

She knew she fell asleep at some point because when she woke up Connor still had hold of her, and before she opened her eyes she enjoyed the warmth of his hand on hers, then her alarm went off and the spell was broken.

'Time to go home, sweetie,' she calls to Aidan, who is hanging upside down on the monkey bars, giggling. Who knows at what. He's a child who likes to laugh, which is a blessing.

She drives him home, knowing her mother-in-law will already be there, having picked up Bridget from school. Julie offered before Kirrily could even ask when she told her about Aidan's appointment.

Once the car is parked down the side of the house, Aidan runs ahead of her to the back door and shoves it open, calling his sister's name.

In the kitchen, Julie is sitting with a mug of tea and a magazine in front of her, smiling tiredly as she looks up.

'Hello, love,' she says. 'Bridget's been doing her homework.'

'Thanks for picking her up.'

Another tired smile. 'Anytime. You know I love seeing them.'

'I'd make you a cup of tea but . . .' Kirrily gestures lamely at the mug.

'Let me make you one.'

'No, no, that's fine, thanks anyway.' Kirrily looks around the kitchen, trying to remember what she had planned to cook for dinner. Potatoes? 'I should start on dinner,' she says.

'Let me help.' Julie pushes her chair back.

'You don't need to, honest –'

'Kirrily,' Julie says sternly. 'You need to let me help you more. You need to let *us*. Roy is itching to get his hands on that garden.' She nods towards the back door. 'You two don't have to manage on your own; we know how hard you're working.'

Kirrily swallows. Her father had always told her that accepting help was weakness, also that it meant other people knowing your business. That's the main reason she ended up looking after four siblings on her own; she resented it then and while she doesn't exactly resent her life now, she knows it's getting to her. All the work, of various kinds, and no end in sight.

'It doesn't seem right.' She tries one last objection.

'To whom?' Julie looks at her enquiringly. 'Who's watching, love? Who's keeping score?'

Only me, Kirrily wants to say, but she doesn't think her mother-in-law would understand. Julie has a kinder view of life than Kirrily has; it's brushed off on her son and is arguably one of the things Kirrily first loved about Connor. He still has it, and still has a kind view of her.

'Okay,' Kirrily concedes. 'Thank you.'

'Now – how about you sit, I'll make *you* a cup of tea and you can watch me peel the vegies?'

Kirrily opens her mouth to object.

'And just in case you're wondering,' Julie goes on, 'I'm not the one keeping score.' She winks. 'Sit. Tell me about the appointment.'

As Julie bustles around the kitchen Kirrily fills her in on developments, and together they make a plan to get Aidan to the specialist and Bridget looked after. By the time Connor comes home, Kirrily feels almost giddy with relief.

CHAPTER THIRTY-SIX

Now that her home has become more fraught, with tensions between Tad and Erik on a permanent low simmer, Alison has increased her without-notice visits to her mother. She keeps telling Frances that she's 'just checking on her', and she suspects that Frances doesn't like being checked on, and there's likely a balance to be found between what Alison needs – respite from her home life – and what Frances wants, but increasingly Alison feels like she might explode if she doesn't spend time with someone who loves her unconditionally and is not demanding anything of her. Frances doesn't even seem to want her company half the time, and Alison should probably just tell her the real reason she keeps turning up at odd times, but there's part of her that doesn't want to admit that her previously pleasant home life is turbulent, and she's starting to resent her husband accordingly. The husband she used to think hung the stars. And maybe he will again. Who knows when that will be.

'How are you, Mum?' Alison says as she bustles in the door holding a bag of grapes. She never likes to come empty-handed.

'Fine,' Frances says, looking bemused, as she tends to.

'Really? You sound a bit snuffly.' Alison peers at her.

'How can you tell?'

'I have school-age kids. I'm like a snuffle detective. They bring home all sorts of lurgies.'

She's through to the kitchen with the grapes, into the fridge they go, then she's turning on the kettle even if she doesn't actually want tea, but it's what you do, isn't it?

'You didn't have to bring fruit,' Frances says, following her. 'You brought some the other day.'

'It keeps you regular!' Alison fake-smiles and hopes Frances can't tell the difference.

'I don't have a problem with regularity,' Frances says darkly, resting one hand on the kitchen table.

'What have you been up to?' Alison says, rearranging the oranges in the fruit bowl on the table.

'Since I saw you two days ago?'

Alison stops moving the fruit. 'Are you trying to make a point?'

'No, just asking. My life isn't so busy that much would happen in two days. How are things at home?'

'Good. Yeah. Fine.' Alison had actually practised telling her mother that she feels like she's losing her mind and asking her if Frances had ever felt like things were just too hard and she wanted to quit – not quit life, but quit *her* life. It's not the sort of conversation they've ever had, though, so she doesn't know how to start it, despite the practice. Yet there's no one else she can tell. No one who loves her enough to not think she's being unreasonable. Only a woman who saw you throw temper tantrums at two years of age won't find you unreasonable if you have one at forty-five.

Frances is giving her that face she gets when she knows something's off but also knows Alison won't tell her. It's the face she used while Alison was a teenager then later when she was still living at home in her early twenties. One night Alison came back after a night out, having been on a date with a man she thought really cared about her only for him to maul her in a laneway outside the pub, thrusting his hand between her legs, doing his best to hurt her and succeeding. She screamed; he put his hand over her mouth; a man standing nearby laughed. Alison had never been so scared in her life. She remembers wondering if this is how she would die, in this laneway, surrounded by cigarette butts, betrayed by someone she really should have known better before she let him take her anywhere. It was only when a group of women emerged from the hotel and one of them called out to her that the man let her go and ran off.

The women got her home that night, and when Alison walked in the door Frances was there, arms folded, almost like she'd intuited that her daughter was about to arrive. She'd asked her how she was and Alison had said she was fine, and Frances had given her the face. The memory of that night makes Alison want to vomit and she's been thinking of it so often lately, to the point where she believes it's been coiled in her cells, waiting for the time when she feels that scared again to be released. What she can't say – to Tad, to Frances, to anyone – is that Erik makes her feel that scared because he's unknowable and, therefore, unpredictable.

'Why don't we sit and have a chinwag?' Frances says now, gesturing to the sitting room. Alison nods and follows her in, trying to think of something to talk about.

'How's the painting going?' Even though Alison is still a little jealous that Joan has some of her mother's attention, she is trying to be interested in what they do together.

'Very well,' Frances replies. 'I'm not any good but I'm doing my best.' She gestures to a sketch propped up against the wall.

Alison glances over and sees the figure of a man. It's not bad – she can see clearly that it's a person, and that he has detail on his clothes, and he's wearing a hat, although she can't quite make out the shape of it.

Alison steps closer to the sketch. 'Is that Dad?' she says.

'Ah . . . no.'

'So . . .' Alison straightens and stops herself from sighing, because she thinks she knows who it is and feels silly for not realising it first up. 'Keith?'

'Well . . . you're close.' Frances has clasped her hands together and her eyes are half-closed. That's when Alison knows who it is:

Albert. The man her mother could never forget. The man her father had to overlook in order to make a family with Frances, be a father to Keith and a great father to her. Because he was, and it hurts Alison that Frances never talks about him – it's as if he never existed – yet here she is making a portrait of Albert. It's pretty much the last thing she can handle at the moment.

'Right,' she says sharply, then she feels like running out of the room and the house altogether. Instead she stalks back into the kitchen and Frances follows.

When Alison was a child, she didn't know that she and Keith did not have the same father; Keith called Gerald Dad and the two were close. It wasn't until she was eleven, at Christmas lunch, that one of her cousins said something about it.

She didn't believe it at first – this cousin had always been mean to her – but the look on her parents' faces told her it was true. It was a relief, in some ways: she had always thought Keith was too different to her to be her brother. But she hated knowing she had been lied to, and that everyone else but her seemed to be in possession of the truth.

'You know,' Alison says as she picks up the oranges again and slams them back into the fruit bowl, 'just because Dad's dead doesn't mean you shouldn't respect him.'

'I do.'

'So why aren't you sketching *him*?' Another orange suffers.

'For all you know, Alison, I'm planning to sketch him next.'

'Sure.' Alison goes to the fridge and opens it, pretending to inspect Frances's milk but really just stalling because she's having all these feelings about seeing that sketch and they're eleven-year-old Alison's feelings, and on top of everything else that's going on for her she really does now feel like she could explode.

'It's possible to hold more than one person in your heart,' Frances says, standing back.

'Is it?' She shuts the fridge door firmly.

'Don't you love both of your children?'

'That's different!'

'It's not. The heart expands as much as it needs to. I didn't need to stop loving Albert in order to love your father.'

'But it would have been nice if you did!'

Now Alison opens the cupboards and the cutlery drawer, trying to get out the nervous energy she feels electrifying her limbs. She's always been a fidgeter; recent events have taken it to extremes.

'For whom? Your father never said anything.'

'Did he even *know*?'

'He didn't ask. It wasn't an issue.'

Alison folds her arms, huffs, and turns to look out the window, to the back garden where the Hills Hoist stands devoid of clothes but covered in pegs. Maybe she should just say what she really wants to say.

'Keith gets preferential treatment because he's Albert's son,' she says, her mouth barely moving. 'He always has.'

She's said it before – after her father died she told Frances how much it hurt her that Gerald would allow and enable Keith to do things that Alison could not. 'That's too dangerous for you,' he would tell his daughter, or, 'You wouldn't know what to do.' But what she really wanted to say was that she knew Frances preferred Keith because she preferred Keith's father to Alison's.

'I can't deny that,' Frances says. She's admitted it before, and said she was 'sorry if you felt that way', as if Alison wasn't stating a fact.

'It's because of *him*.' Alison gestures towards the sitting room. 'And there you are, sketching him like he's the most important person in your life.'

'I sketched him because Joan asked us to draw something from memory,' Frances says. 'Yes, he was the first thing that came to mind. I saw the slouch hat and it went from there.'

Alison rolls her eyes. 'Bloody war.'

'I'm sorry the drawing upsets you,' Frances says. 'I never meant for that to happen.'

'Right, like you never meant to keep his picture in your chest of drawers,' she snaps. But it was a mistake – Alison has never admitted knowing this before because it means admitting she had looked through her mother's belongings, finding the portrait tucked under scarves.

'I didn't realise you'd ever gone through my chest of drawers.'

'Every kid does that!'

'Do they?'

'You didn't?'

'I'd have been belted.'

'What?'

'Your grandparents were of a different generation,' Frances says lightly. 'None of us was permanently scarred.'

'But –'

'I'm sorry you're upset,' Frances repeats, and it makes Alison want to scream because she never seems to be *actually* sorry. 'But I can't change what's happened. I would like us to sit down to tea and chat about other things, if that's all right.'

Alison thinks about it. What would really release her pent-up energy is to yell and scream. But she remembered something she heard once, about how you should be angry at the right person for the right reason at the right time and in the right way. She is angry at Tad and at Erik. And at Erik's mother. She is only mildly upset with Frances. So she should not take out her anger on Frances.

'Yes, it's all right,' she says.

'I'll make it,' Frances offers.

Then they take their tea in the kitchen, near the fruit and away from the sketch, and talk about the weather. Alison is no closer to telling her mother about what's really troubling her yet by the time she leaves she's calmer and feeling more capable of carrying on.

CHAPTER THIRTY-SEVEN

Just as Kirrily was arriving at work today, she saw Wendy heading across the lawn to the entrance of the Duchess, her hair a mess and her rouge too bright, and felt a pang of sympathy. Also a sensation of wanting to rescue Shane from yet another accosting.

She feels sorry for the woman occasionally because she's clearly lonely, given how many men she tries to race off with, and clearly delusional, given that she keeps thinking Shane will be one of them.

'Not interested?' Kirrily had asked him once after witnessing yet another attempt by Wendy to reach over the bar and get Shane in her clutches, literally.

'Not in a million,' he'd replied. Not in a dismissive way. More like he felt sorry for Wendy and didn't want to have to reject her because he knew it would hurt her.

'Not your type?'

Shane had turned towards her with a look on his face that suggested he couldn't believe she'd asked that question.

'I've got enough trouble.' He'd pointed to his head. 'I don't need hers.'

Kirrily didn't know exactly what he meant by 'trouble'. He'd always been stable at work, respectful of everyone, never losing his temper. Maybe he was referring to his recent spell of absence.

She wasn't going to ask him, though. They weren't close enough for that.

Once she'd parked her car out the back, she darted into the hotel and found Wendy ambling towards the bar.

'Hi!' Kirrily stepped in front of her.

Wendy frowned. 'Yes?'

'Wendy.'

'Yes.'

'Kirrily. I work here.' *And you've met me multiple times*, she wanted to say, except she so often has the sense that Wendy's mind is elsewhere that she doesn't know if the woman will have retained the memories of meeting her before.

Wendy looked irritated. 'I'm going in there.' She pointed to the bar.

'I have another idea.'

It wasn't an idea Kirrily had formed earlier but one that had sprung to mind just then, as a way of helping Shane and maybe helping Wendy too. And, sure, Kirrily is hoping there are some brownie points for her in there somewhere, as a way of offsetting the messy way she feels about herself at the moment. Kind of a 'do unto others' method of looking at the world with a little selfish motivation added. Although the whole principle of 'do unto others as you would have others do unto you' is selfish, if you think about it.

'Oh yeah?' Wendy squints at her and runs a hand through her hair, making it even messier.

'How do you feel about art?'

The squint deepens and is now accompanied by a scowl. Kirrily then wonders why on earth she has made this suggestion given she hasn't asked Joan and it's Joan who'll have to take responsibility for the new arrival. She swallows and tastes regret. But it's too late now, because Wendy is nodding and saying, 'Yeah, yeah ... I like it.'

'Good.' Kirrily swallows again. 'There's an artist living here at the hotel and I paint with her. Joan. You've probably met her.'

'Blondie?'

'Yes.'

Wendy nods slowly and her face contorts briefly. 'She doesn't like me,' she says.

'How do you know?'

'Because she's a stuck-up bitch.' Wendy sniffs loudly.

'Right.' Kirrily laughs nervously because she can't disagree. It's nothing she hasn't already thought about Joan – some of the other staff have too. But it's only a first – maybe second – impression because now she knows Joan a little better, she finds her brisk, not stuck-up.

'How about we give it a chance, though?' Kirrily presses on.

'Why?'

'Because it's fun!' *And you could do with some fun*, she doesn't say aloud. Adult life is distinctly lacking in fun; she realised this not long after she left school. Not that her childhood was much fun either. All in all, her life has been not fun. That's probably why she likes doing art with Joan: she doesn't have to take care of or responsibility for anyone or anything, she can just stand or sit and do stuff. Make stuff. Make shapes, pictures. Yes, it's fun.

Wendy shrugs. 'All right.'

Kirrily leads her out the entrance of the hotel and to the right, heading for the rose garden where Joan set today's meeting.

As they approach, she can see Joan frowning in their direction. Frances is perched nearby looking at a sketchpad in her hands and tapping a pencil on it. She's sitting on a bashed-up chair that Shane took from the bar. After someone threw it against the wall, he kept it out the back for some reason, then suggested Joan use it when she said she needed a chair for Frances.

'Hi, Joan!' Kirrily's voice squeaks and she thinks it's the sound of guilt for springing this on an unsuspecting art teacher.

'Hello, Kirrily.' Joan's smile is brief and tight. 'Wendy.'

Wendy puts her hand through her hair again and Joan winces.

'Um, I, um . . .' Kirrily starts. She hasn't thought this part through. 'I invited Wendy to come today because I thought she might like it and I really should have asked you first but it was kind of a snap thing and she may not like it anyway so I hope that's okay but if you really don't want another person that's all right.' She inhales.

'My word,' Joan says, a smile starting. 'What a mouthful.'

Kirrily bites her lip and feels like a kid waiting to be told her punishment.

'Do you like art, Wendy?' Joan asks.

Wendy blinks a couple of times and nods. 'Came top of my class at school,' she says and Kirrily stifles a gasp. Why didn't she say that earlier?

'Really? Which medium do you prefer?' asks Joan.

'Drawing in charcoal.'

'I don't have any but I can get some.' Joan smiles in Kirrily's direction then back to Wendy. 'If you wish to join us, that is.'

Wendy sniffs again. 'I'll give it a go.' She looks at the assorted materials on the ground next to Joan.

'Oh yeah,' Wendy says. 'All the pencils. Nice paper, that. Oils!' She shakes her head. 'Too much trouble.'

'I won't force you,' Joan says. 'Now, there are some lovely American Beauties in there.' She gestures to the rose beds. 'They're the subject for today.'

'What? For drawing?' Wendy asks.

'Yes. Is that all right?'

Joan looks from Wendy to Kirrily, who thinks she sees a flash of irritation but it's too quick for her to be sure. Kirrily really doesn't want to annoy Joan, even if bringing an uninvited person to class is probably the best way to do that.

'Sure,' Wendy says.

'Mm-hm,' Kirrily affirms. Then she takes the pencil Joan gives her and a pad of paper and sits cross-legged in front of a rose bush and its large, gloriously pink blooms. A few seconds later, Wendy sits beside her but Kirrily barely remembers she's there as she starts drawing. Tentative strokes at first, then she stops and stares at the roses, taking in as many details as she can before closing her eyes and trying to remember them. That's what she always used to do, when she was younger: take a mental photo of whatever she was drawing or painting then try to replicate it rather than keep referring to what was in front of her. It was the way she could get the creation to feel like it flowed out of her – that it was something original to her, rather than an attempt at copying what was in front of her. She would check from time to time, particularly if she was painting, as she liked colours to be true to life if possible. But the shapes, the lines, the *feeling* of it – these came from her experience of what she was seeing.

She loses track of time in the most glorious way: not thinking about anything but the art she is making. It reminds her of what she lost after her mother died – the feeling of simply being. When she made art there was no past or future; there was only now. So much of her life since then has been dwelling on the past then trying not to, and worrying about the future then trying not to. It's constant, and exhausting, and she has desperately needed respite from it.

'Time's up,' Joan says when it feels like no time at all has passed, and Kirrily feels a small wave of sadness that her moments here are over. For now.

'How did you go?' she asks Wendy, who holds up a detailed drawing that looks like it could have come from a botany textbook.

'Oh,' Kirrily says, feeling like she's failed a test.

'Not much imagination, me.' Wendy makes a face. 'I just draw it straight.' She gestures to Kirrily's sketchpad. 'I like yours better.'

Their eyes meet and it's hard for Kirrily to tell if Wendy is being sincere or merely trying to spare her feelings.

Joan wanders over to them and inspects both of their work.

'How interesting,' she murmurs. 'Two such different styles. I shall have to come up with some challenges for you both.'

Joan smiles. 'See you next week?' she says to Wendy, who looks surprised, then chuffed.

'Uh, yeah,' Wendy replies, then pats around her hips. 'Where are my cigs?'

'I have no idea,' Joan says, then turns away.

'I have some,' Kirrily says, then checks her watch. 'And I have to go. Walk with me?'

As they head in the direction of the hotel's rear entrance, Wendy chatters about why she likes roses and Kirrily mostly doesn't listen, as the blissful hour of emptiness for her brain – when it was consumed with nothing more than drawing – has given way to the ever-running mental to-do list and her insistent practice of worrying.

At the door, she leaves Wendy with two cigarettes and a spare lighter, then heads to the staff room to see what awaits her.

OCTOBER 1999

CHAPTER THIRTY-EIGHT

When she was younger and the phone would ring, as it is ringing now, Frances would know that it was likely to be a friend of hers or Alison's or Keith's. Gerald had friends but they rarely called the house because they could reach him at the pharmacy, and he liked to keep them separate from his family anyway.

'You're not interested in cricket, dear,' is what he would say when Frances would ask why they didn't see his friends more often. In summer, that is. In winter the answer was, 'You don't like football.'

The underlying assumption was, obviously, that he and his friends were playing or watching those sports, and Frances washed his sporting gear so she knew that he was doing *something*. As he aged, though, there was no more sports gear yet he was still absent for most of each weekend. She never found out where he went; she never asked. That was his business, as far as she was concerned, and she liked having the freedom to do what she wanted on the weekends. It had the side effect of making her not miss him as much as she thought she should when he died. Of course, that might also have been because she didn't love him as much as she thought she should. But she wasn't sure he loved her either. For all she knew it was a mistress he was visiting on weekends and the most pain she had from contemplating that was from realising that she wouldn't have minded if he'd had a mistress.

It is an odd thing to spend a life with a person you are mostly indifferent to, even if you feel some affection for them, yet she knew she wasn't the only one. Some of her friends were in the same boat: they liked their husbands and they were glad to have had good lives with them but they didn't love them much. That was not, they sometimes reflected, the priority. They were women who had grown up during the Great Depression, who had lost fathers, uncles, brothers, cousins, friends in wars. Survival, stability, security – these were far more important than a romantic attachment.

Their own mothers had married the man most likely to take care of them, to protect them and provide for them. That was, they firmly believed, the man's job and neither Frances nor her friends approve of these feminists nowadays not only denigrating the role those men played but insisting that women must do all the caring and providing and protecting to prove they're as good as the man. If women do all of that, though, what's left for the men to do? And how exhausting, for the women to have to do everything! No, no, it's going nowhere good, all of that.

Frances never wanted to behave like a man and she was glad she married a man who felt the same way. Gerald did his bit, and she did hers. Maybe, in the end, when you're building a family and a life and home together, that's what love is. Certainly, having had a romantic attachment and lost it, with only a headstone in the High Country and a lifetime of grief to show for it, she does not think romantic love is the great panacea some movies and books would have a person believe.

Her phone has stopped ringing because she's been daydreaming. That happens a bit, and she also knows that it's unlikely to be anything urgent because she doesn't have a lot of friends left to ring that phone any more, which means it'll be Alison 'just calling to check on you, Mum', or Keith to tell her about his latest 'development'.

It's ringing again. All right, she'll get it this time.

'Hello, Frannie?' says a familiar voice when she answers.

'Margie.' Her sister-in-law is the great family event organiser, so she's probably ringing about Christmas – it may only be October but she's fond of kicking things off early.

'Darl, it's not good news.'

Frances's mind starts whirring, although it doesn't whir at the pace it used to. She misses being quick at things.

'What's happened?' she says.

'Fran, it's Cec.'

Her voice sounds calm but Frances knows. Oh, she knows. She feels it now – her feet tingle and one knee bends without her wanting it to, and her guts are turning to water.

The first time she felt this was when an army man arrived at the house with a letter. Nineteen forty-two. And again as she lost her parents, then her two eldest brothers.

Cec is gone.

'Oh, Marg,' she whispers. 'I'm so sorry.'

'It was quick.'

'When?'

'This morning.'

The whirring starts again. He'd been sick and she hadn't visited. She should have visited. She hasn't seen him in so long. It's so hard to get back to the High Country and he stopped driving when his eyesight went so he wasn't able to get to her. But she felt like she was in touch because she would speak to Margie. Who mentioned he'd been unwell but nothing serious. Not that she said.

So it's been too long. Months have gone by without her seeing the boy she spent every day of her childhood with, as he helped her up trees and across creeks, onto horses and beside rivers.

Months that seemed to go past in the blink of an eye but now they're an eternity.

'It was a heart thing, Frannie,' Margie says, and she's still so calm. 'He died in his sleep. Best way to go. No fuss.' She laughs and her voice catches. 'Just like Cec.'

'Where are . . .' In her shock Frances has forgotten her nephews' names and her niece's.

'Char's on her way. Barney and Dugald are here. They are both here. You wouldn't credit it. They came to help with some fencing and he just . . .'

Now Frances hears a sob.

'It was like he planned it, Fran. To have them here so I wouldn't be alone.'

'He was always a thoughtful man,' Frances murmurs, thinking of her strapping brother darning socks so her mother didn't have to, driving Frances into town when she needed things, taking in Margie's parents when they needed care.

'That he was.'

She hears Margie take a deep breath.

'The funeral will be in a few days, I guess. I'll let you know.'

The funeral. Of course. She'll have to ask Alison to take her.

'You'll come?' Margie says.

'Yes,' Frances says. 'I wouldn't miss it.'

'You can stay here. Please. I don't want you coming up this way and having to go back on the same day.'

Organising to stay somewhere else – thinking about what to do with Colin, about having to pack an overnight bag which she hasn't done for years – is overwhelming in this moment.

'We'll see,' she says.

'Are you all right?' Margie's voice is softer.

'I should be asking you that.'

'You knew him longer, Frannie. You loved him first.'

More memories come to her in a rush: of Cecil in a tie and shirt and shorts, going off to school; of him racing away from her on his favourite horse, his hat held high in one hand as the other clasped the reins; of the day he married Margie and they were all so happy he'd met such a lovely young woman. Gone. All gone.

Except in her mind. He will keep her company there like her other brothers and her parents do. Like Albert does in quieter times when she lets her thoughts roam. Sometimes she thinks old age is nothing but a storehouse of things you want to remember and things you're trying to forget.

'He was lucky to have your love,' she says, and means it with her whole heart.

'And I his.'

They're both silent for a few seconds.

'It's not the best of circumstances,' Margie finally says, 'but I'm looking forward to seeing you.'

'We have a bit to catch up on.'

'We do. I'll call with the date, darl.'

'Thanks, Margie. Talk to you soon.'

Once the call is over Frances walks to her back room, where Colin is curled up in his little dog bed and she can see her garden out the window. There are sturdy trees in that garden, and she needs them now, she thinks.

Colin lifts his head and turns those big eyes her way. She starts to weep a little because she never thought of herself as being all alone in the world but with the last witness to her childhood gone, that's what it feels like.

There's a photo album somewhere. Where? She looks at the low cupboard in the sitting room. Can she get down there? She must.

When she pulls open the cupboard door – last opened years ago, so she's surprised it gives so easily – she peers in and sees a haphazard pile of albums. Reaching in, she feels for the one with the ring-bound spine. That's the album of photos of her brothers and their families.

Tugging it out, she puts a hand on the cupboard to help herself up then takes it over to the couch.

There they all are, at Cec and Margie's wedding. At Charlotte's eighteenth birthday. Two photos out the front of the family home in the High Country.

Her strapping brother. Her tall protector. That's how she'll always think of him, and even as he aged, she continued to feel comforted by the knowledge that he was there if she needed him. A woman needs that sometimes: to know that there's a man to look after her. It's not the fashionable thing these days but she has never felt secure without it. Now he's gone. Now they're all gone. Who will look after her? Her son is no protector.

Fear and vulnerability make her feel weak, and she can't help the tears that arise. Tears that should fall, for Cec. Except she can't let them, because she doesn't know when they'd stop.

She feels a nudge against her leg and looks down to see Colin gazing up at her. Sometimes she understands what he wants and sometimes she thinks he knows what she needs, although she's aware that it could all be fanciful thinking. Today, though, it feels real.

'You're right, Colin,' she says. 'A walk *is* a good idea.'

Normally he has a short constitutional around the block; today she may walk him further. She feels the need for fresh air and sunshine, and trees and sounds of life. So she takes his lead off the hook by the back door and prepares to set out.

CHAPTER THIRTY-NINE

'It's taking too long, Tad.'

Alison is pacing the kitchen and looking at her watch, glancing out the window at the night sky as if that will change anything.

'It will be fine,' Tad says soothingly – if a little condescendingly, in Alison's opinion. 'You're just upset because of your uncle.'

'Of course I'm upset!' Alison snaps, and she doesn't regret it, because he's been spectacularly unsympathetic, in her opinion, since Cec died. Doesn't he know how close she is to Charlotte? Charlotte's father has died and she hasn't even been able to see her to give her a hug because she's been at work, and running the kids around, and doing the washing and everything else for Tad and his children. All three of them. She hasn't even been able to get to her mother to give *her* a hug. Instead, the first time she'll be able to do that is when she picks her up on Friday morning to take her to the funeral. And that just doesn't seem right.

'All right, it's all right,' Tad says in what he probably thinks is a calming voice but it just makes her more irritated. Does he also not know how fond she was of Cec? Of Margie? Doesn't he think it's *normal* for her to be upset?

It was his idea that Erik go and get takeaway for dinner. 'To give you a break from cooking,' he said. She had to stop herself from rolling her eyes and telling him that what would really give her a break from cooking would be him or Erik doing some of it. Taking the children with him was Tad's idea too, so they could 'spend some time together'. Like they don't live in the same house, where Erik could spend plenty of time with them if only he could be more bothered and less surly. He's anti-social. That's the beginning and the end of it.

God, she's short tempered at the moment. She can *feel* it. Cec's death has acted like some kind of release on a valve she didn't realise had pressure building up. Not to this extent. Erik's presence in the house has made her tense, of course, she has known that from the day he arrived. She just didn't realise how much. Or, rather, how much it seems to be changing her personality. There have been pressures in her life before; everyone has them. There has been grief: her father dying, as well as Frances's two other brothers. Her paternal grandparents were dead before she was born, and Frances's parents were distant figures so she didn't feel too sad about them dying, and she was still a child at the time, but with Cec . . .

It's her love for Charlotte that's adding weight to it all this time. She feels sad for her mother and for her cousin, and for her aunt. And for herself. Cec was such a solid figure in her life, always caring but not intrusive. After her father died, he would check on her from time to time, letting her know he was there if she needed anything. She never called on him for help but knowing it was there took a burden away from her. It takes a burden away from anyone, to know that someone would answer their call in the middle of the night and come to their aid. Since they married, Tad has been that person for her. But now he's not. That's what she's been feeling these past few weeks. And it's upsetting her more than she can let on because he would be aghast to know she feels that way – except she can't help it. It's not that she doesn't trust him so much as she can't rely on him the way she used to. Or are those things the same?

She checks her watch again.

'*Tad* – it's been forty-five minutes. That Chinese restaurant is five minutes down the road and we called in that order before they left. Something's wrong.'

'We don't know that.' He has that unbothered look on his face that she used to find reassuring and now finds irritating.

'Exactly – that's why I'm worried.'

Blue and red lights flash through the kitchen window, which looks over the driveway, and Alison rushes to the front door and flings it open in time to see Erik, Sean and Rosie getting out of a police car. Sean and Rosie look distraught but unharmed. Erik looks like he doesn't have a care in the world.

It doesn't matter that they're unharmed, though: this is the moment that she has dreaded because something has clearly happened, something that required police, and her children have been affected by it. She's not upset, though – she's angry.

'*What?*' is all she has time to yell before she runs to her children. Rosie falls into her arms and starts crying, while Sean drops his head, his fringe falling across his face, and she knows it will mean he doesn't want anyone seeing what he's really feeling.

'What happened?' she says to the stocky male police officer who has emerged from the driver's side.

'Mrs Bosko?' The look on his face is one of slight disappointment, like she's let this happen. Which she has. By letting her husband dictate what their children should do. Never again. *Never again!*

'Yes. These are my children, Sean and Rosie.'

'Not, ah . . .' He points to Erik, who is chewing a thumbnail and gazing around.

'No.'

'He won't give us his name.'

'Erik Bosko.' She glares in her stepson's direction but he's not looking at her. Or at Tadeusz, who is standing with his arms crossed near the front door. Coward. Coward! Not approaching to find out what went wrong. In that moment she loses so much respect for him that it makes her gasp.

'Righto. What relation is he to you?'

'Stepson.' She nods over her shoulder. 'That's his father.' Not *that's my husband*. That's not the relationship she wants to claim right now.

'Mrs Bosko, was Erik meant to be driving your children somewhere?'

'To get takeaway.'

'Righto.' He nods, as if this explains everything. 'They had an accident.'

Her chest feels tight, even though she can see the children are uninjured.

'What happened?'

'Travelling at speed, ran into a parked car.' The officer seems bored, as if he's seen it all before. Which he would have. Then something occurs to her.

'They were in my car,' she says softly. Tad suggested Erik take her car because it's an automatic and his is a manual and Erik isn't as familiar with manuals. Nor is Alison.

'Is he insured to drive your car, Mrs Bosko?'

Now the tightness in her chest gives way to a plummeting of her stomach, because she understands what this means: the damage will not be covered by the insurance company.

'No,' she says meekly.

'Righto.'

Tad makes a noise behind her and she turns to see him pointing a finger at Erik.

'Why were you speeding with the children in the car? Or at all?' he barks at his eldest son.

Erik shrugs. 'The kids loved it.'

Rosie looks up at Alison and shakes her head. Rosie had been reluctant to go on the drive given how much she does not like Erik, but her father insisted that she needed to 'give him a chance'. This is what Erik did with that chance.

Alison's eyes meet Sean's and her son also shakes his head. It's not the time to challenge Erik, though, and it's not her job: it's Tad's.

'Where's the car?' she asks the policeman.

'In situ. If I could come into the house, I'll give you some details.'

She nods weakly then turns, Rosie still in her arms, and leads the way, brushing past Tad, who is now pulling Erik by the arm around to the front of the house. Maybe the police will charge him with something. Maybe he'll go to gaol – that would solve her problem. How terrible, to think that. But it's true.

It isn't until she's shown the police officer to the sitting room and the children to the kitchen that she realises something else: without her car, she can't take Frances to the funeral. Apart from the fact that Tad needs his for work, she is not at all confident with manual gears. Certainly not enough to get out of the peninsula, through Melbourne and all the way to the High Country.

That's the point at which she feels like she may actually crack. Not just her children but her mother harmed by this reckless, thoughtless thug who is not only in her family but in her house, and there is nothing she can do to change the situation.

Screaming would be the best thing to do right now, she thinks. Screaming for what a mess her life has become, and all of it beyond her control.

Instead she kisses the tops of her children's heads and goes in to talk to the police officer.

CHAPTER FORTY

Joan could almost forget she has a car with her at the Duchess Hotel. It's not like she needs it regularly. The only time she uses it is to obtain more art supplies – and she'll have to increase the frequency of that particular outing given that Kirrily decided to bring along a friend. Or acquaintance. Kirrily and Wendy don't seem to know each other well, if at all, which has baffled Joan, since Kirrily presumed to bring the woman to what was essentially a private class. Then Wendy revealed her talent for art and kept herself entertained for an hour – more, actually, since she returned after Kirrily started her shift – and Joan realised she wouldn't have to teach her so much as guide her to new subjects. Quite the revelation, really, and a reminder for Joan that she shouldn't judge people by their demeanour.

Of course, she does judge people by their demeanour. Everyone does. This is the reason why demeanour and its elements – grooming, behaviour, presence or lack of manners – are important. Certainly, she thinks they are important. Perhaps that makes her judgemental.

The people she is used to mingling with – her friends in Sydney, Isaac's work and social circles – have demeanours she has been comfortable with. Except she is starting to suspect that she was just telling herself a story about that. Those people superficially ticked the sorts of boxes that are meant to be ticked for a woman in her social position. That did not, in the end, make them her friends because as it turned out she found it easy to leave them behind. All except Genevieve. She misses Genevieve and that's why she still feels betrayed by her revelation to Isaac that Joan was in a grand hotel on the peninsula.

He's called every few days since he left. No further contact from Corinne but, then again, she always preferred to let the men of the family do the dirty work. When her then-fiancé, now-husband, revealed to her that he was still seeing the girlfriend he supposedly dropped before going out with her, Corinne sent her brother to deal with it. The girlfriend was then dropped. Apparently. Joan was never sure. What she was sure of was that Corinne should drop *him*. Instead, Joan was treated to the 'but I love him, Mummy' line over and over until she gave up talking about it. Which is not, of course, the same as giving up thinking about it. Her son-in-law is untrustworthy, and she hates that he is the father of her grandchild. These are thoughts she tucked away while she was in Sydney but which she can now indulge in freely and she enjoys that. While she's painting, she will dream up scenarios in which she rights wrongs and takes revenge for all sorts of things. It's delicious. And tells her that she has spent far too many years policing not only her person and her life and her interests but her thoughts. The only things that are freely hers.

No more. Each time she catches herself judging someone like Wendy, for example, she is going to ask herself if this is what she really thinks or what she is thinking out of habit.

She even realised she was caught in this trap with Frances. When they first met, Joan thought Frances was sweet but that her world was small, because she lived on this peninsula and didn't seem to go anywhere other than the Duchess Hotel. The longer she knows Frances, however, the more she realises she was wrong. Frances has had a rich life, with various strands to it, and she's about to discover other parts of her life because she's driving Frances to her brother's funeral, several hours away.

Joan offered to do this; it's not something, she suspected, Frances would ever ask her to do. They went for a perambulation around the grounds yesterday and Frances waited for a good half-hour before she mentioned that her last remaining brother had died and that she wanted to go to the funeral but neither of her children were able to take her. Frances's daughter couldn't take her because her car had been in an accident and now Alison couldn't come to the funeral at all anyway because she had to sort out a few things. Joan didn't ask for more detail, because it wasn't her business and also because Frances was upset about it, she could tell. And her son . . . well, it sounds like he just refused.

While Joan may not talk to her parents all the time – and they've had their differences, as all parents and children do – she would never, ever say she couldn't take them to a funeral. So she did for Frances what she would do for them and organised to pick her up at home and drive her three hours to the church in Violet Town, where the funeral will be held. Frances had told her that the funeral would be in Violet Town not because it was close to the family home but because that's where her maternal grandmother was from and four generations are buried there.

At least Joan's car would have a good run; that should keep the battery happy, if nothing else.

On the way to Violet Town they talked about Cecil and the childhood he and Frances shared, only a year apart. Their elder brothers were four and five years older than Frances so she never felt as close to them. Cec was, she said, almost like her twin.

Joan observed the changing landscape as they travelled, how dense the trees became as they moved away from Melbourne and its outer limits. The greens were so rich that she wished she had time to take out her paints; instead she would try to remember what she was seeing.

The service is short and lighter in tone than Joan expected.

'He had a good life,' Frances says as it finishes, but as they leave the church, Joan can tell she is unsettled.

'Darl, come back to the house,' says Margie, who had welcomed them both to the church with more warmth than Joan thinks she could have mustered in the circumstances.

'Oh, well, we have a drive.' Frances glances at Joan.

'It's fine,' says Joan, smiling encouragingly. 'I don't mind when we head home.'

Frances nods so slowly that Joan thinks she may have put her foot in it and that Frances may not really want to go to the house.

'We'll see you there,' Joan says, taking Frances's arm.

Margie has already moved towards someone else – that exhausting ballet of the bereaved, having to turn to everyone who turns up for you – so Joan steers Frances away.

'If you don't want to go, I understand,' Joan says quietly.

'I do,' Frances says. 'But . . .' Her eyes drift towards the small graveyard next to the church.

Joan waits. Frances doesn't need prompting from her.

'Albert is in there,' Frances says eventually. 'His headstone is.'

'Is he one of your brothers?' Joan can't remember Frances mentioning the name but she may have just not paid attention at the time. On occasion her brain gets occupied with absorbing visual material – she notices shapes and colours around her – and she can simply not hear words or sounds or music.

'No,' Frances says, then she steps ahead of Joan, who drops her hold and follows.

She comes to a stop in front of a headstone and Joan reads the words inscribed on it:

Albert Jennings
18 May 1923 – 25 April 1942
Always loved and never forgotten

'He died on Anzac Day,' Joan remarks.

'Fitting,' Frances says then sniffs.

Joan looks at the date again. 'The war?'

A slow nod confirms her guess.

'Who was he?'

Frances fidgets, her hands wringing the handkerchief they hold. 'My son's father,' she says softly. 'This is all there is. His body never came home.'

It is not often, Joan thinks, that we stand witness to the whole span of another person's pain. We see glimpses: a memory recounted, a flash of an incident, a tale recounted. Fragments. Shards. Usually something is held back; whether it's to preserve the person listening or the person telling, who can say.

In Frances's face, in her body, in the tone of her voice, Joan sees it all. Understands it, too. Frances the mother of a fatherless son, on her own. Frances trying to make a life and finding her husband, then having her daughter – Joan has heard stories about Gerald and Alison, so she knows that much.

She now knows too that there is a name for the shadow she has always believed Frances carries, the shade of grey – in her mind – that she detected the first time she met her. It is a particular form of grief.

'You still love him,' she states.

Frances turns to look at her, her eyes bottomless, her pain visible. 'Always,' she says.

In that moment, Joan knows why Frances comes to the Duchess Hotel so often. Why she connects to strangers. Why Frances has been so willing to form attachments to her, to Shane, to Kirrily. To anyone who seems ripe for one. Her grief is a well that can never be filled but she keeps trying. Every day, she tries. She shows love to people she barely knows and, whether she is conscious of it or not, she hopes that love will be given back to her. Even if she must know by now that it will never be enough. It will never replace what is lost.

The fact that she keeps trying, though: that may be the most extraordinary thing Joan has ever witnessed.

'What a miraculous thing,' she says, 'to love so much.'

Tears form in Frances's eyes and start to roll down her cheeks. She takes Joan's hand and squeezes it.

'That's good of you to say,' she whispers.

'It's the truth.' Joan squeezes back.

'I don't know where he is.' She sniffs again even as tears keep falling. 'That was the most confusing thing. After he died, I just didn't know where to find him.'

Joan senses that Frances is not talking about Albert's body. 'Don't you think,' she says, 'that you shouldn't look for him outside of your own heart? Isn't that where he is?'

Frances's chin trembles. 'I've never thought of it like that.'

'There's a lot we don't know, Frances. Death, life, how beauty is created, where love goes, how it starts, how it stops.' Joan looks around the little graveyard, at the evidence of people whose relatives loved them enough to mark their deaths with plots and headstones. 'I guess that's why we talk about God. So we can give it a name.'

'I stopped believing in God a long time ago,' Frances murmurs.

'And I understand why. If I were a different sort of person I might be tempted to see God's hand in bringing me here today, to be with you.' She shrugs. 'I don't believe that, but something brought me to the Duchess, and us to each other, and I wouldn't change it for anything.' She smiles and squeezes Frances's hand again.

'Let's go to the house,' Joan says. 'I think there will be people there who love you.'

Frances lets go of her then pats her cheek. 'You're a good girl,' she says.

That term always used to make Joan bristle when it was used by her parents, her teachers, her husband. Today it feels like the most welcome praise.

'Thank you,' she says, then she takes hold of Frances's arm once more and guides her to the car.

CHAPTER FORTY-ONE

Saturday night and the Duchess Hotel is the busiest Kirrily has ever seen it. Now that the weather is warmer on the Mornington Peninsula people are having weddings and parties and the Duchess, with its extensive grounds, its dining room and function spaces, is a popular location. Also popular because wedding and party guests can stay here. William told her the other day that sometimes the hotel is almost entirely booked out for a wedding.

The bride and groom must be well organised to pull that off, Kirrily thinks. She and Connor had a little church wedding and a picnic in a park for their reception. It was all they wanted and until recently she hasn't regretted not making a bigger splash. Unless she's been telling herself that, because now that she sees what other people do, she wishes she'd tried harder with her own wedding. Of course, if she didn't know about the Duchess weddings, she probably wouldn't be revising her opinion of her own. But she does know about them and she can't change that. It's a conundrum that keeps her up at night. Not that specific wedding conundrum but the one caused by her working at the Duchess and seeing and meeting so many different people. Being exposed to so many different stories. Her life was so unworldly before this. In her mind she was cosmopolitan because she read *Vogue* occasionally and went to see foreign films. Now she knows that was merely dipping her toe into a whole ocean of sophistication. The people she meets at the Duchess have these big, interesting lives and she has no idea how to get one, although she wants to try to work it out.

The guest she's going to now, in room 227, probably has one of those lives. They called reception and asked for two more towels, so she's taking the stairs – always the stairs if she can, never the lift, because she's always felt a little claustrophobic in lifts – and walking the hallway with its one floorboard that always creaks.

A strong knock on the door and when it opens she lets out a noise, because standing in front of her is Derek, looking not at all surprised to see her.

'Hello, Kirrily,' he says, smiling in that movie-star way of his, standing back to let her walk in.

Walking into his room is something she has thought about. Maybe even fantasised about, because she's wondered what it would be like to be in his room, with him, with no one else walking past, no one whose presence she need worry about.

'H-hello.' She tries to swallow her nerves but they stick in her throat and she laughs nervously.

He shuts the door behind her then holds out his hands. 'Thank you for the towels.'

She gives them to him. Swallows again, her hands fidgeting with her uniform.

'It's good to see you again,' he says as he puts the towels on the bed.

The bed. The bed he sleeps in. She might have fantasised about that too, not that it's anything she'd admit to *anyone*. Even herself.

'You, ah, have more business in the area?'

Now her hands are twisting the material and it's because she really doesn't know what she's meant to do: he's a guest who invited her in, so that's okay, but her work is done now so she should leave. Except he's not trying to usher her out the door. She has other work to do, though. People will be wondering where she is. Won't they?

'I do.'

Does she imagine that he steps a little closer to her? Or is it that she wants him to?

'I, ah . . .' She swallows again and attempts a smile. 'I don't actually know what your business is.'

'Real estate.'

He definitely steps closer this time. Close enough for her to see his irises properly, to marvel at how blue they are. Close enough for him to lift his hand and tuck a strand of her hair behind her ear. She likes to keep her hair tied tightly back; she has no idea how that strand escaped.

'Oh,' she says. 'So you, um, you're looking at properties around here?'

Her hands are shaking, and she can't tell if it's because she does or does not want anything more to happen with him.

'I have clients here who wish to sell, so I come down to look at their properties.'

Now he's tucking hair behind her other ear, except she doesn't think there's a strand loose. She thinks he's doing it just to be closer to her.

Her heart is beating so fast she gasps; he doesn't seem to notice.

'You're so beautiful,' he murmurs, standing right in front of her, his body square to hers, taller than her so she is looking up, noticing faint lines on his forehead, the perfect shape of his nose, his lips, the strength of his chin.

Maybe she examined Connor's face like this, once upon a time; she can't remember. She also can't remember him ever looking as closely at her as Derek is doing. She's never before thought that her and Connor being together just *happened* but it feels like that now: they met, they spent time with each other, she liked it, she liked him, he proposed, and his proposal made her feel wanted and safe. Once she felt wanted and safe, she was in for the duration. She just didn't know that a man could make her feel the way Derek is doing right now. So *seen*. So appreciated.

Kirrily knows that women should want to be valued for more than their looks – should want other people to recognise them for being smart and strong and wise and brave – but every now and again what she really wants to hear is that she's pretty. That she looks nice. Because it's a compliment, and compliments make the days – the endless days of work and housework and responsibilities and lists – lighter.

'Beautiful' was never her aspiration, yet here is Derek saying it to her. And if he wanted to provoke a response in her, he's getting one.

'Thank you,' she whispers.

Derek puts his hands on her shoulders, and she wonders if it's to stop her shaking.

'Are you nervous?'

She nods.

'Because I'm a guest?'

'I . . . No.'

His thumb strokes her cheek and his skin is so warm, and his touch so reassuring, that she closes her eyes.

His lips are on her other cheek and she sighs.

'So beautiful,' he murmurs near her ear and she leans against him.

As his lips find hers it's the least surprising thing to happen to her today.

His hands are cupped around her chin and her hands find his back as their kiss deepens. Kirrily feels like she's falling into a vortex, and she is conscious of not being conscious of anything but this kiss.

When Connor kissed her the first time, it was nice. Over time they learnt what each other liked and kissing became fun. But they haven't kissed in a long time. And he has never kissed her like this. Like he desires her more than anything or anyone else.

She pulls Derek closer into her and he wraps his arms around her. A movie-star kiss to match his movie-star handsomeness.

Then she feels it: guilt. Guilt and remorse. Shame. This man is not her husband. This is not something she should ever be doing.

She steps back.

'Sorry,' she says, her hands falling by her sides.

'I'm not,' he says, looking slightly amused. 'You seemed to be enjoying it as much as I was.'

Does Derek know she's married? Surely he's seen the ring on her finger? She never wears her engagement ring to work but her wedding ring doesn't comes off. How laughable that seems now. But she can't use that as the excuse for why she stopped, because it should have been a reason why she didn't start.

'I, ah . . . You're a guest. I shouldn't have done it.'

'I won't say anything. If that's what you're worried about.'

'No, I'm not. Just, ah . . . I have to go.'

She hurries past him and he grabs her wrist with a light touch.

'Kirrily, I wasn't just saying that so you would kiss me. I think about you . . . a great deal.'

These are the words she longed to hear – that he would think about her as much as she thinks about him. Not that she will say that. Not that she will ask what he intends with her. She has to get out of here and tell herself that she won't ever do this again.

'Thank you,' she says softly, then pulls her hand from his and opens the door, not looking back as she almost sprints down the hallway to the staircase.

CHAPTER FORTY-TWO

As the days lengthen and the southern hemisphere moves through spring towards the golden light of summer, Frances appreciates the opportunity to still be here, on this planet. Cec's death rattled her, which is to be expected, but it also made her realise that she may not have many days left of her own. Sure, once she's dead she won't know what she's missing. Or she thinks she won't.

She's not convinced that a person just stops once their body dies. After her father died, she believed he visited her. By then she was living far from the High Country, with sea breeze on the air rather than alpine chill, and he died at home, in his sleep. A civilised way to go, just like Cec. For several days in a row, she would wake up to find her alarm clock had stopped at the exact same time: just after three. No one knew the time her father died but she liked to think it was just after three, and that he was telling her that he wasn't quite done. He was on his way out but he was saying goodbye to her a few last times.

She mentioned that to Cec once, how she thought their father didn't just slip away without them noticing.

'Oh yeah,' he said, like it was the most normal thing in the world. 'He keeps putting his boots by the back door.'

Cec was living in the house they grew up in, their family having made the decision that he would run the property, and their parents had moved to a smaller building on the premises. The boots, Cec told her, were showing up by the back door of the original house, not the door of the house their father died in. It was a mystery, he said, then winked. 'But it's not, really,' he said. 'Dad wants me to know he's still in charge.'

It was reassuring to learn that her logical brother believed in whatever magic happened between this world and the next; still more reassuring that she wasn't losing control of her faculties, which she'd thought she might be.

Their father's death, however, was not the one that really got her to thinking; her two oldest brothers' deaths didn't do that either. But Cec, well, he was only a year older than her. Close enough to spook her. So she's making herself take in each day, soaking up the sights and sounds and smells, because she may need to take them with her, wherever she goes.

That's made her pay more attention around the Duchess Hotel, too. She's always loved its gardens and now that Joan is creating opportunities for her to stop and observe them more closely, she's relishing them.

Actually, they probably go hand in hand: learning from Joan and paying closer attention to the world around her, with extra motivation provided by the fact that she's now more aware of her mortality than ever.

So she arrives a little early for Joan on this Friday afternoon, and takes a seat next to the cactus garden. She has no idea why the Duchess has a cactus garden but according to the old photos in the hotel's library it's been here for a while. The plants even look the same, although is it possible that a cactus can survive for decades? She'd like to think so. After all, she can be a little spiky herself and she's still here.

'I knew it was you,' says a man's voice over her right shoulder and she knows it's Shane's. 'I'd recognise that blue rinse anywhere.'

'Get away with you, you cheeky boy,' she says, swatting away the hand he's put on her shoulder. She's never had a blue rinse, although she did think about it once upon a time.

He pats her cheek and moves in front of her.

'Taking in the view?' he asks, nodding at the cacti.

'Waiting for Joan. Art class.'

He nods. 'I know.' His smile is uncertain. 'I thought . . . I'm going to ask if I can join you.'

'Don't you have to work?'

'William said he'd get someone to cover me for an hour. Thought that painting might be good for my morale or something.' He makes a face. 'I must be bringing the mood down.'

'He knows you suffer sometimes,' Frances says with a sympathetic tone. 'It's good he acknowledges it.'

'I guess.'

Shane looks behind her, towards the hotel. 'Joan's on her way. I'll go and help her with the equipment.'

'Oh yes?'

Shane frowns. 'What does that mean?'

'What sort of equipment do you want to help her with?' Now that Shane has turned up for class, Frances is even more convinced he's sweet on Joan.

His cheeks go red, then he laughs. 'Now who's being cheeky?'

'Never me.'

She looks over her shoulder and watches him walk towards Joan, who is struggling with all the gear. Frances knows that Wendy and Kirrily will be coming today – Wendy bailed her up in the bar yesterday, a little more sober than usual, and acclaimed her prowess with a paintbrush and how Joan said she was a natural.

'Which I *knew*,' she said, a little too close to Frances's face for her liking.

It is Wendy she can see now emerging from the hotel entrance, but who knows where Kirrily is. Hopefully not sneaking around with that guest. The one Shane told her about, only because he was worried about Kirrily and wanted Frances's advice.

Not that Frances will say anything to Kirrily. Actually, she will say something if she thinks Kirrily is about to do anything really stupid. It's hard to judge that, though, when you're only going off one person's report. Perhaps she should ask Shane to keep an eye on it for her. Or perhaps that is poking her nose in where it doesn't belong.

As Joan and Shane draw near it's clear that Joan is not pleased about something. Probably about Shane joining their little group. She has enough trouble keeping up supplies as it is, she told Frances the other day, not from an expense point of view – the source of Joan's funds is still a mystery to Frances and she'd love to know what it is – but logistics. How is she meant to have enough paper, pencils and so on if she doesn't know who's turning up each week? What if Wendy starts inviting people willy-nilly? It could get a little out of control.

Out of control. There's a thought. Wendy is convinced she has a romantic future with Shane, of which Shane is unaware, but now he's going to be here with her, making art . . . Wendy may take it as a sign that they are destined for each other. And Frances has no inclination to warn him because she's quite interested to see what happens.

'Frances,' Joan says through pursed lips.

'Joan. Good to see you have a helper now.'

'Mm.' Joan practically dumps her easel on the ground and throws her large canvas bag onto the seat.

Shane raises his eyebrows in Frances's direction, looking a little abashed.

'Did you invite him?' Joan demands.

'No. He invited himself.'

Joan looks furious for a second then composes herself. 'I'm not an art teacher,' she says to the air. 'I'm a painter.'

Now she turns to Shane. 'I can't teach you. In fact, I firmly believe no one can be taught how to do anything creative.'

He sighs. 'I didn't mean to –'

'I can teach technique, *sure*.' Now it's Joan's turn to sigh. 'But . . .' She throws her hands in the air.

'I'll leave,' Shane says, gently placing the easel he's been holding against the seat.

'No,' Joan says sharply. 'You're here now. I just . . .' More sighing, bordering on huffing. 'It's a surprise. That's all. I need to figure out how to do this. As I said – not a teacher. Up until this point I thought I was just showing Kirrily and Frances how to do a handful of interesting things.'

Shane frowns. 'That sounds like one definition of teaching.'

Joan glares at him.

He raises his hands in surrender. 'I'm being sincere,' he says.

Now Wendy is upon them and Kirrily is approaching from the side of the hotel.

'G'day,' Wendy says, chewing gum.

'Don't put that gum near my paints,' Joan warns.

'It's Nicorettes.' Wendy keeps chewing. 'Thought I'd give up smoking.'

'Again?' Frances asks.

'Yeah.'

Wendy smiles at Joan. 'So – cactus today?'

Joan nods.

'Great. Love 'em.' From the large bag over her shoulder, Wendy extracts a drawing pad. 'Brought my own stuff. Let's get going, eh?'

Shane puts his hands in his pockets.

'Oh, all right,' Joan says. She points to her own bag. 'Take some paper and pencils out of there and I'll show you what to do.'

'Hi, gang,' Kirrily says as she arrives. 'Shane?'

'Yep,' he says.

She shrugs. 'Cool.'

Without another word, Kirrily gathers her equipment and doesn't even ask Joan for a task.

'Frances, why don't you sit with me,' Joan says quietly after she's set up Shane in a position and told him what to do.

'Love to,' Frances says. 'In fact, I'd be happy to just sit and do nothing.'

'And not draw? I don't think so.' Joan looks just like a strict school teacher and Frances laughs, which earns her a bemused expression from her friend.

'You can't fool me, Joanie – you're not that tough.'

'Don't tell the others,' Joan says under her breath. 'I have to keep them in line.'

Frances glances across to Shane, who seems to be observing them out of the corner of his eye.

'I'm sure Shane would be happy for you to keep him in line,' she says, perhaps indiscreetly, but also because she quite likes the idea of Shane and Joan becoming closer.

However, Joan frowns. 'What do you mean?'

'Nothing,' Frances says quickly, then picks up a pencil. 'Now, what am I doing?'

Joan gives her instructions and Frances nods, then spends the next almost-hour trying to follow them. Mostly she lets her mind wander, thinking about Cec, about Margie, about the generation she's part of disappearing. It doesn't make her sad so much as mystified, how humans come and go from this planet in waves, as it's always been, yes, but that doesn't make it any less strange. One day she won't be here. One day none of them will be. But these trees around them will go on, and so will the ocean, and so will the sky, and in the steadiness of all of that she finds some reassurance. Perhaps that's why Joan is always asking them to draw the natural world: because it's all that lasts. That's a good enough reason for Frances.

CHAPTER FORTY-THREE

Sean and Rosie have taken to disappearing on Sundays and Alison hasn't been able to stop them. They're colluding in it, obviously making plans to take off and not tell their parents where they're going. After they've had their breakfast they head for their rooms, then the next thing Alison knows they're gone. They come back hours later and won't answer questions about it.

At fourteen, Sean is old enough to roam but because Rosie is only twelve, and a girl, Alison is increasingly upset about her disappearing. She knows Sean would be looking after her – he's a considerate, caring boy – and she also knows that she shouldn't try to restrict Rosie's movements because she's a girl, but the fact remains: *she is a girl*. Girls in this world have so much to worry about. Sure, she would rail against her own mother for trying to tie her down, probably because Frances used to say Alison was 'too precious' to be running around. To Alison's ears that sounded condescending, like she was too delicate, not hardy enough, and in light of Frances's stories about how she used to do all the same things as her brothers, Alison took it as criticism. Now she wonders if she didn't completely misread it – and her mother. If she had just taken it at face value, she might not have thought that Frances didn't care about her. Because when she thinks that Rosie is too precious to be out all day without supervision it's because she means it: her daughter is too precious *to her*.

The reason for the disappearances is clear: Erik. He hangs around the house on the weekends, doing who-knows-what because he doesn't read or do anything resembling an activity. His hobby is picking fights with Tad, who instead of walking away from them tends to engage with his eldest son and prolong the arguments.

The fights have made Alison want to leave home as well, so she can't blame her children. Instead, she sits in her own misery about how much her family has changed in such a short space of time, and confusion because it seems to her that the family was not as solid as she believed if their unit could be so easily upset. Surely it can't be that one person is so destructive.

Except the evidence is in her quiet house. No sounds of Sean watching television or whatever Britney Spears tune Rosie is passionate about at the moment. Alison is dubious about the lyrics of 'Baby One More Time' but she knows if she tries to stop Rosie listening to it, that will just make the song even more appealing.

Instead her mother is here, sitting at the kitchen table, glaring at Erik, who is leaning against the bench waiting for the kettle to boil.

Frances insisted on coming over today, so Alison went and picked her up in her newly repaired car. Colin is here too. For some reason Frances wanted to bring the dog and now Alison is glad, because he's a pleasant distraction from the heaviness of tension in the house. So maybe that was the reason. Maybe Frances, with her long life experience, knew that a dog could be an antidote.

'What do you think you're doing?' Frances says sharply and Alison jumps, thinking the remark is directed at her. But then she sees that Frances is still glaring at Erik.

'What?' he says, with a disdainful look on his face.

'In this house.' Frances inhales noisily. 'With my daughter and my grandchildren. *Your behaviour*, Erik. *What do you think you're doing?*'

'None of your business.' He turns his back to her and picks up the boiled kettle.

'It *is* my business. This is my family.'

'Yeah, well, I'm not in *your* family.' His back is still turned but Alison thinks she can hear him snicker.

'You're Alison's stepson, so that means you are. No matter how much I may wish it otherwise.'

'Mum!' Alison gasps as Erik's head whips around.

'Stupid old bag,' he mutters.

'Stupid old bag who can see right through you.' Frances is still glaring.

Tad enters the room and looks from his son to his mother-in-law.

'What is going on?' he says, his eyes meeting Alison's.

'My mother was expressing an opinion,' Alison says, emboldened by this increasingly feisty version of Frances. She's seen her mother stroppy before but this is something else – Frances looks as though she could take up arms.

'More like stating a fact.' Frances now turns her glare to Tad. 'What are you going to do about this, Tad?'

'About what?'

He blinks, as if he's confused, but how can he be? It's not as if Alison hasn't told him repeatedly that something has to change. It shouldn't require her mother to be the catalyst.

'This house is in disarray.' Frances turns towards Alison, who is taken aback to see something she hasn't before: softness. Directed at her. It makes her feel as though her mother is in league with her, which is also not something she's familiar with.

'My daughter is distressed,' Frances continues. 'And it's your fault, Tadeusz.'

Tad's mouth hangs open, then he closes it and frowns. 'We're adjusting,' he says.

'No. My daughter should not have to *adjust* to you at this stage of your marriage. Adjustment happens in the first year. Maybe two. If it's still going by the third year, you need to divorce. You are well past the third year.'

'I can't turf my son out on the street.'

'Right.' Frances looks at Alison again. 'And where *is* Sean?'

'That's not what I –'

'I know it's not. But think about this: you do not want to turf *Erik* out on the street while *Sean* is roaming the streets with *Rosie* in tow, and there's nothing you have done to stop that either.'

'They sneak out!'

'They're *children*! It is your job, as their father, to ensure that they never want to sneak out of their own home.'

Alison feels an unfamiliar mix of fear and excitement as she observes her mother in full flight. Never before has she seen Frances so worked up about anything, although part of her wishes she could have been this agitated about Keith from time to time. Perhaps this is a version of a speech she's always wanted to give him.

'And what do you have to say for yourself, Erik, apart from attempting to insult an old woman?' Frances's focus is back on Tad's eldest son, who has been dunking a teabag in his mug for longer than strictly necessary.

'Nothing.' More dunking, his eyes on the mug.

'That's pathetic.' Frances says it lightly, as if it's a joke.

'Rack off.' Erik replies.

'Erik!' Tad sounds shaken more than upset.

'Why don't *you*, hmm?'

'Frances, that's inappropriate!' Now Tad sounds agitated. 'He's my son!'

'What's inappropriate is you letting your guilt for past behaviour affect the family you have built here, with Alison.' Frances reaches across and, to Alison's surprise, takes her hand. 'My girl is hurting. I have been watching it for weeks now and saying nothing. But I'm saying something now.'

She squeezes once and lets go.

'To be clear, Tad, it's not entirely the boy's fault.' She nods at Erik. 'He hasn't had much of a role model. That's *your* fault. But think about what you're showing Sean and Rosie now. What they see is a grown man behaving like a spoilt child and getting away with it. Where does this end?'

Erik and Tad glance at each other then look away.

'My house is too small for the kids and Alison,' Frances says quietly yet firmly. 'But if you push me, Tad, they can move there and I'll move in here, and then you'll really know you're alive.'

Alison can't help the yelp she makes as she considers what it would be like to have Frances running this house.

Frances pushes herself to standing.

'Alison, let's go. I think we'll have morning tea at the Duchess, don't you? Maybe we'll find the kids en route. And they can take Colin for a walk.'

Never did Alison think she would want her mother to chastise her husband – mainly because Tad has never needed to be chastised – but she's oddly thrilled by it now. So this is what it's like to have your mother stand up for you. She could get used to it.

'Sort it out, Tad,' Frances says as a parting riposte before she puts her handbag in the crook of her arm and toddles out the front door and towards the car.

'I'll be back in a while,' Alison says to Tad, because she has to say something, and she leaves the house still worried about everything but lighter too: she's not alone in this any more, and there is something freeing about that.

CHAPTER FORTY-FOUR

'I am not planning to come back, Genevieve.' Joan's throat feels tight, and she clasps the phone even tighter. This is the second call from her friend this week, after three last week, after none for several weeks. Joan thought that Genevieve had accepted her decision to stay at the Duchess Hotel indefinitely. Clearly not.

'Ever?'

'For the foreseeable future.'

There's silence. They've always had the sort of friendship in which there is constant conversation, even if it's frivolous. Joan supposes that she is the cause of this silence – her decisions, her actions. Although she likes to think that if Genevieve did something similar, she'd be understanding. More understanding than Genevieve is being.

'How's Adelaide?' Joan says to end the stalemate. Adelaide, Genevieve's daughter, used to be best friends with Corinne until Corinne's husband had a falling-out with Adelaide's boyfriend over something that seemed so trivial at the time that Joan can't even remember it. Maybe a round of golf? Or, just as likely, a business deal gone south. In the world she used to live in, the stakes for each were equally as high.

The world she used to live in: that's how she thinks of it now. Not the life she will return to one day.

This change has come upon her unconsciously and she realised it had happened when she referred to the Duchess Hotel as 'home' the other day in conversation with Frances.

Or perhaps she is kidding herself and she's really in limbo, and it's limbo that is home. Maybe the next phase of her life is somewhere, something, she can't yet identify. It may even be in Sydney, but it won't be the life she had.

She supposes that her money will run out eventually – she hasn't checked to see how much is left – and Isaac will divorce her. Divorce feels like an inevitability but also not, because he keeps calling her too.

'She's fine,' Genevieve says tightly. 'Busy. The shop is going well.' Adelaide has a boutique in Double Bay with expensive clothes and even more expensive customers.

'That's wonderful,' Joan says warmly.

'And Corinne?'

'She seems to be fine.'

'You haven't spoken to her?' Genevieve sounds accusatory.

'She wrote a letter. Mainly telling me what I need to do rather than what she's doing.'

More silence. Genevieve clears her throat. 'I would think she misses you,' she says.

'And I miss her. But, Gen, as I've told you, I missed myself more. That sounds selfish, I know –'

'It's not. Joan, really it's not.' Silence for a second, two, three. 'Look, there are *plenty* of days when I think about taking off.'

That's an admission and a half. Usually Genevieve is the standard bearer for idyllic suburban life.

'So why don't you?' Joan asks.

'Because I have obligations.' It's said in a haughty tone that Joan doesn't appreciate.

'Right,' she says. 'And you think I've skipped out on mine.'

'You have!'

'What about my obligations to myself? Why am I – why are you – expected to sacrifice myself and what I want just to keep other people happy? Especially now, when my children are running their own lives?'

She imagines Genevieve is thinking about that, and it does bear thinking about. Joan, of course, has had plenty of time to think, and talk to Frances, in particular. They both watch Kirrily running herself ragged taking care of her family and doing her job and worrying about everything.

'People have been asking about you,' Genevieve says, obviously not willing to answer Joan's question.

'That's nice. I've had some letters. So clearly my current place of residence is not a secret.'

'Did you want it to be?' There's an edge to Genevieve's voice that Joan hasn't heard before.

'Well, I didn't take out an ad in *The Sydney Morning Herald*.' They both know that Genevieve was the only person to whom she told her location, although after Genevieve told Isaac clearly the information hadn't been contained.

'So it's my fault, is it?' Now the edge is a barb.

'No, I'd say it's Isaac's fault.'

'What's the poor man supposed to do, Joan? He's desperate.'

Joan feels her grip on the phone growing tighter still and suspects she is holding her breath too.

'I know how he feels,' she says softly.

Then she hangs up.

Then she sits down in the big armchair that is a feature of the room but which she often forsakes for the sofa. But the armchair is closer and its sturdiness is what she needs.

Never in her wildest dreams would she have imagined that Genevieve would give up on her.

Perhaps she and Isaac are having an affair? That would explain why she's so keen to take his side. Joan feels oddly unmoved by that prospect, although rationally she knows it's more likely that Isaac is badgering Genevieve and something had to give.

The phone rings and Joan jumps. Then she gets to her feet, picks up her room key and leaves the ringing behind, taking the stairs down to the foyer, which is moderately busy on this Wednesday afternoon, before walking into the bar, where Shane is polishing glasses.

'G'day,' he says. 'Usual?'

'Um . . .' Joan takes a seat in front of him, which she doesn't usually do, and he looks surprised accordingly.

'Maybe something stronger?' Shane suggests. 'Like a whiskey, no rocks?'

'Yes, please. Double.'

She watches him pouring it – really watches him, watches his hands. They are elegant. An artist's hands with long fingers. Not something she's noticed before, not even when he was sketching the other day. His hands didn't help him with his sketching, which was spirited but far from competent. Oh well – everyone has to start somewhere.

'Do you mind if I come back?' he's saying to her as he puts the drink in front of her and she wonders if she's missed anything.

'Hm?'

'For art. On Friday. Do you mind? I really liked it.'

'No, I don't mind.' She picks up the glass and takes too big a sip of a liquid that feels like fire in her throat. Before she has a chance to react, Shane puts a glass of water next to the whiskey and she drinks half of it.

'Not a regular whiskey drinker?' he says, smiling.

'No. But it seemed like the thing.'

He nods. 'That kind of day?'

'Yes.'

'You'll tell me if you want to.'

'Maybe.' She gives him a look that she hopes he can read: she doesn't want to talk about it.

He nods again. 'How about that Mondrian, hey? Any good?'

Joan laughs, surprised. And it makes her feel better, so she keeps laughing.

Another patron sits up at the bar and Shane moves away, but he keeps glancing in her direction and it makes her feel if not less alone, then more cared for than she did.

CHAPTER FORTY-FIVE

One of the parts of growing older that Frances does not appreciate is that professional people she has come to rely on – her doctors and dentist, specifically – retire and she has to find new ones. It would really be convenient if they could stay working until she dies, saving her the trouble of having to learn to trust someone whose competence can only be detected in the execution of his or her job, by which time she may have jammed something into Frances's gum or he may have misdiagnosed her headache and failed to find a brain tumour. Not that that's likely, but how can she be sure?

It's a good idea to rely on recommendations from others, of course, but she's not sure she wants her GP to be the same as Alison's. Yet here she is, in Alison's car being driven to an appointment with Alison's GP, squeezed in after Alison finished work for the day. All because Frances said something offhand about her glasses not doing the job any more as her eyesight seemed to be getting worse.

'How long have you known this Dr Chen?' she says as Alison drives her towards Mornington.

'Since, oh . . . before my first pregnancy. He's been great. Got me a good obstetrician. Knows all the right specialists. That's why I think he's right for you, Mum.'

'Because I need a lot of specialists?'

'Well . . .' Alison glances nervously in her direction. 'Maybe?'

'Because I'm old?'

'Well . . .'

Frances knows she's putting her daughter in a spot. Alison can hardly say, 'No, you're not!' because they'll both know she's lying.

'It's all right,' Frances says. 'I know I'm old.'

'Ageing gracefully!' Alison titters.

'I'd rather not,' Frances mutters.

There's silence for a few seconds.

'Age?' Alison says. 'Or age gracefully?'

'Both.' Frances wonders how frank she should be with her second child. A parent likes to protect their children from the realities of life – because they're not always pleasant – but that probably ends up doing both parties a disservice. Forewarned is forearmed, and all that.

'Age catches a person unawares,' Frances says, looking out the window at passing houses with their varied façades, some with neat gardens, some with no gardens, some with gardens that look like they used to be cared for. All the different places to live, to be; all the different lives a person can lead. So many combinations of how things can end up. Frances thinks about that a lot now that she has more time for thinking. She thinks about how her life would have been different if Albert hadn't gone to war. Or if he had and he'd returned and she hadn't had Keith by then so she and Albert would have started their life together properly. Or if she did have Keith and Albert returned to a son he had only known through letters.

A thousand and one directions her life could have gone in and possibly they would all have ended up with her sitting in a car with her daughter, being driven to see a doctor who is likely to tell her what she already suspects: she's going blind. Slowly but definitely. Which will really make it difficult for her to keep up with the art classes.

'I swear I was thirty years old yesterday,' she goes on. 'You're too young to understand that.'

'No, I do,' Alison says softly. 'And the graceful part?'

'Who needs it? Grace takes time and effort. It's easier to be outrageous.'

Frances smiles but as she's still looking out the window, Alison wouldn't have seen it.

'Do you ever . . .' Alison starts, then pauses.

'Yes?'

'Do you ever wished you'd lived a different life?'

Now she has Frances's attention.

'Do you?' Frances asks, because she suspects Alison's question has everything to do with Alison and nothing to do with her. And maybe a lot to do with what's happening in Alison's home life, which has not yet improved despite Frances's intervention, such as it was. Which irritates Frances, it really does. Tadeusz needs to take command of the Erik situation.

'Sometimes.' Alison grips the steering wheel tighter. 'Sometimes I wonder what I would have been like if I'd grown up where you did. You know – on the land. In the mountains.'

'You'd have been different,' Frances says. 'Just as I would have been different in a city. Our environments shape us, no doubt. Why have you been wondering about that?'

'Because, Mum –' Her voice catches. 'Because I want to understand you better.'

Frances sits with this information. Alison has not exhibited much curiosity about her to this point. Does she think, perhaps, that her mother is dying and that's why her eyesight is failing? That might make her sentimental. More sentimental. Alison will cry over cute cards about dogs and her children's baby photos. But she's never asked Frances much about her upbringing or wanted to know about her family beyond Charlotte, Margie and Cec. Once, sure, for a school project about family trees. And when Rosie's eyes turned out to be green and Alison wanted to know if there were green eyes amongst Frances's relatives.

'Don't take this the wrong way, Alison, but may I ask why?'

'Your brother died,' Alison says, sounding upset. 'I didn't go to the funeral even though I wanted to. I let what was going on at home wreck that. And I knew you would go without me but then you took that Joan and I . . .' Now she's definitely upset. 'Am I that easily replaced?'

There's a lot to untangle from what her daughter has said, so Frances thinks about it before she opens her mouth.

'She's not "that Joan",' is what she leads with. 'She's Joan. She's my friend.'

'You see her more than you see me!'

'You're busy. She's not. We have time to see each other. She had time to drive me to the mountains. You weren't able to. It's fine.'

It's said without emotion but Frances does feel a little agitated: who is Alison to tell her who to take to a funeral?

'I would have gone!'

'But you couldn't, love.'

'I know I couldn't! And you didn't even talk about Cec that much! It's Margie you talk to.'

Alison's practically panting and Frances can tell – because a mother knows her daughter, even if they're not as close as they could be – that she's worked herself up into a state about this well before they got in the car. There's something else going on here, and Frances is determined to find out what it is.

'I didn't talk about Cec much to you because, well . . .' She stops and thinks about her brother. About how she's going to explain this to Alison, who has always had a fractious relationship with Keith that is neither of their faults, really; rather, it's just the way life has worked out.

'Cec was as obvious to me as the air,' she goes on. 'We were always together. Sure, our lives went separate ways, as they do when you're adults. But he was always with me. I thought about him all the time and it felt like he was just next to me. So it never occurred to me to talk about him a lot. Or my other brothers.

They're still with me. That's why I may not seem so upset about Cec's death. He's with me, like he ever was.'

She sighs.

'Maybe that means I carry around a lot of spirits. Even when people are still alive, I carry them with me. You and your brother – Alison, I carry you too.'

And Albert. Except carrying him has felt harder and yet more inevitable than anyone else. Because with his spirit comes the thousand directions her life did not take and the one it did – the one without him. She can't imagine telling Alison about that, though, because to say it out loud to her would be to admit that she wanted a life in which she had never had to meet Alison's father, let alone marry him and have a child.

'Do you love me, Mum?' It's a whisper; Alison sounds like she's ten years old.

Frances looks at her daughter properly while Alison focuses on the road ahead. 'Of course I do. I always have. Always will. After I'm gone, you'll be the one carrying me around. Maybe you'll wish you weren't.'

'I won't mind.' It's another whisper. 'And I love you too. And I want you to know that if the doctor says your sight is going, I'll help you. You can move –'

'We're not discussing that,' Frances says sharply. She can't believe they've just had a nice moment and Alison is using it to start up again about moving her into a home. 'Not yet, anyway,' Frances adds, because she's a realist. 'I'm not rejecting your help, love. I'm just . . . not ready to be infirm.'

Alison sniffs and swallows and Frances sees that her cheeks are wet. 'Don't be upset,' she says. 'We'll figure things out.'

'Okay, Mum.'

Alison puts her blinker on and turns into a street Frances has never seen before, then starts looking for a parking spot.

CHAPTER FORTY-SIX

Maybe smoking is all she and Shane have in common, Kirrily thinks, as she leans against the cold stone of the Duchess Hotel, waiting for him to appear. She takes a drag, looking out to sea, ignoring the fact that the stone is not flat so there are little points of it digging into her back. Instead of lying on a bed of nails she is leaning on Duchess stone.

Each night since Derek kissed her, she has almost longed for a bed of nails to help her atone for what she knows was a mistake but which she can't get out of her mind.

Since Derek kissed her. That's not entirely correct. She kissed him back. She didn't just stand there and let him press his lips against hers, nor did she stop him. She kissed him back. She *enjoyed it.* She's been *thinking about it.*

That's not correct either: she's been fantasising about it more than thinking about it. In every spare moment she has her eyes closed and she remembers what that kiss was like. How his lips felt on hers. How she felt like she was melting inside and her skin had turned fluid. Whether that was because Derek was a very good kisser or she simply wanted him to kiss her so badly she can't tell.

This is why she needs to talk to Shane. To confess to Shane, because he has that air of being priestlike in his trustworthiness with a secret while earthy enough to tell her to pull her head in if that's what is required. And she is sure it is, but she hasn't been capable of doing it yet.

Partly it's because she saw Derek again after that kiss. The next evening, he passed her in the second-floor hallway and his hand brushed against hers right after he stared into her eyes and the look she saw there was something she could only describe as hungry.

Desire is not something she's used to. Wanting, yes. *Desire* – the feeling she has for him, the one he seems to have for her – is not part of her life. She wants a cigarette; she wants food; she wants comfort; she wants company; she wants some respect from her husband and affection from her children. She wants Aidan to live without pain and Bridget to have more fun, because being the sister of a little boy who needs regular medical attention is the opposite of fun.

But what she feels now – what has been in her veins and her nerves and her skin for several weeks – is different. It feels more irresistible than any of her wants, even the one for a cigarette. That's how she knows it's not an addiction; it's something else.

She's read novels where characters feel so strongly about each other that they will do anything to be together, including hurting other people, and she's never understood it. Now she does. Now she thinks about how long Connor will hate her if she leaves him for Derek.

Not that there is the option of that, because Derek has only kissed her and told her she's beautiful. That's not a promise of anything. She just wishes her body knew that.

'Contemplating the meaning of life again, are we?' Shane has appeared, who knows when, because Kirrily has been so lost in thought.

'Something like that.' She smiles weakly. Now that he's here she feels nervous about confessing.

'Or something more serious,' he states as he lights his cigarette and looks at the water. 'Rough out there. Guess I won't be swimming after work.'

'Do you ever?'

'No.' He grins. 'But I'm sure I will one day. Bring the togs and get down to the beach. Quick dip after my shift ends. You could join me.' He looks at her pointedly. 'Maybe it'd clear your head.'

She makes a noise that could sound like agreement if he wanted it to.

'So . . .' He drags on his cigarette, holds the smoke in his lungs for a couple of seconds then exhales. 'What *is* going on in that head?'

'Oh.' Connor once told her she'd never make a good poker player because her emotions were always written on her face. It seemed to be beside the point that Kirrily wasn't interested in playing poker. But she remembers it because clearly she isn't good at hiding what she's feeling; not to Shane, anyway. Maybe not to Connor either, although he's barely looked at her lately. It's funny how you can live with someone and not actually *see* them.

'Um,' she adds.

'Let me guess,' Shane says. 'A certain guest?'

'He kissed me,' she blurts, watching Shane's face for condemnation or anger or anything that will punish her the way she thinks she should be punished.

Shane nods slowly, smoking.

'A kiss,' he says. Then he glances around, presumably to check for witnesses, which *she* should have done before she confessed so quickly.

'How was it?' He says it innocently enough.

'Shane!'

'I'm not asking for technical details. I'm trying to understand why you look this upset. Was he aggressive?'

'No!'

'Right.' More nodding. 'So it was good?'

She presses herself into the wall and is rewarded with more points of stone sticking into her.

'Yes,' she whispers.

'Very good, I'm guessing.'

Their eyes meet and she hopes that he can see written on hers the memory of the kiss so she doesn't have to give him details.

'Right,' he says. 'Good enough that you're feeling bad about it.'

'Why would you say that?'

'If it was a bad kiss, you'd have forgotten about him already. You know – he wasn't the fancy boy you thought he was.'

'Fancy boy?' She almost laughs at the term.

'My mum used to say that about a couple of my friends. They were handsome. Liked the grooming. Good clothes. Fancied themselves with the ladies. So . . . fancy boy.'

'Right.'

'But this mate of yours *is* a fancy boy and your head is turned.'

She closes her eyes and presses harder against the stone. Maybe she'll draw blood; that would be fitting.

'What do I do?'

'What do you want to do?'

'That's not what I asked.'

'Kizza, what do you want me to say?'

She feels his hand on her wrist and realises he's standing next to her, then he's put an arm around her and is pulling her in for a hug. They've never hugged before. Never even got close enough. But it's just what she needs and she can't believe he detected that.

'Don't cry on my shirt,' he says as she sniffs. 'You've got mascara on and I don't want to have to explain it.'

She laughs and he pats the back of her head before letting her go.

'You've got yourself in a mess,' he says, and she likes the fact that the statement doesn't let her off the hook, because she doesn't deserve to be. Yes, she has got *herself* into this.

'I can't stop thinking about him,' she says.

'Must have been a *really* good kiss. Don't think my wife ever said that about me. I need to up my game.'

Kirrily frowns. She didn't think he was still married. 'Oh, so you're . . . ?'

'Not back together, no,' he says. 'Just not divorced yet. And that's how I know marriage is hard and sometimes we do things that aren't the best for it.'

He is standing in front of her, looking like he's about to take her shoulders and give her a shake.

'Do you want to stay married to Connor?' he asks.

'Yes.' It's her automatic answer but she knows her voice sounded weak.

'You don't seem too sure.'

'I do! I do. I'm not . . .' She shakes her head, trying to clear it, but it doesn't work. 'It's not like Derek asked me to marry him.'

'No,' Shane says flatly. 'And for all you know he's married anyway.'

This has occurred to her and she's dismissed it because she doesn't want to think about what it means – that he would kiss her despite it. It's bad enough she kissed him despite *her* marriage. She needs him to be virtuous and free of impediment. In her fantasy – the one where she has a romantic life with a dashing man – he is free to be with her and helps her overcome her guilt about what she's done to her family. And oh, yes, she has gone too far down the road of imagining what a relationship with him would be like.

'He could be,' she concedes.

They're silent for a little while.

'What do you want me to say?' Shane repeats, softly.

'I want you to tell me I'm a terrible person.' She almost hiccups it out.

'Not going to say that because it's not true.'

'Isn't it?'

'One kiss?' His laugh is dry. 'That just makes you a *person*, not a terrible one. C'mon, Kizza – you're running yourself ragged with the house and the kids and the job. Of course you wanted a kiss with that bloke. It's a bit of a lift, isn't it? Made you feel good?'

She nods slowly.

'I'm not going to judge that,' he says. 'Don't let the sky fall in because of a few seconds of you feeling good.'

Now his face hardens a little.

'But don't make a habit of it. That's when things start to change. That's when you risk it all.'

From the look on his face, she thinks he has personal experience of this. Not that she will ask him. Despite her confessions to him, she's not sure they're good enough friends yet.

'I won't,' she says, and it's so feeble that she knows he won't believe it any more than she does.

'I mean it,' he says, pointing a finger. 'Think carefully about what happens next. No one knows but me. That would change.'

There would be consequences, is what he means. The very consequences she has contemplated and which she can't say part of her isn't tempted to provoke. Except she can't do that to her children. If she doesn't care what happens to her, she does care what happens to them. She just hopes she remembers that when she sees Derek next, as she surely will.

'All right,' he says, looking at his watch. 'Break's over.'

She half-smiles and drops her cigarette, grinding it under her shoe before picking up the stub to take it inside.

'If you think,' he says as he holds open the door for her, 'about doing it again, tell me first. Will you remember that?'

'Like you're my priest or something?'

'Aren't I?'

In the dim light of the interior – before they reach the brighter lights of the foyer – she can't see his face, so she doesn't know if he's teasing her or not.

'See you, Shane,' she says before she goes back to the laundry.

'You will,' he promises as he turns towards the bar.

CHAPTER FORTY-SEVEN

Sunday mornings used to be lovely in her house, Alison thinks as she listens to the quiet of children not stirring and wanting breakfast. Rosie and Sean aren't as keen to spend time loitering in the kitchen, or the sitting room, or anywhere, in case Erik shows up. This home, which used to be a place of harmony and connection, is now a site of disjuncture, and Alison does not know how to bring back what she took for granted.

On Sunday mornings the kids would lazily emerge and ask for whatever breakfast they wanted – that was the day they could have pancakes or Coco Pops, anything they weren't allowed to have on other days because Alison tries to keep them eating sensibly. If it was pancakes, or anything that needed cooking, Tad would make them. He'd make whatever Alison wanted too.

There hasn't been any cooking on a Sunday morning for several weeks. There hasn't been any quiet snuggling on the couch on a Sunday afternoon either, and they used to do that every week while the kids mooched around. Now Tad seems to be unwilling to touch her in front of his son – perhaps he thinks it will offend Erik or something – and Alison feels like a woman he used to know once, or someone he regretted taking out for dinner. He isn't choosing her any more. He isn't choosing their children, their life, their future. He's not honouring what they have created together, the love that she thought was so strong, and now she can't help wondering if it was never there, for him at least. Was he pretending all this time?

She told Charlotte about it the other day when she was apologising, yet again, for missing Cec's funeral.

'Dad wouldn't care, Ally,' Charlotte said. 'He knew you loved him.'

'But I wanted to go for you. For Mum. For your mum.' Alison could feel tears packed into her chest but it would have felt rude to cry so she left them there.

'We know you love us too. Funerals are just . . . a thing. A thing we have to do. A ritual.' Charlotte sounded weary as she said it, not sad as Alison would have expected. 'They aren't a chance to make a naughty-or-nice list.'

Alison had laughed at that, and so had Charlotte, then they'd talked about the reason why Alison couldn't go to the funeral and that led to talking about Tad.

'He may not know what to do,' Charlotte said. 'It's not as if he's faced this situation before. I know you haven't either, but . . .'

She left it hanging there.

'Women are better at this stuff?' Alison offered.

'Better at knowing that we need to be better at it,' Charlotte said. 'Because everyone expects us to be. Including other women. Including ourselves.'

There was silence on the line.

'I guess the world would fall apart if women stopped caring about keeping everyone together,' Charlotte went on.

'Why is it our job, though?'

'I have no idea. But I know what it looks like if we stop doing it.'

'Chaos?'

'Chaos and confusion.' She laughed. 'And I don't want to live like that.'

'So . . . I shouldn't be so harsh on Tad?'

'Oh, you can be a bit tough. You're his wife and he needs to take care of this so it doesn't affect you or Sean or Rosie so badly.

But maybe try telling him that you understand it's difficult. That there's no neat solution. Especially since your mum put her foot down. He may feel outgunned.'

After Frances made her feelings known, Tad didn't say a word and Erik skulked off somewhere; Alison is still waiting to talk to her husband about it. Which is why she's waiting in the kitchen, hoping he'll appear, knowing her children have probably taken off again. And she's so *tired* of worrying about it all. Some days her tiredness feels like the most compelling thing: like it could make her leave them all behind for a day, a week, a month, just for a break.

Like Joan left. Frances told her the story, and at the time Alison thought Joan's behaviour was appalling. Now she finds it appealing.

'Alison.'

She's been distracted and not noticed that Tad has entered the room.

'Hello,' she says like a stranger to the man she's still sleeping beside. He looks terrible – he hasn't shaved in a couple of days; his skin is sallow and his hair is all over the place. It's possible he's looked like this for a while but she hasn't exactly been observing him closely.

'Would you . . .' Tad sighs and rubs a hand over his eyes. 'Would you like some pancakes?'

Their eyes meet and she sees that he's making a peace offering. It's up to her if she takes it in the spirit in which it's offered.

'I would,' she says. 'But it's not the same if the children aren't here to have some too.'

'They are still asleep.'

She looks at the clock on the wall, showing a quarter past eight. It's possible he's right.

'Or have they snuck out?' she says.

'No, asleep.' He sighs heavily. 'I checked.'

'Where's Erik?'

He shrugs. 'He did not come home last night.'

Alison doesn't want to know how Tad knows that; maybe he sat up waiting, because he didn't go to bed when she did. Why hasn't he worried about their children being out somewhere unknown? That's what she wants to ask, but it would sound like she's starting a fight. Which she would be.

She bites her bottom lip as she considers what to say next. There are so many paths to take now, when before there was only one: forward, together. United in purpose and opinions and so many other things. Does she really have to be the peacemaker still? Forever? She thinks of her mother's fury when she let Erik have a piece of her mind and feels emboldened – not to do something similar, but by Frances's strength. Love takes many forms; one of them is taking up weapons to protect what you hold dear. Yet those weapons can also take many forms.

Charlotte went through a phase of liking Hindu goddesses. She took Alison to some art exhibition in Melbourne and they looked at depictions of Kali, Lakshmi, Saraswati and others whose names Alison can't remember. She remembers Kali, though, because Kali had many arms, all holding weapons. She didn't understand why a goddess would need a spear, a trident, a bow and arrow.

'*Pushpabana*,' Charlotte said as they looked at it. 'Flower arrow. Kali sometimes has a flower arrow. Her heart to your heart. Piercing the darkness.'

While Alison didn't love the weapons, she loved the idea of the flower arrow. She just didn't know why. Until now.

'I love you, Tadeusz,' she says, uttering words that used to be their common currency, transforming her anger into something far softer, aimed at his heart.

His eyes widen then fill with tears. When she was younger Alison hated it when men became emotional. It was their job to be stoic, she thought. Who could she depend on if *they* started crying? Then she realised it was because she thought of crying as a weakness, because it was something only women were meant to do. And she wasn't weak. Crying always made her feel better.

Crying cleared the way for something to come through. So his tears don't scare her. They don't make her think he's weak. Instead, they show her how much she means to him.

'I love you too, *kochanie*.' He sits beside her.

'We need to find a way through this,' she almost whispers, not knowing if Erik is nearby. 'We have to find a way to keep this family together. Because . . .'

Now her own eyes fill with tears, and he takes her hand and nods.

'It has gone too far,' he acknowledges.

'I want my children to feel safe in their home. *I* want to feel safe in my home. He's not safe, Tad.'

His sigh is long and broken. 'I don't know what to do,' he says.

'I don't either. But it's not my job this time.' That's her second arrow, aimed at showing him who she is and what she will stand for.

'It is not,' he agrees. Then he lets go of her and stands. 'I will think on it.'

He looks around the kitchen. 'I still wish to make you pancakes,' he says.

'And I still wish to eat them. I'll wake the kids.'

A thud from above tells her that she may not need to. She and Tad look at each other and smile.

'Thank you,' he says and she nods her acknowledgement before leaving to check if Sean has fallen out of bed or decided to kick a football around his room.

CHAPTER FORTY-EIGHT

'You absolutely, fundamentally, cannot be here.'

For Joan this is a statement not of rejection but of fact, because she is looking at her dearest friend – that is, the woman who until recently she had considered to be her dearest friend – and failing to comprehend how and why Genevieve is standing in the foyer of the Duchess Hotel with two suitcases and a grin, like she's sprung a lovely surprise on Joan.

Her presence, however, is not a lovely surprise as far as Joan is concerned. It is an invasion: of her privacy, of the sanctity of this place, of the very life she is trying to live now. Genevieve blabbed to Isaac about her location and now, what? Joan is meant to think everything's wonderful and welcome her effusively? She thinks not. And she really wishes Frances were here, because she believes Frances could come up with some stern words for Genevieve that Joan will struggle to muster because as much as she is cross at Genevieve, she still loves her. They have known each other too long and been through too much together for it to be otherwise.

Like the time Genevieve lost a baby at twenty weeks gestation, and it was Joan she wanted in the hospital with her as she sobbed into one hand and clutched her friend with the other. Joan was being the friend she wished she'd had when Rachel died, because she didn't have Genevieve then.

Or the time Joan's son Nathan fell off his bike and split his head open, and for a while there the doctors thought he might have brain damage. Genevieve scooped up Corinne and looked after her while Joan spent day and night at the hospital.

'Well, I *am* here.' Genevieve keeps smiling as she hoists her handbag higher up her shoulder.

'Why?'

'Why not?'

Genevieve keeps smiling and now Joan thinks it's a tactic, to put her off. To break down the objections that Genevieve would have guessed she'd have because she knows Joan and knows she can be pig-headed on certain matters. Like this one: the Duchess is her fortress, and she does not appreciate having its walls breached by what she considers to be marauding forces.

'Have you left Stephen or something?' Joan has never known Genevieve to be a copycat but, then again, she never knew her to be a tattletale either.

'For now.' Genevieve's expression falters.

'Are you being serious?'

'I need a break. I'm not just copying you. Honestly.'

'I don't care if you are.' Joan pauses to consider the weight of what Genevieve has told her. Stephen has been the same kind of husband as Isaac: distracted, more interested in work even at the times he doesn't need to be, such as at this point in his life when he's had a great deal of success and can afford to step back somewhat. As with Isaac, the more successful he's become the more success he's chased. Isaac's behaviour made Joan realise that he was mainly – perhaps only – interested in success at work, not at home. Perhaps it's the same for Stephen and Genevieve has only now realised it. Not that Joan wanted to start a trend. Not really. Maybe a little. There's part of her that likes the idea of a quiet revolution.

'Do you care that I'm here, though?'

Genevieve's question could be read in two ways, and Joan thinks she knows it.

'If you're asking if I *mind* if you're here,' Joan says, 'yes, I do. But if you're asking if I care that you are upset enough with your husband to leave him, well . . . Of course I care about that. Because I care about you.'

'And you think I didn't care that you left Isaac?' Genevieve says tensely.

'That's a big . . .' Joan presses her lips together while she thinks about what to say next. Because it's possible that their friendship hinges on it. 'I think you care, yes. But given that you told him where I am, my impression is that you cared about him more.'

'That's just not true!'

They stare at each other, two friends on the verge of becoming foes, and Joan sees how her actions – and hers alone – have led them here. She made the decision to leave and did not tell Genevieve until it was done; then, having told her, she did not want her friend to remediate the situation. Nor did she invite her to be as close as they had been. In short, she did not treat her like a friend. She has treated Frances like a friend; even Shane. She has confided in them both in the way she would usually confide in Genevieve. How quickly she switched allegiances, then she condemned Genevieve for doing that, as Joan perceived it.

When the truth, Joan believes, is this: she can't be without a friend. No one can. There are loners who tell themselves that they don't need anyone, that they can manage just fine with no confidants. But that is a wretched existence that could be altered with a little care and attention. She has given care and attention to Frances and Shane and been rewarded with their friendship. It was easy, in retrospect, to make those connections when she wanted to. Yet she dropped the connection with Genevieve.

Actually, that's not true: she took it for granted. They have been connected for so long that she assumed Genevieve would be on her side, and by her side, forever.

Now Genevieve is here, likely to show how good a friend she is and Joan is trying to think of reasons why she isn't. What she needs to do is stop taking a defensive posture and instead realise that her friend is still her friend. And, if she makes the effort, she is still Genevieve's friend too.

'You're right,' Joan says at last. 'It's not true.' She sighs loudly, performatively, not proud of doing it but wanting to buy herself some time to think. 'I'm just . . . rattled that you're here. It feels like . . .' She grasps for the right word.

'An invasion of your privacy?' Genevieve says gently.

'No. It feels like one world has bled into another and I'm not sure how to react.'

'Then don't.' Genevieve pinches her arm. 'Just be. Let me take care of myself. And you take care of yourself. And maybe you'll let me spend some time with you.'

'That sounds terribly formal.' Joan looks at her watch. 'Why don't we meet in the bar in an hour? It's over there.' She nods in its direction. 'I'll introduce you to Shane. You'll like him.'

Genevieve looks mildly shocked.

'He's the *bartender*,' Joan explains. 'Not my boyfriend. If that's what you're thinking.'

'Is it wrong to say I might have been *hoping*?' She grins.

'Ha ha. One hour.'

Genevieve nods and Joan turns away and starts to walk up the staircase without another word. She's going to need the hour to assimilate her old life and new, and to think about whether she actually wants to do that at all.

Behind her she hears Genevieve giving her name, saying she has a booking, but Joan doesn't hear how long it's for because she has turned up the next flight of stairs.

CHAPTER FORTY-NINE

Joan has barely mentioned her friend Genevieve so Frances is surprised to be introduced to the tall, solid-boned brunette with carefully blow-dried hair and a cracking smile full of straight teeth. Joan's hair has never looked that neat – or maybe it did when she lived in Sydney? Maybe Sydney people are required to have hair that looks like it takes a full can of hairspray each day. Frances will ask Joan.

'So you're, ah, visiting?' Frances says, trying not to sound like she's a little bit jealous, because she might be. She's had Joan all to herself these past few weeks and has come to presume that will continue, even though she's half-aware that Joan could leave at any time. The Duchess Hotel isn't her home; nor is the state of Victoria.

'Yes!' Genevieve says, showing all those teeth. 'Well, staying. Like Joan.'

'Have you left your husband too, then?'

Frances is now wondering if leaving husbands and moving into hotels is also a Sydney thing to do. She knows they breed them a little looser up there – her husband used to say that New South Wales is full of crooks, including the police force, but never offered proof – so perhaps they're more mobile around marriage than the folk she's used to.

'Not left. Just . . . a break. A me-break.'

'A you-break?'

'A break for me. Not from him. If that makes sense.'

'Sure.'

Except it didn't really, not to Frances, who never took a break for herself. That's not what happens, not in her world. When she still lived on her parents' property breaks were only granted by bad weather, and even then they had some work to do. Once she had Keith, well, it was clear straightaway that you never have a break from being a mother. Not while they're small.

She knows Joan's children are grown up, so she presumes Genevieve's are too – maybe that's why they're both taking breaks. One thing is for certain: she is not going to ask Genevieve how her husband is coping without her. When Frances was in her fifties, she needed to have some surgery that required a couple of nights in hospital and all anyone asked her was how Gerald was going to feed himself. Not how she felt, not how the surgery went. She had to send Alison to check that he knew how to make toast, because she'd started to wonder if she was married to a helpless man. Turned out he was fine.

'So you paint?' Frances asks the newcomer.

'No!' Genevieve laughs. 'I didn't even know Joan could. How odd is that?'

'Quite odd, yes.' Frances wonders how they can be such good friends if Genevieve didn't know something that Frances sees as being fundamental to Joan's identity. One day, probably not too far away, she'll have Joan in her memory, not her present day, and she'll think of her with brush in hand, or pencil and sketchpad, and that will be the version of Joan she'll remember best.

It's an odd thing to anticipate someone's departure, and Frances doesn't usually, but she can't help thinking that Genevieve's presence means that things are going to change. That Joan is going to leave now that she's being reminded of what she's left.

Or maybe Frances is being a sentimental old duck and she should remind herself that she's survived much worse than losing a friend. If, in fact, that is what will happen.

'Right, Gen, I'll put you with Kirrily,' Joan says as she smiles distractedly. 'To observe today, all right? I don't have enough tools for everyone.'

Frances looks across to Kirrily, who seems irritated. Maybe at the newcomer, maybe at life in general. That girl has been out of sorts a lot lately, and Frances has tried chatting to her but she hasn't found out anything. Shane isn't talking either.

'Where am I?' Wendy has bowled up with a cigarette in hand – clearly the Nicorettes did not last – and her ratty old bag over her shoulder.

Joan points to the sundial a few metres away. 'There. I think you should have your own project.'

'Rightio.' Wendy puts her cigarette in her mouth and puffs away as she opens the bag and pulls out her own brushes. 'Am I good enough to paint on my own?'

'Wendy, I think you know you are,' Joan says. 'If you need *motivation* to do it, well, here it is: go and do it. Or else.'

'Ha!' Wendy's laugh turns into a raspy cough.

Frances detects a tall figure next to her and turns, surprised at who she finds there. 'William!' she says. 'Are we in trouble?'

'Not at all. And you're never in trouble, Frances. Although I believe Shane is often trying to get you *into* trouble.' He winks and Frances wonders what Shane has been telling him.

And they may not be in trouble but Joan looks unsettled.

'Hello, William,' she says meekly.

'Joan.' He nods in that courtly way he has, like everyone he meets is higher ranked and he's acknowledging them. 'This group is growing quite large.' He looks around at the assembly.

'I didn't mean it to,' Joan says quickly.

William holds up a hand. 'It's not a problem. In fact, I think it's an enhancement. I'm merely wondering if we should . . .' He tilts his head from side to side, like he's considering something, although Frances is sure he wouldn't have walked over here without a plan. 'Formalise things,' he says. 'Give you some space inside, perhaps, to save you having to find a new location each time? We have a small function room that is rarely used on a Friday afternoon.'

'Oh,' Joan says. 'That's very nice. But I like to paint things outside. That's why we move around.'

'Of course, of course. Perhaps you could think of it as a meeting place, then? There's a cupboard there we could use to store your equipment.'

Joan's eyes have narrowed. 'Why?'

'Why?'

'Why would you offer this? Are we upsetting someone by being out here?'

'No.' He laughs heartily. 'Not at all. I, ah . . .' He nods as if to summon her over, which pleases Frances because he's standing right next to her so she'll get to hear everything.

'We'd like to *pay you*,' he says to Joan under his breath. 'To run a proper class.'

'Pay me?'

'You're teaching, aren't you?'

Joan makes a face. 'Yes.'

'Would you be open to the occasional guest joining in?'

She frowns. 'Perhaps.'

'Maybe hanging some works in the hotel?'

'Ah . . .' Joan's face relaxes. 'You want cheap decoration.'

'No! No.' William shakes his head vigorously. 'We want a story, Joan. We want this story to be part of the Duchess Hotel's. You, the art you're making, that you're encouraging . . . It could only happen here, couldn't it? The hotel has inspired this. That's a lovely thing to share with guests.'

Joan gazes at him and Frances can see she has her thinking face on; Frances has come to know it well.

'You know that I don't live here?' she says. 'That I may leave at any time?'

'Yes,' he says. 'But I don't think you'll leave us without notice. That's not . . . you.'

He smiles at her kindly and Frances marvels at how observant the man can be. He's always picking up things about people that she may take an age to detect. It must be a talent, because she's not sure if a person can learn that. Or maybe they can, but they have to be really interested in others, and in her experience people are mostly interested in themselves. Including her. She knows she is not the best conversationalist, not the best observer, no matter how often she's thought she should be.

'May I think about it?' Joan asks.

'Of course. And I realise I've taken up quite a few minutes of your hour, so I'll leave. *Adieu.*' He nods again and Frances half-expects him to click his heels together but he does not.

'What a thing,' she murmurs to Joan. 'You're becoming part of the furniture!'

Joan nods slowly and says nothing, so Frances leaves it and picks up her pencil. She's sketching a rose today, even though she's sure she'll be bad at it. But as she watches Joan moving amongst the others, checking on their work, offering assistance, she admires her quiet determination and hopes that Joan will take up William on his offer, and also hopes – more than anything – that Joan will stay.

CHAPTER FIFTY

In the romance novels Kirrily read as a teenager – seeking escape from her life and an assurance that her future might offer her something more thrilling – there were rarely couples who were having affairs. Usually it was a handsome, rich single man and a beautiful, relatively unsophisticated young – always young – woman who met and fell in love. Complications came in the form of family members who disapproved or something that caused the man or the woman to move away, not a spouse.

So she doesn't have much of a template for how to manage her attraction to Derek, and the stories she did read about affairs always ended badly, which should tell her something. Except she wants to feel this attraction. That's what the novels can't really express: how much you want to be wanted, how you want someone to tell you you're beautiful. There is the theory of this, of course, and characters may talk about it, but it's quite another thing to be *in it*.

Being in it is what she was not prepared for. Having her brain filled with thoughts of a man who is not her husband, to the point of being distracted constantly, letting her toast and tea go cold, barely holding it together as a mother – this is nothing she knows how to manage.

Meeting Derek for lunch today, here at the Portsea Hotel, is not likely to help her, either. Yet when he found her last night, in the laundry room – and she doesn't know how he did – and told her he'd like to see her for lunch, she said yes straightaway. It's Monday, so the children are at school; normally she'd be doing housework or cooking large amounts of Bolognese sauce to put in the freezer. Having lunch won't take too long, she rationalises, and it will just be a nice chat. Won't it?

She feels nervous – sick with it – as she waits for him at a table. She's early, of course, and she didn't want to sit in the car, or sit outside at the hotel where there's a wind blowing. The view from inside the hotel is magnificent so she's not missing out on anything, although she glances from the window to the doorway so many times that her neck starts to ache.

As he enters – right on time – he doesn't look surprised to see her. She doesn't know whether to stand or stay seated. How do they say hello – with a kiss? He solves it by coming over to her and kissing her cheek.

'You look beautiful,' he says and although it's an easy thing for any man to say in order to get a woman onside, she appreciates it, given she's wearing her best dress in a moss-green and her favourite necklace with a green stone set in gold. Or fake gold. She's never really been sure. It was her mother's and there's no way to check.

'Thank you,' she says. Is she meant to pay him a compliment? Is that how these things work? And why is she even wondering how these things work? This man is not her husband and as he's a regular guest of the Duchess Hotel there's undoubtedly a rule about her fraternising with him. Although *fraternising* is too mild a term.

'Thank you for meeting me.' Derek sits forward in his chair and his eyes stare into hers. He puts one hand on the table, almost like he's about to reach across and take hers. Which she cannot allow. They're having lunch. Hand holding means something else.

'That's okay,' she says meekly. She should probably act as if she's doing him a favour, gracing him with her presence and giving him her time. That's what she read in a magazine once, that men should be grateful for women's attention, not the other way around. If only she believed that.

'Have you been here before?'

She remembers a lunch, long ago, when Bridget was a baby and she put her in a basket on the seat next to hers and she and Connor sat and looked at the view and sighed and wondered how on earth they were parents, and they were thrilled about it at the same time.

'Once. A while ago.'

'Only once? I would think everyone in the area would come here often. I know I would.' He smiles and glances out the window. 'Although the view at the Duchess is spectacular, so perhaps you don't need this one.'

She shrugs. 'Sometimes I forget to look while I'm there.'

He's still staring into her eyes and she feels rattled. 'Have you worked there long?'

'For a few months.'

She's not good at making conversation, at least not with him. Maybe not with anyone. It's been a while since she's needed to develop a connection with someone. Not that she needs to develop one with him. Or that she necessarily wants one. Isn't that what this lunch is for, to work out if she even likes him beyond thinking about how handsome he is and how soft his lips are?

'You're probably wondering why I asked you to lunch,' he is saying and she stops looking at those lips.

'Yes,' she concedes. 'Guests don't . . .'

'They don't usually ask staff to lunch?' He nods. 'I know. But I don't think of you as staff. You're simply a beautiful woman I'd like to get to know better.'

That makes it sound like he thinks she's available. And, yes, by kissing him she acted like she was. Except he *must* have seen the ring on her left hand. Or maybe he's not observant. Maybe this is all a big misunderstanding, even though it's also a misunderstanding if he thinks she's married because he's probably going to want her to have an affair with him, and she –

'You look upset,' he says, and now his hand definitely moves closer to hers, which she leaves on the table possibly because she doesn't know what's good for her.

'I'm just . . .' She swallows. 'I'm married.'

'I know.'

Does she imagine that his smile is a little sly? 'Yet you're here,' he says.

'You . . .' How does she say what she wants without it sounding desperate? *You are the most handsome, dashing, intriguing man I've ever met and I wish you would sweep me away from my life so I can have just a smidgeon of excitement before I shrivel up forever.*

'You're very appealing,' is what she actually says.

He laughs. 'I've been told that before.'

That's an arrogant statement but he says it with a little shrug and she forgives him.

'I'm sure you have too,' he says, and she forgives him even more.

'No.'

'What?'

Now he does take her hand and while her instinct is to pull back, she relaxes into his touch.

'Clearly you're associating with the wrong people,' he says, his thumb rubbing her palm in a way that makes her insides flip-flop.

'Um,' is all she can manage in reply.

'I'm not here to ask anything of you,' Derek says, 'other than that you be here and be yourself.'

Who is that, though? Maybe he can tell her, because she is so used to being one Kirrily at home and one at work and there were other versions for her family home and school and friends and church, when she was a child. *Be yourself* is a confusing phrase. For her; for everyone, she thinks. We're all different versions of ourselves depending on where we are and with whom.

'That's nice,' she says.

There's a waiter hovering nearby so she takes back her hand and looks at the menu. Then they order, and they make light chitchat about the Duchess and the people who frequent it, and the whole time Kirrily feels like they're building towards something – a declaration from him, perhaps, that he actually *does* want something.

It isn't until they are leaving and he leads her around the side of the hotel that he presses her against the wall, with the sea to her left and his right, and kisses her throat softly, then her collarbone, then her lips, and while her instinct is to not allow him to do that either she lets him, and she lets herself be there and, maybe, be herself – the version of her who wants to be desired, to be appreciated, to be seen by a man who has seen the world and knows what he wants and right now he wants her.

Minutes pass, maybe longer. Then he stops kissing her and brushes his hand along the top of her head.

'I won't be able to see you for a while,' he says softly, with a peck on her lips. 'But I will see you again.'

As he leaves she leans against the wall as if she's holding it up, not the other way around, and waits for her breathing to slow down and the shaky feeling in her arms and legs to subside.

Once she feels able to walk she makes her way to her car, and realises that she is late to pick up the children from school, and decides she won't apologise for it, to them or to herself.

CHAPTER FIFTY-ONE

The beach at Sorrento is a very pleasant spot, with its placid waters and moored boats – probably used only twice a year, those boats, like the ones moored in view of Joan's house in Sydney. For years Isaac said he wanted a boat but she kept reminding him that he wouldn't have time to use it. Maybe he's bought himself one now that she's not there to stop him. Maybe she should ask Genevieve, who's standing next to her on the sand, shoes off, pants rolled up, brush in hand.

Joan's letting her paint even though Genevieve doesn't have much of a clue about it. She's only allowing it to be civil, and because this trip was Genevieve's idea.

'Don't you ever go anywhere but here?' Genevieve said last night in the dining room as they finished their soup. 'You'll run out of things to paint!'

Joan had to concede she had a point.

Given she has her own car with her at the Duchess Hotel, Joan knows she should explore the local area more. Yet apart from driving Frances to the High Country, she has only ventured to the shops for art supplies, paperback novels and sweets. She never let herself have sweets while she was married to Isaac; she had to keep her figure.

While she was married to Isaac. That's the phrase she's started to use in her head. A past-tense phrase. Somewhere between arriving at the Duchess and finding herself teaching a random crew of art students, she put her marriage in the past. Which, she presumes, means it's over. At least for her.

The sweets may be part of it. The art is definitely part of it. Pleasures she has denied herself for so many years because she had to look a certain way, be a certain kind of woman. The empty kind. That's what she has realised about the life she was living: she was expected to be a vessel that everyone else could fill with their wants and needs. Including her friends. Because she has suspected even Genevieve of only liking her – loving her, as Genevieve says she does – for what she has been able to do for her. How supportive she's been, how helpful, how present. Joan is not sure whether that says something about her or about Genevieve but she can't say she's thrilled at the realisation.

She does not feel that way about the friends she has made – or started to make – at the Duchess. Frances seems to like her company, likes just to be with her; the same with Shane. Those are the only two she would call her friends for now, but she is fond of Kirrily. Even fond of Wendy. Actually, she's not – she admires her talent. The woman presents like a cyclone and paints like a zephyr. Quite the achievement.

Joan has long thought that her own ability to express herself artistically is part of who she is in the world, which is why she hasn't done it for so long. An empty vessel has nothing to put on a canvas. Now that she is filling herself up instead of letting other people do it, she has something to offer. And she does think of her art as an offering. It would be grandiose to say it's an offering to the world yet would it be any less so to say it is an offering to God? In those moments when a brush is in her hand, it certainly feels holier than anything else in her life.

These are not thoughts she can share with anyone; not yet. Because they do sound grandiose in her head, if not too odd for polite company. And polite company is who she is, what she's been, for so long. Not that she doesn't like manners – they certainly have their place. She's simply not interested in being polite for the sake of it any more.

Not even to Genevieve, who is still hanging around, insisting that she too is taking a break from her life when Joan is sure that she's on the phone to Stephen, her husband, every day. They've always seemed closer with each other than Joan has ever felt with Isaac. Which is sad, when she lets herself feel anything about it. She's lived so many years with that man and isn't sure if he even likes her.

'Don't be too ambitious,' she says as Genevieve attempts to slap some paint onto the paper she's using for practice. 'Small amounts can go a long way.'

'Is that code for something?' There's an edge to Genevieve's voice but her face is impassive.

'No. Why?'

Genevieve waves a dismissive hand. 'No reason.'

'Gen, I really have no patience for anything like this.' Joan knows she sounds tetchy but they've been on edge with each other this morning. In the car, on the way here, Genevieve made a remark about how she was 'neglecting her family' and Joan took it personally, probably because it was personal. Then Genevieve didn't like Joan's response. On it went. Two grown women not saying what they really mean, so Joan is saying it now.

'Like what?'

'I get the feeling you want to say something to me on a subject other than painting. And that's keeping me from painting. Our purpose in coming to this spot is to paint, no?'

Genevieve pulls her sunglasses down from the top of her head, so now Joan can't read her eyes. In response she pushes hers up.

'You said you came here to see me,' Joan goes on, 'and you're seeing me, sure, but you're also being odd.'

There's a snort. *'I'm* being odd?' Genevieve practically throws paint on the paper.

'Gen, really, just say it.'

'Fine. You're selfish.'

Joan almost smiles because she knows that 'selfish' is one of the worst insults Genevieve could choose – in her own mind. Once upon a time, only a few weeks ago, it would have stung Joan and Genevieve knows this. For a woman to be called selfish, when she is meant to be selfless – when she is trained from girlhood to put others first, to be sweet, to be kind, to make sure her needs are never the priority – is to set out to wound.

Except the word bounces off Joan now. Perhaps it's because she has developed armour against it, although she is inclined to believe that coming to the Duchess, and everything that has happened since, has stripped her back to her essential self. She is bare before the world, and she feels more protected than ever.

No, it's more likely that the word has lost the power to hurt her. Genevieve's use of it shows that it means something to her, however. She thinks Joan will be upset. Or she wants her to be upset. Because Joan being selfless helped her too.

'Yes,' Joan says. 'I am.'

Genevieve's eyes widen then she looks away. 'So you're proud of it.'

'Did I say that?'

'Admitting it means you are.'

'No, admitting it means admitting it.'

'For God's sake, Joan, just stop this!' Their eyes meet and Genevieve's hazel irises look like they're aflame.

Joan regards her old friend and sees a woman who is as trapped as she once was: inside the parameters set for her by others, inside the cage they have become. The sad thing is, as Joan discovered, that she will have to make her own key for the lock on that cage. No one is going to come along and let her out – including Joan. Because Joan could open the cage door and it won't mean Genevieve will walk free.

'Stop what?' she asks softly.

'Stop . . .' Genevieve exhales and it sounds like a hiccup, as if she's about to cry.

'Stop doing what I want to do?'

Genevieve turns away from her.

'I know that what I've done is inconvenient for a lot of people,' Joan says, standing next to her, both of them looking out at water that is glistening in the sunlight, at seagulls that are hovering above it. 'But it's not inconvenient for me.'

'What about all those other people?' Genevieve sounds calmer.

'They're all adults. I don't have any dependents now.'

There's a noise and Joan glances across to see Genevieve taking her hand to her nose, sniffing. 'That sounds so sad,' Genevieve says.

Joan smiles wryly. 'Not to me. It sounds free.'

'Is that what you want – freedom?' There's mystification in Genevieve's voice and Joan pities her, right then.

'It's what I *have*,' she says, and she feels it suddenly: in her chest, in her shoulders, in her neck, in her jaw, in her entire face. Like she's a bird opening its wings for the first time, feeling the breeze beneath it, travelling higher. Like the bird that spontaneously emerged through her hand onto the page, weeks ago.

That's what she wants to do: travel higher. Up there she can see more, do more, be more. The possibilities of her life have no limits like they do here on earth. If she lets herself be free, who knows where she will go. Who she will be.

That's why she is still at the Duchess Hotel, still so reluctant to re-enter her life. She is on her way to soaring, liberated from everything that has bound her, and she is defiantly uninterested in being tethered again.

'It's what I need,' she says quietly, glancing at the friend she used to know so well and who used to know her. But Genevieve doesn't want to go where she's going, and Joan understands that means she may be going alone. That will not deter her.

They spend an hour or so mostly in silence, painting, then Joan drives them back and as she farewells Genevieve on the Duchess

Hotel stairs she wonders if she'll ever see her again. The path she is taking is not one she expects others to accept, and while she has found companions here at the Duchess, she knows that she may need to leave others behind. She's also been on this earth long enough to know that relationships may have natural endings – and that this doesn't mean they have failed. Her friendship with Genevieve has not failed, but it may have ended, through her own actions. This is for fate alone to know.

NOVEMBER 1999

CHAPTER FIFTY-TWO

'I've been thinking,' Alison had said to Frances as she took her to the green grocer at the start of the week.

'Mm?'

'I'd like to join you on Friday afternoons.'

She held her breath after she said it, sure that Frances would think she was trying to hone in on something that was hers and hers alone. But Alison's motives are purely selfish: she wants something to take her mind off what's happening at home, to remind her that there are other things in the world apart from surly stepsons, plus it would give her a different connection to her mother, and maybe help bring them properly closer. Sure, they spend time together – a lot. Between Alison's visits and phone calls and helping Frances around the house, they are in each other's lives. She's still not sure, though, if she'll ever be properly in her mother's heart. This might be a way to get in there.

'Are you interested in art?' Frances said.

'I don't know.' Alison braked at a red light and smiled in her mother's direction. 'I'd like to find out.'

'Do you have time?'

'I'll make time, Mum. I'd like to do this with you.'

'All right,' Frances said. 'That would be lovely.'

The light changed, but not before Alison grinned.

'Great!' she said. 'Shall I pick you up at a quarter to this Friday?'

'Oh no, love, I'll walk.'

'Okay.' Alison felt a little rejected – which mother doesn't want to arrive with her daughter?

'Nothing personal,' Frances said. 'I just like my walk.'

Alison nodded and wondered if that was the truth.

'But I'll look forward to seeing you at the Duchess,' Frances added.

So here she is at her first class, with Joan looking slightly put out because Frances didn't mention that Alison was coming so she's worried about supplies or something.

'Sorry,' Alison says. 'I can go and get some.'

'Not today,' Joan says distractedly. 'There's no time. We'll work something out.'

She forages in a large bag and extracts a sketchpad. 'It's not new,' she says as she hands it over, 'but it will do.'

'If you give me a list of things I need, I can go to the shops,' Alison says, feeling embarrassed that she's put Joan out. The paragon Joan, her mother's special friend.

Then a man walks towards them and she remembers Shane from seeing him inside at the Duchess. Part of her wants to feel jealous because she knows the way Frances's face softens when she talks about him; part of her is glad that Frances has an alternative son. That's what Alison called him once, although she was being snarky at the time. Later she realised she shouldn't have been so mean about Shane, because her mother has been disappointed by Keith; they all have. Who can blame her if she wants to spend time with a man around her son's age who doesn't treat her badly?

'Hello,' he says as he nears. Then he glances at Frances and raises his eyebrows before smiling at Alison.

'New classmate,' he says.

'It's not a class,' Joan remarks. 'It's a gathering.'

'Like a coven of witches?' Shane says lightly.

Joan purses her lips. 'It's an hour of art, Shane,' she says. 'Or art hour, if you prefer.'

'Art hour at the Duchess Hotel. I like it. Got a ring to it.' He nods as if he's still considering it.

'Maybe we could have a poster made,' says Frances.

Joan doesn't answer her. Instead, she gestures to the view in front of them. They're standing on a bluff that forms part of the Duchess property – Alison wouldn't have found it without her mother leading the way from the front entrance of the hotel. Frances says this part of the grounds is not usually visited by guests because it's barren compared with the rest of the surrounds, all rock and scrub, buffeted by the wind most of the time.

'It takes a local to love it,' she said, although locally grown Alison isn't yet sold. What is she meant to paint here? It's not very colourful. Maybe that's why Joan gave her a sketchpad instead of paints.

'What should I do?' she asks Joan.

'Just sit and observe for a few minutes,' Joan says as another two women arrive, one younger than the other. Kirrily and Wendy, she guesses, then Frances's introductions confirm it.

As the late arrivals go about their business, Joan comes back to her.

'A few minutes,' Joan repeats. 'Then draw what you want to document. Don't think about it too hard. Don't try to make it good. Good is a subjective assessment. This is an exercise, not a test. So be free.'

She smiles then and Alison feels the warmth of it, like she's been invited properly into this group. No doubt she has Frances to thank for that, since Joan probably wouldn't let in just anyone.

Frances herself is sitting on a chair and giving no indication that she's about to draw or paint anything.

'What are you going to do, Mum?' Alison asks her.

'Contemplate the meaning of life,' Frances says drily. 'Then try to put it in a picture.'

Alison laughs and is rewarded with a twinkle in her mother's eye, before Frances gestures to a nearby bush.

'That,' she says. 'I'm going to draw that.'

Alison nods, then finds a place to sit herself so she can follow Joan's instruction and observe.

'Don't aim for an imitation,' Joan is telling Shane, who is standing next to Frances but facing in a different direction, looking at a nearby shed. 'There's a lot of detail in the building and you can come back to that. So go with the strongest lines today.'

'Any tips for what should I do?' Frances asks with a smile as Joan turns towards her.

'Your best.' Joan smiles back.

Alison can see the bond between them and now she does feel a little jealous. Has Frances ever smiled at her like that – like they're equals? No, she doesn't think so. Because they're not equals and can never be. The balance of mother to daughter is invariably tipped in one direction, with each one thinking it's tipped the other way. For the first time, Alison realises that Rosie will likely think this about her one day.

Alison looks over to where Wendy and Kirrily are standing close together but not talking to each other. Wendy looks like she's studying for a test, concentrating on whatever she's doing, frowning with it.

'She never shows us what she's working on,' Frances mutters. 'She's always saying that we'll have to wait and see. Maybe she's painting rubbish?' Another laugh. Her mother is so light-hearted here.

Shane picks up his easel and moves it next to her, so now she has her mother on one side and him on the other.

'Better view of the building,' he says, then he busies himself with what's on his easel.

After a few minutes of observing, Alison looks at the pencils Joan gave her and wonders which one to choose. She'd had this idea that being in the class would be this effortless flow of just creating something; silly of her not to realise that there are choices to be made, including which tools are needed.

'I usually start with a 2H,' she hears Shane say.

'Oh. Okay.' Alison looks amongst the pencils.

'This one.'

Shane hands over a pencil of his and Alison is looking at what's written on it. She's always liked to check details.

'How are you getting on?' Frances says.

'We're still sorting out the equipment,' Shane replies.

'I have no idea where to even start with this,' Alison mutters, gesturing to the paper in front of her.

'I'll get Joan,' Frances says.

'No! No.' Alison purses her lips. 'I'll figure it out.'

'It takes some getting used to,' Shane says. 'Not that I'm used to it. But I like giving it a go. It's a bit of fun.'

'Fun?' That's what Alison was hoping for but she doesn't know how to achieve it.

'Aren't you here for fun?'

'Um . . .'

Alison looks at Frances. 'I'm here to spend time with Mum,' she says.

'You can't have fun at the same time?'

'Well . . .' Alison shrugs. 'I guess so.'

'Joan isn't marking anyone's work,' Shane says lightly. 'I was worried she would but we're all just here to, y'know, spend some time doing something different. I wouldn't have ever thought to draw something if I hadn't started coming.'

Alison takes up the pencil and puts it to the page, then takes a breath. 'Okay,' she says.

'Just start,' Shane says. 'What's the worst that could happen? It's a pencil. You can rub out anything you don't like.'

'True.'

It would be so convenient, she thinks, if she could rub out the things she doesn't like in her life at the moment, but maybe that's part of the benefit of coming to this class: she has control over what she does here; she can destroy it if she doesn't like it and keep it if she does. Instead of an hour of just not thinking about what's worrying her – as if it's truly possible to forget about it – she can give herself this one hour a week to be completely in charge of what she makes and unmakes. It's so appealing. No wonder people like it.

So she starts and doesn't like what she does, and rubs it out, and starts again. By the end of the hour, she has a semblance of something and, best of all, she has lost track of time. When Joan starts packing up and Kirrily quickly departs so she can start work, Alison turns to her mother.

'Can I come back?' she says.

'I reckon you can,' Frances replies. 'Help me up, Shane.'

Alison stands back as Shane gets her mother to her feet and sees that there's something else she can appreciate about this gathering: other people are here to help. That's something she could use more of too.

CHAPTER FIFTY-THREE

The hardest thing as a mother, Kirrily thinks, is to know your child is in need of help and you're not able to provide it. It's especially hard when the help is of the medical kind – not about picking him up from the ground or putting a Band-Aid on his knee – because never in her entire life will she have the skills to do what needs to be done for Aidan now.

'We need to take steps,' is what the burns specialist told her when she and Aidan made the visit to Melbourne to see him. Melbourne is so close yet they needed the whole day to travel there, wait in the rooms, have the appointment and travel back, and it was a reminder of how isolated the peninsula can feel when you really need something that can't be provided there.

Steps was such a mild word for what was proposed.

'He'll need skin grafts to repair the places where the skin is stretching beyond its current capacity,' the doctor said. 'We'll take them from the places where he's not burnt.'

'The same places as before?'

The doctor looked impassive. 'Adjacent to them. I know it's painful.'

'It's awful.'

Kirrily tried to block out the memories of what it was like before and now she is going to have a new round of them.

'I appreciate that,' he replied.

No, you don't! That's what she wanted to scream at him. Except she knows there is no other way. There is no permanent solution to this. There is only repair and restart, over and over again. Connor kept growing until his mid-twenties, and he's so tall. If Aidan goes the same way they'll be back here, in this office, at the hospital, each time he has a growth spurt. And each time, what is she meant to tell her son? How is she meant to explain that his parents only took their eyes off him for a minute and that he's the one who has to suffer for it?

It is no comfort whatsoever when people say things to her like 'bad things happen to good people'. She knows that. She also knows that good people can do bad things. That's what her whole situation with Derek is. Or she needs to tell herself that it is, because she thinks she's a good person. Wants to think that.

When the doctor tells her that Aidan has to go through more hell, though, it's the worst feeling in the world.

Actually, it's not. Because the worst feeling would be if no one could help him, and thank God they live in a place where there are doctors and nurses and hospitals are not too far away, even if it means he'll have to go back to Melbourne for the operation and one of them – her, most likely – will need to stay with him. Connor has to work, and his parents can look after Bridget.

The planning for it all runs through Kirrily's head as she sits in front of the dining room table, the television on a low volume across the room showing some old movie as she folds clean laundry and makes a mental list of what needs to be done for her son before he goes into hospital. What she and Connor need to organise for themselves, including money. Their private health cover will pay for a lot of it, but not all. There will be a gap. This is why she's been working, she tells herself. This is why she's been saving. This is why she's felt so stressed the past few months. This is why she has not been herself.

There it is: the rationale she's been using to excuse the way her thoughts keep going to Derek and how much she wants to be with him.

'I thought you were coming to bed?'

Connor's voice makes her jump.

'I'm, um . . .' She presses one of Aidan's singlets flat then folds it in half. 'Not tired yet.'

His hands on her shoulders make her jump again.

'You worried about the op?' he says, sounding concerned.

'Um . . .'

Once upon a time, she would have told Connor everything that was on her mind. She never censored her thoughts or feelings around him, and she believed he was the same. The mundane, the profound, the inane, the amusing, they just said it and it kept them connected. Each of them knew how the other was feeling about life and in that way they never found themselves in a situation where they upset each other, because they were always talking. Some men don't talk to their wives – she knows that from other staff at the Duchess Hotel – but he's always talked to her. Or he used to.

It's been a long time – she can't remember how long – since they've chattered away to each other like that. They're disconnected now, and it's both of their faults. He could have kept talking to her even if she stopped talking to him. The reverse is also true. And it's so hard, she thinks, to get back to the way they were. Almost like learning a new language: the language of each other's interior lives. The easier path, the one that requires less effort, is to make no effort at all to restore their relationship. It's to continue co-existing in this house, with these children, getting by, doing the best they can, not hoping for more and wanting less. That's not much of a life, really, but it'll have to do for now. Unless she changes things, and the changes she's been dreaming of don't involve Connor. She doesn't want to think beyond that, to the fact that they don't involve the children either. Because in romantic daydreams, you don't take your children along.

'Sweetie?' Connor's hands are still on her shoulders, and he kisses the top of her head. 'I'm worried too.'

He's letting her off the hook, presuming that she's distracted because she's worried about Aidan. Which is partly true. Mainly she's worried about everything.

'I know,' she says, patting his hand.

Connor moves to sit beside her. His eyes are bloodshot, and his hair is going in a hundred different ways at once, like he's woken from turbulent sleep. Maybe he has – he went into their bedroom a while ago.

'He's going to be all right,' Connor says, but the tone of his voice is at odds with his statement. He sounds scared, the way Aidan does after a nightmare.

'I hope so,' Kirrily says, wanting to be the realist. Someone has to be, because they need to make plans for what happens if he's not all right. He may end up in hospital for days or weeks. Or he may be fine this time and another time they'll be back in hospital and it won't work that time. The happy-go-lucky Connor she met would have told her not to worry about things that haven't happened yet but that Connor wasn't a parent. That Connor didn't know how bad it feels to have a child you can't help.

'Mum will help with Bridge.'

It's the plan they've already discussed – that Connor's mother will arrive early and pick up Bridget and her belongings, take her to school and take her home, while Connor and Kirrily drive Aidan to Melbourne. The plan is for one of them – probably Connor – to come home after the surgery but Kirrily knows her mother-in-law will expect to keep Bridget with her, for as long as it takes. It's a consideration and kindness Kirrily appreciates. Now they just have to wait for the date for the surgery. The specialist's secretary said she'd let them know when he could fit them in.

'Thanks,' she says, although she doesn't know who she's thanking. It's something to say.

'Aren't you tired?' Connor puts his hand on her arm.

'Yes. Aren't you?'

'Beyond.' He runs a hand over his hair, back and forth. No wonder it looks like a dog's breakfast.

'Go back to bed,' she urges.

'Not without you.'

He picks up some of the laundry and starts folding, and it makes her want to scream. This was her time alone, to think, to worry, to long. To forget. Now he's invading it, and she knows he just wants to help, which means she can't tell him to go away, because no one wants to be told to stop helping. Besides, if she tells him that now he may never help her again, and they may need each other, her and him, over the coming days.

'I don't know what's going on with you,' Connor says softly, still folding. 'You don't tell me anything any more. But . . .' He stops and gives her the crooked smile she knows so well. 'I'm not going anywhere. I love you, Kick.'

They stand together, breathing.

'Just so you know,' he adds. 'Maybe I don't say it enough.'

You don't say it at all, she wants to reply. Except he just has. And she hasn't. And she should.

He doesn't wait for it, though. Just stands, kisses the top of her head again, and pats her shoulder. 'I'll wait for you in bed,' he says. Then he leaves her alone with her thoughts and her worries and her longing, and she doesn't find them such good company any more.

CHAPTER FIFTY-FOUR

'Are you comfortable, Mum?' Alison practically leans over and tucks Frances into the chair like she's tucking her into bed, and Frances wants to tell her that she wasn't *uncomfortable*, but Alison works from a presumption that old age is inherently uncomfortable and Frances, while not liking it, is coming to accept it. Because that's what you do for your children, if you wish to keep them in your life: when you disagree with them, you mostly keep it to yourself unless or until you reach a point when you can't. And when you can't, you know that there may be a price to be paid in the form of silent treatment, glowering, sighing, eye-rolling or increased tucking-in behaviour.

'Yes, love,' Frances says, smiling as genuinely as she can. She's not sure if Alison has ever been able to tell the difference between her real smile and her fake smile. Don't women get good at the fake smiles? From childhood they're told to smile and because implicit in the order is the fact that they don't, in fact, want to smile it's set up early: smile when you don't want to smile, just so everyone else can pretend that you like them or approve of them. Smile at the boy you don't like because he likes you and if you don't smile, he'll get angry. Except smiling means he gets the wrong idea about your feelings towards him.

This was a trap Frances found herself in once. Before Albert. She never told anyone. Not even him. Definitely not him. But he never told her to smile; he didn't have to. She always wanted to smile around him. And after him there was Gerald, who never told her to smile either, mainly because he didn't look at her that often.

'Want to watch *Blue Heelers*?' Alison sits on the couch and pushes some pillows behind her. She invited herself over, like she did last week on the same night. Escaping the tension at home, obviously, because she's given no indication that it's abated and Frances doesn't think it prudent to keep asking, because Alison will tell her if there's any news.

'Certainly,' Frances says. She has been a viewer of the program since it started a few years ago and it's set in a Victorian country town and that's familiar to her. Although she has never known a country town to be as crime ridden as the Heelers' Mount Thomas.

Alison picks up the remote control just as there's a knock on the front door.

'Who would that be?'

'I have no idea,' Frances says. Her neighbour Phyllis has stopped her tirades about Colin, presumably having realised that the other corgi is to blame, and Colin himself is lying next to her feet. So he can't be the cause of a nighttime visitor.

Alison is down the hallway and opening the door before Frances has time to think further. Low tones head her way, then she sees Keith following his sister into the room.

'Hello, love,' she says, putting her hands on the arms of the chair to push herself up.

'All right, Mum?' he says, looking nervous, scratching the back of his head.

Alison is peeved; Frances can tell.

'It's late for a visit,' Frances says, gesturing to the couch, but he takes the other chair across the coffee table from hers.

'Yeah, yeah.' His laugh is as nervous as the expression on his face, and he keeps looking furtively at Alison.

'What's wrong?' Frances asks.

'Wrong? Nothin'!' More head scratching.

'Don't you want your sister to know?'

'What?' Now his laugh is high-pitched and, if Frances is being honest – not that she wants to admit this to herself – creepy.

'You're uncomfortable about Alison being here.' No point in pretending otherwise, Frances thinks, otherwise his obfuscating could go on all night.

'Just wasn't expecting it.' He folds his arms across his chest.

'Are you feeling okay?' Now it's Alison doing the asking.

'Sure, sure. Um . . .' Keith glances around the room. 'I just need to talk to Mum about something.'

'You can tell me in front of Alison.'

Alison looks almost smug about that, and Frances wishes it hadn't sounded like she was taking sides. Except her daughter has always been trustworthy. Solid.

'So Uncle Cec's funeral – went all right?' He's not laughing now, and Frances is taken aback at the introduction of the topic since the funeral is now in what she would call the middle-distant past.

'As all right as a funeral can go,' she says, feeling tension in her neck and shoulders. What was it her father used to say about horses? You can tell what they're thinking by observing their bodies. She wonders what he'd make of her body and its reaction to her own son. It's like her body knows that something's amiss, and her mind is about to catch up.

'Poor old bugger,' Keith says.

'How would you know?' Frances says sharply. 'You hadn't seen him in years.'

'Oh, you know.' Keith appears unbothered. 'Dying and all that.'

'He isn't aware of it. He's dead.'

Keith nods quickly.

'What's this about, Keith?'

'Nothin'. Nothin'.' He sniffs. Scratches his head. 'So . . . he leave a will?'

Frances bites her bottom lip and risks a glance at her daughter, who looks stricken. Probably because they both know now why

Keith is really here, and Alison will find this as unseemly as Frances finds it upsetting.

'I imagine so,' Frances says. 'Not that I'd be in it. If that's what you're wondering.'

There's a flash of something across Keith's face and as it passes Frances feels something she's never felt before around her son: fear.

'Why would I wonder that?' he says and his voice is deeper than it was before, and hard.

'Because you asked about the will. It's an unusual question. Considering you haven't once asked how I feel about my brother dying.'

The fear is still there, sitting on her chest. Ah, that's why her shoulders and neck tensed first: bracing themselves for the weight of what was to come. Fear wrapped around disappointment. A heavy bundle for a mother to carry.

Keith shrugs. 'Sorry,' he says, and Frances knows he's not.

'Do you need money, Keith?' Alison asks quietly.

'Why would you say that?' He's defensive again and of course it's because he has something to protect – the truth of his finances, his life, his messes, who knows.

'It just seems like you might.' Alison smiles briefly and her eyes meet her mother's. Frances can see some steel in them that she has rarely seen before.

'Yeah, maybe,' Keith concedes. 'But I don't need it from you.'

'That'd be a change,' Alison says, and Frances is surprised: when is Keith asking her for money?

'Well, you're not getting it from Mum,' Alison adds firmly, sitting up straighter. 'I think you know she's hardly swimming in it. You got it all when Dad died.'

'Yeah. Dad.' His laugh is caustic and it pains Frances accordingly.

'What happened to your investment in Melbourne?' Frances asks, wanting to put him on the spot.

'Didn't work out.' He sniffs.

'Right.'

'I want you to stop bothering Mum about money,' Alison says.

'I'm not bothering her.' His eyes, glittery, turn towards Frances. 'Am I, Mum?'

This is one of those moments when a parent disagrees with her child and knows she should keep it to herself. But it's also the point at which she knows she can't, because keeping up a fiction will ultimately damage parent, child and anyone in the vicinity. Except Frances's impulse to make things all right for her eldest child is so strong that for a second she forgets that if she bites her tongue and doesn't say what she thinks, she'll be preferring him over her other child. She'll be letting him be right and Alison wrong. Perhaps she's always done this – not consciously. There's no part of her that loves him more than her. Yet she's preferred Keith over Alison, over and over again, and that has allowed him to reach this point, where he presumes she'll be on his side over Alison's. It's a habit he's developed. A habit Frances must have allowed, if not fostered. A habit she now must break.

'You are,' she asserts, pushing herself up to stand, noticing Alison doing the same thing. 'You've come here late, making no sense. Upsetting your sister. And I'm missing my *Blue Heelers*.' She hopes that by mentioning the TV show she'll make it sound like this is a light family spat, not the total change in dynamic she feels it to be.

'Oh well,' he says, waving his hands around. 'Can't have you missing *Blue* bloody *Heelers*, can we?'

There's another knock at the door and this time Frances jumps.

'Frances!' she hears a call. It's Phyllis's husband, Lloyd. She recognises his voice because Lloyd is always calling out to their cat in the back garden.

'I'll go,' Alison says.

Keith keeps his eyes away from Frances's until Alison returns.

Alison raises her eyebrows as she comes to stand closer to Frances. 'He says Phyllis saw a strange man coming into the house late and wants to know if we're being robbed. She sent Lloyd over to check.'

A strange man. Yes, that just about describes Keith these days.

Keith always waits for Frances to come to the car when he visits so Phyllis would never have seen him. God bless her busybody-ness – just this once.

'I presume you set him straight,' Frances says.

'I said the strange man is just leaving,' Alison says, her chin lifting defiantly.

Keith makes a face. 'Fine.' He turns to go and doesn't say goodbye, then he's out the door, slamming it hard enough to make whatever point he thinks he's making.

'I'm sorry, Mum,' Alison says, taking her hand. She never does that.

'Not your fault,' Frances says, but she feels like it must be someone's. Hers. Gerald's. Albert's, for leaving her. No, she can't blame a man who went to fight for his country and died doing it.

'Tad and I will sort it.' Alison's voice is so gentle and reassuring that Frances feels herself relax, and the mention of Tad's name suggests that some kind of resolution has happened there.

'Come on,' Alison continues, 'I'll put the telly on.'

They both sit down, and after a few minutes they sit back, and the show helps Frances forget for a while. Although she knows when she tries to sleep tonight, she'll be worrying about what's to become of her son, and what, if anything, she can do about it.

CHAPTER FIFTY-FIVE

It isn't fair of her, Joan realises, to ask William to keep her room empty considering she doesn't know how long she'll be gone. The hotel shouldn't lose money on her. But she doesn't want someone else in the room and she isn't sure she could continue to pay for it, either, since William informed her that her last cheque did not clear.

That should have embarrassed her but instead it enraged her, because she is confident she knows what has happened: Isaac has found out about her bank account and cooked up some legal means of freezing it. He'll have said that she's left him and put joint assets in the account so she shouldn't be allowed to use the funds, and given that whomever he's talked to at the bank is someone he likely plays golf with or goes sailing with, they would have just gone along with his request.

The worst part is she should have guessed this would happen. She's seen him do it for other men – friends of his whose wives have left and who asked him to 'help me out, mate' with some legal thing. It was the currency of their social set, the helping-out with things which now, as she looks back, she realises were mainly about stymieing a woman either so she returned to the marital home or was so thoroughly ruined that she had to start a completely different life.

Of course, in Joan's case the ruination is her own choice. Which means Isaac is trying to financially starve her out of it and force her to come back to him.

Well, it's worked. She's here in their driveway, with a petrol tank that is almost empty because she had hardly any cash and only enough to fill it once on the way up the Hume Highway. William offered to lend her money; so did Shane. But she didn't want them having to pay compensation for her husband's deeds.

'You *are* coming back, right?' Shane had said as he poured her a drink she didn't ask for, waving off payment.

'I hope so,' she had said, wanting to down the whole glass at once.

Then William had said of course they'd keep her room because they presumed it would be hers for months anyway, and not to worry about money because she hasn't yet accepted payment for the art classes. Which is hardly an even exchange – there's no way her classes are worth the cost of her room – but he insisted.

Frances was the last one she told about her departure, dropping past her house on her way out of town, hoping she would be there.

'You're what?' Frances had said, blinking in the morning sunlight as they stood in her front garden.

'I have to go home,' Joan repeated.

'No, you don't.' Frances had looked quite indignant, enough to make Joan smile.

'I do. Isaac has stopped my money.'

'Your money?'

'Yes.'

'*Your* money?' Now she looked confused.

'Yes.'

Colin was sniffing around both of their feet and Joan felt an almost overwhelming desire to pick him up, take him inside and stay with Frances forever. It was a better idea than going back to Sydney. At least Frances would be nice to her.

Frances pursed her lips. 'My son did something similar,' she said, then she put her arms around Joan and hugged her tightly enough that after a few seconds Joan gasped for air.

Joan didn't ask for specifics, figuring Frances would provide them when she wanted to; instead, she said she'd let Frances know when she was back and almost skipped to her car because she was starting to cry and she wasn't prepared for it. Crying is not something she is fond of doing, originally because it ruined her make-up, then because she didn't want to be thought hysterical – hysterical being a label always meant pejoratively. 'Stop being hysterical,' Isaac said to her once not long after Corinne was born and she was exhausted. But her own mother said it to her as well, so she thought it must have been true.

Now she knows better: she wasn't hysterical, just reasonably tired of everything life was throwing at her. Nor is she hysterical now, as she waits for Isaac to come home from work. She has a key to the house, of course, but doesn't feel like it's her house to enter any more. For all she knows he's installed her successor.

She hears his car before she sees it, then he pulls in next to her and as she turns to look at him, she's fairly sure she sees a smirk.

'You came home,' he says once they're both out of their cars.

His arms are open, like he's going to hug her, so she hugs her handbag to her chest. If before there had been a sliver of her that still thought they may stay married, it's slipped away now. So there will be no hug.

'I had to,' she says, turning away from him and walking towards the front door. 'You cut off my funds. *My* funds.'

'They're ours,' he says, then pushes the door open.

'They're *mine*. That money was in a separate account.'

'That account is a joint marital asset now.' He says it so lightly, so assuredly. 'For all I know you put some of my money in there too.'

'Money you made while I was running your entire life,' she almost hisses. She doesn't move further than the grand entranceway with ceramics displayed on the wall and a John Olsen painting Isaac likes to tell everyone he 'picked up before Olsen was Olsen'.

'Do you not understand, Isaac,' she goes on, 'that if I hadn't run your households, raised your children, maintained your friendships, that you wouldn't have had the time or energy to have the career you've had? You and your friends, all of you, relied on your wives doing everything. Then once you've reached a certain point you act as if it all happened by magic. How have things been since I left?'

His facial expression falters a little then corrects itself, back into his mask of confidence and supremacy.

'You've had to hire people, haven't you?' Joan says calmly. She's trying to make a point, not start a war.

'Yes. A housekeeper.'

'Oh – a housekeeper?' She looks around and indeed the house looks spotless. 'I imagine that's not cheap.'

He stares at her.

'And how many fun couple-y dinners have you been to? No, wait – I'm sure you've been invited to plenty because everyone feels sorry for you. Just as they did when Andrew and Nicole broke up. Nicole was never seen again but Andrew was invited everywhere and set up with every available woman under the sun.'

'You and I are not breaking up,' Isaac says with a surprising amount of passion.

She looks at his face – the confusion there – and wonders what he thinks has been happening these past few months.

'You're here, aren't you?' he says. 'You came back.'

'I came back to get a lawyer and sort out this mess with *my* money,' she snaps.

'The children want to see you.'

The children. Not children any more but, yes, *their* children. She does miss them, even if she doesn't miss the way they treat her. The way she has let them treat her.

'I will see them,' she says. 'And I will have to stay here because you've left me no choice.'

'It's your home,' he says, almost pleadingly.

'Isaac, let's get this straight: this is a hostage situation, not a home.' She has practised this line, wanting to make an impact, wanting to wound, wanting to shock him because she knows he thinks of himself as a kind, generous man, mainly because she's always reassured him that he is. And, as she could have predicted, he looks appalled.

'How can you say that?' he says hoarsely.

'You've trapped me. No money. Nowhere to go but here. I'm not *willing* to be here, so that means you've taken me hostage.'

'But I had to do something . . . They said . . .'

So he's had advice, probably from one or more of his colleagues. Maybe the barrister who's on wife number three or the QC who has a secret second family. The great, the good, the morally upstanding of this city.

'And the something had to be money?'

She says it wearily, knowing the answer. For him and his friends it's always about money. And the status money brings. Perhaps she has been a status symbol for him all these years, and he thinks money bought her. But it didn't. At the start it was his sense of fun and adventure, his kind eyes, his warm hands. That was so long ago.

When he doesn't answer and looks away instead, she takes it as her dismissal.

'I'll go to the guest room,' she says.

He doesn't stop her, but he does go out to the car and bring in her suitcase.

CHAPTER FIFTY-SIX

It's taken Frances a few days to recover from Keith's last visit. Actually, strike that: she hasn't recovered. She may never. It is a sad and sorry day when you realise that your son is not – perhaps has never been – the man you expected him to be, not because you were waving some generalised expectation in his direction but because you raised him in a certain way.

Keith didn't have a father for his first years but he had a grandfather and uncles, and those uncles were men Frances admired, whose values she believed in and lived by herself, and she had thought her son had absorbed them too. Maybe there was something else going on that she didn't see – maybe there was shame attached to those early years that he picked up on.

Or maybe she should realise that, try as hard as she did, he just went bad.

That's probably the more difficult realisation, that nothing she did – nothing her family did – had an impact. She could have raised Keith in a paddock and he might have turned out the same way.

Alison told her that his behaviour wasn't Frances's responsibility, or hers.

'He's had all the love in the world, Mum,' she said the day after his visit. 'And all the opportunities. If he doesn't make the most of any of it, that's not our problem.'

Except it is. Because he keeps making it their problem. By turning up out of the blue and scaring them – yes, he scared them. Or scared Frances, but she thinks Alison was rattled too.

She doesn't want to feel scared. Not at her age. Instead of growing a thicker skin as she's grown older, she feels like she's more exposed to the world. The hard things feel harder. The joyful times are therefore fewer, and she clings on to them. Joan's art class had become a regular joyful time but now Joan's away and Frances doesn't approve. That's what she's come to discuss with Shane.

'What are you going to do about it?' she says to Shane as he brings her a shandy. The bar is quiet so he has time for a chat; he hasn't said that but she's going to corral him into one.

He looks bemused. 'Do about what?'

'Joan not being here.' The shandy's a little on the sweet side. Shane must have been distracted when he made it. Usually he gets the balance right.

He puts his hands on his hips and looks at her like she's a little touched in the head. 'What am *I* going to do about it?'

'Yes. I can't do anything – I'm an old lady.'

'Old harridan, you mean.'

'Sit down, you rude individual. Then we can talk properly.'

He does as he's ordered, pushing his chair against the wall and turning out so he can survey the space. Not that there's much likelihood of clientele arriving – it's the middle of the afternoon in the middle of the week, which is the quietest time for the Duchess.

'You can do plenty, Frances. Including this. I don't know Joan well enough to do anything.' He doesn't look at her as he says that last part.

Frances takes another sip of her drink. 'But you want to.'

Now he *is* looking at her, almost like a child caught nicking biscuits from the pantry.

'Do I?' he says softly.

'I reckon you miss her more than I do.'

There's a touch of sadness in his smile and Frances thinks she shouldn't have raised this subject. She didn't mean to put him on the spot, more wanted him to feel understood. Maybe she's no good at understanding men, though; maybe that's why her son behaves the way he does.

'Yeah, I miss her,' he concedes. 'But probably just the same amount as you.'

'I wasn't sure I was going to like her, you know. She seemed a bit – mm, stuck up.' Frances remembers Joan's nose literally being in the air and thinking that she couldn't be friends with a woman who turns her nose up. Then she realised Joan was guarded and that's how she put up her defences. The more she's got to know her, the more she's realised that Joan has played a role for most of her adult life, and while Frances has often felt the pressure to be a certain way, she's always remained true to the girl she grew up as: sturdy, no-nonsense, with a side of dreamer. Through all the challenges she's had, she's never had to pretend to be someone else and she reckons that'd be quite a burden, so it's no wonder Joan is slow to let people in.

'She *is* a bit stuck up,' Shane says, laughing. 'But I like that about her.'

'Oh yes?'

'You have to work to gain her approval. So when she finally decides she likes you it means something.'

Frances considers this in light of people she's known and how they behave. And her own behaviour. Her mother did always want her to be friendly to everyone, but her brothers – Cec, in particular – said that if she was friendly to everyone, people wouldn't know if she really liked them or not. It was a conundrum, and she thinks now that maybe she tended towards her mother's way of doing things just because she was the closest example to follow. So maybe she was more influenced by others' expectations than she thought.

'It doesn't feel right, her not being here,' Frances says. 'I know she was never going to be here forever, but . . .' She sighs, mainly for effect, and sips her shandy.

Shane's forehead wrinkles. 'Why can't she be here forever? I mean, not in the Duchess but . . .' He sweeps a hand around. 'Here. In the area.'

Frances thinks about this. 'Because she may not belong here. She has children in Sydney. She would have friends.' Although Frances doesn't know about that, given what Joan has told her about Genevieve.

'She has friends here,' Shane says, although he doesn't sound convinced.

'It may not be enough. This place was meant to be her waystation.'

'On the way to what?'

He looks so serious that Frances wants to laugh, but then she remembers that he's serious about this because he's serious about Joan, and she fears that there's only heartache ahead of him there. Joan doesn't seem to be in the market for a new fella and even if she were, Shane may not be him.

'To whatever her future brings,' is what Frances offers him.

She has to say something, though – Shane was her friend well before she met Joan, and it is Shane who would command more of her loyalty, if push came to shove on that matter.

'What does she mean to you?' she prods, gently.

There's a look on his face – the sort of look that says he's considering pretending that he doesn't know what she's talking about – then it passes.

'I admire her,' he says. 'She's strong. Courageous. Doing what she's done.'

Frances waits.

'I know she's gone back,' Shane continues. 'For now. But to leave in the first place, when she was unhappy . . . A lot of people wouldn't. It's harder to do that than to stay, I reckon.'

Now he looks pained, and Frances is sure he's thinking about how his own marriage has dissolved; there weren't fights or tears, not really; it just seemed to disappear while he and his wife weren't looking. He's told her that he should have put in more work and that he has regrets. Also that he doesn't know which work he was meant to do because he was just doing the things his father did, thinking they would still apply this late in the twentieth century when the women have different expectations of life than his mother's generation did.

Shane wouldn't be the first man to make that mistake and Frances can't blame him for it, given that there's no handbook. Sure, there may be plenty of books of advice about relationships but they don't tend to agree with each other. It's a confusing world. It was simpler for her, she thinks, living on the land when the roles and work of men and women were more clearly defined by the demands placed on each. Women simply couldn't physically do many of the tasks the men could, and the men respected that the women played roles that were different but just as valuable. Of course, there were inequities – she's just not sure they were worse than the way things are now, when a good man like Shane finds himself adrift because he's not sure which direction he's meant to go in, or if any of the directions are suitable to begin with.

'I agree that she's courageous,' Frances say. 'But we're not going to figure out what she's doing by talking about it.'

A loud group of three men in suits walks into the bar and Shane swivels his head.

'I should go,' he says.

'I know.' She lifts her shandy. 'It's all right; I have company.'

He laughs and it sounds a little sad. 'You're a good friend, Frances.' As he stands, he bends down to kiss her cheek. 'Thank you.'

'Not sure what I've done to deserve that.'

'You put up with me,' he says, then leaves before she has a chance to rebut his statement.

CHAPTER FIFTY-SEVEN

After Alison joined Frances's art class – or should she call it Joan's art class? – she needed to find a space at home where she could practise drawing. She didn't mind being disturbed while she did it, but she wanted to be able to leave her paper and pencils in place and not have them moved or riffled through while she wasn't using them. In other words: she wanted a space of her own. Not a room, just a space.

As part of her rapprochement with Tad, she asked him to find her one, and he had immediately grinned and announced, 'The garage.'

They never put either of their cars in the garage, preferring to leave them in the driveway or on the street. The garage was therefore a refuge for sporting equipment that Sean and Rosie used to need, a bicycle Tad rode for a few months on a get-fit campaign, and some tools that he used from time to time. Alison hardly went in there, which was ridiculous considering it was part of her home. But she had no need. It had never been a space that had a function for her.

There was a room above the garage that they had always thought the kids could use as a rumpus room when they became teenagers, but it has no furniture, no heating – a necessity in these parts – and threadbare carpet. So it's not overly welcoming and therefore not a space she wants to be in either. Which is why she initially baulked at Tad's suggestion.

'That room isn't very inviting,' she said.

He shook his head. 'Not the room. The bench.'

There's a long workbench in the garage which houses some of those tools but is otherwise unused. Alison walked out to the garage, switching on its bare-bulb light to inspect the size of the bench, and she saw it was perfect.

That very night she sat down, wrapped up in a cardigan against the cool spring air, and drew one of the tools, just for practice.

While she took up the art class to spend time with Frances – to understand her a little better, perhaps – she's enjoying it, both the quiet time and the opportunity to express herself. Charlotte went through an arty phase once and Alison was slightly sceptical of it, given that it went hand in hand with her not cutting her hair or styling it in any way, wearing some colours that Margie described as 'strong' – that is, not suitable for Charlotte – and talking about garrets in Paris, which everyone knew was ridiculous because Charlotte doesn't like the French. Something about smelly cigarettes and smellier cheese.

The phase didn't last long but the impression did, and thereafter Alison associated being artistic with a life change. Or a life phase. Either of which wasn't something she thought she wanted. Now, though, with all the changes that have happened against her will, the idea of creating change, literally, with her hands, is appealing. Plus drawing is fun. Fun is underrated, she has decided, and she has not had much of it in her adult years.

So she has been spending time in the garage at night, when she can, and she leaves her drawings in a stack weighed down by a rock from Sean's terrarium. The drawings are not always realistic, either – sometimes they're fantastical. One night after Erik was surlier than usual, she drew him as a dragon. It didn't look like him, of course. Although the dragon had hair like his.

That's one of the things she likes about making her own creations: in her world dragons can have hairstyles.

She hasn't shown the drawings to anyone and they haven't asked – the kids don't even know she's drawing, because they're usually in bed by the time she's in the garage – so when she walks in this night and sees her creations scattered across the bench, she feels violated, then upset, then afraid, like her secrets have been exposed to the world and she is going to be found wanting.

Then she is angry, because there's only one person who could have done this.

She almost sprints back to the house.

'Erik!' she shrieks from the kitchen as she enters via the back door.

Tad looms in the doorway to the sitting room. 'Alison?' he says, looking concerned.

'He's ruined my drawings,' she says, which is not technically but emotionally true.

Tad takes her arm. 'What do you mean?'

'They're all over the place. Scattered. It has to be him.' She can feel herself getting puce, then her breathing speeds up. This must be what proper anger feels like – the type she's never allowed herself to feel. The type Keith inspires but she tamps down to keep the peace in the family.

'Erik!' Tad yells.

A door slams at the back of the house then Erik is there, looking annoyed. 'What?' he says.

'Have you been in the garage?' Tad asks.

Erik's eyes flicker to Alison's then away. 'Yeah. So?'

'Did you touch Alison's drawings?'

He looks irritated. 'They're right there. She didn't hide them.'

'I didn't issue an invitation to touch them!' Alison says, wishing her voice wasn't so high-pitched.

'So? How was I meant to know?'

He has a point, of course, but that doesn't change how outraged she's feeling. What he's done is bad manners.

'The same way I know not to go through your things in your bedroom.' Alison tries to lower her voice for that one.

'But they weren't in your *room*.' He crosses his arms.

'This house is ours,' Tad says. 'That means it's *all* her room.'

'Yeah – and none of it's mine, right?' He looks hateful in that moment, his lower lip jutting out.

'That's right,' Tad says, surprising Alison. 'You are my son but you are Alison's guest.'

Tad and Alison exchange glances.

'Which means you need to respect her things. And her privacy. You still haven't apologised for damaging her car.'

Alison watches as Erik looks like he wants to explode. He's probably used to getting his own way all the time. No siblings to disrupt that. Not even a father to tell him what he could and couldn't do.

Which is why she still tries to think well of him, despite all the reasons not to. He's a boy who didn't know if his father cared. That's something she finds hard to reconcile with the Tad she knows, and it is so strange to think that Tad can be perceived as one sort of man by his eldest son and ex-wife and another sort by her, Sean and Rosie. It's not something she will ever be able to reconcile or resolve. Maybe that's just how life is.

She drew a flower arrow the other night, while she was thinking about the whole situation. All their names were written into it, in small letters. It was one of the drawings arrayed on the bench, so she knows Erik saw it. She just doesn't know how he interpreted it, if he did at all.

'Whatever,' he says, although it's softer.

'You're not going to apologise?' Tad pushes.

Erik half-turns his head away. 'Not tonight.'

He leaves quickly and Alison wonders if there's half a promise in what he said. Not tonight, maybe sometime.

It's a start.

CHAPTER FIFTY-EIGHT

This house is just as lovely as it was when she left, and no more lived in. It's as if Isaac hasn't been here at all; perhaps he's been staying at a hotel. Or the housekeeper is really meticulous. She should ask him if that's true. Except she's avoiding him as much as she can, and luckily this lovely house is big enough to make that possible.

She hasn't told anyone she's back. Has been tiptoeing around the suburb, going for walks at times when her old friends – acquaintances, as she thinks of them now – will be at lunches or groups or classes. Whatever it is that they all do that fills their time. The same activities she used to do but she can barely remember them now. It's as if living away from here, albeit for a handful of months, has changed everything.

Certainly she has not missed any of her Sydney friends the way she has missed Frances. Even Shane and Kirrily. Three people who opened their hearts to her and did not demand hers in return, which made her more likely to show it. She didn't, though – she was guarded with them. Or she thought she was. Painting so that they could see what she painted, teaching so that they could share her passion, this is how she shows love. It's not the acceptable way. A woman is meant to be warm and effusive and affectionate. That's not her; it's never been her. But she is passionate and focused and determined when it comes to the one thing that sets her alight: art. It's taken her too long to come back to the essence of herself. Although she does not want to think of the intervening time as wasted years. She had her children. She made a life. That's not nothing.

The key turns in the front door.

'Mummy?' It's Corinne's voice.

Joan wanders in from the 'small' sitting room, which is bigger than her room at the Duchess and adjacent to the large sitting room that lies beyond the front door.

'Hello, darling,' she says.

'Is Daddy home?' Corinne puts down the basket that holds her sleeping daughter, the one Joan should feel guiltier about not seeing more.

'No.'

'Good.'

Joan feels herself tense, as if Corinne is going to attack her now that she knows there are no witnesses. It's a little ridiculous, and melodramatic, but being in this house feels like she's on a stage performing the role of her former self rather than the authentic self she left on the Mornington Peninsula.

'Why is that good?' Joan asks, wanting to get it over with.

'Because I know there's something he's not telling me.' She puts her hands on her hips. 'You and I don't always get along, Mummy, but it's completely not like you to do what you did. What did he do?'

So her daughter is more astute than Joan gave her credit for; what a pity her son isn't the same. Nathan hasn't spoken to her since that one phone call at the Duchess, and she knows that Isaac has told him that she's home.

Except Corinne isn't exactly right: it's more what Isaac didn't do, hasn't done, all these years. He has not been interested in her other than in what she can do for him. Is this the sort of thing a mother can tell her daughter? She will have to test it in order to find out.

'He didn't pay attention,' Joan says. 'To me, to you, to our lives. He didn't *care*.'

'He does care!' Corinne says.

'I knew you wouldn't believe me.' Joan feels petulant saying this but it's out before she can stop it.

'I didn't . . . I didn't say that. I'm just . . . confused. He's always said he cares. He says "I love you" each time we talk.'

'Saying and doing are different things. Anyone can say "I love you" regardless of whether they mean it or not.'

Corinne's face falls.

'He does love you,' Joan adds hastily. 'But I don't think he loves me.'

There: it's out. She wasn't even sure if she believed it until she said it, but now she has it feels right.

'Mummy!'

If Joan thought Corinne would receive this information like an adult, she was incorrect: her daughter looks like a child who has been told her cat died.

'That's just not true!' Corinne adds, her voice wobbly.

Regardless of the dead-cat expression, Joan needs to talk to her daughter like an adult because she can't protect her from reality any more. Corinne is a mother herself now; things are going to happen to her, to Natalie once she grows up, to other people she loves. Life is never as fixed as anyone thinks and it does no one any good to pretend otherwise. She thought her life was fixed when she had Rachel and four months later it felt like it was over.

'He used to love me,' Joan says, trying to be reassuring. 'But somewhere along the way . . . I don't know when it happened, darling. I became his maid, really. That's all I've been good for.'

Now Corinne looks shocked and Joan realises she's perhaps thinking about her own husband and whether he's going to turn out the same way. Joan has no insight there and the only person she can focus on saving at the moment is herself.

'So why is he trying so hard to get you back?' Corinne demands.

Joan shrugs. 'I could guess but I don't think it's because he has really missed *me*. That's because he doesn't really know me. I have hardly known myself.'

It's important that she accepts her own role in what's happened in this house, in their lives, in their family. By not being who she really is – all the parts of her, including the wild ones that want to paint all night and dance all day, the ones she has sublimated all these years so she could be a good wife and mother – she's let everyone down. Not that she thinks Isaac will accept this or give her back her money because of it. But she has to be truthful to her daughter, at least. There is still time for Corinne to learn from where Joan went wrong, and not hide herself in her own marriage or from her own daughter.

'That's sad, Mummy.' Corinne steps closer to her. 'That's really sad.'

'What would have been sadder is never coming to this realisation,' Joan says. Then she puts her arm around Corinne and kisses the side of her head. 'I have to save my own life, my darling, so you can learn how to save yours if you need to.'

Joan is surprised to find herself crying. Tears are not something she indulges in if she can help it. But she lets them come, lets them fall. Through their haze she feels that one thing is true: she loves her children, enough to not let the connection drop again. Whatever comes next for her, she will commit to that.

'Does that mean you're not staying?' Corinne murmurs.

'In this house? No, I'm not. Where I go after that – who knows?' She smiles with her cheeks wet. 'My paints are still in Victoria.'

'Your paints?' Corinne steps back, and Joan remembers that Corinne still has no idea about what she's been up to. Because she hasn't told her. And if she's going to tell her, she should go back to the beginning.

'Have a seat, darling,' she says. 'This may take a while.'

CHAPTER FIFTY-NINE

Well, it's official: her knee is not improving. So she'll have to go to the doctor. Which means asking Alison to take her. And these days Alison is strung tighter than a Stradivarius, with all the hullabaloo at home, so Frances doesn't really want to bother her but there's no one else to ask. It's not as if Keith would ever help.

It's all so tiring in the considering of it – the logistics of healthcare when one is unable to take care of it all oneself – that Frances reckons there are some days when it would be easier to just close her eyes, go to sleep and stay asleep for the foreseeable future. Except that is not how sleep works, no matter how much she'd like it to. One wakes up eventually.

She could always start taking sleeping pills. Gerald was fond of them, saying they knocked him out good and proper. The idea of being drugged to sleep never quite appealed to Frances, but she was younger then and her knee didn't hurt.

Colin is a consideration, obviously. If she slept for days, there would be no one to feed him. She couldn't do that to him. Mind you, now he's back in the good books with Phyllis next door she could always turn him loose and hope for the best. Phyllis might take him in.

You see, this is what happens when a person spends too much time alone: they start conjuring up all sorts of schemes that are neither sensible nor feasible, and if said aloud, they'd sound a little cuckoo. She feels a little cuckoo some days. Her knee is preventing her getting to the Duchess as often as she was and she misses the company. The midday TV shows don't really cut it. She is missing Joan most of all; it's been over a fortnight and, with no contact from her friend, she's imagining all sorts of things, like Joan never talking to her again.

'Eh, Colin?' she says, as if he knows what she's thinking. Or saying. She's not one of those people who thinks her dog is a person, but she talks to him often enough that the casual observer might suspect she is.

He lifts his corgi head and sniffs the air.

Outside she hears a car tearing along the street. It's become popular with hoons, that street. So she couldn't turn Colin loose – it's not safe for him to be out there. That means she'll have to keep to a normal sleep–wake cycle.

A knock at the door gives her a little fright. She isn't due for visitors, and an unexpected visitor probably means Keith. Who she doesn't want to see because it would mean he wants something. Not that he's bothered her for a while, now he seems to have accepted that she doesn't have any money to give him. Alison hasn't heard from him either. So maybe it's not him. Maybe it's the neighbour on her other side, who wants to put in a new fence.

She needs both hands on the arms of the chair to push herself up and she takes her time to get to the door, although whoever is there doesn't seem to mind because there is no further knocking.

'Hello?' she says meekly through the closed door. Can't be too careful with the hoons around.

'Frances, it's Joan,' comes the response.

Joan! Her Joan! Their Joan!

Frances turns the lock as quickly as she can and opens the door to see her friend looking exactly as she did the last time she saw her. Which, admittedly, was not that long ago, but for all Frances knew Joan had gone into hiding and changed her hair or something.

She opens her arms and Joan steps into them, hugging her as tightly as Frances hoped she would.

'Hello,' Joan says into her hair, then Frances releases her so she can take another look at her.

'We missed you,' she says.

'I missed you too.'

'Come in, come in.'

They walk down the hallway and Frances gestures for Joan to take a seat.

'Tea? Biscuit?' she offers; Joan shakes her head.

'I won't stay long. I need to get to the Duchess and find out if I still have a room.'

'You do. I've been checking.'

Joan looks momentarily stricken. 'That's so kind.'

Frances waves off her compliment. 'That's just being a friend. Besides, William's been hoping you'd come back. He says you add something to the place.'

'Mm.' Joan still doesn't look too happy.

'What is it?'

'I just don't know . . .' She sighs. 'I don't know if I'm staying in the area permanently.'

This is not what Frances wants to hear but nor is she surprised: Joan is not from this area and while she may have stayed longer than she planned, there are other people and places who, no doubt, need her.

'Well, I'm pleased you're back,' she says. 'Even if it's not for long.'

They sit for a few seconds in silence, Frances hoping Joan will tell her more.

'I have money again. I went and found myself a more expensive lawyer than the one Isaac was using and he sorted it out. I'm lucky William didn't ask me to pay up straightaway. He's been very understanding.'

'We would have helped you,' Frances says. 'If we'd known.'

Joan frowns. 'I would never have asked you to do that.'

'And that's why we would've. Between me and Shane and Kirrily we could have worked something out.'

'Thank you but I could never impose. You all have enough to pay for and think about.'

'They'll be so pleased you're back. We've kept up the art. Although William moved us indoors.'

'Oh? I think he's been wanting to do that for a while.'

'Something about an art show.' Frances gestures to some drawings she has propped up against the wall. They do not include a sketch she made of Joan, which she must have known to keep hidden since she wouldn't want Joan to see it yet.

Joan stands then walks over to inspect the drawings.

'Who's the little girl?' she asks.

'Alison. I had a photo of her and I thought . . .' They had another minor squabble the other day and afterwards Frances had pulled out her photo albums, reminiscing about Alison's childhood and pondering how things had changed between them, mainly because their lives had changed. She selected a photo of her daughter at the age of five and decided to draw it – perhaps later paint it – as a gift.

'It's lovely.' Joan smiles. 'I hope you're going to show her.'

'We'll see,' Frances says, because if it's not completed to her liking, she won't be showing anyone else.

'And how are the others – Kirrily?'

'Still pining over that fella.'

'Oh dear.'

'I know – hopeless. He's a rogue, I'm sure of it. But she needs a bit of a distraction, poor love. She's working so hard.'

'And Shane?' She says it slowly, like she's not sure she should mention his name.

'He misses you.'

There, no mistaking her meaning. She's not above scheming to get Shane and Joan together so Joan stays in the area. Or maybe that means they both move away? Her plan may go awry there.

But they're both good people and they deserve to be happy. Joan's husband doesn't sound like the sort to make her happy.

'I'm sure you've kept him busy.' Joan looks back to the drawings. 'So we'll have a class tomorrow, I guess. Given that tomorrow is Friday.'

'Wendy may be a bit miffed.'

'Oh?'

'She's enjoyed being top dog while you've been away. Gone to her head.'

Joan laughs. 'I can't wait to see that.'

Then she walks over, bends down and kisses Frances on the cheek. 'But I should go. I just wanted to see you before I went on to the hotel.'

'I'm glad you did, love. Help me up.' She holds out a hand.

'Stay there, please.'

'No.' Frances keeps her hand out for Joan to take. 'You're a guest here and I always see guests to the door.'

'All right.'

Joan helps her up and Frances takes her time ambling down the hallway, opening the door to let Joan out.

'I wish you were back for good,' she says as Joan is halfway out the door, 'but most of all I wish for your happiness.'

Joan turns. 'And I for yours.' She blows her a kiss, then walks through the gate and to her car.

Frances waits to watch as she drives away.

CHAPTER SIXTY

Three weeks. It's been three weeks since Kirrily has seen Derek and she wants to know what that lunch was for if he's going to stay away. There she was, daydreaming about him, wondering when she'd see him again, worried about Aidan's surgery, completely distracted at work and at home – which of course Connor noticed – and as time has gone on that distraction has intensified, not waned. The only respite she has is during the art class, when she can focus only on what is literally in front of her on the easel and forget about everything else for an hour.

She has considered that he meant to do this: wind her up then leave her spinning. Except how does that benefit him if he never shows up again?

The other possibility is that something has happened to him. She has no way of knowing – she doesn't even know his last name. Not that he knows hers, but he knows how to reach her: at the Duchess.

It wasn't him she was thinking about this morning, though, when she snapped at Connor during the usual breakfast flurry when Aidan wanted Fruit Loops and Bridget wanted toast and eggs and Connor was trying to navigate his way around them to make his coffee and get on the road. It was the fact that they still don't have a surgery date for Aidan and with each day that passes he gets more anxious about it, which makes her worry too.

'Watch it!' she said testily as Connor trod on her foot, trying to manoeuvre around her.

'Sorry, babe.' He grabbed her and kissed her temple and she recoiled. Which was not a nice thing to do, especially in front of the kids, because Bridget saw her and looked upset.

'Daddy didn't mean to do it,' she said, as if Connor was the one at fault.

'No, I didn't.' He kissed Bridget on her crown. 'See ya, chickadee.' A kiss for Aidan. 'See ya, mate.'

Then he was gone and she felt wretched, so she snapped at the kids about taking too long with their breakfast, which did not make her feel better at all, and just left her asking herself when she'd ever learn that taking out her woes on the ones she loves is never the solution.

Except sometimes she feels like she can't help it. She knows it means she takes them for granted, especially Connor. But she reaches a point where she needs to get her feelings out and they happen to be in the way. Or maybe that's yet another excuse she's made up for herself.

Her feelings were stuffed back down again when she arrived for work earlier than usual. William had asked if she could cover someone in the dining room at lunchtime, just clearing plates and so on, then do her usual shift. Given the kids were already at school and he said she could take her hour for the art class, she agreed. The art class was the clincher: she needs that hour. She needs the time to get things out and onto a page.

After lunch service, she busied herself in the laundry – there's always work to do there – before four o'clock came and she made her way to the function room William has designated for them. The room is fine, she thinks, but it's not the same as being outdoors. Yet she has no wish to debate with Wendy the merits of this or that spot in the grounds. While Wendy is a good artist, she has a different sensibility to Joan, and Kirrily knows whose she prefers.

So for the time being she'll sit in the room and make the best of it.

That is, until she walks in and sees Joan talking to Frances and involuntarily squeals before dropping her art bag and running over to hug her.

'Oh,' Joan says as she squeezes her tightly. 'That's enthusiastic.'

'You're back!' Kirrily breathes. 'Back-back.'

'Just back.' Joan pats her cheek. 'Good to see you.' Then she narrows her eyes. 'How are you?'

'Yes. Good. Fine.'

Kirrily doesn't want to answer that question truthfully so instead she fossicks in her bag and brings out her supplies. She's facing the door when Shane walks in, so she can see what moves across his face in quick succession: confusion, wonder, elation.

'Joan,' Shane says softly.

'Hello, Shane.'

Kirrily watches as their eyes meet and tries not to look from one to the other like she's at a tennis match. She risks a glance in Frances's direction and sees her frowning.

'When did you get back?' Shane asks.

'Yesterday.'

'And you're staying here . . . at the Duchess?'

'I am.'

His face falls and Kirrily can guess why: he'd want to know why Joan didn't come to see him at the bar. And the reason probably is that Joan wasn't as keen to see him as he was to see her.

'Joan, would you take a look at what I've been working on?' Kirrily says, hoping to give Shane some time to adjust to this realisation.

'Certainly.'

Joan wanders over to where Kirrily is setting up her easel and her drawings, one of Aidan and one of Bridget. She's proud of them and pleased that the children sat still long enough for her to draw them. Aidan in particular was interested in the process, asking her questions. Bridget just sat and read her book, but that's how Kirrily wanted to draw her anyway.

'These are very good,' Joan murmurs just as Wendy arrives, stops and looks somewhat annoyed to see Joan there.

'Oh. Joan,' Wendy says, then she plasters on a smile.

'Hello, Wendy.' Joan smiles quickly in her direction then gives her attention back to Kirrily's work. 'You're really coming along well,' she remarks. 'What else have you been working on?'

Kirrily looks to Frances for direction, not knowing if she should reveal the other sketch she's been working on, of Joan herself. Frances nods then winks.

'A portrait of someone you may recognise,' Kirrily says, pulling it out of her portfolio but feeling shy as she presents it. How weird, really, for someone to see a drawing of themselves.

Joan's expression is one of concentration as she studies it, then her face relaxes into a smile.

'Me?' she says, laughing. 'Why would you draw me?'

'We all did.' Kirrily looks at Shane, hoping he doesn't mind her dumping him in it. 'Because we missed you. Didn't know if you'd ever see these, though.'

Joan looks at the others in turn and Frances is shaking her head while Shane looks away.

'Didn't bring mine,' says Frances. 'You'll have to work for it. By staying for a while.'

Joan's mouth opens but she doesn't say anything.

'I didn't bring mine either,' Shane says, but he clenches the sketchpad under his arm more closely to his side, so Kirrily presumes he's fibbing.

'Yeah, didn't like mine,' Wendy says, almost hurling her bag to the floor. 'So you're back?'

'For now.'

'What about . . .' Wendy flings her hands into the air. 'This. The class. What are we meant to do if you're coming and going?'

'From what I hear you have it under control,' Joan says mildly. 'And William tells me there's some sort of show coming up?'

'Yeah,' Wendy says in a tone of voice that suggests Joan is an idiot.

'You can tell me all about it as we work.' Joan glances around the room. 'But not in here. Let's go outside.'

Wendy makes a strangled noise but she picks up her bag and stomps out of the room.

'Clearly I've turned into an enemy in the time I've been away,' Joan remarks to Frances.

'Not you, love; she's given up the fags,' Frances says. 'Again.'

Joan and Frances leave, and Shane is left watching them.

'Are you okay?' Kirrily says.

'Yes. Of course I am.' He smiles that fake bartender-smile she sees him get sometimes when a customer is being rowdy and he's about to tell them politely to leave or be escorted from the premises.

'Okay,' Kirrily says. 'But I haven't given up smoking so I'll be taking a ciggie break at some point tonight if you want to join me.'

Instead of answering, though, he just smiles sadly and stands back for her to walk through the door first. So she grabs her easel, drawings and bag and does just that.

CHAPTER SIXTY-ONE

It was three days ago when the phone rang in the sitting room and Frances went to answer it.

'Frannie,' said the familiar voice on the other end.

'Margie.' She glanced towards the kitchen, where Alison seemed to be engaged in finding missing grocery items.

'How've you been?'

'Good.'

She and Margie had been speaking regularly since Cec died – even more than they used to – and that meant she didn't need to say much more than 'good' as an update.

'Listen,' Margie said, and Frances could hear pages turning.

'I'm listening.'

'Funny. No, look – listen – I, ah . . .'

There was silence for a couple of seconds and Frances got an odd feeling in her gut. Not a premonition – she doesn't believe in those. But a feeling. Margie is never lost for words, so whatever she was trying to tell Frances couldn't be good.

'What is it, Marg?'

'Look, Frannie, I've been going through Cec's things.'

'Mm.'

'Papers. Letters. The amount of crap the man held onto . . .' There was a loud sigh, more rustling paper. 'We're lucky no one lit a match near the shed, I tell you that.'

'You could have just thrown it all out. He wasn't going to miss it.' It was Frances's attempt at levity, although not a good one.

'There's a letter from Albert,' Margie said quickly, and that feeling in Frances's gut turned into a pain.

'Right.' She needed to think – why would Cec have had a letter from Albert? They weren't friends. Albert was friendly with all of her brothers, certainly, but she wouldn't have thought them to be letter-writing friends.

'After he left for the Pacific,' Margie said. She knows the whole story because she had already married Cec by the time Frances gave birth to Keith. There have been no secrets between them on that score. Although it now seemed as though Cec was keeping at least one.

'Cec never mentioned it to me.'

'He wouldn't have, darl.'

That sounds ominous. Frances swallowed. 'What's in it?'

'I'm just going to say it,' Margie said. 'All right? I'm just saying it.'

Except she didn't say it. She was silent for a second, two, three – too many.

'Then say it,' Frances prompted. 'We're both grown-ups.'

There was the sound of a strangled sort of noise and, once more, the movement of paper.

'Albert wrote to Cec to say that he couldn't marry you,' Margie said quickly. 'He said that he trusted Cec more than the other boys to tell you in a calm way.'

That pain in Frances's gut was now a knife twisting deep inside, piercing her past, the foundations of her life, every belief she's built her life on.

It was stunning, this pain. It caused her to lose her balance, to put out a foot to steady herself. And she must have made a noise because out of the corner of her eye she saw Alison in the doorway.

'Frannie?'

'I'm here.'

'Are you all right?' Marg asked.

'I . . . don't know.'

'Lord, I shouldn't have said anything. Cec kept it from you all these years. I should have too. But I just thought . . .' She paused. 'I thought you had a right to know. Albert intended to tell you. Maybe Cec thought it was better to let it be. But was it?'

It was a good question and one Frances couldn't answer; might never be able to, because life's hypotheticals are like that.

'I don't know,' she said truthfully.

She really wanted to lie down. Lie down, close her eyes and not think about anything. Because it felt like the day she found out Albert was dead all over again. This was the day her idea of him died, and who was to say which grief would be harder.

'I should go, Margie,' she said quietly.

'I shouldn't have said anything.' Margie sounded upset.

'No, you should have. The truth is always better in the end.' It's what Frances said to reassure her sister-in-law although she wasn't sure she believed it.

'All right. Bye, Frannie.'

But what she wanted to say was: *Why did you take that away from me?*

She knew why, though: Marg was quite aware of how much Frances had clung on to Albert's memory; she'd probably had her opinions of it too but never said anything. Cec never raised the subject but he'd listen if Frances talked about it, and in those early years, before Gerald, the talk was regular.

Frances turned slowly around to face her daughter, whose eyes were wide and mouth slightly open.

'Mum,' she said, stepping forward, holding out her hand to take her mother's. 'What did Margie say? Is she sick? You look so shocked.'

What could she tell her child – that the man who has loomed over their entire lives was more of a phantom than she thought? That she had immortalised – lionised – someone who, by the time he died, probably wasn't thinking of her at all? Perhaps there was more in the letter, giving his reasons, but . . . those reasons didn't matter any more. Almost sixty years had gone by. Those reasons were ashes.

'I am shocked,' Frances conceded. 'And I'll tell you about it later.' She summoned a smile. 'Why don't you go to the shops? I'm just going to sit for a while.'

'I don't think I should leave you.'

'I'll be all right. Nothing a cuppa won't fix.'

That's the remedy she learnt at her mother's knee: cuppas for dead relatives, bad news in the district, letters from the army. For strained friendships, for churlish children, for times when you just need comfort and there's no exact reason why. It was the remedy she needed now.

'If you're sure?' Alison's frown was so deep Frances reckoned her forehead may disappear.

'I am. Honestly.'

She smiled and headed for the kettle, flipping the switch and turning her back to her daughter, to let her know the conversation was over.

Frances knew she'd have to see the letter, though. It wasn't that she didn't believe it existed but that she needed to see it for herself. Whether that was to close that long chapter in her book or because she knew she required more convincing, she couldn't say. She may be an older personage now but that doesn't mean she knows everything or doesn't get confused about her life and what goes on in it. When she was young – when she became a mother for the first time – she looked forward to growing older and feeling wiser. It's never happened. Perhaps it doesn't happen for anyone, and other people are just better at pretending it does. But she's not going to pretend. You're on your own if you pretend, unable to ask anyone to help you because you don't want to confess that you don't know everything. And we all need help.

When Frances told Alison that she planned to see Marg, Alison offered to drive her, and Frances accepted. Something changed between them after that phone call – it was as if Alison saw her as a person for the first time, not just as her mother, and she's changed her tune. Started to ask more questions about Frances's younger years, about what it was like to grow up on the land – questions she and her brother never asked when they had all the time in the world to do so. Frances presumed it was because they weren't interested or that they thought she didn't have a life before them. It's such a conceit that children have, maybe a necessary one: *your life only began with me*. She doesn't remember thinking that of her own parents but, then again, she's not a reliable witness to her own life. Memory is selective and she has clearly selected only the best memories of Albert, for example, the ones in which he adored her and was going to cherish her forever. He clearly had no such intention.

They've had an uneventful drive into the High Country and as Alison parks the car next to the house, Marg emerges from the side door, waving.

'Good to see you, Frannie,' she says with a loud kiss on Frances's cheek. 'And Ally girl, look at you! Even more beautiful than last time I saw you. Why didn't you tell me she's getting more beautiful, Fran?'

'Because you would have told me I was boasting,' Frances says.

'True.'

Marg's smile is sadder than it used to be; they both have things to be sad about, Frances thinks, so it's no surprise.

'Come in, come in,' Marg says, holding open the screen door. 'Kettle's boiled; scones are on the table.'

Of course they're going to be fed straightaway – it wouldn't be the country otherwise.

Scones, jam, cream and tea are consumed – hold the cream for Frances – then Marg leads them into the sitting room, which has remained mostly unchanged since Frances's parents lived here. The sofa is newer but the sideboards are the same, as is the good china on display. There are photographs of Frances's parents and grandparents, in the same spots they've held for decades. These things are unchanging even as her understanding of the life she had here has changed.

'So . . .' Marg picks up a single sheet of paper from the coffee table and holds it out to Frances, who sits first then takes it, extracting her reading glasses from the pocket of her cardigan.

She thinks of who she was in 1942: not much more than a girl, working hard for her parents and worried about her beau, pregnant but not aware of it for four months because she was always so busy on the property that at the best of times she would lose track of when she was bleeding.

That slip of a thing, with her whole life ahead of her, believed she was loved by a kind-eyed young man and she was waiting for him to return. By the time she was told he wouldn't, she knew anyway, because she was so sure he'd have got word to her if he was all right.

That wasn't true, though. He could have survived that war and never got word to her again and she would still have had Keith and been wondering what happened.

As much as she knows the danger of indulging what-ifs, she does it anyway, holding this letter she doesn't want to read from a man she swore never to forget.

There is it, on this yellowed paper, in his strong cursive. He'd sent her letters, before this – she memorised the date and contents of every one of them once she knew there would be no more. They have gone with her throughout her life, from house to house. Perhaps she'll add this one to them, then burn them.

I was hasty, the letter reads, *in offering marriage to your sister. In truth now I do not believe we are suitable for each other. Could you please let her know? I will write to her once I receive word that you have done so.*

So few words to say something that means so much, and so cowardly to ask Cec to do it.

The date of the letter was two days before Albert was killed; who knows when Cec received it. She will never know why he decided not to tell her about it, and she'll probably spend the rest of her life wondering if that was a cruelty or a kindness.

'I'm sorry, Fran.' Marg pats her arm and kisses the top of her head. 'I know how you loved him.'

Alison moves in her seat and sniffs, causing Frances to look up. She's surprised to see tears in Alison's eyes.

'I'm sorry too, Mum,' she says, then she leans over and hugs her, burying her face in Frances's neck like she used to when she was a child.

It's just what she needs, Frances realises as she returns the hug – to be reminded how much she is loved by the people who are still here. The ones she has not given her full attention to because she has been wrapped up in a fantasy of a love that wasn't as real as she thought it was.

What a waste of years. What a waste of emotion. That is what she's most sorry about.

'Thanks, love,' she says into Alison's ear and squeezes her a little bit harder.

After a minute or so, they let go of each other and smile through their tears.

Marg takes them on a drive around the property, which Alison has never seen properly. When she was young they didn't visit that often, for reasons that probably had everything to do with their lives being busy and the property not being close to the peninsula. But once a habit isn't formed, it's hard to make, so that lack of early connection to Frances's home translated into a lack of interest in adulthood.

On their way back to the peninsula, however, Alison asks questions about Frances's childhood, the work she did, amazed at how much physical labour was given to such a young person.

'It was the only way,' Frances explains. 'The farm couldn't function if we didn't all muck in. Children are perfectly capable. We don't have to cosset them so much.'

Alison purses her lips and Frances guesses she's said something wrong. But she's talking about her own parenting as much as anything: Keith and Alison were not given the sorts of tasks she was. She wanted them to have fun.

It's not something she is inclined to delve into now, and the rest of the drive home is spent talking about cattle and the High Country and the life that Frances has now, for good, left behind.

CHAPTER SIXTY-TWO

She'd forgotten about how the screaming made her feel. After Aidan was burnt and in hospital, he'd need to have his dressings changed. She would be there for that – she made herself be there for that. Because it was the worst part. He would scream and scream and scream as they removed dressings and bandages then put him back together again, and she would feel it so intensely that she would almost black out.

Her mother once told her that she felt it each time one of her children was hurt and Kirrily didn't quite believe it, because she thought it would work the other way too and she'd have felt something when her mother was so sick, but she didn't. Apart from sadness.

Once she had Bridget and Aidan, though, she got it: if they hurt themselves, she'd feel tears spring to her eyes. That's when she understood why her mother was always telling her and her siblings to 'get on with it, kids' when they were hurt and cried – she didn't like feeling upset any more than Kirrily did. Than she does.

Aidan has been crying as his pain relief wears off and she feels it so deeply it's like someone has put a hot knife into her heart. That is followed by a sense of utter helplessness because she can't do anything for him.

At the time he was burnt and so distressed, her limbs would feel like they were on fire and all she wanted to do was hold her boy to make both of their pain go away, except it would only have made it worse for him. And, therefore, for her.

Connor never had as intense a reaction. He was distressed, but not to this extent. It caused resentment in her that was futile and ridiculous, because he wasn't the one who carried Aidan in his body for nine months. That's the reason she feels her boy's pain now: once upon a time his flesh was hers, his nerves were hers, his breath was hers. They were one. And each time he cries in pain it feels like they are again.

'Mummy,' he says weakly from his bed, where his wrist is stuck with a cannula so the drip can give him fluids, and once again he's swaddled. He's cried himself into a sort of stillness.

'It's all right, darling, you can go to sleep,' she murmurs, picking up his free hand and kissing it.

'Mummy – Bridge?'

He's been asking for his sister but Kirrily and Connor are united in not wanting her to see this. She didn't see him the first time, and they want to spare her the same sight that is upsetting them.

'Soon, darling,' she tells him, because it's not untrue: at some point in the near future, he'll go home from hospital and his sister will be there.

She holds his hand until he falls asleep, then places it gently on the bed, picks up her handbag and goes outside for the only break she'll give herself.

Kirrily remembers the first time she tried smoking. She was sixteen, and it wasn't at school. Her father thought it must have been, when he caught her down the back of the garden one day, hiding behind a gum tree, thinking no one would see her – that he wouldn't see her – even though smoke was curling away from her and the tree was visible from the sunroom at the back of the house. Maybe she wanted him to catch her. Maybe she wanted him to notice just one thing about her, considering he relied on her to raise his kids and spent most of his spare time elsewhere.

With women, with grog, with mates – she didn't know. As long as she had her siblings fed and presentable – or, even better, asleep in bed – when he came home, he didn't seem to care. Who knows what happened after she left them but she had put in her time. Now they barely keep in contact with her and she wants to ask them if they couldn't tell how much she loved them by all the time she put into them. It's not a subject she can afford to dwell on too much, though, because otherwise she'd be so upset that she'd never get anything done. And she has to get things done.

So, no, she didn't take up smoking at school. Not even with a school friend. It was with Tony, who was a few years older and whose dad ran the local milk bar. Tony was sweet on her, she knew, and he chatted her up whenever he saw her. She let him, although she didn't feel the same way. Any attention is good when you're sixteen, though, isn't it?

Around the corner from the milk bar that day he offered her a cigarette and she took it, having been curious about what she'd seen some of the girls at school doing. They looked cool; she wanted to be cool. Probably every sixteen-year-old does.

It wasn't love at first puff but there was something about the ritual of it – light, inhale, exhale, stand, contemplate – that was appealing. It helps as she lights, inhales, exhales, stands and tries not to remember her son's anguished cries. Instead of letting thoughts crowd her brain she watches the flow of people on the footpath a few metres away from where she's leaning against the hospital wall, near a small semicircular garden that has a bench. The bench looks like one in the grounds of the Duchess Hotel. She wishes she was there now, just working, able to focus on one task at a time, or having a laugh with Shane.

The other day he was asking her questions about Joan – as if she'd know anything – and she teased him about having a crush.

'Men don't have crushes,' he said, but he looked away from her and she thought his cheeks turned a little pinker under their brown exterior.

'Sure they do,' she said. 'My husband had a crush on me for months. That was even the word he used.'

'Guess he isn't a man, then.' Shane laughed and she knew he was joking but it made her think: what is a man, to her?

If you'd asked her that six months ago, she'd have said Connor was the living definition of it: solid, reliable, trustworthy, strong, loving, capable. Those were qualities she'd always thought a man should embody and when she found them in him, she grabbed them with both hands – after they became clear to her. He revealed himself to her as slowly as he revealed his feelings about her, and she liked that too, that he didn't rush her, didn't make her feel unsafe or uneasy.

Now that she has experienced a rush, though – now that she has felt a little unsafe and uneasy – she has to wonder if she hadn't been exposed to enough different types of men. Maybe her definition of a man was just a definition of Connor. Maybe she needs . . . more. Or different. Is that wrong? Is she being ungrateful? She's definitely being silly. Although it's not Derek himself she thinks may offer her an alternative, especially since she hasn't seen him in weeks; he's just shown her that there are other ways of being in the world.

As she smokes, she looks around her at the men and women coming and going from the hospital. Mainly at the men. Not to perv, just to look. To observe.

There's a short man dapperly dressed, holding a patent leather briefcase, with a pocket square and a tightly knotted tie. He is chatting to the taller man next to him, who is also in a suit but who couldn't look more different, with his jacket unbuttoned and half of his shirt hanging out, although, mystifyingly, his tie is also tightly knotted. Two different men, one style of dress, and it's all in the details.

Joan said that to her the other day when she was trying to figure out how to make her painting of a rose look better.

'The colour's right,' she said, 'but you are missing some details. The details are what make it realistic rather than impressionistic.'

She walked over to the actual rose and pointed at various things that Kirrily then took the time to scrutinise. Then she put those details in the painting, and it did look so much better.

So she looks at more details of passing men and lights another cigarette – why not take ten minutes instead of five, since Aidan was asleep when she left? – and it's a fun game. Right up until she watches a man whose details she knows quite well strolling up a footpath on the other side of the driveway from her, holding the hand of a child, a woman on his other side.

Of course she knew Derek was married. There was never a suggestion that he was not. So it can't be the fact of seeing it that is causing the great thud in her chest and the buzzing in her middle. Can it?

She should leave immediately, before he sees her, but her feet feel stuck and she wonders if this is what it's like to not be able to look away from a car crash, the way people say. Except the car crash is the fantasy she's made for herself with this man who is laughing, putting his arm around the woman, still holding the child's hand. And she's in the crash, not watching it. So there's no escape, especially not when he turns to speak to the child then his head lifts and he sees her.

Her mouth opens, although there's no way she's going to call out to him.

His eyes go hard and the rest of his face follows.

Derek, who was so handsome to her, now looks like someone else.

Kirrily closes her mouth and throws her cigarette to the ground, stomping on it as if she could stomp out the past few seconds, breaking his gaze to do it.

When she looks up, Derek and his family have moved along. Realising they're likely heading for the same doors she needs to enter, she hurries to get ahead of them, rushing towards the lifts, pushing the buttons frantically, hastily walking through the first open doors.

She ignores the nurse on Aidan's floor who calls out a hello as she passes, just wanting to get to her son's room, to the temporary shelter of it, far from wherever Derek may be, so she can start to count the number of pieces her fantasy has shattered into and, with it, her whole sense of how she can manage her life now. Because that's what it's been doing for her: holding her together.

'Hi, darling,' she says as she enters and sees him awake again. How long was she gone?

Aidan snuffles and turns his head from side to side slowly, like he's trying to work out where he is, in the way of someone still in the limbo between sleeping and waking.

'You're here,' she tells him, and for the first time in a long while she knows that she is too.

CHAPTER SIXTY-THREE

It's been many weeks since Joan has sat in the bar of the Duchess Hotel and done nothing else apart from observe the comings and goings, sip a glass of wine and not think about much. She has a lot to think about – her whole life and what's to become of it – yet today she finds her brain is mostly still. The constant whirring of maybes and could-Is and should-Is is still, and she puts it down to being in this place, where there is so much other activity that she can actually be still inside the storm.

The tricky bit is that she can't live here forever. She's already paid far too much to accommodate herself in a place that has a tariff better suited to a weekend stay. It's been worth it, for the time to just *be* and the unexpected sense of belonging she's found here, but it's not sustainable in the long term. Living on the Mornington Peninsula probably isn't either. While she loves the drama of its seaward beaches and the prettiness of its sheltered side, since returning from Sydney she's found herself longing for the light on the harbour and the ripples of water in the coves near her house. She's been dreaming of things she might paint and walks she might take, of spots where she can sit and look at the world then try to make something of it through pencil and brush. This is a longing she can only have conjured by being absent and it is starting to tell her where her home is. If only her heart were there the way it is here, with people she has come to cherish.

'Penny for your thoughts?' Shane says as he hovers over her table.

'They're worth more than that,' she says, arching an eyebrow.

He laughs and nods. 'I'm sure they are. May I?' He gestures to the vacant seat opposite her.

'Of course. But it must be a slow day if you're taking time to sit.'

'Slow enough. Bugalugs behind the bar –' he gestures with his thumb – 'can handle anything we need. It's good experience for him.'

She doesn't know who Bugalugs is; perhaps she'll never find out.

'I wanted to thank you,' Shane says, 'for the art class. I wasn't sure about it at first but it's really . . .' His face softens. 'Grown on me.'

'You didn't seem unsure,' she says, remembering that he presented as quite enthusiastic about it.

'I wanted to be there,' he amends quickly. 'I just didn't know if I'd like the art.'

They look at each other and she thinks she understands what he's trying to say, but doesn't want to make any presumptions.

'I've been painting at home,' he goes on. 'Nothing much, just splashing colours around. Found a big bit of canvas at a hardware, thought I'd give it a go.'

'That's wonderful,' she says, and means it, because she can see how this man who holds so tightly onto his emotions might need to get them out. As we all do. She held onto hers for too many years and let go of them by driving her car down the Hume Highway. If she'd found a way to do that earlier, who knows where she would be. Or maybe she'd still be at the Duchess Hotel. Life seems to bring us to the places where we're meant to be just when we're meant to be there. No amount of revising the past changes that. So maybe she was always meant to be here, talking to Shane, and he to her; we can never know the significance of the part we play in other people's lives or us in theirs, not fully. Everyone is the centre of their own universe and may misjudge the size of the planets orbiting around them or the length of their orbits.

'I'm not going to ask you to look at it or anything.' He laughs nervously. 'It's just paint on a canvas.'

'There are many ways to make a picture.'

'I guess.' He glances around the bar, which is as quiet as it was five minutes ago.

'So . . . do you know if you're staying on?' he says after a few seconds have passed.

'At the Duchess? Or in the area?'

'Both. Either.'

'I haven't made up my mind.' This is the truth: while there are parts of her life in Sydney tugging at her, she can also see how she could make a life on the peninsula and be quite content. It wouldn't be something she'd ever planned for herself but that really describes the whole of life. Even when we do the things we planned, they have a way of surprising us.

'Is there . . .' Shane exhales loudly then sits forward, his elbows on the table. 'Is there something that could persuade you to stay here?'

Joan considers this – it's a valid question.

'Maybe if my children were here,' she says, for as fractious as things can be with them, being so far away from them permanently is not something she thinks she can sustain.

'Oh.' He sits back. 'I guess that's a stumbling block, yeah.'

'Did you forget I had children?'

'No,' he says quickly. 'You have two – Nathan and Corinne.'

She smiles warmly. He's really a kind man; considerate. With problems, but he seems to manage those.

'You've been paying attention,' she says.

His gaze is direct, his eyes holding hers. 'I tend to when it comes to you.'

The whole conversation has been leading to this, she knows, and she had to let it. If she'd tried to pre-empt it, to save him from what she's about to say, that wouldn't have been kinder. Men need to do things, she knows – it's in the doing that they feel like they've achieved something. Of course, they like the doing to be acknowledged, but if she'd prevented him from doing what he set out to do, that would have led to more awkwardness than was necessary.

'I appreciate your close attention,' she says. 'I have noticed it.'

They're still looking into each other's eyes, and she thinks that if she were already divorced, or never married, and she met this man she would want to build a life with him. But she also thinks he wouldn't be interested in that if she were different, and those circumstances would make her different. He likes her as she is now: trying to figure things out, not quite sure what will happen. Unless she's being ungenerous.

'You're attracted to me,' she states, because there is no point in leaving it unstated.

He swallows. 'I am. From the start.'

'And you are a not unattractive man, Shane, I can tell you.'

There's an expression on his face but she can't read it before it's gone.

'It's more than attraction,' he says. 'That's not even the half of it.'

She can feel what he wants to say as tangibly as if he had made a sculpture of it and placed it on the table between them.

'I appreciate that too,' she says quietly. 'But I think you know that it's not returned.'

This time she can read his expression, and it looks like relief, which is not what she expected.

'Are you sure?' he says.

Now she's confused, because she doesn't believe she's ever given him an indication that she feels strongly for him.

So she laughs lightly, mainly to give herself time to think.

'I'm fairly sure,' she says. 'Have you seen evidence to the contrary?'

'Nah,' he says, his face relaxing into a smile. 'It was worth a try, though.'

'You're not upset?'

'At you? That will never happen. You've given me more than I could have hoped for. You've been my friend. You've treated me like someone who still has a chance.'

'What do you mean?'

'The way I've been sometimes . . . People have given up. My wife . . .' He stops and sighs. 'I don't blame her. But after she left everything felt a bit hopeless, you know? Then you came along. You chatted to me; you stood up to me.' He laughs. 'I liked that. And you taught me art. No wonder I fell in love with you.'

He's taking one last shot, and she admires him for trying.

'Are you in love with me or in love with how you feel about your life now?' she says.

'Can't it be both?'

'Certainly.' She nods slowly. 'I do love you, Shane, but not in the way you might hope.'

'Not right now.'

She laughs. 'I can't quite believe we're discussing this like it's something other than a matter of the heart.'

'Why not? We're both middle-aged, right? If we can't talk about this like grown-ups, we're doing something wrong.'

He has a point: they're past the stage of life where romantic promises and dreams mean anything in light of what they know to be true about what is required to stay in a relationship. It makes more sense to discuss it rationally, even if that doesn't seem like a rational thing in itself.

'True,' she avers. 'But I'm still married, and I don't know if or when that will change.'

'So . . .' He frowns. 'You're not leaving your husband?'

'I imagine it looks like I've left him already.'

'Well . . . yeah.'

'As you said, we're middle-aged. Things may be more straightforward in one way but they seem to get more complicated when it comes to marriages. Or getting out of them.' The prospect of divorcing Isaac – of all the ways he could tie things up, putting her in an unwelcome stasis – has made her pause. No doubt the system is designed to keep women like her – perhaps all women – in the marriage because it can be punitive to get out of it. She needs to gather strength if she's to do it.

'If he doesn't appreciate you, leave him.' Shane says it so matter-of-factly, like that's all there is to it. And maybe it is. Yet she has no interest in leaving one man for another. If she leaves Isaac, it will be for herself.

'A good principle,' she says.

If she were to attach herself to someone, she likes to think she'd choose Shane. She's attracted to him – she too has known this from the start, but we can be attracted to many people throughout life and it doesn't necessarily mean anything. He has been clear in his intentions towards her, and she enjoys his company. Lifelong commitments have been formed with less. But now is not the time, and she is also old enough to know that timing is everything.

'I'd take care of you,' he says softly.

'I know you would,' she replies. 'But I just don't know what comes next.'

He takes her hand, and she doesn't resist.

'Just . . . keep me in mind, would you?' he says. 'Once you know where you are and what you want. I just want to be considered.'

She leans across and presses her palm to his cheek.

'I promise,' she says.

He puts his hand over hers for a second or two, then releases her other hand and stands.

'I'll be here,' he says, then he leaves her and walks back to the bar, where Joan can see Bugalugs looking agog in their direction. She turns away so he can't see her tears.

DECEMBER 1999

CHAPTER SIXTY-FOUR

In the days after they visited Margie to see Albert's letter, Alison checked on Frances more than usual. While she couldn't understand exactly what her mother was feeling, because she had never been in the same situation, she has lived with the ghost of Albert for most of her life. So she has her own relationship with him and the alternative path her mother might have taken. The path that would have meant Alison never existed.

It feels oddly comforting to know that even if Albert had lived, that path would likely not have been taken – although who knows, given that Keith exists in both versions of reality. Alison has probably spent too much time thinking about all this, pondering how there are potentially infinite versions of all of our lives rolling out across the universe, and we pick one and stick with it not knowing that the others exist. Or maybe they don't exist. Maybe everything about our lives isn't real.

She really ties herself in knots over that.

'You think too much,' Tad told her the other night as they tried to watch a movie but she was restless – she knew she was – fidgeting and sighing. 'Go out and draw.'

Drawing has become the way she gets the thoughts out of her head. The dragon version of Erik was just the start of it. Now she creates all sorts of fantastical creatures representing aspects of her life that she can't control but wants to at least manage. She wishes she'd discovered drawing earlier – perhaps it would have helped her through the adjustment period when Erik arrived.

They're not exactly getting on better now but there's no overt antagonism. And he's leaving Sean and Rosie alone, in that he's not teasing them. Neither of them has reported that he's been mean.

The house is calmer. Or maybe that's just her perspective at night, from the garage.

The other day she asked Sean how things were going and he did his usual avoidance tactics of turning his head away and not looking her in the eyes, then mumbled, 'Yeah, okay.' That's his new code for 'good'. If he'd said only 'okay', that would mean 'bad'. Alison has worked this out by observing him in conversation with Rosie, who seems to understand him at all times. Her children have made a world of two to which she needs an invitation, but she's not sad about it: they're growing up, detaching from their parents; it's what happens. She's just glad they are close; she and Keith never were.

The changes in their house, and in her mother's life, have made her think seriously again about the project she started a while ago: moving Frances in with them. Originally she'd wanted to build a granny flat but Keith blew the money for that; she doesn't want to let that stop what she believes is a solid plan. Having Erik in the house has shown her that five people can live here. Of course, Frances would make six. But she has a plan for that too.

Tonight she has pencil to paper and Tad sitting nearby. It's his new thing: he brings a book to the garage and sits on the old chair they put here years ago, intending to throw it out. He doesn't talk; he reads. They didn't discuss it, he simply started doing it, and she likes it. Actually, she loves it. She feels cared for. She also feels like he is *with her* again. There will be bumps in the road – there always are – and Erik will likely cause most of them, but if she and Tad can show up for each other, if they can remember to keep demonstrating that they care, they'll manage. That's the work of life: not grand gestures, not promises, just being there for each other so that when there's a wobble, they can right themselves. If they hadn't done that since the start of their marriage, they would not have made it through the past few months. Somewhere underneath all the strife, though, she knew that he loved her and he knew she loved him, and they both knew they were stronger together than apart.

'I've been thinking,' she says as she lets her hand roam over the paper. The process is odd sometimes, almost as if she's not conscious of what's happening, then she has to look and see what she has created.

'Mm?' He looks up from his book.

'I do really want Mum to live here.'

Tad nods slowly and closes his book.

'We've discussed the pros and cons,' she goes on. Ages ago, when they were first talked about it, they went through everything. The only thing Alison would add would be a pro: having Frances in the house would be a form of bulwark against Erik's behaviour.

'We have,' he agrees. 'But . . .'

'Where would we fit her?' Alison asks.

He nods again.

'I've thought about that.' She points up.

'She cannot live above the garage!'

Tad looks so startled that Alison laughs.

'You didn't let me finish,' she says. '*Erik* could live above the garage. We need to spruce the place up. Put in some heating. But it's big enough, and there's a loo here too. And a shower.'

The garage used to house the laundry, which is now in the house, and the previous owners had turned the laundry into a small bathroom. So Erik could be mostly self-contained, which would suit him and the rest of the household too. She doesn't know why they didn't think of it earlier.

'Then Mum could live in his room.'

'A family of four becomes a family of six,' Tad says, raising his eyebrows.

'We always have been. Just not in the same place.'

They stare at each other for a few seconds. Alison has missed this, the way they can just be with each other in silent acceptance. She welcomes its return.

'Now you just need to convince her,' Tad says.

'I'm hoping it won't be convincing so much as encouraging.'

'The dog will come too?'

'Oh.' Alison hadn't thought about Colin. 'Yes, I guess he has to. Is that all right?'

Tad looks thrilled. 'Indeed.'

'So . . . that's it? Mum moves in? If she agrees.'

Her husband's warm smile is the only affirmation she needs.

'Thank you,' she says.

'No, *kochanie* – all the thanks are to you.'

He blows her a kiss then opens his book again, and when Alison turns back to her pencil and paper she sees what she's been creating without realising it: a flower, petals open and turned up. Towards the sun, she guesses. Yes. It has to be.

CHAPTER SIXTY-FIVE

It was four months ago when Joan first walked to the window of this hotel room, saw a glimpse of the Southern Ocean and felt a part of her let go while other parts were still being held tightly. The view gave her a sense of expanse and possibility even as she felt like that wasn't possible. Or that she didn't know how to embody those things, even though she knew she wanted to. And knew she had to.

Leaving Sydney, leaving Isaac, leaving her children and her friends and her life, leaving the Joan she knew behind, was unplanned yet once she arrived at the Duchess Hotel, it felt like her flight was inevitable. She had just been waiting for the day when she could travel back to herself, and what better place to do that than literally travel to where she knew herself as a child, dreaming, playing, seeing beauty in the world and determined to keep finding it.

That was the part she forgot so completely that she didn't even know she missed it until she found it again: she wanted to return to putting beauty into the world. That's what her art had always done, or it seemed to her it did. She used to question whether there was actually any value in that – it wasn't a practical thing, like baking bread or being a surgeon. Was it even a worthwhile pursuit?

After a while, after she sold some paintings and people said nice things to her, she realised that there was no other pursuit. Putting beauty into the world was all that mattered, because its opposite was cruel and diminishing. And to do nothing was unthinkable. To be on this earth for such a short time and *not* put beauty into the world – to not try to make the days better for other people, and for herself – was inconceivable.

That, then, is what she has been pursuing here: beauty that is shared with others. She could have painted in private, in Sydney, not telling anyone, getting away with it because Isaac wouldn't have paid attention anyway. But that would have been a selfish act, because – no matter what others may think of the art she makes – she wants to create beauty for people. And, as she has discovered at the Duchess Hotel, she wants to encourage others to do the same.

That work can be done anywhere. And she has made a decision about where that should be and how she should do it, although she still wants to discuss it with someone who has a vested interest in the answer but who she also knows to be sensible: Frances.

Descending the staircase of the hotel to meet Frances in the bar, Joan wonders how many more times she may do this. The Duchess has never felt like a permanent home but it has been homely enough that she's become attached to it and she'll be sad to leave it. As she must, because even if she stays in the area, she can't stay here forever.

Entering the bar, she sees Shane and Frances chatting, their easy familiarity evident in their body language, in the way they smile at each other. People are so interesting to observe; Joan knew this once upon a time, when she used to watch everything closely, but she forgot it in the years since. One of the great pleasures of her life has been rediscovering it.

'Hello,' she says, and Shane turns, smiling at her with that same familiarity as well as a certain sadness in his eyes that she knows she has caused. He's been a little less eager to engage with her since they had their heartfelt conversation, but she won't tell him what he wants to hear just because he wants to hear it. If she has learnt nothing else from the changes in her life over the past few months, she knows that she needs to do what is right for her, not anyone else.

'Hi, Joan,' he says, his voice catching.

'Hello, Joan love.' Frances beams. 'Take a seat and Shane will bring us our usual.'

There is so much implied in 'our usual': an established friendship, routines around it, no need to explain anything. She has come to love Frances and knows that if she leaves the Mornington Peninsula, she will miss her forever.

'So what's up?' Frances asks after Shane has left.

There's no point being coy and asking what she means – they know each other too well.

'I think I know what I want to do next,' Joan says. 'But I don't know the exact shape of it yet.'

Frances wrinkles her nose. 'I've got some news for you, Joanie – and take it from an old duck – you may never work that out.'

While Joan should know this – it makes sense – the way she flinches involuntarily tells her that she doesn't yet believe it. She *wants* to figure it out. She wants to know what to do next. The alternative is that she freefalls through the rest of her life, although her sense of trepidation about that suggests that the main reason she may have stayed in Sydney, with Isaac, for so long is that at a subterranean level she wanted the predictability because the alternative was terrifying. Not knowing what happens next is exhilarating in short spurts. Can she handle it for the rest of her life? Can anyone?

'But I want to work it out,' she confesses to Frances.

'Love, trust me – just when you think you have it sorted, life will change it on you. I stopped worrying about controlling things a long time ago.'

'How did you stop?'

Frances shrugs. 'A war took it out of my hands.'

'What happened – with Albert – didn't make you try to control things more?'

'What would be the point? That only leads to disappointment. If you're lucky. Usually it leads to pain.'

They sit quietly for a little while.

'He didn't love me,' Frances says, so softly that Joan almost doesn't catch it.

'Who?'

'Albert.'

'But he did – you've told me all about him.'

'There was a letter.' Frances picks up the drink Shane has silently deposited and takes a sip. 'He told my brother he didn't want to marry me.'

'But . . . when? I mean – at what point did he write it?'

'After he embarked. From wherever he was.' Her laugh is dry. 'I can't even say it happened at a particular time in a particular place because that war meant those details couldn't be put into letters.'

'How long have you known about this?' Joan can only guess how sad Frances must have felt when she found out.

'Not long. Margie found the letter in Cec's things.'

'I'm so sorry, Frances. I know that's the standard thing to say – but I am. No one wants to have their heart broken all over again.'

Frances stares at her. 'That's it, isn't it? That's why . . .' She sighs and shakes her head. 'I've been blue,' she continues. 'Going over it. Wondering why it feels so bad this many years later. Why should I care? But that's it – my heart was broken again.' She pauses. 'It's funny how you can be a grand age like mine and still feel nineteen inside.'

Joan thinks of herself at nineteen: painting, being free, the future wide open. She didn't have plans then, wasn't trying to control anything. Turning away from the life she built as an adult has been an attempt, most likely, to recapture who she was at that age. So she and Frances are not that different. It makes her think about others she knows and cares for: is Genevieve, for example, stuck at a certain age and trying to relive it? Is Isaac? Is Shane?

Maybe we never grow up. Maybe adulthood is a veneer. These are not questions she will have answered today, if ever. And that, she knows now, is all right.

'If that's the case,' Joan says, 'I like nineteen-year-old you.'

Frances looks away for a few seconds. 'You know what? I think I like her too.'

'She did really well. Coped with a tragedy, raised a son and a daughter, and now she's in an art class. And so much in between.'

'So much,' Frances says. 'It's been a good ride.'

'It's not over yet.'

'And yours is just starting. So tell me: what are you planning?'

'I think I need to go home. Back to Sydney, that is.'

Frances looks downcast then recovers. 'I see,' she says. 'I guess it was too much to think you'd stay with us.'

'Believe me, I thought about it. But . . .' She glances towards Shane, who is gazing at her with affection, and she feels grateful that he has felt moved to offer that to her.

She also feels the momentousness of her decision: she's at a river crossing and there's no clear way of knowing what awaits her on the opposite bank. Turning back is the safe option, of course. But she doesn't want that.

Or maybe she could see it another way: she's in the river, right now. Water is up to her waist. The current is strong. But her footing is sure, and she has one thing that will help her greatly: courage.

The same courage that has made her recommit to her art when it feels like she is revealing all her vulnerabilities. That Frances has had all these years in just living. The courage Shane had in telling her how he feels. That Kirrily has each day but which she believes she doesn't have. That each and every person has in their own way, although they may not recognise it either, let alone acknowledge themselves for it.

She has courage in her belief that whatever is on that other river bank is what she wants, even if she can't see what it is yet. And she will be carried there by something else she has allowed into her life, as the giver and receiver – love. All shades of it, all different strengths. She can't always see that either, but she knows it's there.

'I can't keep pretending that my life is mine alone,' Joan says. 'I don't exist on this planet solo. I need other people. And it is not a bad thing that they need me. I've had time to figure that out and I plan to be a better person because of it.'

Frances seems to consider this. 'Your friends here are better people because of it too,' she says.

'Thank you, Frances,' Joan says, her voice wavering. 'I don't know what would have become of me without you.'

'You'd have sorted yourself out – you're the type. But it's always nicer, isn't it, when someone can give you a hand?'

'It is,' Joan agrees, then she raises her glass to clink it to her friend's.

Frances winks, takes a sip, and calls Shane over for a chat.

CHAPTER SIXTY-SIX

Frances can't pretend that her last conversation with Joan didn't rattle her. Joan was talking like she was about to leave the Duchess imminently. Having gone through that once already, Frances feels ill-equipped to have it happen again so quickly. No guarantee it will be quick, of course, but she knows Joan enough to figure that once Joan makes up her mind about something she doesn't muck around.

So Frances has been in a philosophical mood ever since then, wondering about life and what she needs from it. It's okay to need things from life, she reckons, provided you put back into it. If you give some attention to the world around you, to your nearest and dearest. There's a balance to be struck, and the trick is in not tipping things too much one way or another. Don't take too much, don't give too much. Hold something back for yourself while letting out enough to care for others.

It's a lesson most of the women she's known haven't learnt or were encouraged to never learn. But Joan's shown her the way: she gave far too much, then she swung it back in the other direction and now she's aiming for balance.

Which has meant that Frances has looked at what she needs and she has realised that, a little like Joan, she needs to swing things back in the 'take' direction. Or at least in the 'take a little more' direction.

She needs to clear some things out first, though. Out of her head. Out of her life. Specifically: the letters Albert wrote her. They have represented a fantasy life she has held on to for six decades too long, and if the letter Margie found hadn't forced her to realise that, Keith's ongoing behaviour would have. She idealised and idolised that boy simply because he represented something that was really nothing to do with him: the life she thought she was going to have with Albert. If she treated Keith with kid gloves, it would be like making sure no injury came to that fantasy life. Except Keith is a human, not a dream. Definitely not a dream in any sense of the word. Yet treating him as such meant that he grew up thinking human consequences didn't apply to him, and she's suffered as a result.

So has Alison. Her Alison. The child who has stuck by her, tended to her, put up with her crotchetiness and her persistence in living in that fantasy life – never spoken of out loud but once she knew about Albert she knew what was going on, because she isn't stupid – and has never let her down.

Alison deserves a mother who no longer holds on to relics. Who now, finally, wants to live in the present instead of grieving the past.

'Come on, Colin,' she instructs her dog as she picks up the yellowed stack of paper that used to represent so much to her. Now it is nothing but a talisman of a mirage.

On her way towards the back door she takes a box of matches from the kitchen, then steps out into the early summer day.

She doesn't visit this back garden as often as she should, mainly because she keeps herself cooped up inside. Out of habit, really. Gerald liked to garden, and at the old house they had a nice range of plants and trees and bushes. This garden is small, with a couple of garden beds, and mostly paved. Which is handy for what she's about to do.

Sitting on a wrought-iron chair that Alison gave her when she moved in, she manoeuvres herself carefully – as one does at this age – and puts the letters on the stone. Immediately Colin has a sniff.

'Out of it, Colin,' she instructs, gently swatting him.

He gives the stack one last nudge then obeys, trotting off onto the grass, where he lifts his leg against the one tree to be found there.

There's no breeze, which is handy for Frances as she lights a match and drops it onto the letters.

As the flame catches, she feels nothing. She expected to feel something. She thought there'd be, oh, a pang, an ache, a sense of regret.

Nup. Nothing.

It's not as if the words in those letters weren't memorised decades ago, even though she kept rereading them.

The whole thing was pathetic even before she knew that Albert had changed his mind about her. She has wasted so much of her life wishing that very life were different – to what end? This is where she is right now, an old lady in an old house in a cold part of the world that comes up nicely in summer, with a smattering of friends and no talent at art.

'Mum!' The call comes from the side of the house, where there's a narrow passageway.

'Back here!' she calls in return.

Paper burns so quickly. The stack is almost gone as Alison appears.

'Mum!' she calls again, sounding panicked.

'It's all right, love.' Frances gestures at the flames that are already dwindling. 'Albert's letters,' she says, then looks into her daughter's eyes.

'What?' Alison says. 'Why?'

'Why not?' Frances takes her daughter's hand. Something she hasn't done since Alison was a little girl.

'Because of that letter Margie found?'

'That was the push I needed. But . . .' She waggles the hand. 'I should have done it years ago. In fact, I should never have kept them at all. Once I knew he was dead I should have closed that chapter and moved on. But I didn't.'

Their eyes meet again.

'I'm sorry.'

'Oh, Mum.' Alison lets go of her hand and hugs her instead, awkwardly because she has to bend down. 'There's nothing to be sorry for.' Alison straightens up. 'It's just life.'

And it is, isn't it? It's taken her daughter to say it so plainly. Frances can keep castigating herself for something she can no longer change, or she can just accept that it's life and get on with things. There's so little time left in which to do so, and there is life left for her to enjoy. First, though, she needs to confess something.

'I don't think I want to live here any more,' she says, nodding back at the house. 'On my own.'

She knows she's conceding to Alison's campaign to move her into care, but part of realising that she needs to move on and embrace life is accepting that it will be more easily done if she's not trying to manage on her own.

'What . . .' Alison scratches the back of her head. 'What prompted this?'

Frances shrugs. 'I'm old. I'm tired. I need help.'

'You know I'll help you.'

'Yes – you can find me an old person's home to live in. That's the plan, isn't it?'

Alison frowns. 'What do you mean?'

'That's what you've been hinting at?'

Alison's still frowning. 'No.' Now her face relaxes. 'Mum, I want you to move in with *me*.'

It takes Frances a minute or so to digest this. Alison has never said this is what she wants and Frances had never guessed it, either. So she'd presumed it was an old people's home that Alison wanted to put her into. All this time, has it not been the case? That changes things.

'You know that if I move in Colin has to come too?' she says, because it pops into her head.

'Of course.' Alison smiles. 'I'd hardly ship him off somewhere.'

'What about Tadeusz? Have you asked him?'

'Tad wants me to be happy,' she says. 'And I told him that if his son can move in, so can you. The house is big enough. Besides, Erik is moving into the room over the garage.'

'That sounds like a reward for bad behaviour,' Frances sniffs.

'He's been . . . better.' Alison half-smiles. 'We seem to have something in common.'

Frances's eyebrows go up. 'Oh?'

'He reads fantasy novels. And I . . .' Alison looks slightly bashful. 'Draw fantastical creatures.'

'When?' Frances has only ever seen Alison draw whatever is around them at the Duchess.

'At home. I've been drawing a lot. Erik saw some of them.' She smiles. 'We got talking.'

This is not enough to make Frances think the boy isn't troublesome, but she likes the fact that he's at least talking civilly to Alison about something. Maybe they'll make an adult of him yet.

'That's nice,' she says. 'So he'll be in the garage and I'll be in the house.'

Alison nods.

'And having me there would make you happy?' Frances asks, a little incredulous at the idea that her old mum living in the house would make Alison's life better. She knows she's at an age when things are going to start getting difficult, maybe not this year but maybe next, and definitely down the road.

'Why do you think I've been badgering you about it?' Alison says quietly. 'Nothing's more important to me than you, Mum.'

Well, that makes Frances want to cry but she doesn't let on to Alison. She's still her mother and a show of some kind of bravado comes naturally.

'I see,' she says, then spies Colin trying to dig up one of the garden beds. 'See what a nuisance he is?' she says, but with affection.

'I can use him to turn over our soil,' Alison replies with a smile.

They stand there watching the dog getting his snout dirty, then Alison helps Frances off the chair and they head slowly inside. When they walk into the house, Frances has the strangest sensation of knowing that everything will be all right. It is the first time in her life she's felt that and it makes her momentarily sad that she's had to wait so long, yet she feels freer than she has been since those days, long ago, when she raced her horse away from her parents' house and through the trees, wind in her hair and at her back, not a care in the world and no limit on her time. If she closes her eyes, just for a second, she's there, and she's here, and in her cells and her marrow, in her breath and bones, the feeling is exactly the same.

CHAPTER SIXTY-SEVEN

Once her mother had agreed to move in with Alison and Tad and the children, they started talking details. Alison contacted a real estate agent to start the process of selling the house. Frances didn't need to be living in it for that to happen, so they could start packing up straightaway.

They moved Erik into the room above the garage after Tad found some secondhand furniture at a shop in Frankston. Nothing fancy, but it's not as if he – or Alison – had anything fancy when they were that age. Erik seemed pleased to have his own space, and Sean seemed a little jealous that it wasn't him moving into the garage.

Before Erik moved, Alison considered what it would be like to have him living above her while she spends her nights drawing, but figured there might be benefits for them both. He would feel like someone cared enough to be around him while not intruding, and she could adjust more to him being around. Because there's no sign of him going anywhere else, and he's always going to be Tad's son.

The room that was Erik's and is now Frances's has its own en suite, so she'll have her privacy. The kids were looking forward to having their grandmother in the house because, as Alison told Frances, they like her company.

'That's news to me,' Frances replied.

'What do you mean?'

'I would have thought kiddies had better things to do than talk to their old gran.'

'Mum! They're always chattering away to you.'

Frances, in fact, can get Sean talking more than he does to anyone except Rosie.

The night before the move, Tad and Alison went round to pick up some knick-knacks and other small items; Shane is coming to help move some things, although most of the house's contents will be sold.

When Frances told her that Shane would be helping Alison started to protest – they could hire movers, she said – then she realised that having Shane around might make Frances feel more reassured about what's going on. She has to remember that Shane is to Frances what Keith has never been: a reliable son. And since they've been spending time together in the art class, Alison has come to appreciate why her mother likes Shane so much: he's solid but not boring; naughty yet not mean with it, and he adores Frances, which Alison appreciates.

While they were there, Phyllis from next door came knocking and Alison answered the door.

'What's going on?' Phyllis said to Frances, who appeared behind Alison.

'I'm moving out,' Frances said.

'Where to?'

'My daughter's.'

Phyllis looked upset. 'But I barely got to know you,' she said, and Frances looked as surprised as Alison felt. She'd always had the impression that Phyllis wasn't fond of her mother.

'I didn't know that you even wanted to,' Frances replied.

'No.' Phyllis sighed. 'I guess not.' She tapped the edge of the door. 'Sorry to see you go.'

'I hope you're not troubled by any more corgis.'

Phyllis flushed. 'Sorry about that,' she muttered, and turned to go.

'It's fine, Phyllis,' Frances said. 'Water under the bridge.'

'Mm.' Phyllis pulled a face. 'Maybe I'll see you at the bowling club?'

'I don't bowl.'

'Not yet.' Phyllis gave her a sly little smile then headed off down the path.

On the morning of the move, Alison watches as Shane carries small items into the house, then worries that they're taking up too much of his time.

'Aren't you going to be late for work?' Alison asks him as he carries a lamp inside.

'William's giving me a bit of leeway,' he says. 'Since it's your mum who's moving. He said I should take care of her.'

'Oh, that's nice.'

'He wants her back at the Duchess as soon as possible,' Shane says, then turns to Frances. 'Not sure he's that happy about you missing a day to move.' Shane plugs in the lamp and turns it on. 'There you go,' he says. 'Adds to the ambience.'

'What do you know about ambience?' Frances says.

He looks amused. 'I run a bar.'

'Right.'

'Just a couple of boxes left,' he says as he heads back out to his car.

'Does everything look okay?' Alison asks as she glances around the room, Colin nudging her heels. He seemed to switch allegiances the second he trotted into the house.

'It does.' Frances smiles.

'I realise it's not like having your own house with all your own things, but . . . I hope you'll be happy here, Mum.'

It will take some adjusting, Alison knows – Frances hasn't lived with anyone since Gerald died, and Colin doesn't count. But she truly believes it's the best thing for them all. Her mother deserves to have someone care for her. We all do.

'I've set up an easel in the back sunroom,' Alison says.

'I thought you were in the garage?'

'It's for you.'

'For me!' Frances chortles. 'I don't think that's necessary, love, but thank you for thinking of it.'

'You don't enjoy it?'

'I do. But I'm not very good at it, as you know.'

'Who defines "good"? If you enjoy it, doesn't that make it good?'

'I suppose.'

Shane reappears with a box. 'Photos,' he says, setting it down.

'Thanks, Shane,' Alison says, and he nods in acknowledgement.

She and Frances look at each other and Alison hopes her mother can interpret what her look means: Keith should be here helping. Yet Frances hasn't heard from him in weeks, she knows, and he doesn't return her calls. Presumably she's of no use to him at this point in time, and nor is Alison. She would feel sadder about that – for her mother's sake – but she knows now that she has no control over his behaviour, or anyone else's. People do things because they want to do them; sometimes those things are good, sometimes they're bad, and when it comes to Keith, she has to accept that they're not likely to be good.

Shane starts unpacking the box. 'Where would you like these?' he says.

'By the windowsill,' Frances answers.

He carries a few frames over and starts arranging them, and he's putting them in the same order Frances had them at the house. Such care, Alison thinks. He loves her mother, and for some reason that makes her feel proud.

'All right, ladies, now I do have to get to work,' he says once he's finished, then he grins, bends down and kisses Frances's cheek.

'Bit more of a walk to the Duchess, isn't it?' he says, and he's right: Alison's house is probably too far for Frances to walk.

'I'm going to take the bus,' Frances says, 'but not all the way. The constitutional does me good.'

'See you tomorrow, then.' He winks. 'And see you later, Alison.'

He waves his goodbye then mother and daughter are left alone.

'Welcome home, Mum,' Alison says, wrapping Frances in a hug. Frances hugs her back harder and longer than she ever has, and that's all the reassurance Alison needs that everything is, even for this moment alone, in its right place.

CHAPTER SIXTY-EIGHT

It's funny to see Wendy buzzing around the function room, acting all efficient. Kirrily remembers when she first started coming to the Duchess Hotel, tipsy in the middle of the afternoon, talking a million miles an hour and none of it making any sense. She would plonk herself down on a seat in the foyer and never seemed to have anywhere else to be.

Now she's directing William to put a certain painting in one spot and another painting in a different spot, acting like it's *her* art show. Which she probably feels like it is, since she was running the art class while Joan was away. But Joan is in charge. Anyone who meets her knows that.

Kirrily has brought her own work to display: a portrait of her children, curled around each other in bed, asleep. She went in to check on Aidan one Saturday morning and found Bridget with him, and they were so deeply asleep that she knew she had time to grab her sketchpad and at least start a drawing. After that she painted over the sketch, observing them as they moved around the house to capture the colours in their hair and the tint in their cheeks.

Connor found her doing it one time and put his hand on her shoulder, not saying anything, just standing and watching her work. It was comforting. But at the time it wasn't his touch she wanted. That was before Aidan went to hospital. Before she knew that her daydreams were just that and she had to let them go. She misses them, the way you can only miss something that will always be hypothetical. A wish, a promise, a fantasy. That's all Derek was. If that, actually, because she made him into something he never really held himself out to be.

It is Connor who has come with her today, leaving the children with his parents, telling her that he wants to see what they've all been up to in this class.

'Joan,' Kirrily calls, waving as Joan enters the room. She then walks over, smiling.

'Can you believe madam over there?' She nods towards Wendy and laughs. 'You'd think she's after William's job.'

'He looks pretty happy about it,' Connor remarks.

'Oh, Joan – I'd like you to meet my husband, Connor.'

They shake hands and Joan looks from one to the other.

'You didn't tell me he was such a strapping, handsome fellow,' she says, and Connor blushes. He's never been good at receiving compliments.

'I guess I take it for granted,' Kirrily says without thinking, and as soon as it's left her mouth she knows it's true. She glances up at him and sees hurt in his eyes. 'I'll have to stop that,' she goes on. 'I should never have started it.'

'He'd be worth painting.' Joan nudges her. 'That way you'd really get to appreciate him.'

It's not said pointedly but Joan's point is made regardless.

'That's a good idea,' Kirrily says, and when she smiles up at him this time he looks happier.

'She's a great artist,' he says to Joan.

'I agree. I hope she'll keep it up.'

Just as Kirrily feels a flush of pride, Shane walks in with Frances not far behind him, and he looks to be carrying both of their works, one under each arm.

Frances is limping a little – she's mentioned something about her knee but Kirrily hasn't really noticed it before now. Or maybe it was something else that was troubling her. It's not that she wasn't paying attention when Frances talked about it – well, maybe it was. Too wrapped up in her own drama. That's been the story of her life these past few months. When she thinks about what's gone on – what she has allowed to go on – it's like she's been in a fever of some sort that is now abating, leaving her feeling wrung out yet calm, because she knows she can survive something so torrid. It's not a fever she wants to experience again; she's only glad her whole life didn't burn up in it.

'Hello, loves,' Frances says as she comes over to them. 'And you must be Connor – you can be a love too.' Her smile is as warm and welcoming as Kirrily is used to.

'I am,' he says. 'And you're Frances.'

'Only old duck here – is that how you guessed?'

Connor smiles kindly. 'No. Kirrily pointed you out once when I visited her at work.'

'Didn't realise you'd ever visited here,' Frances says. 'Welcome back to my home away from home.'

'Hers too, I think.' Connor's smile flashes, then his hand is on her shoulder in that reassuring way he has, just letting her know that he's there. Something else she's taken for granted.

Joan leads Frances away and they stand together near where William is moving a painting around on the floor, looking flustered.

Kirrily watches as Shane props up a drawing in the spot where Wendy tells him to, laughing at the expression on his face, a mix of dismay and fear that tells her he's worried that Wendy's going to try to tell him how to run the bar next.

'I should go and rescue Shane,' she says. 'I've told you about Shane, haven't I?'

Connor nods. 'Barman. Vietnam veteran.'

'That's him.'

Before she can go to Shane, though, he sees her and hurries over.

'Help,' he says, 'Wendy's sending me spare.' Then, turning to Connor, 'Shane, mate.'

'Connor.'

They shake hands and Kirrily marvels at how simple men's interactions can be. She could never get away with introducing herself to someone as 'Kirrily, mate'. And maybe she doesn't want to. Being tangled up in a conversation isn't such a bad thing.

'What's she doing?' Kirrily says to Shane.

'Telling me that I shouldn't have brought a *drawing* because a *drawing* isn't what she was looking for.'

'I didn't realise it was her show.'

'None of us did. But she's decided. It's like she's on a mission.'

Just then Wendy starts wagging her finger in William's face and Kirrily laughs.

'A mission to annoy William,' she says.

'He's big enough to take care of himself. Anyway . . .' Shane shakes his head. 'Why are we doing this show again? No one's going to look at it.'

'William said it would enhance the hotel and let people know the Duchess is a destination for more than just fine rooms, food and views. Or something.'

'That sounds like something he'd say. All right, well, back to it.'

Shane winks then he straightens his shoulders and heads back towards Wendy.

'It's funny,' Connor says, 'seeing these people. I had started to wonder if they were real.'

There's something in his voice – a quavering – that makes her feel uneasy.

'Why wouldn't you think they were real?' she says tentatively.

'When you started leaving early on Fridays, I . . .' He glances away. 'I don't know, I thought maybe there was something else going on.'

That uneasy feeling has now turned into something like cement in her gut. Has he come here to tell her that he knows about Derek? In front of everyone?

She swallows. Might as well get it over with.

'Like what?' she asks.

Now she has his full attention, his eyes boring into hers.

'Like another fella,' he says, but he doesn't sound angry, just . . . resigned.

'Why would you think that?' Her voice is slow, steady. She can't let on, can't do that to herself now. Or to them. Yes, she betrayed him; no, she doesn't think she should tell him. The impulse to unburden herself is there but it's selfish, because it's about her trying to feel better by confessing. It will not help Connor. She doesn't ask to know everything about him and hopes he would never ask that of her.

'Because you've been so weird. Not wanting to go near me. We haven't had a proper conversation in weeks . . . until now.'

His hand is back on her shoulder, and she almost feels herself deflate with relief.

'I have been weird,' she says. 'I've felt weird. I . . .' She wonders how to phrase it. 'I've been feeling lost. Like I don't know what I'm doing with my life. What I'm good for.'

Now he takes both of her shoulders and stands in front of her, staring into her eyes.

'Please don't ever think that,' he says, his voice low and strong. 'You're so caring and loving towards me, towards the kids. You don't know what you mean to me. To them. Maybe I don't say it enough.' He drops his head. 'You've always stood by me. When we married, I didn't amount to much. You didn't care.'

'But that's not true,' she says, remembering how hard he worked then – as he does now – and how determined he was to make a life for them.

'It felt true. So I know . . .' He squeezes her shoulders. 'What it's like when you feel like you're not much chop. But believe me, you are.' He wraps his arms around her. 'You're the best and I love you. I'm going to tell you more often.'

She stands, hugging him, letting him care for her, catching Frances's eye and seeing her nod slowly, not like she's giving her approval but like she understands.

After a few minutes have passed, Kirrily lets him go. 'I'll tell you more often too,' she says softly.

'Kizza!' Shane calls.

'Kizza?' Connor looks amused.

She sighs exaggeratedly. 'I wish he wouldn't. But he does.'

She kisses Connor on the cheek then wanders over to Shane, who is holding up his drawing. 'I don't think it's too bad – do you?'

'I'm not the best judge,' she says, then laughs at his hurt expression. 'It's *fine*, Shane. None of us is Rembrandt here.'

'Thank God,' he mutters, 'that bloke's paintings are boring.'

Kirrily glances back to where Connor has perched himself on a table, arms folded, watching the scene around him. She could get used to him being interested in her life. Not the life she shares with him but the one that has been just for her, that she has always thought no one else would care about. The life she's started to express with the people in this room and on the canvas she's brought here.

Maybe he has a life, too, that he hasn't shared with her. She wants to know what that is. And there's time to do that, and also no time at all, because she's wasted enough of it.

Connor waits for her while she helps set up everyone's works the way they want, then he takes her by the hand, back to their car, back to their children, back to their life.

CHAPTER SIXTY-NINE

ONE DAY IN JANUARY 2000

The light here really is beautiful.
Joan exhales as she looks across the water to small boats moored, barely moving in this patch of the harbour on a warm day with no wind for seagulls to ride.

This little patch of bush next to the water's edge, where she can sit and look and dream and be, is where she spends her days now. It won't last forever, but it's impossible to estimate how long a creative process will take. She may have enough paintings in a month, or six months. The good thing is that there's no limit because the exhibition she is working towards is her own and the local gallery owner told her to take her time.

'Love your style,' he said as he reviewed the work she'd already done and brought to show him. 'This will do very well here. Just tell me when you're ready, sweetie, and we'll set you up. You know you're in the right place too? Margaret Preston.' He winked. 'Lived in Mosman. And Grace Cossington Smith won the Mosman Art Prize. This place is *lousy* with art, sweetie. Lousy!'

Basil, his name is. Joan suspects it isn't his real name, but she's often thought it odd that we are all saddled with the names our parents chose for us, not the names we might choose for ourselves. She's also wondered how much names determine destiny. Joan is hardly evocative of someone with a life that is anything other than suburban.

And yet: Joan of Arc. When she was a child, her father used to call her 'my little warrior' and tell her it was because of Joan of Arc. She forgot about that until she was sitting in her room in the Duchess and remembered feeling so proud that he thought her a warrior. Then she thought maybe she could be a warrior now too – for her future, for her happiness. No one else will take up arms on her behalf, and she did it by going to the Duchess. Now she's doing it by re-entering the life she left, on her terms.

It was the hardest decision of her life to leave the Mornington Peninsula behind.

'You're being unreasonable,' Frances said when she told her she was leaving the next day. It was said with love, but the intent was real enough, Joan could tell.

'I'll visit,' she said as she hugged her goodbye, and she meant it. The place feels like a second home to her now.

Kirrily was her usual circumspect self as Joan said her farewells, but Joan saw the glint in her eye and knew that her erstwhile student would continue to create in whichever way gave her joy.

Shane was the hardest goodbye because she had become more attached to him than she thought. Not romantically, she doesn't think. But perhaps she doesn't know. Indeed, she's not sure if she knows what romance is. In retrospect, Isaac didn't so much as romance her as compel her with his arguments about how they should be married and she, thinking that was what she should be doing with her life anyway, agreed. He was very attentive at first, and then not. Shane has been constantly attentive, letting her know of his regard for her. It does turn one's head, that kind of behaviour.

She had to leave him, though. They would always be friends, she told him, and she meant that too. The past couple of weeks, since her return to Sydney, she's been half-expecting him to turn up. That *would* be romantic. Except she is back living in her marital home, albeit in a separate bedroom to Isaac, while she organises herself.

'There's no need to leave,' Isaac had said when she told him she needed her own space. 'We can work something out.'

'You mean you want to work it out so I never leave,' she had replied.

'Well . . . yes. I still love you.'

'You tried to financially starve me out of the Duchess, Isaac,' she had said crossly. 'I'm not going to forget that.'

Of course, it had worked: she'd returned to Sydney that time. This time, however, she's here because she wants to be. It feels like home again. The light, the trees, the water – they mean things to her that someone else may not understand yet are more profound than her need to escape the nitty-gritty of her life.

'What can I do?' he'd said.

'What do you mean?'

'I want us to be together.'

She had almost laughed at him then, at how naïve he seemed for a man so experienced in the ways of the world.

'Isaac, I'm not the same woman any more,' she said. 'So I can't live the same life.'

She could tell he didn't understand; it is, however, not her job to enlighten him. If he wishes to figure it out for himself, they can talk. In the meantime, she has plans.

There's a two-bedroom flat on Queen Street, not far from where she's sitting now at Curlew Camp; she would be able to walk here, even carrying an easel. It is up for rent and she had a look at it; the real estate agent told her not to spend too much time thinking about it. Today is the day by which she needs to make a decision, he said.

She called Genevieve to tell her about her plans. It felt normal – right – to let her know. There was no sense of oddness between them. It was as if there had been no schism, and Joan felt it almost as an elastic band between them, one tugging, one yielding, in a way they can sustain, she hopes, forever.

'Dad said I would find you here.'

Joan turns and smiles at Corinne, with Natalie in her arms.

'Did he? I thought he didn't listen when I told him details.'

'Mu-um.' Corinne makes a face. 'He's trying.'

'We're all trying, darling.' She holds out her arms for the baby. 'Aren't we?'

'She's a little fussy today.' Corinne hands over her child then sighs, smiles and looks across the water. 'This really is the most magical spot,' she says. 'I can see why you love it.'

'Me and generations of people before me.' Joan puts a finger to Natalie's nose and coos at her. This child has been an important factor in her return: during her last, forced visit to Sydney she enjoyed seeing her so much that the prospect of barely seeing her hurt. An actual pain, which surprised her. She felt that when her children were small and didn't expect to experience it with a grandchild. Yet of course this small human has captured her heart, with all the euphoria and pain that comes with that.

'Perhaps you could join me,' Joan states without looking at her daughter. 'You may like to paint too.'

'Me?' Corinne laughs. 'Hardly. Remember what I was like at school?'

'But that's often a matter of how you're taught. I could teach you.'

Corinne smiles at her and there's pride in it. 'I guess you have experience now,' she says.

'I do. Against my will.' Joan presses her lips to Natalie's head. 'And I miss it.'

They had one last class before she left, everyone there: Frances, Kirrily, Shane and Wendy. Even William came along, just to watch. They gathered on the spot where they had the most expansive view of the sea, and Joan told them to look around and paint whatever caught their eye first.

Shane painted her. She felt flattered, then wistful, and she thinks about it sometimes.

Frances posted her the drawing she made that day, signed, along with a note telling her that they're planning to keep gathering on Friday afternoons to paint and draw and that Wendy's running the class now.

She'll call Frances sometime this week. But Frances is the only person she'll stay in touch with. No doubt she'll hear about the others, and they about her, so she won't ever be too far away. Shane will call her if he wants to talk.

Her life is in Sydney now even if her son still isn't talking to her. Corinne has said he'll come around; he's just being a tantrumy child who wants his mummy on tap. Which told Joan that Corinne has possibly always thought of him this way.

'What's so good about painting, Mum?' Corinne asks as she continues to look outwards at the view.

'The freedom. The fire.' Joan briefly closes her eyes and feels in her body what it's like when everything is working, when her hand seems to move without conscious thought and something pours out of her. It's like dancing without moving her feet. And so hard to explain to anyone else.

'The fire?'

'The fire of creation.' Joan laughs. 'It's a feeling – a heat. Electricity, I suppose. When you're making something and it feels *right*. I can't describe it better than that. But I'd love to help you find it.'

Natalie wriggles and Joan holds her up, turning so her granddaughter can look over her shoulder at the gulls in the water.

'I don't have the time,' Corinne says.

'We all have to make time for it,' Joan says. 'I've learnt that. Life is half full without it.'

'At least you said half full, not half empty. Otherwise I might have taken that personally.' It's said lightly but meant seriously, Joan can tell.

'You and Nathan could never be emptiness for me, even when he's being difficult. But there's more. To me. To you. We are not just vessels for what other people want us to be. I mean that, darling. I don't want you to get to the point I did.'

They smile at each other.

'How can I?' says Corinne. 'You're here. I know you will help me.'

'I will.' She pats Natalie's back. 'And I'll keep helping myself too.'

Joan turns towards the water once more and Corinne draws alongside, holding out her hands, and Joan gives her granddaughter back.

'So you paint here – just here?' Corinne asks.

'Most days.'

'Would I paint here, if I were painting with you?'

Joan feels a surge of hope. 'If you want to.'

Corinne briefly places her head on Joan's shoulder. 'I think I might,' she says.

'Natalie can come too.'

'I was hoping you'd say that.'

They both stand, with trees around them and light dappling through their canopies, with noise in the undergrowth from lizards or whatever is in there, birds flapping overhead and paddling in front of them. There is richness, in this spot, and, if Joan chooses to look for it, in her life too. She doesn't need to travel far away to find it. It is next to her; it is under her feet; it is in the sky above. It is in her hands as she paints, in her mind as she dreams, and in her heart.

Whatever comes next, she is wide open to it. She is ready.

ACKNOWLEDGEMENTS

Many thanks to Fiona Hazard, Rebecca Allen, Lee Moir, Rebecca Saunders, Louise Stark and all at Hachette Australia for their support of my writing, and to editors Nicola O'Shea and Samantha Sainsbury, proofreader Julia Cain, and publicist Laura Benson.

Thank you to Christa Moffitt for always creating the most beautiful covers.

Thank you to my agent, Melanie Ostell, for steady counsel and stimulating conversations.

Thanks and love for their support to my parents, Robbie and David, and my brother, Nicholas. Thank you to my beloved friend Jen Bradley for her love and support. Thanks to the luminous Isabelle Benton for being her, and to Anna Egelstaff, Chris Kunz, Neralyn and Col Porter, Tammie Russell, Kate Sampson and Jill Wunderlich for their support.

Thanks to Ruth Anstice and Diana Mitchell for being my Bushcare buddies, and to Rachael Johns for riding the podcast road with me.

Huge thanks to Matt Joe Gow, Kerryn Fields and Amber Lawrence for being inspirational artists, and to Ashleigh Dallas, Fanny Lumsden, Hayley Marsten and Luke O'Shea for their wonderful music. The influence of these and other Australian country music artists on my life and writing is impossible to measure but deeply appreciated.

Love all ways to Shiva Rea.